THE SALESMAN

Also by
Joseph O'Connor

Fiction

Cowboys and Indians
True Believers
Desperadoes

Nonfiction

Even the Olives Are Bleeding:
The Life and Times of
Charles Donnelly
The Secret World of the Irish Male
The Irish Male at Home and Abroad
Sweet Liberty: Travels in Irish America

Drama

Red Roses and Petrol
The Weeping of Angels

Screenplays

A Stone of the Heart
The Long Way Home
Ailsa

THE SALESMAN

Joseph O'Connor

Picador USA
New York

Picador ® is a U.S. registered trademark and is used by St. Martin's Press under license from Pan Books Limited.

Library of Congress Cataloging-in-Publication Data

O'Connor, Joseph, 1963-
The salesman / Joseph O'Conner.
p.   cm.
ISBN 0-312-19998-8
I. Title.
PR6065.C558S25   1999
823'.914—dc21
98-51067
CIP

First published in the United Kingdom by Martin Secker & Warburg Limited

First Picador USA Edition: March 1999

10 9 8 7 6 5 4 3 2 1

For Jonathan Warner, in fond memory.

PART I

Prologue

Glen Bolcain, Dalkey Avenue
November 1994

When I open up my diary for those terrible months at the end of last year, my love, I see once again that the first time I ever laid eyes on Donal Quinn was that October morning in Court Number 29 of the Four Courts when the air reeked of mildew and dusty old leather-bound books. I was surprised when he came in. I suppose I must have thought that people would at least look up and fall silent when the three guards led him in and brought him up to the dock; but they didn't, they just kept right on talking, the clerks and solicitors passing papers and thick folders to one another, the chuckling senior counsel for the defence unfolding a paper-clip with his teeth, the cops around the court softly laughing and nudging, or strutting about in a businesslike manner as though trying to get themselves noticed by somebody important.

In he came, bold as you like, with the air of a man who owned the place and was not about to sell, the burly men in dark uniforms around him more like some royal retinue than prison officers. Father Seánie put his fingertips on the back of my wrist, told me to try and be calm.

I think the first thing that struck me about him, as he climbed the steps to the dock, was his smallness. He had tiny hands and dainty, elegant feet. He moved quickly, jerkily, like a vicious little winter bird. He had on a blue tie with a pattern of melting black and white clocks, one of those chain-store suits that look good in a shop window but cheap and sad and saggy in the daylight, also a pair of battered old training shoes, which seemed a little odd to me, given the circumstances. He had sideburns. His arms were short and thick. There was something revoltingly efficient about him. He could easily have been taken for a boxer.

His hair was much lighter in colour than it had appeared in the newspaper photographs: sandy red, poorly cut into an old-fashioned pudding-bowl style and slightly thinning at the crown. It looked like maybe he had cut it himself. He showed very little interest as the other three accused were marched up and put into the dock beside him. I did not see him glance over in the direction of the jurors – eight men and four women – even once. He sat looking bored, his shoulders slumped, listlessness personified, his head lolling a little to one side.

Although it had rained for almost a week without stopping, it was a hot day for October. The courtroom was stuffy and airless, it felt like a place that was in some fundamental way dead. The plump registrar was sweating heavily in his bench below the judge, and I had the distinct impression that the tipstaff was actually asleep at the side door. I remember one of the lawyers asking the judge if anything could be done about what she called the atmosphere in the court and the judge did not know at first what she meant. When the lawyer made it clear that she was talking about the air supply, the judge smiled and adjusted his wig and made some kind of joke which I could not quite hear, although a few of the solicitors laughed in a whinnying, dutiful way. A cadaverous young garda had to go out and get a long wooden pole with a hook on the end to open the sky light. While all this was going on Quinn peered around, his eyes rapidly blinking, and waved to a girl in heavy make-up who was sitting up in the public gallery between two scrawny-looking youngfellas in sunglasses and green and white track suits. He blew her a kiss with his cuffed hands. He looked so harmless and far-away. I suppose he looked a bit like a movie star.

I think it was around then that one of the prison officers ambled over to me and said hello. He was a large, pink, vaguely damp-looking man with a head like a bullet. 'Isn't it Billy?' he went, 'Billy Sweeney?' He shook my hand, told me that I had changed his life and saved his marriage. Big toothy beam, breath smelling of meat. I did not know what he meant. He winked conspiratorially. I had sold him his satellite dish, he said, and he punched my shoulder; what the hell was I doing here?

I don't think I will forget the look on his face when I told him.

As the hearing proper began and the garage manager went up to give his evidence, Quinn bowed his head and began to stare at the courtroom floor, resting his chin in his cupped palms. He must have sat like that with his gaze fixed on one spot for a whole half-hour. He seemed absolutely immune; if I tell the truth, some part of me almost envied him. Occasionally he would tap his fingertips against his cheek-bones as though he was listening to music. I remember a chubby little guard shoving him in the back at one point to make him stand up and listen to the judge. He was a bit jumpy from then on and I noticed that he had the habit of jerking his neck to snap his hair out of his eyes, which were small like the rest of him and quite narrow although they often took on an expression of surprise – or even shock – for no apparent reason.

As the first hour wore on I studied him. I got to know the small things. A good salesman has an eye for the small things. Sometimes his lips would move as though he was speaking to himself; other times his teeth would gnaw at his top lip, or his darting tongue would lick at his thin moustache. In the days and weeks after that first time I would often find myself thinking about him, particularly very early in the mornings, for some reason. Often these would be the first things I would focus on when I awoke: the sharp-remembered sight of him licking his moustache, the image of his mumbling lips, the strange squeak his grubby sneakers somehow made as he ground them on the floor of the dock. It was odd. Sometimes I even found myself imagining that I was him. I suppose I must have wanted to know how he felt.

Few things that happened during the whole trial would compare to the force of the first time I saw him. I stared at him, pet, that first time. I felt the hatred bubble up and fizz through my veins until it seemed to me that the rage was about to burst open like an egg in my stomach. It actually became interesting to me, almost as an objective thing, just how far that sensation would go. I felt such a pure clean contempt for him – it was like something boiled right down to its essence – that for a while I found it difficult to concentrate on anything that was being said, by the lawyers, by the officials, by Father Seán beside me; even the judge's occasional words were quite impossible to connect with, they seemed to come echoing from some distant place that did not include me. I could not stop looking at Donal Quinn. But I don't think he even noticed me once.

Just before lunch he beckoned his solicitor over to the dock. I could see him nodding furiously and squinting his eyes at her, I could hear the hiss of his voice. She went to the front of the court then, a slim and intense-looking young woman with thick dark hair and a Northern Irish accent.

'My Lord,' she said. 'Excuse me. I've a request in relation to my client.'

'Go on.'

'My client has been in extreme pain for some days, my Lord. With his wisdom teeth.'

Someone giggled in the public gallery. The judge peered down at the solicitor and took off his glasses, an expression of disbelief in his hooded eyes.

6

'My client is in great distress, my Lord. He tells me he can't concentrate on these proceedings with the pain. I'm respectfully asking your Lordship to grant an adjournment of one day so the matter can be attended to.'

The judge sighed, his ancient face hawklike against the wine-red curtain behind him. 'Have the State anything to say about this?' One of the main prosecution solicitors shook his head. The judge drummed on his wrist with a pen for a few seconds. Then he turned to the dock, looking flushed and uncomfortable, as though he wished that he were somewhere else. He seemed to stare at Quinn for a moment or two before glancing back down at the file on his desk.

'Wisdom-tooth pain is very severe, my Lord,' the solicitor said. He ignored her and continued flicking irritatedly through his papers.

'I see here that your client is serving with the armed forces, Miss Harding. I thought Irish soldiers were trained not to whinge about a bit of pain. God help us all now if we're ever invaded.'

More people laughed at the back of the court. Quinn's face was dark with anger. 'Well?' said the judge.

'May it please your Lordship,' the solicitor said, 'my client had the rank of private in the defence forces and indeed served a three-month tour of duty in the Lebanon, as part of the United Nations peace-keeping mission to that country. But he's no longer with the army, my Lord.'

Someone made a loud scoffing sound at the back of the court. The tipstaff awoke with a jolt.

The judge nodded and wrote something down. Then he glared towards the dock again, his scarlet face shining and moist. 'I'm going to let you see a dentist, Mr Quinn. Officer, take the accused out and make the appropriate arrangements, will you? I'll grant an adjournment until tomorrow morning at ten o'clock.'

'Thank you, my Lord,' the solicitor said. 'I'm obliged to the court.'

The judge's face was inscrutable. 'I'm sure we're all happy to safeguard the constitutional rights of your client's wisdom teeth, Miss Harding. And happy to hear he's possessed of *some* wisdom at any rate.'

'Yes, my Lord. Thank you, my Lord.'

Quinn glanced up at the ceiling and I thought I saw in his glazen eyes a faint, almost embarrassed smile.

I now believe that was the moment I decided I would kill him.

Chapter One

S ince these things must begin somewhere, I suppose I should start with the first time I met your mother. You will remember my telling you that Seánie and I and some of the other lads from Ringsend had a little skiffle band when we were kids. We were called the Raytown Rhythm Kings, if you don't mind, and we were going to be huge. A fat lad called Noel Bascombe played the drums. Buckets Bascombe, everyone called him. We used to tell Buckets that he was huge already. He could have worn his stomach as a kilt.

I played the piano whenever we could find a piano; other times I strummed on an old banjo or a big battered guitar with a terrible action and thick steel strings that made my fingertips ache and bleed. Seánie Ronan – Father Seán – played this beautiful semi-acoustic red Hofner guitar which he had ordered from a catalogue sent him by an aunt who lived in Chicago.

The last time I bumped into Noel was in town, about a year ago now, just shortly after that dreadful night and what happened to you. It was one of those dark and spattery Dublin autumn afternoons that make your skin sting and toes ache with the cold. I was rushing down Grafton Street, late for something, when I glanced up and happened to notice this enormous flabby man staring in the window of Brown Thomas and recognised him straight away, though I had not seen him in an age. I went over and tapped his shoulder. I was right, it was Buckets. The hug he gave me nearly broke my back. He lives in Milwaukee, Wisconsin

9

now, married to a Lebanese girl, his third marriage, he hadn't been home in nearly twenty years, he told me. He was driving a train for Amtrak over there. I told him I had given up the teaching some years earlier – I lied about how many years – and was selling TV satellite dishes. He laughed. 'Look at us, pal. Remember we were gonna be big rock 'n' roll stars, Billy? I guess we talked the talk, but we didn't walk the walk in the end, huh?' Lightning flickered and cracked in the sky over Trinity College. Hailstones started to surge down into the street. We stepped into a doorway, Buckets cursing the weather.

'How's that eldest girl of yours?' he asked me then. 'I guess she's a respectable married lady now?'

I told him about Lizzie emigrating to Australia and marrying Franklin. I showed him a photograph of her, another of Conal and Erin, whom he said did not look like twins. I remember noticing the Americanness of his accent when he pronounced their names. He called me a glamorous grandad. Then he asked about your mother. He seemed sad when I told him how it had not worked out between us, and shocked at the news of her death. But when I told him what had happened to you, his gentle rheumy eyes actually filled with tears. He kept saying your name, over and over. Maeve. Little Maeve. After a while I was actually sorry I had told him, he was so upset. He insisted on coming out to the hospital with me later that evening, the two of us silent in the taxi all the way out the coast road towards Dun Laoghaire, the wild grey waves splashing over the sea wall at Booterstown.

Afterwards we went to the bar of the Royal Marine Hotel. He drank a few Irish coffees and I had tonic water. His face was very white and there was a fearful blankness in his eyes. He kept trying to get me to have a drink. 'What's the matter, Bill, don't y'like it no more? Or don't tell me you're one of these damn waistline watchers now?' I told him I liked it too much, how it had been one of the big things between your mother and me. He attempted a smile. 'Jesus. Things sure don't work out the way everyone says, Billy, do they?'

A few weeks later a padded envelope arrived at home with a Wisconsin postmark. Inside was the photograph Buckets had promised me that evening when I had seen him off at the guest-house, an old creased-up snap, mottled by mould, of the Raytown Rhythm Kings playing a gig in Beechwood Avenue Tennis Club on a December night in 1963 when I was seventeen years old. There we are on this tiny stage with a low ceiling, Seánie out front, collar turned up on his black leather jacket, red Hofner slung low down to his crotch, white shirt open to his navel. His damp quiff is in his eyes, with a few strands clinging to his wide sweaty forehead. I'm at the back strumming a guitar and looking a little down in the mouth. Buckets is wearing his sister Bernice's pink sequined blouse and pounding the snare drum, his eyes closed tight, his cheeks puffed out. Beside him playing a tea-chest bass is Frank English, a nice quiet lad from Hope Street in Ringsend. I have not seen Frank in thirty years and have no idea now what ever happened to him in the end.

Seánie was so handsome in those days, what all the Ringsend girls used to call a dazzler. He had sleek black hair that did not curl up like mine, sallow skin, gleaming white teeth, cheek-bones you could hang your hat on, as my mother used to say. He had a way of looking straight at you when you were talking that made you feel like you were the only person in the world. He would listen attentively to what you were saying; often he would say something back to you about it much later, as if he had really been thinking about it in the meantime. He was easy and relaxed, I never once saw him get flustered by anything. The girls just loved him. He had one trick I often saw him do: when a nice-looking girl came into the room he would wait casually until she noticed him, then he would glance back, take his cigarette out of his mouth, do his full-beam dazzler smile, drop the cigarette nonchalantly on the floor and crush it out with his foot, *but never once taking his eyes off her.* It was a small enough thing, but it always worked.

There he is in this photograph, doing the dazzler smile. Christ, what a nightmare he was.

I think we were about half-way through our set that night when I saw this slim beautiful girl in the middle of the crowd, right beneath the revolving mirrorball, dancing with another girl. She had on a blue knee-length dress with short sleeves and white polka dots. Her black hair was tied up on top of her head. She was wearing some kind of pendant that seemed to glitter on the soft part of her neck when the light from the mirrorball would catch it. She was so lovely, she reminded me of Audrey Hepburn. She and her friend were wonderful dancers. They wheeled around and swung each other back and forwards, the two of them laughing together as they swayed their hips and snapped their fingers in time to the music. From time to time apprehensive-looking boys would approach and ask them to dance but mostly the two girls would shake their heads and say no. I could not stop looking at your mother, the way she jived and twisted and threw back her head when she laughed, the lightness of her and the way the blue dress with the white dots moved on her slender body. Late one night recently I was driving up from Limerick through a full-force gale when on the car radio, over the wail of the rain and wind, I heard Seamus Heaney read out an old love poem with a phrase in it – the liquefaction of her clothes: I don't mind telling you, pet, that brought me right back to the very smell of the night I met Grace Lawrence, perfume, sweat, clean hair, cheap aftershave on the hot damp air, the very feel of the grit on the tennis club dance floor, and the liquefaction of her clothes.

Towards the end of our set she sauntered off with her friend and disappeared down the back of the room. When we finished playing, the others went to the changing-room but I hung around in the hall, hoping to see her and maybe speak to her. I walked up and down for a while, feeling light-headed and strange. The second band came on. Couples started slow-dancing. I could not find your mother anywhere. After a while I gave up and decided to go and have a drink. That was when I noticed her again.

She was in the queue for the mineral bar, four people ahead of me in the line, her long tanned arms around a girl in a flowery trouser suit and a boy wearing denims and leather. All three were chatting together and laughing. I strained to hear what your mother was saying but it was no good, I could not make out the words. I remember she took the thick blue hairband off her head and let her hair fall down around her shoulders. She combed through her hair with her fingers. I looked at the side of her face. She seemed heartbreakingly beautiful then. She and her friends got to the bar and ordered their drinks. Then they stood to one side and swigged from their bottles, the three of them looking at the dancers and nudging one another.

The band was playing a Christmas carol. A ludicrously tall girl in a Santa Claus outfit was crooning the words, swaying from side to side in uneasy rhythm to the drummer's brush sticks.

> *In the bleak mid-winter*
> *Frosty wind made moan,*
> *Earth stood hard as iron,*
> *Water like a stone:*
> *Snow had fallen, snow on snow,*
> *Snow on snow,*
> *In the bleak mid-winter,*
> *Long ago.*

By now I was at the bar myself and only a few feet away from your mother. She had her back to me and I could see the tops of her bare brown shoulders. I ordered drinks for the lads and myself and paid for them. I was just about to take up the bottles and leave when your mother turned around giggling to put her lemonade bottle on the bar and I caught her eye. I felt a flutter in my stomach. I did not even have time to think about it, I just asked her straight out if she wanted to dance. She peered at me for a second with a quizzical look but then she just shrugged and said yes, all right. She turned to the boy and girl and asked them to mind her bag.

The band started into a new song. We walked to the edge of the dance floor. Your mother put her hands on my shoulders, and I put mine on her hips. I remember the warm silky fabric of her dress. We danced so far apart it was as if there was another person dancing between us. For a few moments she said nothing at all to me, just stared around the hall with a self-conscious grin, sometimes snapping her long hair out of her eyes or whistling. It intrigued me that she whistled: I don't think I had ever met a girl who whistled before. Then she gazed into my face – the pupils of her glittering eyes were wide and dark – and asked me was I always this quiet. I couldn't think of anything to say so I simply apologised. I could feel myself blushing. She smiled gently at me and said she didn't mind. In fact, she told me, she liked boys who were quiet when they danced and didn't interrogate you like a bloody policeman.

'Because some of them,' she said, 'soon as you're out on the floor it's what's your name and where do you go to school and where do you live and what kind of music do you like? And of course' – here she put on a stupid voice and made her eyes bulge – 'do you come here often?'

'And do you?' I asked her.

'No.' She peered at me. 'But I'm glad I did tonight.'

'I am too.'

'I'm sure you are,' she smiled.

She moved closer to me and curled her arms up to touch my shoulder-blades.

'So why did you come anyway?' I said. 'Is it because it's Christmas soon?'

'No, I don't believe in Christmas,' she said.

14

When I finally got home to Raytown that night the house was dark and silent. My lips were numb and dry with cold. I sat in the kitchen for a while drinking tea and eating toast, while the lights blinked red and gold on the Christmas tree. I looked at the tiny figures in the crib on the mantelpiece, the kneeling shepherds, the virgin in blue, the camel missing one hump, the chipped and misshapen Magi. I went up to my room, put on the bedside light and undressed. It was so very cold that night, I remember shivering, and ice forming on the inside of the windowpane. I took a blanket from the bed and wrapped it around myself. Your Uncle Stephen, who would have been about ten at the time, woke up and asked me was anything wrong, but I told him no, nothing was wrong, everything was fine now, and he fell back asleep, stuttering the names of the stars, which for some reason always used to feature in his dreams when he was that age. I got a pencil and an old copybook and wrote out the words of the song to which your mother and I had danced.

'*Vulpecula,*' he sleepwhispered. '*Andromeda. Draco. Perseus.*'

I have the copybook still and came across it again only recently, in a drawer downstairs stuffed with tangled fairy lights, strings of bright tinsel, sheets of crepe paper, angels made of tin foil. There is a map of Ireland on the salmon-pink front cover, along with my name and birthplace in Irish, '*Liam O'Suibhne, Baile Atha Cliath*', and an intricate Celtic cross. The inside cover has printed on it the names of all the signatories of the 1916 proclamation along with their dates of birth and execution by the British. There is only one piece of homework in the copybook, an essay about what I had done on my summer holidays that year. All the other kids had written about trips down the country to see their relations, or building sandcastles on Dollymount strand. I wrote about going to the moon. There it is, 'My Summer on the Moon' by Liam O'Suibhne. And there on the inside back cover are the date and the words to the song, in red fountain pen, tiny scribbled letters, somehow fitted in beneath the printed panel containing the names of the thirty-two counties of Ireland, with their chief towns, important rivers and major industries, and the motto 'Ireland Unfree Shall Never be at Peace'.

Aquila. Delphinus. Arcturus. Castor. Ophiuchus. Pleiades. Camelopardalis.

1963 *December 12*

I can feel a new sensation in the place;
I can feel a new expression on my face;
And I can hear the guitars playing lovely tunes,
Every time that you walk in the room.

★

When Seánie and I arrived for the second day of the trial we were a couple of minutes late. The traffic had been very bad on the drive in from Dalkey; an oil truck had jackknifed on the dual carriageway outside RTE, and Nutley Lane had been closed. It was clear when we got to the court that something was badly wrong. Reporters were crowded around the door, shoving each other, trying to take pictures, being warned to stop and held back by a line of guards. Some of them shouted at me as I tried to get in, asked me how I felt about what had happened now. Before I could answer or even speak two guards had grabbed Seánie and me by the arms and were dragging us through the scrum and into the court. As we pushed our way in I saw that the detective was on his feet and trying to speak to the judge. People in the public gallery were clapping and shouting. The solicitors and young clerks at the defence table were searching frantically through thick files and books. The judge banged his fist on the bench. 'Silence! I've more to do now than contend with empty-headed persons who are here, as far as I can see, for their own amusement and entertainment. There'll be no further disruption of these proceedings. There'll be complete silence this minute, I'm telling you now, or everyone will be put out immediately by the guards. Now go on, superintendent.'

The detective coughed. 'Yes, my Lord, I'm afraid it's my duty to inform the court that the prisoner Quinn unfortunately absconded from custody at about five-thirty yesterday afternoon and has not been apprehended since.'

Lizzie came over to me and gripped my wrist. Seánie's mouth was open wide. One of the defence solicitors stood up and started jabbering something about a mistrial application. I could not concentrate on what he was saying. I think he wanted the jury sent out. An argument started. I remember certain words being angrily shouted – Supreme Court, justice, constitutional rights – and then, before the jury members had quite left, the detective raised his hand and asked for permission to address the court again. The defence solicitors objected furiously that it was a matter for counsel, but the judge told them to sit back down. Quinn's solicitor stayed on her feet, arguing that the jury should be removed immediately if the detective was going to be allowed to give evidence.

'God, hold your horses, can't you, Miss Harding? They're going. And then I'll hear the detective for a minute, it isn't evidence. Superintendent, what measures have you in hand to deal with this very unfortunate turn of events?'

'My Lord, my officers are out now looking for him and I'm confident of an imminent arrest. I would urge your Lordship not to take any action by way of entertaining a mistrial plea. The prisoner Quinn has been known to my colleagues and myself for some time. He has a record of serious violent crime in the south inner city. I've had occasion to interview him many times. He comes from a well-known criminal family and has been in trouble before. Your Lordship will recall that his brother was shot dead in a criminal feud in the city last year.'

A solicitor I had not heard speak before jumped up and shouted. 'My Lord, this is absolutely outrageous. Three or four of the jury are still present in court. There's an application before you in relation to the matter. And what Detective Doyle has just said is irrelevant and absolutely can't be admitted. I'll have to insist on the immediate removal of the full jury if he's going to be allowed to abuse the court in this way again.'

'Yes, yes, Mr Duggan, I know. That can't be admitted, detective, you know that well enough. Or you should know it. Now if those few jury members could please leave the court.'

The last of the jurors filed out through the door.

'My Lord,' said the detective, then. 'If you could grant a short adjournment . . .'

The judge held up his hand. 'You know well I have the greatest sympathy for the gardaí in these difficult times and so on. I think you'd agree that I'd very rarely be found wanting when it comes to the gardaí. But what am I to do here? There are procedures, you know. How in the name of God did this man accused of such a serious violent crime manage to escape from the State's custody?'

'It seems he overpowered the dentist, my Lord, and managed to climb out of a rear window of the premises. Using the drainpipe.'

There was a roar of laughter from the back of the court.

'You do realise how that sounds, detective?'

'I know, my Lord, but . . .'

The three in the dock started shouting. They tried to get to their feet, jostling and squirming, and had to be held down by the prison officers. A crowd of people in the public gallery clapped and cheered. The three managed to get back up; they screamed curses at the judge. 'Hey you,' one roared. 'I fucked your wife. *I fucked your wife*!' A warder got him into a headlock. A gang of policemen ran into the court with their batons drawn.

'Take them down,' the judge shouted.

The detective rushed over to me and started to say

something I could not make out because of the noise. Lizzie was in tears beside me in Franklin's arms. I noticed Hopper from the office sitting in one of the benches with his head in his hands.

'Silence,' the judge was yelling, 'I'll have order now or I'll clear the court this minute.'

You may be wondering, I know, exactly why I am doing this now, writing down these words that will reveal to you what was to happen between Donal Quinn and myself in the weeks and months after I decided to end his life and started making my plans. Indeed, I am wondering myself. After only these few pages, I am already a little fearful of the sheer futility of trying to put these things into words. It feels a little like trying to freeze running water.

A good salesman knows the things words can do and the things they can't.

But I do in fact have my reasons.

Once, many years ago, when I was in Carlow Mental Hospital for the first time – I think you would have been seven or eight around then – the consultant psychiatrist asked me to take a week and write down all the important things in my life. Just that. He felt it would be good for me, he said. Most recovering addicts found this a helpful thing to do.

It was a strange experience because it was only in the writing out of the story that I realised what the important things had actually been. That might sound incredible to you but believe me, it is true. In those years I was too close to the everyday to be able to see anything with objectivity. I wrote for a whole week, usually quite late at night or very early in the morning when my bewildered fellow patients were at mass down in the hospital chapel. I wrote until I had a hard red blister on my writing finger, then I went back and showed the psychiatrist what I had done. He looked through the two full foolscap notebooks for a while.

He seemed disappointed and even a little disconcerted. This was all fine, he told me, but there was no feeling in it.

I had no feeling. That part of me had maybe died, he said. It was all facts. I will always remember the strange expression on his face when he told me this. Your life, Mr Sweeney, is all f-f-facts and no f-f-feelings.

It was just my luck to get the only psychiatrist with a stammer in the whole place.

You should try to remember your feelings was what he reckoned, more specifically, your f-f-feelings about your choices. That was what made you f-f-fundamentally human, the nature of the choices that you had made. Every person is the sum of their choices, he said, each one of us is a story, a mix of desires, experiences, f-f-fantasties: I needed to write my story if I wanted to f-f-fully recover.

I was tempted to tell him to go f-f-f, but I suppose I felt a bit sorry for him. I went back to the ward and wrote for a while, then I gave it up. But in the long silent hours I spent listless and tranquillized, in a cocoon of artificial warmth punctuated by occasional oddly obsessive, random neural firings, I would find myself thinking incessantly about that word. Recover. An interesting word. To recover is to be healed of an illness, of course, but it is also to reclaim. When a ship sinks at sea the bodies of the drowned are recovered. Stolen goods are recovered by the police. And there is another meaning too, of course, to cover up again. You see, pet, for some reason, lately I have been thinking about what the psychiatrist said to me all those years ago.

I suppose I have been wanting to recover. Hence these words.

There is another, more important reason for doing this now. Last month your doctor and I had a conversation that has stayed with me. He told me that no change could be expected in what he called your condition, at least in the short term. You would not wake from the coma that Donal Quinn and his three brave friends put you into. But you would not die prematurely either. You might awaken in a year, or five years, or thirty years. It was possible and actually quite likely that if you did wake your memory would have gone in parts, or even completely, and that when you tried to recall the important events of your own life nothing would be there. Just a hollowness. A computer, he said, with the hard disc taken out and thrown away.

It was also possible that there would be long-term motor-neuron damage or muscular atrophy. You might never walk normally again. You might well be at least partially blind or deaf. Perhaps you would have lost the power of speech. I found this especially a terrible thought, you who were always so full of endless brave talk, like your mother. These things were notoriously difficult to predict, but you would not die prematurely, he was certain of it. You were in a hospital, after all, it was the safest place you could be.

He took off his glasses and peered at me, an impatient scowl on his suntanned, handsome face. 'Lookat, Mr Sweeney, your daughter could live a deal longer than yourself,' he said, and he poked me a few times in the stomach, '"specially if you don't lose a bit of that spare tyre and give up the fags. You're a heart attack waiting to happen.' You know how amazingly arrogant these doctors can be. 'Now,' he went, 'if you'll excuse me, I've work to see to here.'

In the days afterwards, the doctor's remark began to preoccupy me. It was just a throwaway comment, I was aware of that. But a good salesman knows that a throwaway comment can be more powerful than any other. No force in the world can pierce the armour of the heart like a well-timed throwaway remark. In the car, out on the doorstep, at the warehouse, back at the office, I found myself thinking about what the doctor had said. I began to try and imagine what would happen if I were to die before you. My intention was not to be morbid, but the truth is that you cannot treat your body the way I had treated mine for years and then expect to live to a hundred. I know that. I am not holding my breath for a telegram from the President. So I decided to write these events down, just some things that I thought you should know – and one or two things that I am not at all sure you should know, but I am going to tell you anyway – about me and your mother, some things that you and I never had the chance to discuss and most probably never will now, and some things that happened when I decided to take the law into my own hands and murder Donal Quinn.

If you ever do wake up, these words and pages will be here for you. I intend to see to that. I do not have high hopes, they are after all only marks on a page, black stains and justifications, and no substitute at all for what you deserved from me. But they might help you to understand something small of where you came from, the bright mad love we felt for you, the evanescent love we had for each other. I confess that I do hope for that little, or that much.

A salesman has to have his hopes. It is not a way of life for a pessimist.

Let me apologise to you now if I tell some things the wrong way around, or incompletely. A forty-nine-year-old man should still have a good memory, but my drinking years I mostly remember as a blur, or more precisely, a set of vague stories and unconnected incidents involving somebody else, a man on the run from love who has nothing at all to do with me. It is not that I have forgotten those times exactly, I just remember them distantly, out of shape, out of their chronology, in the wrong colours.

In fact sometimes, I have discovered, I clearly remember things that never happened, or events at which I was not even present. I could swear to you, for example, that I attended Seánie's investiture as a priest. If somebody asked me now to describe that scene, I could, I know it, down to the details, the chubby bishop, the smell of incense, the shimmering blue of Seánie's robe. In my mind I can see him walking slowly up the aisle with that smile on his handsome face, then lying face down in front of the altar with his hands outstretched. I can see that he is wearing new shoes and has not thought to take the price tags off the soles, and as a result the people around me in the chapel are trying not to laugh. But I know that I was not there that day. It is a simple fact, I was not there. I have seen photographs and I suppose down through the years I must have talked to him and others about it. But I was not there. I could swear I was, but it would not be true.

A good salesman will swear to things he knows not to be true.

Chapter Two

Early enough the other morning I was gunning it down to Portlaoise with the car full of satellite dishes and decoder boxes to be distributed among the indigenous peoples of that region when I heard on the *Pat Kenny Radio Show* that the Beatles were about to re-form. A middle-aged man came on from the Irish Beatles' Fan Club, then Pat Kenny interviewed Pete Best – you may or may not know that he was the one who left the band – about the old days and the Cavern Club and meeting John Lennon and all the rest of it. Pete Best is now working in an unemployment counselling centre in Liverpool, apparently.

Fuck me, I thought to myself, imagine taking career advice from Pete Best.

When the interview was over Pat Kenny played that old song, 'Love Me Do'. I hadn't heard it in so long. It sounded absolutely wonderful, that lazy feel, the nonchalantly sullen delivery, the nasal twang of the lyrics, the hollow thunk of the drums, the doleful honk of the harmonica. When I was your age, Elvis was hot. Little Richard was red hot. But in those days, whenever I heard 'Love Me Do' I thought of smoky industrial Merseyside, ice cool in the morning mist. That morning I turned up the radio and sang along loud. Anyone passing me by on the Naas dual carriageway must have thought that I was some kind of a basket case. But it brought back memories, I can tell you.

One important thing for you to know about Seánie was that he was always a fixer. He was simply one of those people who knew how to get his hands on things that others found difficult or impossible to find. I'm thinking about spare parts for cars, real leather footballs, bottles of poitín for some of the old Ringsend ladies, rare cigarette cards needed to complete a collection. Seánie was the youngfella to see. He knew people everywhere, he had contacts the way the other kids in Raytown had acne. That little gurrier would've got on great during the war, my mother always used to say about him, and I knew what she meant. He would definitely have been one of those spivs in a hound's-tooth jacket, the pockets all stuffed with plump lemons, stolen watches, sheer silk stockings. So when it was announced that the Beatles were going to play a concert in Dublin – this would have been early in 1964 – it did not really surprise me that Seánie had got his hands on four tickets despite the fact that the show had completely sold out in ten minutes.

I remember still the way he laughed out loud when I asked him where he had got these precious tickets. He did a gesture which he was fond of in those days, tapping the side of his nose and winking. I think that he had seen someone do this in a film. Seánie was always susceptible to films. I looked at the tickets and touched them and held them up to the light. I stared at the words 'The Beatles' printed on them, in exactly the same slim black typeface that Ringo had on the front of his bass drum. I thought they would disappear if I blinked too hard.

'The Beatles,' he laughed. 'The fuckin' Beatles, Billy. In *Dublin*. If that isn't a ticket to ride I don't know what is.'

I handed them back and asked him if I could buy one.

He clicked his tongue and peered at me. Oh, he didn't know, he said, they were worth a rake of money. He'd been offered two quid each for them by a fella he knew in work. Seánie worked as a runner in a bookie's shop at that time and so always seemed to know people with money. There was absolutely no way I could afford two pounds. My own job in the storeroom of Randall Electrics paid thirty shillings a week and of course I had to give half of that to my mother.

I was broke all the time, or at least badly bent. But I stared at those tickets, love, and I thought about the Beatles and I suppose I just spoke out without really thinking.

'I'll take one off you anyway,' I told him, 'if you let me have it on the never-never.'

'What?' he went, pretending to splutter, 'is it a dollar a week? Are you jokin' me, man? Are you hoppin' the ball or what?' (A dollar was Seánie's word for five shillings. For some strange reason, I think to do with music, Seánie used to talk in Americanisms back in those days.)

'Let me buy one,' I said, 'and I'll give you piano lessons for it.'

He burst out laughing. 'Buy me arse,' he said, 'amn't I givin' you two of them. One for you and one for what's her name. That posh Jewish mott above in Harrington Street.'

It was actually several years after I met her that Seánie finally stopped referring to your mother as that posh Jewish mott above in Harrington Street.

He put the two tickets into my breast pocket. I was absolutely speechless. I told him that I did not know how to thank him. Which was true, I really didn't. This was above and beyond.

'Well, shag off and don't be annoying me, so,' he said, then, which was Seánie's way of telling you that thanks were not absolutely necessary.

Seánie knew that I had been completely smitten by your mother. The Saturday night after I had first met her he had come back up to the tennis club dance in Ranelagh with me but she had never showed. The next week was the Christmas dance and I was sure she would come to that, but again she didn't. I wondered what to do about this. I had discussed with Seánie the idea of calling to her house to talk to her but he had advised against it. Seánie was full of advice.

'Let's face it, man, you've been blown out,' he told me. 'I don't know what you're bellyachin' for, there's plenty more motts about the place.'

There followed one of Seánie's frequent lectures on how girls could sometimes be funny and you had to get used to their strange and unpredictable ways. That only annoyed me even more. Your mother was not a girl, after all. Your mother was Grace Lawrence.

The next afternoon I took a half day off work and waited for your mother outside her school. I did not feel too good skulking around the gateway like a peasant and she took so long coming out that I thought I must have missed her. When she finally emerged I barely recognised her. She was wearing her school uniform, fat clumpy shoes and carrying a satchel and a hockey stick. Her socks were down around her ankles. Her shins were grazed and bruised, I remember noticing. She was with two or three of her friends. When she saw me waiting across the road she did not seem taken aback in any way, and I suppose that surprised me. She just said something which must have been amusing to the gang of friends and they glanced over at me and laughed before walking on. Your mother came across the road with a warm smile on her face and said hello.

'God,' she said, 'I'm embarrassed you seeing me in this awful get-up, look at the bloody state of me.'

We sat on a bench under some fir trees. I smoked a cigarette. For the first few minutes things were easy enough between us. I asked how she was getting along, she told me fine. She was studying for her Leaving Cert at that time and had plans to go to university. A raindrop fell from a branch and hit her bright face. When I think of it now, love. If we had only known that afternoon what was going to happen to all your mother's plans. But it was very hard work, she told me, especially the maths. You know the way your mother always was with maths. Trigonometry was the worst, she told me, it was enough to set a person stark staring mad.

Then I think I said to her that I had been wondering whether she was avoiding me. She seemed suddenly to get a little peeved. She said she had been studying hard and just had not felt like going to the dance for a few weeks. Also she had been invited to a Christmas party at a friend's flat in Leeson Street on one of the Saturday nights. There were far more interesting people there than anyone you would meet at that stupid dance. There had been writers and painters, she told me, and different kinds of musicians; people with something to say for themselves. You'd meet some awful old bores up at that bloody dance, she said.

I suppose it hurt me to think that your mother felt people at the dance were boring, since that was where she had met me. But perhaps, I figured, she was just saying this to test me in some way.

'So who did you go to this party with?' I asked her.

She peered at me with a bold and sullen expression, the same one I would often see on your own face when somebody crossed you. 'That's for me to know and you to find out. And I'm old enough to do as I please, thank you.'

'I didn't say you weren't,' I told her.

'No,' she snapped, 'well I didn't shaggin' well say you did, did I?'

This was not going quite as well as I had planned.

We sat there for maybe a minute or two without saying anything, her long fingers fiddling with the frayed ends of her hessian satchel. I noticed that she had chipped pink varnish on her fingernails, and also that the backs of her wrists were covered with hieroglyphics of thick black felt-tipped pen. After a while she nudged my arm.

'Why anyway, young Sweeney?' she smiled. 'Would you be jealous if I'd went with a fella?'

'No,' I told her, 'I'd be interested, that's all. But you can do as you please I suppose.'

Wrong thing to say, as it turned out. Her eyes narrowed. 'Oh, can I? Is that right? God Almighty, thanks for the bloody permission, Lord Muck.'

'You're welcome,' I said, and I lit another cigarette. A

group of middle-aged people whom I took to be teach-
ers came out through the school gates. They stared at
your mother for a moment but she did not look back at
them. Then they stared at each other, like small confused
woodland animals of some kind. They climbed into a little
Volkswagen and drove off. I remember being surprised by
how many of them had fitted into the Volkswagen.

'Well, I didn't go with any fella actually,' she said. 'I went
with some girls, for your information. And with my cousin
Ronnie. He writes poetry and got himself invited. He's in
Trinity College like I'm going to be. If any of this is your
business.'

There was silence between us for what seemed to me a
long time. I must have thought about just getting up and
going home, but for some reason I stayed. I told your mother
that I had been thinking about her over Christmas, which
was the truth. I had thought about little else. She did one of
her dismissive sighs. She peered up into the sky, then down
at her scuffed knees.

'Well, I suppose I thought about you too,' she said, in a
very gentle voice and without looking at me. Then she just
nodded and peered across the road as though something
interesting was going on in the school's front yard.

'It made me feel warm inside to think of you opening your
presents,' she said. 'did you get good ones?'

I told her about Christmas in our house, how my grandparents had come up to visit from Oughterard and spent
the whole holiday moaning about the length of the journey
and the dirt of Ringsend and the spectacular rudeness of
Dubliners, how my granny smelled of turf and mist, how my
grandad played the piano standing up, like Little Richard,
or so Seánie had laughingly said, how everyone in the family
had given me either a book or a book token, all except for
my sister Nessa who'd gotten me a sub to the *NME*, how my
father had sat down blind drunk to the dinner table and told
everyone he hoped they truly enjoyed their meal this year

29

because he could feel in his bones that this was definitely his last Christmas on God's earth. Just like he'd been saying every year for as long as I could remember. That made her laugh. And I liked it when she laughed. It was exciting, and it made me laugh too. I felt closer to her then.

'So do you want to know a secret?' she asked me.

'Yes, all right.'

'Will I whisper it to you, Billy?'

'If you like.'

She leaned close to me and put her hand on my shoulder. 'I walked down from Harrington Street to Rathmines Church early on Christmas morning and went in. And lit a candle for you, so you'd have a happy little day. That was very bold of me, wasn't it? But it was interesting. I was never in a Catholic church before.'

She looked at me and smiled.

'So you see now,' she whispered, 'you must have been on my mind after all, young Sweeney. Despite your thinking I was after forgetting all about you.'

This struck me as a very good moment to ask your mother if she wanted to come with me to see the Beatles. Always be selling, as they say in my trade.

Your mother sat back from me and scoffed. She folded her arms and told me to stop messing, the girls in her school had been trying to get tickets for weeks but with no success. Tickets for the Beatles could not be had for love nor money. One of the girls was practically engaged to a youngfella who worked in the Adelphi Cinema, where the concert was going to be held, but even he couldn't get any passes. I took the two tickets from my pocket and showed them to her. Without saying anything. Not a word.

Her eyes widened.

'Billy Sweeney,' she said.

She snatched them out of my hand and stared at them. 'Oh my God,' she said.

All week long I looked forward to our date. When the

evening finally came I ran home from work. Literally. I took in a pair of shorts and an old singlet so that I could run home to Raytown when the shop closed. I wolfed down my tea and then I must have spent half an hour in the bathroom trying to comb the curls out of my hair. My father and your Aunt Molly, who was only a toddler then, caught me spraying myself with anti-perspirant and laughed at me. 'Would you look at your brother,' Dad went, 'preening himself like one of the birds out the back yard.'

'What's that under your arms, Billy?' Molly tittered disgustedly. 'Is it *hair*?'

'No, love,' my father howled. 'It's feathers.'

'Billy the bird,' Molly laughed.

Your mother was waiting for me under Clery's clock on O'Connell Street, as we had agreed. I saw her from the top of the bus as it pulled up outside Eason's across the way. She was wearing dark blue jeans and a blue velvet jacket that came down to her hips. She looked like some kind of impatient angel as she stared at her watch and peered up and down the street.

'I thought you were after standing me up,' she smiled.

'No, I was kept in at work.'

'Poor young Sweeney,' she said. 'Are they getting their money's worth out of you?'

The street was full of policemen and reporters and boisterous crowds of teenagers. It reminded me of an old newspaper photograph my father had once shown me of a famous riot that had happened during the 1913 Dublin trade union lock-out. Outside the cinema a gang of Teddy boys in full lurid regalia had converged on an old Morris Minor which they were bouncing and hefting on to the pavement. They all seemed very drunk. I remember the wildness in their eyes. Two policemen ran across the street and grabbed at one of them but he slithered out of their grip and ran away, roaring with laughter and brandishing a beer bottle. As he sprinted over towards Parnell Square one of his leopardskin-pattern shoes fell off and I saw an old lady pick it up and start to slap him around the shoulders with it.

It was very hot inside the cinema and the air seemed damp and sweet. Dark red and gold curtains hung across the front of the stage. Many of the young girls were screaming as we pushed through the crowd to find our seats. There were gardaí and first-aid men from the Order of Malta lined down both sides of the hall. Loud rock and roll was playing over the speakers. I remember Buddy Holly and Fats Domino, Jerry Lee Lewis hammering a piano, Gene Vincent lazily hiccuping 'Be-bop-a-loola, she's my baby'. When the house lights went out the screaming suddenly loudened. Your mother turned to me and smiled.

'This is great gas, isn't it?' she said.

The cinema remained in darkness for whole minutes. Then, from the upper balcony, a spotlight snapped on, spreading an undulating disc of whiteness across the gorgeous scarlet curtains. There was some kind of announcement but it could not be heard above the applause and cheering. The curtains slowly parted. Another spotlight illuminated the back of the stage. There, on a small podium, was Ringo's drum kit. The screaming became frantic. The guards and first-aid men linked arms and tried to keep the crowd in their rows but it was useless, the young girls and boys ran at them, clambered over them, scuttled under them, all trying to get up to the front. Your mother put her fingers in her ears. The screaming got as loud as I thought it could possibly get. One more spotlight flickered on, picking out a flap in the curtains at the side of the stage, through which could now be seen four black silhouettes. And then the screaming got louder still.

John Lennon strolled on first, wearing sunglasses and a leather cap, smoking a cigarette and waving to the crowd. Then came Paul McCartney, who did a thumbs-up sign, saluted and plugged in his bass guitar. A wail of feedback echoed around the cinema. George and Ringo ran on a few moments later and bowed. Then all four stood at the front of the stage and bowed several times in perfect unison. There were piercing screams and wild, anguished cheers. Ringo clambered up on to the podium, took a pair of sticks from his jacket pocket and bashed a few times at the cymbals and drums. Paul ambled over close to George and shouted something at him. John strummed a couple of loud power chords on his beautiful Rickenbacker guitar. And then it started. I could not believe it. This was Dublin. This was where I lived. Nobody famous ever came to Dublin. When you looked for Ireland on the weather map in my father's *News of the World*, the Republic would actually be missing: all you would see was Northern Ireland, an island now, floating a few miles off the Mull of Kintyre. I lived in a place that did not even exist. But here were the Beatles, in the same country and city – in the same *room* – as me and Grace Lawrence. The only other famous person who had ever appeared in Ireland before was the Virgin Mary. But that was in Knock. So I missed it.

And anyway, the Virgin Mary didn't sing 'Twenty Flight Rock' quite the way John Lennon did. To tell you the absolute truth, love, I wanted to scream myself at that moment, and if your mother had not been with me, I believe I would have.

I think the first song they played was 'She Loves You', but the screaming was so loud that I could not make out the words. There they were, John Lennon at one microphone, George and Paul at the other, bopping from side to side and stamping their feet in time with the clatter of Ringo's drums. All around me people were dancing with their arms about each other, jumping up on to their seats, waving scarves and posters and record sleeves in the air. I was actually shaking with excitement by the time they had finished the song. The whole floor of the cinema seemed to be bouncing up and down. Fainting girls were being passed through the crowd. My shirt was completely soaked with sweat. I remember your mother nudging me and pointing out a girl of about sixteen who was a few rows in front of us and to the right. Her hands were clamped to the side of her face, her head was swaying from side to side and she was shrieking as though she was in some terrible agony.

The more they played the louder the screaming got. They did 'I Saw Her Standing There' and 'Good Golly Miss Molly', then 'Please Mr Postman' and 'Dizzy Miss Lizzy' and 'My Baby Says She's Travellin on the One After 909', then 'All My Loving', 'Money' and 'Till There Was You'. It was a good half-hour into the concert before the screaming began to die down at all.

My own favourite Beatles' number at the time was 'Love Me Do'. I particularly liked the part where John Lennon sings 'so please, plee-hee-*hease*' and then stops for just the smallest moment before going on 'love me do', the harmonica riff and so on. But that night in Dublin when they got to this part, John Lennon did something unforgettable. He sang it just like he had on the record – 'so please, plee-hee-*hease*' – and then they just stopped playing. For maybe thirty seconds. He actually *strolled away from the microphone* and up to the front of the stage and shook hands with someone in the audience before finally slinking back to his place and laughing and hollering out 'Love me do'. It was the coolest thing I had ever seen in my life. And as for the audience, I had never heard anything like the squealing that filled the cinema at that point. It was actually quite disturbing. It certainly didn't have anything to do with music, but then, as your mother used to say, music often doesn't.

I remember that at one stage your mother and I were trying to dance in one of the aisles but the crowd had simply got too unruly by then. People were falling over seats and stampeding from side to side of the hall as they tried to get up to the front. During one particularly strong surge towards the stage your mother was pushed up hard against me, but when the crowd flowed away again she stayed where she was for a moment, pressed into my chest with her arms around my waist, before stepping away from me and beginning to jive again. She kept coming up to me and shouting in my ear but I could not hear a word. The Beatles started into 'I Want to Hold Your Hand'. Your mother turned to me, grinning as she mouthed the words, and then she held out her hand and raised her eyebrows in a silent question. I took it in mine and kissed it. She laughed and rolled her eyes but she did not take her hand away. The concert finished with 'Twist and Shout', John Lennon howling and barking into his microphone while the rest of us joined in, what seemed like every last person in the building, including, I noticed, several of the gardaí and most of the first-aid men. I had a sore throat for a week afterwards.

Outside the cinema we waited for Seánie and his date, a nice girl called Angela Bledsoe who I think was a dress designer from Drimnagh, but we could not find them anywhere. The scene was chaotic. Television cameras had been set up in the street. Newspaper photographers had clambered up on to the plinth of the Parnell monument to get a better vantage point: I saw one chap actually swinging one-handed from the statue of Parnell as he pointed his camera down towards O'Connell Bridge. The police had blocked off the entrances to Henry Street and Abbey Street. Someone said there was a full-scale riot going on in the back lanes that led to the stage door behind the cinema. Young people were lying on the pavements in hysterical tears. The noise was constant, shouting, screaming, car horns, and chants, instructions being bawled through bull-horns by the police. Your mother and I decided not to wait any longer so we walked quickly up towards Grafton Street and she linked her arm in mine. Just outside the front gate of Trinity College we bumped into two girls she knew from Clanbrassil Street. We stopped and chatted to them for a few minutes and told them all about the concert. She introduced me and I shook hands with the girls. It made me feel excited to have been seen in public with Grace Lawrence.

Bewley's was closed so we went into a little coffee bar around the corner on Duke Street. It was a strange dark place that smelt of musk and peppermint. There were lurid posters on the walls advertising communist meetings, Republican demonstrations, folk music concerts. A young woman in a red floppy hat sat in a corner staring at a rose which she waved from side to side in front of her eyes. At the next table, singing in Irish under his breath, was a handsome, very tall man who looked like an Apache. Your mother asked for a cappuccino and I ordered one for myself too, even though I did not actually know what a cappuccino was. When it arrived I was relieved.

'That was mighty,' she said. 'I can't believe we're after seeing the Beatles.'

I told her I couldn't believe it either. She did not seem to be listening to me.

'You know,' she said, 'all the girls in school fancy the knickers off Paul. But I prefer George, he looks more sad, you'd want to mother him, wouldn't you?'

'I don't know,' I said.

'No,' she said. 'Well, I suppose I'd worry about you a bit if you did.'

She sipped her cappuccino and licked the froth from her lips.

'And do you like their songs too?' I asked her. 'Or just the way they look?'

She grinned. 'Looks aren't important to me, young Sweeney. Amn't I hanging around with you?'

She could take care of herself, your mother. I wouldn't want you to think she couldn't.

'Ah no, they're great,' she said, 'I mean they were bloody brilliant tonight. And there's only one Beatles. But I think I prefer the Rolling Stones in a way. I prefer bad boys, they're more sexy. Tell us anyway, are you a bad boy yourself, young Sweeney?'

She laughed before I could think of an answer. 'I'm only messing with you,' she said. 'I'm an awful bitch, amn't I?'

'No,' I said.

'I am,' she said. 'If you'd any sense you'd gallop away full speed.'

We drank more of our coffee. I reached across the table and took her hand. She twined her fingers through mine and looked around the café. She started to whistle.

'So how d'you know how to dance then?' she asked me, after a while.

'My sister Nessa taught me to jive. She's a great dancer. She's won competitions for it.'

'Runs in the family,' she said. 'You're a nice dancer yourself, Billy. I love dancing too.'

We finished the coffee and called for the bill. I told your mother that I wanted to pay. She shook her head and took out her purse. 'You will not, *go raibh maith agat*,' she said, 'I'll get my own.' She insisted on giving me the money for her coffee and we even halved the tip.

We went out into the street and walked up towards Stephen's Green holding hands. She started to chant in a gentle singsong voice, 'We saw the *Bea*-tles, we saw the *Bea*-tles,' then she glanced at me and winked. 'Wait till I tell them in school, Billy. They'll only be raging.'

We talked about her school for a while. There were a lot of Protestants there, she said. I told her that I didn't think I knew any Protestants.

'No,' she said, 'well, they're like us Jews. They have horns and tails too, of course. The only difference is, Protestants are blond.'

She had good friends in school, she told me. She hoped they would all still see each other when they finished the Leaving Cert and went to college or got jobs. Of course, one or two of them were hard enough to keep in touch with already, she laughed, all the ones with steady boyfriends. Girls were awful for that, she said: as soon as they got a boyfriend you could kiss goodbye to them. They'd drop the oldest pal they had in the world for some louse of a boyfriend, she said, and you'd be lucky to hear from them ever again.

'So do you have a boyfriend?' I asked her.

'God, of course. Loads of them. Poor Daddy's nearly worn out beating them away from the door.'

'I wouldn't be surprised if you did. I think you're lovely.'

'Stop it, Billy. Don't be embarrassing me.'

'Well you are. I think you are.'

'Oh I know. Gorgeous.'

We walked on. She started whistling again, which I was beginning to realise was something your mother did when she was thinking.

'You're an odd fish,' she said, 'do you know that, young Sweeney?'

'Why's that?'

'Well, do you really think I'd be strolling down the public street holding your paw like a gom if I'd a boyfriend?'

'I don't know,' I said.

'No,' she said, 'well, you don't know much then, do you?'

'I know I'm very fond of you,' I told her. 'I like being with you.'

She tossed her hair and did her mock scowl. 'God, you're fierce bloody serious, aren't you? You're like a little pope.'

We stopped into an Italian chipper on Camden Street and bought some lemonade and fried fish. Then we walked on together, eating from the oily sheets of newspaper. She asked me about work. I told her a bit about Randall's but I could tell that she was not very interested. I asked her more about school.

'I love English,' she said. 'That's what I'm going to study in Trinity.'

I told her I liked English too, especially poetry. She said her favourite poet was Patrick Kavanagh. I told her that my father had met him once, in some pub in town, and that he had been very drunk. Her eyes seemed to shine, I noticed, when she talked about poetry. When I quoted to her from a Yeats poem which my mother loved, she squeezed my hand hard and said it was so sad that it made her want to cry. Before too long we came to her street. Her house was on the corner, a tall red-brick building, with a twelve-arm candelabrum in the window.

'Thanks, then,' she said. 'It was a great night, really.'

She folded her arms and peered at me.

'So are you not going to kiss me then?' she said. 'Some boyfriend you are, Billy Sweeney.'

I couldn't think of anything to say.

'Come here to me,' she said. 'I won't bite, you know.'

I took a step towards her. She put her arms around me and held me close. She signed and rubbed her nose against mine, smiling up at me. I said her name out loud, Grace. I liked saying it. She said my name a few times. Then she began to kiss me. Her lips were soft and they tasted of vinegar. We kissed on the mouth for a few minutes and then she lowered her mouth to my neck and kissed me there. I remember my lips brushing against the fineness of her long hair, and then she put her hands on my head and asked me not to move, just to stay still for a minute. We stood in each other's arms and she stroked my face. I was trembling with happiness.

She took my right hand, raised it to her lips and kissed it.

'You've such lovely hands, Billy,' she whispered. 'They're so gentle. It's the first thing I ever noticed about you.'

'I don't want to let you go,' I told her.

She laughed softly and kissed me on the lips again, moving her tongue inside my mouth this time. 'God, Billy Sweeney, where did I get you?' she sighed, then pulled me close to her once more. I remember her hands in my hair.

'She loves you, yeah, yeah, yeah,' she lilted, her lovely face tilted playfully to one side. Then she turned away, blew me a last kiss and walked quickly across the street and into her house.

Two days later an envelope arrived for me. It was from your mother, a card she had bought to thank me for bringing her to the concert and a poem by Emily Dickinson, which, she told me, she had copied out of her Leaving Cert textbook.

> *Wild nights – Wild Nights!*
> *Were I with thee*
> *Wild Nights should be*
> *Our luxury!*
>
> *Futile – the Winds –*
> *To a Heart in port –*
> *Done with the Compass –*
> *Done with the Chart!*
>
> *Rowing in Eden –*
> *Ah, the Sea!*
> *Might I but moor – Tonight –*
> *In Thee!*

'My heart is in your port, Billy Sweeney. And yours in mine. Aren't we lucky?

'I love you, always.

'Grace.'

Chapter Three

The judge delayed the new trial for a month to give the police some time to find Donal Quinn. His description and photograph were broadcast on *Crimeline*, along with a short, computer-enhanced clip of slow-motion video from the robbery and an acted-out reconstruction of the minutes before and after. His picture was published in all the newspapers, hung on the walls of post offices and train stations up and down the country, and I believe in the North too. But by the beginning of last December he still had not been found.

His escape and disappearance provoked a new surge of publicity about the case in the newspapers. ACCUSED IN STUDENT COMA CASE STILL AT LARGE was one of the headlines, under a photograph of you taken at your debs dance. SIX WEEKS AND NO SIGN OF 'SYRINGE MAN'. What had happened seemed to capture people's imagination. There were editorials, angry columns, protests from women's groups, calls for action from the Rape Crisis Centre and the trade unions, statements from the Council for Civil Liberties, speeches in the Dáil. A delegation of women TDs and senators demanded an urgent meeting with the Minister for Justice. The detective in charge was transferred to another unit. Callers rang up late-night radio shows to tell the presenters how they felt about what had happened to that poor girl, how they simply could not understand how one of the animals who had done it had been let escape. As the date for the new trial approached they actually had problems down at the hospital because so many reporters turned up asking questions about you. The staff had to call in the guards more than once. When you were taken up to Belfast for the operation a whole fleet of cars followed, the reporters sticking their cameras and microphones out the windows and shouting at us to look at them; the same story when we brought you back down, except this time there was even a helicopter above us, hired by one of the English television companies. Back in Dublin they had to hire security guards at the hospital and post them round the clock on the door of the intensive care ward. I got letters of sympathy from people all over the country and a few from abroad. I even got a note from President Robinson.

Late one night just before the hearing was due to start again, a reporter from one of the English tabloids called out to the house – he came right up the drive to the front door and banged on it – and asked if I had any photographs of you as a child which I could give him or sell him. He told me that he would be willing to pay very good money for a nice picture of you in a ballet tutu or on a horse, something like that. You with Father Christmas, maybe, what with the festive season coming up. His editor, he grinningly explained, would cream his jeans for a picture of you with Father Christmas. I looked at him and smiled. Then I opened my mouth and screamed at him. Just screamed, no words or anything, just let out a nice loud blood-curdling screech. You'd want to have seen him cantering down the driveway.

The trial was resumed in the first week of December. On the first morning Seánie picked me up at the house and we drove in to the Four Courts together. All the way in he tried to make conversation about other subjects, how Lizzie was doing, how long now before she and Franklin would return to Australia, the friends they were staying with down in Wicklow, different bits and pieces of news on the car radio, various plans he had for the holiday. After a while I asked him to switch the radio off. I was afraid that there would be something about the case on *Morning Ireland*: if there was, I did not want to hear it. We drove on through the rush hour. Before long Seánie stopped talking, I suppose he had run out of things to say.

The streets and shop windows were full of Christmas lights. There was a clown on Baggot Street Bridge handing out cans of Coca-Cola to people stuck in the traffic. At the side gate of Trinity College a choir was singing 'Once in Royal David's City'.

The huge circular hall of the Four Courts was full of people. When we came through the front doors a murmur went around and everyone turned to look at us. Silence came down. I remember flashbulbs going off. I looked up at the dome; there were golden stars on it, beautiful perfect stars. A reporter came over and asked me how I felt on this difficult occasion.

'Did you think that bloody question up by yourself, pal?' Seánie snapped, and the guy opened and closed his beak a few times – I suppose he must have been surprised that a priest would talk like that. The reporter swallowed and blushed and said he was only trying to do his job. Seánie told him to fuck off and do it somewhere else unless he wanted to wake up with a crowd around him.

I was surprised by how humane the guards were. I'd had plenty of dealings with guards in my drinking years and never liked them much. But that morning they were decent enough, I have to admit. They took us down to the basement of the Four Courts where there is a dreary little coffee shop the colour of a cancerous lung. There were soldiers at some of the tables. A couple of paper streamers had been strung along the ceiling and there was a nylon Christmas tree beside the cash register. I did not want to eat anything, but one of the guards, a kindly older man whose bent nose gave him the look of a retired prizefighter, kept telling me I should have a sandwich and a cup of tea, because it was going to be a long day.

Before too long the new detective in charge of the case came in. He was a tall, chain-smoking, heavy-looking Dublin man who didn't say too much. He had on a neatly pressed dark civilian suit, shiny black patent-leather shoes which seemed strange on his massive feet. He sat down at the table, nodded a gruff hello and lit a cigarette. There were one or two small last-minute details he wanted. He wrote down my answers in a thick notebook with yellow pages, sometimes letting ash fall on to the page and brushing it away with the back of his enormous hand. His eyes moved a lot, I noticed. Even though his head and his large body did not move too much, his eyes would flicker around and seem to take in everything.

A good salesman learns to read people's eyes.

After a while he ran out of cigarettes and I offered him one of mine. He peered at it with a seemingly suspicious expression that might have made me laugh had the circumstance been different, before finally reaching out to accept it.

'Fierce, the old coffin nails,' he said, taking a light from Seánie.

He took a deep drag. 'The wife's never done at me about jackin' them in. Has the ear fairly worn off me, she does. Even got me to do the hypnosis there last year. But it didn't work.'

'No,' I said. 'It wouldn't work for me either.'

He nodded. 'Waste of time and money. But the women are never done talkin', are they?'

'That's true enough,' I said, wishing he'd just shut up and get back to his writing.

Which he did. He wrote for another ten minutes or so, ignoring the noise around us. I remember feeling very tired. I would have loved to run out of the place and home, back to my warm bed. Hopper and Liam turned up from the

44

office, which was good of them, I must say. They sat down with us and had coffee. Hopper started talking too much, which is a thing he does when he's nervous, but I noticed that the detective was not looking at him. He was staring at the doorway now, with a scowl on his face. 'Shay,' he said curtly to one of his men. I turned around to look at the door. A photographer was skulking there, trying to take pictures of us with one of those long lenses. 'Listen,' the detective hissed at the guard, 'go and tell that fuckin' rubberneck to make tracks, will you, Shay, before I have to go over there and break his face for him.' The young guard leapt up and went to the photographer and threw him out.

The detective looked at me. 'Don't worry about that waste of space,' he said. 'If he comes nosin' around here again he'll be carryin' his balls home in a plastic bag.'

He went back to his papers then, scribbling facts, checking forms and notebooks.

A bell rang loudly on the coffee shop wall. The detective's face darkened. 'I suppose that's starter's orders,' he said. 'Are you right so?'

We all went up to the courtroom: Seánie, myself, the lads from work, the detective and the guards. Lizzie and Franklin were in there already when we arrived. Dominic was standing down at the back with his parents and some of your college pals. The detective wanted to know who he was. I told him he was your boyfriend from university. For some reason he wrote his name down in a notebook.

The press gallery was packed, some of the journalists were standing. The public benches were also completely full, except for a row of seats up near the front, on which someone had left pieces of paper with the word 'Reserved' scribbled on them. These were meant for us.

We made our way up to the seats and sat down. The room was stiflingly hot, it smelt of sweat and wet dirty hair. The tipstaff came in, followed by the judge. There was a bit of bowing and scraping and then the three accused were led up the steps from the cells beneath the court. All four names were read out: Mathew Kelly of Plunkett Avenue, Dublin 1, Gerard Paul Davis of Mangan Terrace, Dublin 1, Eamon John Malone of no fixed abode, and Donal Michael Quinn of Michael Collins Buildings, Dublin 1.

A young policeman went up to the witness box and took the oath. He had a quiet and nervous voice, he sounded as though he might have had a sore throat. His hand seemed to be shaking a little when he raised it and promised that he would tell the truth.

The prosecution counsel asked him if he had been on duty on the night of an armed attack on a petrol station at Stillorgan Avenue. He licked his lips and said yes, he had, then he asked the judge if it would be in order for him to consult his notes. The judge nodded.

The guard took out a notebook, flicked through it for a moment and began to read.

'My Lord, Garda Con Healy and myself were on mobile patrol duty from Donnybrook station on the night of 19 August 1993, when we were called by radio to an incident at the Quasar Petrol Station at Stillorgan Avenue. This would have been just after midnight. When we arrived at that premises there was evidence of an attempted robbery in the shop area on the forecourt. A young woman had been violently attacked and was almost unconscious. The assistant manager, a Mr Seamus Lyons, was present and identified her as a Miss Maeve Sweeney of Glen Bolcain, Dalkey, County Dublin, an employee of his. He added that another of his part-time student employees, a Miss Sinead Dwyer, had seen a group of four youths hanging around on the forecourt in a suspicious manner on previous evenings.'

'I object, my Lord,' said one of the defence lawyers.

The judge took off his glasses and peered down at him.

'Yes, Mr Brennock?' he sighed.

'My Lord, that's hearsay. The guard can only say what he himself found.'

46

'Garda?' said the judge.

'I don't understand, my Lord.'

'You must only give your own evidence.'

The policeman gaped around. 'Who else's evidence was I giving?', he said anxiously.

There was loud laughter in the press gallery.

'Yes,' the judge said, 'thank you, ladies and gentlemen, I'm gratified that you're all so amused. When you've finished in the playground you might try to remember that this is certainly no occasion for levity. And that the guard is doing his best for us after all.'

The judge turned to the policeman. 'Now, guard, disregard what you were or weren't told and tell us only what you saw yourself. Was the injured party, Miss Sweeney, actually unconscious or not, for example? Would she have been capable of speech?'

'Well yes, judge, but she was in a very bad way and severely injured.' He raised his hand to his face. 'Here,' he said. 'There was an awful lot of blood. She would have been in great pain, my Lord. There seemed to be deep wounds to the head and the upper chest and arms. The top she had on and the skirt were nearly torn off her. Her tights had been pulled down around her thighs.'

'Right, Go on, then, guard.'

He looked into his notebook again. 'Well, there was evidence of a violent struggle and an attempted robbery. The cash register was lying on the floor and attempts had evidently been made to smash it open. Con – that's Garda Healy, my Lord – immediately requested backup from the station. Two squad cars and an ambulance arrived shortly afterwards. In the intervening time I conducted a preliminary search of the crime scene. Underneath a retail display unit in the shop I found a hypodermic syringe full of blood. Garda Healy told me that this would be infected blood and would have been used by the criminals as a weapon. He said criminals with Aids were in the habit . . .'

'I object to that' shouted another solicitor.

The judge put his hands to his face. More snuffles and giggles came from the press benches.

'Well, my Lord, with respect, neither Garda Howard nor Garda Healy could possibly have personal knowledge of whether or not the blood in the syringe was infected. Nor even whether it was real blood or tomato juice. And they certainly couldn't know who brought it into the shop. It's hearsay again. I'm sure as a public servant the guard would have a good knowledge of the Irish language and would know the old expression '*Dúirt bean liom go dúirt bean lei* – a woman said to me that a woman said to her, et cetera.'

The judge sighed. 'All right, yes. But you know, really Mr Lynch, if we're going to have all these objections we could be here until kingdom come.'

'Yes, my Lord. Thank you. But I'm only thinking of my client's rights, after all. My client's rights are extremely important.'

It was at that point that I got up and left the court.

Chapter Four

A round the time that the trial began again, I got into the habit of driving around late in the evenings. This was something I had begun to do in the period immediately following that dreadful night at the garage. In those first weeks and months of your absence from the house I would often discover myself lying awake at three or four in the morning, still half-waiting for you to come in from some party or nightclub, half-expecting to hear your voice and Dominic's downstairs in the kitchen. I found the new silence disturbing and strange, it seemed to wrap itself around the house like a blanket. I would get up in the dead of night and make a sandwich or a pot of tea. Sometimes I would watch part of an old film on ITV or some terrible gameshow. I joined a video club in Dun Laoghaire which was open twenty-four hours, and sometimes I would drive down there and wander up and down the racks in the blueish light, with little enough idea of what I was doing or what exactly I was looking for. The girl who worked there must have thought I was insane. She was a student in UCD, she told me one night, doing an MA in ancient Irish history. Her name was Gráinne, her parents had named her after the legend of Diarmuid and Gráinne. I wondered what Cuchulain or Ferdia or any of those muscle-bound lads would have thought, if they could have seen us talking about them, there in the video store at three in the morning, the two of us sipping bitter black coffee out of styrofoam cups, while *The Silence of the Lambs* played on the multi-screen behind the counter, Hannibal Lecter snarling into his hockey mask.

There were times back then when I would drive around all night long. I found that I was gravitating back to the places we had gone, Grace and I together, when you and Lizzie were children and our lives had some kind of order and shape. I am thinking of Brittas Bay, Arklow and Enniskerry, the usual places to which Dubliners go, say, on a Sunday afternoon or a warm bank holiday, all in a convoy of a hundred thousand cars. But on those bitter autumn nights I would almost always be alone on the roads. I would often drive down to Glendalough, where I would park the car and look at the lake for a long time, and the bare trees and the round tower, so black and slim against the sky, which always seemed bright even on the moonless nights.

As the trial started up for the second time, I found that I began to be attracted back to these places late at night. Sleep was out of the question. I would get up, climb into the car and simply drive. One night I drove up through the quiet and lonely roads to the Sally Gap, where I knew I could get the BBC World Service clearly because of the altitude. I remember sitting in the car, smoking, listening to the radio with its news of wars and revolutions, earthquakes and volcanoes, all in these exotic far-away places. I remember too that I thought that night about what had happened to you, and then about the terrible events that were taking place around the world, and that I tried to see if I could in some way connect these things. That seemed important, I did not know why then, and still do not now. I must have fallen asleep, because I remember that just before dawn a young policewoman on a motorbike woke me by shining her flashlight into the car. She looked very frightened. I think she thought I must be dead.

I got out of the car feeling confused. She seemed relieved and offered me a cigarette. And then we simply talked for a while, as the sun came up red over the Sally Gap. She said that I looked like a person who had troubles. I told her that I was and explained about the trial. She knew about it, of course, and tried to be sympathetic as she encouraged me to go home and rest. There was not a lot more she could say.

She and I stood on the edge of the Sally Gap and looked down at the lake for a while. I remember great discs of pale light on the surface of the water, the croaking of birds, the sun glimmering on the lumps of quartz and granite embedded in the barren black moraine. Hardly a word passed between us for perhaps ten minutes, but as the sun rose I felt strangely close to her. She asked me if I was sure I was all right to drive. I told her yes. She climbed on to the motorbike and sped away down the hill. I slept in the car for a while more, then drove in to the trial.

Later that afternoon, when the day's hearing was over, I was delivering some dishes to a shop out in Bray when something odd happened. I had a bad headache from exhaustion. The shop was very crowded – I remember a gang of rowdy, red-faced children playing with a computer, Christmas music blaring on a stereo. I had brought in the last of the boxes and was just about to leave when I saw an unusual looking young man come in and begin to look around at the shelves of radios and CD players. He was clean-shaven, with thick black-rimmed glasses and shaved inky black hair, but something about his gait and bearing seemed familiar. For some reason I found it difficult to take my eyes off him. I remember wondering whether he was one of your college friends or someone Lizzie might have known in art school, because he was dressed like a student, in jeans, a black turtleneck and a leather motorbike jacket. Anyway, I was late for another delivery so I left, dawdling for a moment just to check the display in the window.

He caught my attention again. Through the glass I saw him jerk his head, as though to snap the hair out of his eyes. Rain started to fall. I walked back towards the car, still wondering who he was, had he been out to the house on some occasion, had he perhaps been a guest at your twenty-first party, was he a friend of Dominic's? I had the car key in my hand and was about to open the car door when something occurred to me. That gesture, that thrust of the neck. Why would he have that gesture? He had short hair. He did not need to snap his hair out of his eyes, it was shaved so short that his scalp could almost be seen. It was a gesture that a person with long hair would have. Or a person who had shaved his head only recently.

I walked slowly back up to the shop and looked at the window display again, the cardboard blue and green planet earth with the red plastic satellite. My eyes drifted upwards. I could see him moving slowly around the shop now, poking at switches on the radios and stereos. He strolled across to an electronic keyboard and held down a chord. He seemed to be trying to limp, but every so often he would break into an arrogant birdlike strut that I was sure I had seen before. He jerked his neck again. My heart began to speed up. I felt my mouth go dry.

I went slowly back into the shop. My glasses steamed up in the heat. After I cleaned them I walked around for a while, pretending to look at the washing machines and fridges. I kept trying to get a proper look at his face but he had his head bowed and kept it that way. He moved down an aisle of television sets. I followed, pushing through the customers until I was standing right behind him. I could see his reflection clearly in the mirrored pillar. It was obvious that he had recently shaved off his moustache, you could still see the redness around his upper lip. An assistant came over and asked if he wanted any help. He muttered something about cassette players. When I heard his voice and accent my blood seemed to freeze. He snapped his hair out of his eyes again. Twice. It was then that I was certain who it was. There was absolutely no doubt about it.

Trembling, I left the shop and ran down the street to the car. I tried to ring Store Street garda station on my mobile but Duignan's direct-line answering machine flicked on. I kept trying the number but it was no use. A minute later in the rear-view mirror I saw Quinn leave the shop and cross the street, limping heavily now, with a package under his arm. My heart was thundering. I tried to remember back to the day I had seen him in the court. I did not think he'd had a limp; certainly none of the descriptions that had been circulated to the papers had mentioned this. It was clearly part of the disguise, like the dyed hair, those ridiculous glasses.

I phoned Directory Enquiries and got the main switchboard number for Store Street. I dialled quickly and got through this time, a young woman's voice answered, sounding brisk and efficient. I was about to speak, I may have been *begun* to speak. I saw him on the pavement just down the street, buying a newspaper from a stall.

And then, suddenly, a thought occurred to me, as clear as the moment when a migraine lifts.

I switched off the phone and put it down. I climbed out of the car. I could still see him, perhaps a hundred feet away from me now, looking in the window of a butcher's shop, stamping his feet in the cold, puffing out mouthfuls of steam. After a moment, he walked on.

I started to follow him down the street.

It had begun to rain harder, people were running. His limp was completely gone now, he was striding along fast, his feet splashing through the puddles. Thunder cracked in the sky. I trailed him all the way down Quinnsboro Road, past Duncairn Terrace, across the train tracks and down on to the sea front. He turned the corner by the train station and disappeared from my view. I ran to catch up.

As I came around the corner a woman's umbrella caught me in the face. When I looked again, the sea front was completely empty, I could not see him anywhere. Over on my left the waves were white-capping. Far out in the bay I saw a small fleet of what looked like pleasure boats turn and head back in towards the shore. A flash of lightning sparked and ripped over the headland.

I went back to the car drenched to the skin and sat in the passenger seat for a while. For some reason what happened for the next hour or so is very vague in my mind. I recall the seat being wet, the window misting up. I remember smoking a lot of cigarettes, feeling dreamy, playing the radio for a while. And on the way home – yes, I do remember this – there was an account of that day's court hearing on the six-thirty news.

It was much later that night when the rain finally stopped. I drove down to Dun Laoghaire for a walk on the pier and some fresh air. My head was buzzing with pain and tension, I was so confused that I had not been able to eat anything. I was half-way down the pier and looking at the gulls when I could have sworn I saw you standing by the bandstand, a string of Christmas lights spilling a wash of vivid colour over the upper half of your body. You were gazing over in the direction of the beaming lighthouse as though it was something miraculous or maybe sacred from some far-away and better world.

I stood shocked and still outside the public toilets for a while and watched as the young woman turned and raised the collar of her long white raincoat and walked quite quickly back in my direction towards the town, hands thrust into her pockets. A tall stately grey heron lifted up from a bollard as she passed it and the bird stalled in the air above her, its huge wings outstretched and arched like those of an angel in some astonishing old painting. But the closer she came to me, the less like you she was; and by the time she was level with me and I could see her features clearly I wondered what the hell I had been thinking. She was not like you at all. But then, how could she have been?

That night I had a terrible dream about a teenage girl I came across perhaps twenty years ago in Belfast, tarred and feathered on a side street. When I went up close to help her, she had your face. And then there were dreams of flying. Not like a glider or a bird, but more like a long-distance swimmer, having to pull my aching arms and kick my legs hard through the sticky, treacly air to stop myself crashing to the ground.

Next morning outside the courtroom I asked Duignan if there had been any news of Quinn.

'We're following a number of leads,' he said. 'Checking out his regular haunts.'

'Where would they be?'

He shrugged. 'Pool halls, pubs in the inner city. Drinking clubs.'

'Why around there?'

'It's his territory. He'd be lost anywhere else. He's no money, no clothes, no contacts. He'll be holed up in some flat around there. He won't stray too far. They never do. He'll poke his head out like a rat one of these nights.' He clapped his hands. 'And we'll be waitin' on him, don't worry.'

Sweetheart, it was tolerable – in truth, it was almost even pleasurable – to sit in the court that day. I listened to the medical evidence, the fingerprint expert, I watched the lawyers argue and the jury fidget and yawn. The word 'truth' was mentioned many times. The importance of ascertaining the truth. And all the time, I told myself, I knew one part of the truth that nobody else in the court knew. I knew the truth about Donal Quinn.

At about eight that night I went back out to Bray to look for him. I could tell you that I had planned it – I suppose I must have – but if I did I was not aware of it. I simply got into the car after dinner and drove those five miles from Dalkey. It was almost as though it was nothing to do with me. In my mind's eye I recall the car seeming to drive itself, like one of those luridly-coloured carts on a roller-coaster track.

When I got to Bray the amusement arcades were very full; it was so close to Christmas. I could see the sparks of silver and orange spat out by the black dodgems. I could hear the screams and wild laughs and the rock music booming from every doorway. Couples were kissing in the alleyways and bus shelters. The smell of fish and chips filled the air, mingling with the sickening smell of candyfloss and cordite from the dodgem arenas. Up on Bray Head I could see the black cross looming against the sky. I remember walking past a bar and hearing a jazz band inside belting out the Saint Louis Blues. The door of the bar opened as I passed and I got a wave of that hot manly smell of drink and cigarettes. Somehow I managed to keep walking. I did not see him anywhere that night, although I looked around for what seemed to me like hours.

Before long it became a habit to go out to Bray every night as soon as the day's proceedings in the court were over. When I close my eyes and think back to those insane nights I am able to see the whole sea front. There is the snooker hall, there the crazy golf, the helter-skelter, there the ghost train with the fat laughing phantom painted in white on the wall and the leering skeleton on the doors. There, just down the way, is the roundabout with the nightmarish blue horses caterwauling at the silver-foil moon; next to that, the machine where the boys punch a boxing ball as hard as they can and see if they can ring a bell. I got to know it all so well. The streets of Bray became almost as familiar to me as my own house.

The first few nights I saw nothing. But then he would be hard to see, I remember telling myself, because he was so small. And then one night – maybe the fourth or fifth – I did see him, I was sure of it. Down by the huge, inflatable rubber castle surrounded by a gang of jostling kids in black leather jackets, there he was. By the time I parked the car and got closer he had gone into the slots palace. I went in and looked around for a while. The place was full of old people, some of them in slippers, all of them shovelling plastic cups of change into the fruit machines. I could not find him. I hung around for a time playing electric roulette. I kept winning. It was one of those machines where the rotating wheel is divided into five or six triangles of different colours and you bet on which colour is going to come up. I had twelve or fourteen bets in a row. I just kept winning. I bet more and more money and still I kept winning. It started to frighten me actually. I had to stop playing.

The next night I saw him again. It was raining quite hard and I was driving slowly along the wet main street, red and green Christmas lights reflecting in all the shop windows. Half-way down the street and just outside the tall morbid-looking church a shouting match was going on between a gang of teenage lads. One chubby youngfella had been pushed up hard against the church railings and another was bawling senselessly into his face, pulling hard on the lapels of his jacket. A third, who was perhaps a little older and very heavily muscled for such a small-framed boy, suddenly ran at the other two, flailing his arms and screaming. All three fell on the ground in a scramble of punches and kicking feet.

I drove on a little way down the street. I was still looking for Quinn, of course. But what I had seen outside the church was on my mind. I felt that I should do something to break up the fight. I wished I had not seen it, because I hate to get involved in other people's situations, and these days you would not know how something like that would turn out. A cosh, for example, or even a knife would not be a surprise. A syringe. But I had seen it, and now I knew that I would have to do something.

Plenty of times in the past, people saw me in similar trouble and just kept on walking. A good salesman remembers his hard lessons.

I drove on, looking around myself for a place to park. Soon I came to a part of the street where there is an all-night kebab shop. I do not know what made me glance up at the window – perhaps it was the Christmas lights – but for some reason I did. He was there, in the queue by the counter. I recognised him immediately, that emaciated face with the scar across the forehead, the cropped black hair, the sideburns, the Buddy Holly glasses, also the way he moved: tight, controlled, disciplined. Like a soldier. It was definitely him, there was no doubt at all in my mind. Beside him was a tired-looking girl in baggy jeans and a knee-length black leather coat. The Merc behind me, a taxi, started honking furiously and flashing its headlights. I had to drive on. I went around the corner on to Quinsboro Road and pulled the car up on to the footpath. I switched on my emergency lights. As the taxi overtook me the driver rolled down his window and yelled, but I did not hear what he was saying. My heart was pounding. My palms, I noticed, had started to sweat. The steering wheel was actually damp.

There are times in every life, I think, when the things you have fantasised about are suddenly on the point of coming true, depending on the action you take or do not take, depending on the range of your choices. And those are very dangerous times.

As I got out of the car I saw him up ahead of me, crossing the street very quickly. I followed. He was jogging along with a plastic shopping bag over his head to keep off the rain. The leather-coated woman was with him, trotting behind. They went into the cinema. A loud bus, leaking diesel and smoke, cut me off just as I was about to follow and cross. By the time I got into the picture house the lobby was empty. There was a bored-looking young woman behind the counter. I went over and knocked on the window, which had been decorated with bell-shaped sprays of artificial snow, and a foot-long poster of Santa Claus, onto which graffiti genitals had been scribbled.

'There was a youngfella here a few minutes ago,' I told her, 'buying a ticket. He was with a girl.'

She peered up at me. 'You don't say, Sherlock.'

'He's my son,' I said. 'You see, he's not well, love, I've drugs for him here that he needs, he's an epileptic.' I patted my pocket at this stage. I may have also pursed my lips.

A good salesman can tell believable lies.

'Well, there's three screens here,' the young woman said. 'And I can't remember which one he's after goin' into.'

She gave me a ticket for Cinema One and I went in. The film had started. Up on the screen a blonde woman in a torn silk dress was running frantically through a multi-storey car park. A black man on a motorbike chased after her with a long knife in his hand. I stood at the back for a while but could not pick out Quinn anywhere. I could feel myself breathing so hard that I was afraid someone would hear me.

I came out and waited for the film to end, but he was not among the people who left. I felt angry now, frustrated to have lost him. I got into the car and drove down through the jangling, lit-up streets to the sea front. I sat there without getting out and looked at the sea. The water was grey and white. Although it was cold that night – I see in my diary that it went down almost to zero – I had to open the window, because I felt so light-headed. When the waves broke on the shore they threw a crunch of stones up on to the beach. The air smelled of seaweed and urine and hamburgers. Gulls wheeled around in the air, wailing like amorous cats as they rose and fell in the breeze. Down near the water sat a line of paddle boats shaped like laughing animals, all chained up together in the wet sand.

I could see the mail-boat, passing Howth far off in the distance. I switched on the radio. It was playing a carol service.

> *In the bleak mid-winter*
> *Frosty wind made moan*
> *Earth stood hard as iron,*
> *Water like a stone*
> *Snow had fallen, snow on snow,*
> *Snow on snow,*
> *In the bleak mid-winter,*
> *Long ago.*

I closed my eyes. I tried to breathe more deeply and calmly.

And just then, for some reason, your mother stalked across my mind like a ghost. Such a sharp and immediate sensation, it was as though she was there in the car with me.

I always feel that she is some way close to me around Christmas. Perhaps this is because I met her at Christmas, and also her birthday, as you know, was St Stephen's Day. And I think it would have been around Christmas 1966 that she told me she could not marry me. We had been to a dress dance in a hotel, it might have been the Gresham. I knew there was something on your mother's mind because she had not wanted to dance much. At the table she had seemed preoccupied and irritable. After only an hour she had asked me if I would mind leaving early.

Out in the street I asked if she was feeling sick. She shook her head and tried to smile. She was not sick, she said, she just wanted to talk to me about something that could not wait any longer. I suppose I must have got a sinking feeling. We had been arguing recently, and sometimes when we fought she would threaten to finish with me.

She asked me if we could go for a walk. And yes, I suppose the hotel must have been the Gresham, because now as I sit here and write a picture comes back to me of the two of us walking up towards North Frederick Street and into the Garden of Remembrance, our feet slithering on the icy flagstones.

There was a distracted and far-away expression in your mother's eyes that night. I had not seen it before and it unnerved me. We sat on a bench by the cross-shaped, frozen pond and she looked away from me, up at the sky, and then at the towering black statue of the Children of Lir, which had been draped with green, white and orange fairy lights. When I took her hand she squeezed my fingers very hard. Tears filled her eyes and started to spill down her cheeks. I put my arm around her shoulder and she gave a small, timorous sob. I asked if she wanted a cigarette – she had started smoking by then – but she shook her head.

'I probably shouldn't,' she said, and wiped her face with her sleeve.

'And why's that?'

'Because I'm pregnant, Billy. I'm going to have a baby.'

Her hands were shaking when she said it and her lips were trembling. I looked at her for a while. I asked if she was sure and she nodded. She had been to a doctor in town. She had not gone to the family doctor because she had been afraid that he would tell her parents. A girl in college had known about this discreet, gentle doctor and had made the appointment for her. There was no doubt whatsoever about it. She was going to have a baby in six months.

I was astounded, love, because I thought that we had been so careful. I simply could not figure out how this had happened to us. I think that I probably said nothing at all for a while. It was desperately cold in the park, so cold that I thought it was going to snow. I remember feeling this terrible, absolute certainty that I would always remember this conversation and what was about to happen. It was the first time in my life that I ever had that sensation. I held your mother's quivering hands and kissed them. I wished I could do something to stop her crying. After a while I told her it did not matter to me that she was pregnant, we could get married anyway.

'It's not the first time this ever happened to people,' I said, and I remember trying to laugh. 'I mean to say, it's not like we just met last week, is it? It's been two years now, after all. It's nearly time we named the day, that's what my Da keeps telling me.'

'I don't think you understand, Billy,' she said.

'I do, Grace,' I said. 'Of course I do.'

She shook her head. 'It's not yours,' she said.

She knew who the father was, she told me. He was not somebody she loved, and he certainly did not love her either. It was just a stupid thing that had happened and she was ashamed of herself. She had been to a party in college and had too many drinks. She had ended up going back to this person's flat afterwards. Things had happened, they had lost control of themselves. She could not say that she did not know what she had been doing, because she did. And now it was too late. She said all this to me very calmly, as though it was a speech she had written down and learnt by heart. It was only when she spoke about how we could not even think of getting married now that she began to get visibly upset once more. She hung her head and wept into her hands.

I held your mother as tightly as I could and told her that I did not care about any of this. I do not know how long we must have sat there with me telling her again and again that I did not care. I pleaded with her, love, I am not ashamed to tell you. I begged her. I said that we could get married and she could have the child and we would bring it up together. We would be a family together and nobody would ever interfere with that. I told her there was nothing in the world that could ever stop me loving her, not even this. But she did not believe me, or would not, and perhaps she was right, after all.

Because of course I did care. I did care.

When she dried her eyes and started to speak again there was a coldness about her that terrified me. She seemed immune and detached, she would not even look at me. She had made plans, she said, and they did not involve me any more. She told me that she could never see me again. She was going to leave in a minute or two and she did not want me on any account to follow her.

After she had left, I sat there feeling shell-shocked and stared at the pond. To be honest, this is another of those times about which I do not remember very much. A few minutes ago I put down my pen and began to rack my memory, searching for some tangible thing to tell you about exactly how I felt that night after your mother left, but the truth is that I can recall nothing for a few hours except the unmerciful bitterness of the cold, the glint of the lights on the statue of the Children of Lir, the doleful sound of country-and-western music coming from one of the dancehalls out on Parnell Square. And ice. Ice on the water.

Much later, at about ten o'clock, an attendant came over and told me that I would have to leave now, he was locking up for the night. I left the park and walked down the street, looking for a pub. I could not find one, so I went into the bar of the Gate Theatre on Parnell Square. I had some drinks there and then the play must have ended because I remember the room being suddenly very full of wealthy-looking men in sharp suits and women in fur coats and pearls. I stayed for a while and had more whiskeys and Coke. I think I must have got into an argument with somebody, because after a while an usher in a royal blue military-style uniform marched over and asked me to leave.

I went out into the street feeling badly drunk. I did not want to go home. I did not want my mother to ask me why I was back so early. I wondered where Seánie could be. He did not have a telephone at home – none of us in Ringsend had phones in those days – so I could not ring him. I was desperate to talk to somebody. I remember just walking around aimlessly for a while and I think I might have been sick in an alleyway behind the GPO. Then I recall being on Leeson Street, where the late-night drinking dens used to be at that time. I had somehow got it into my head that Seánie would be in one of these clubs. I managed to talk my way into one place, which was tiny and flashing with white light and full of dancers in Santa Claus hats. Of course, Seánie was not there. I had some drinks. When the club closed it was after four. I walked up and down Leeson Street for a while, then I sat on the cold steps outside one of the Georgian houses. I remember a prostitute going by and staring down at me for a few moments before walking on, her heels clacking on the pavement. Next thing I recall is being woken up by a milkman just after dawn.

Shortly after that Christmas I heard that your mother intended to go to England to have the child. There was a convent in London where an order of nuns took in young women who were pregnant without wanting to be. She wrote to me before she left to say that she had quit college. She was going to have the baby and give it up for adoption in America. She was never coming back to Ireland. She said that she might write again when she had settled down in London, but, in fact, she never did.

I managed to get her address in London from one of her college friends, but the letters I sent were always returned unopened. Then they began to come back marked 'Not known at this address'. Finally they stopped being returned at all and I stopped writing.

One day I plucked up the courage to call at her house in Harrington Street. Her father opened the door and let me in. The house smelt of polish and warm bread. He was a broad, handsome man before he got sick, your grandfather, distinguished-looking and vaguely aristocratic in his bearing. He had a beautiful warm accent, half Dublin and half East European. Yes, he smiled, he knew exactly who I was. Grace had often mentioned me to his wife and himself; in fact, he chuckled, they were a little surprised never to have met me before now. She was getting on very well over in London, he said. She sometimes telephoned on a Sunday night but no, he did not have an address. She was always moving around, what with her new job over there. She was working for a travelling theatre company and was never in one place longer than a week or two. I realized then that he did not actually know what had happened. He clearly had no idea about the child. His wife and himself had not exactly been keen on Grace taking a year off college, he laughed, 'But then, you know my Grace, she has definite ideas about everything, like all the modern young women, isn't that right?' Next time she telephoned he would be sure to pass on my best regards and say that I had been asking after her. I wrote out my name and address and asked him to be sure to give them to her. It was very important that she write back to me. He laughed, winked and clapped me on the shoulder. 'I like your style, Billy,' he went. 'Faint heart never won fair lady, isn't that it?'

He promised to tell her it was urgent that she get in touch immediately but of course the months passed and no letter ever arrived.

One night in the following October, I suppose, or November, when I got in from work the house was empty apart from my mother, who was sitting at the kitchen table by herself. She had sent everyone out to the cinema, she told me, because she thought that she and I should have a talk. Somehow she had found out that Grace had been pregnant. She was very sad to hear it, she told me, but sadder to hear about how I had treated her, abandoning her like that and sending her away to England to have the child by herself.

'The girl's only a child herself, Billy,' she told me. 'It isn't right what you've done.'

I think I might actually have laughed at this point. Then, when I told her that Grace's baby was not mine, she went quiet for a while. I thought that she would be horrified, but she did not seem to be. She spent some time peering at the tablecloth, scraping at a tiny lump of grease with her thumbnail. In the end she just sighed and looked across at me.

'What about St Joseph?' she said, and laughed softly. 'That child wasn't his either.'

'I'm not St fuckin' Joseph, Ma,' I told her, 'in case you hadn't noticed.'

'Oh, I had, love,' she said. 'Don't worry.'

She got up from the table and went to the shelf over the sink. She reached around into a space behind the shelf and took out two rolled-up pound notes. She slapped them down on the table.

'That's for you,' she said. 'Get over to England and fetch her back here where she belongs.'

I looked at the money. 'What about Da?' I said. 'Won't he throw the head if he hears you gave me that? That's your Christmas money, isn't it?'

'I've discussed it all with Daddy,' she said. 'He agrees with me. You'll have to go over and get her.'

'I'll go at the weekend.'

'No, son. Go tonight. Go now. We could all be dead by the weekend.'

That very evening I took the boat from Dun Laoghaire to Holyhead, then the overnight train to London. I arrived in Euston station around dawn. I walked around the wide, empty streets for a while – it was my first time in London and I knew nobody. I had a cup of milky coffee in a half-empty Wimpy bar. As early as I thought decent I went to the convent and asked after your mother. At first the old nun would not even admit that she had ever been there. It was confidential, she told me, that was part of the sisters' mission, to offer a secret place to women who needed it. But eventually she took pity on me and said yes, she could not truthfully say that she didn't know who I was talking about. I was talking about the attractive Jewish girl, wasn't I, from Dublin? She had left some months ago with the baby – a beautiful healthy baby girl, whom the nun thought would already have been adopted by now. Nobody knew where she was.

I went to the last address I had for your mother, a small flat over a newsagent's shop run by a kindly Pakistani man in a dirty winding street behind King's Cross station. The flat was empty, he told me. There had been a fire up there recently and the tenants had gone. He had never met them himself, he said, but they had seemed like a nice, quiet couple. Yes, definitely a couple. A dark-haired young girl, nice looking, very slim, and a slightly older man. Never caused any trouble. Kept to themselves. The girl had liked dancing, he said, that was one detail he knew about her, because one night his wife had called up to her with some food and a few small things for the baby. The door of the flat was open and she had been dancing to the radio, and his wife had thought it so funny to see her dancing like that, all by herself.

He did not know who the landlord was. I could leave an address if I liked.

The next morning I arrived home in Dublin. As the boat pulled in to the quay at Dun Laoghaire, workmen were putting up a long neon sign on the terminal wall: 'Welcome Home for Christmas to all our Returning Emigrants. *Nollaig Shona*'.

All this I remembered in my car that night in Bray, with an ache as palpable as a once-broken bone on a cold morning. Mist began to appear in the bay. A foghorn gave a lugubrious moan. The radio crackled as it played.

> *Angels and archangels*
> *May have gathered there,*
> *Cherubim and seraphim*
> *Thronged the air –*
> *But only his mother*
> *In her maiden bliss,*
> *Worshipped the Belovèd*
> *With a kiss.*

I started up the car and drove home. Ice was forming on the roads.

I felt sure that everything in my life was about to change.

Chapter Five

The trial resumed shortly after Christmas and went on for just over a fortnight. It would have been significantly shorter but all three of them had insisted on pleading not guilty, despite the force and extent of the evidence against them. I attended the hearing almost every day with Seánie. I swear I do not know how I could have got through that dreadful time without him.

Early in the morning we would go down to the hospital together to visit you. Sometimes Seánie would invite me to pray with him, but I was never able to do this. I found the small details of your situation the most distressing – the forest of Christmas cards by your bed, the blue rubber identity tag on your wrist and the plastic tubing around your frail neck like some awful parody of jewellery. The vulnerability of your bare feet. That sounds utterly ridiculous, I know. And yet, to a parent, small things – a child's bare feet – can awaken the most visceral protectiveness. After the hospital we would have a silent breakfast in a café in Dun Laoghaire, drive into town in his car, turn up at the court just before ten, sit through the morning session, wait for the next extraordinary horror to reveal itself.

Whole days were wasted with legal arguments of various kinds: the jury would have to leave and then it would all start up, seemingly endless words about what could be admitted as evidence and what could not; precise, measured talk of statutes and precedents and ancient acts of parliament. There were times when I wanted to stand up and scream,

'My daughter is lying half dead not five miles from here. Stop talking! I want no more talk.' It was like drowning in a sewage of putrid words.

Often I would get the sickening feeling that something else would go wrong and all three of them would get off, just like Quinn, but through some lawyer's trick or semantic sidestep. I actually grew to despise some of the barristers, so vulgarly polite and smilingly obsequious; even the prosecution counsel irritated me almost beyond belief. He seemed pompous and over-educated, he loved saying the Latin phrases and ornate adjectives of the law, he would roll them around his mouth like a priest saying high mass. I became obsessed with the thought that they would be acquitted. I started to dream about meeting them walking down an exploding street with your clothes in their hands, all three of them laughing together about what they had done. In this dream I would keep running at them, trying to do some kind of violence to them, but always, always, just when I was close enough to strike I would wake up shuddering, my mouth dry and my eyes hot, the damp sheets wrapped tight around my legs and arms like manacles.

One afternoon around the middle of January, Superintendent Duignan took me to one side after the hearing and said he was not sure whether I would want to keep coming into the court every day. For a while he hedged about his reasons for saying this, but finally I forced him to speak honestly. Photographs of your injuries would be shown to the jury the next morning, he told me. He had seen them himself and they were not pretty, was how he put it. He could not absolutely guarantee that I would not see some of these photographs in the courtroom. People who were not used to court procedures often seemed to think that evidence could only be seen by the jury, but this was not always the case. There would be copies of these photographs floating around the court. If I happened to see them, they would be upsetting for me. He had teenage daughters himself, he added, in a tone of voice which I think was supposed to be in some way significant.

I told him that I had seen you on the night of the attack and almost every day since. I had talked to your doctors at length about your chances. I had sat in the ward with you for hours at a time just watching to see if you would stir. The twitch of a finger, the curl of a lip, these would have been victories to me. It had never happened. Not once in all the hours and nights. Never. There had been many such nights when I'd thought that you had actually died. Curved lines on monitor screens, grey waves gently undulating across sheets of computer paper had been the only proof that I was wrong. I had sat in that ward and watched people old and young being dragged in bleeding and broken around you. One night I had sat there until dawn while the teenage boy in the bed next to you had slowly died. Jesus Christ, I had brought his parents coffee and sandwiches at four in the morning and seen the expressions on their chalk-white faces. I had sat there until I could not stand it any more, until the doctors had asked me not to come at night any more and when I did visit, not to stay for hours at a time. I'd had to talk to your six-year-old niece and nephew, down a telephone line to Australia, and face their confused questions. I had answered the phone to friends of yours who were out of the country and had no idea of what had happened. I'd had to explain to them that you might die soon, while they stood in noisy bars or telephone boxes on the other side of the planet, asking me if this was some kind of twisted joke. I'd had to watch one morning when a doctor young enough to be my son rushed in to start your heart beating again with his bare hands.

'It's not that I feel sorry for myself, detective,' I said, 'but there's nothing in a photograph could hurt me now.'

He sighed and pinched the bridge of his nose. 'Mr Sweeney, I don't know if you understand. In some of these photographs your daughter wouldn't be dressed.

She'd be partially naked. They have to show all the injuries to the jury.'

I told him I would be there and that was more or less that. He nodded.

'I know I'd be too,' he said, 'if it was me. But some people are different. I just thought I'd better warn you.'

In the event, I did not see any of the photographs. But I heard the sound that the men and women in the jury box made when they saw them. I won't ever forget that sound, love, or the image of the middle-aged jury woman who always wore pearls weeping into her hands, or the sight of Duignan hanging his head and peering at the floor, or the quake in the judge's voice when he started to speak again after those moments were over.

And then the day came for the security video to be played in the courtroom. In the darkness I saw your shoulders and the back of your head on the screen, the cash register on the counter in front of you. You were listening to a radio – some corny country music station – and bobbing your head from side to side in time with the music. A black strip ran along the bottom of the film, with flickering white digits and letters. The four of them could clearly be seen coming into the shop, wearing motorbike helmets. They did not run. They walked. They swaggered, like half-drunk lusty boys ambling into a dancehall. The lens was slightly unfocused, or perhaps the film itself was faulty in some way, because they seemed to move like phantoms and leave ghostly imprints and pale tracings of themselves as they slid across the screen. The country song kept playing as Kelly closed the door and stood by it with his arms folded. Quinn vaulted over the counter and pulled an iron bar from his jacket. He started threatening you while Davis and Malone tried to hammer open the till. He screamed so loud at you that the speakers buzzed and rattled in the courtroom and one of the officials had to turn down the volume. You said nothing. You stood wedged into a corner with your hands above your head and said nothing. Quinn screamed again. The other two took out crowbars and began to hack at the till. Then Kelly rushed across and clambered over the counter, waving the syringe. This is my blood, he screamed, I have Aids! He held it in your face and said he would use it if you did not open the till straight away. Did you understand this, he wanted to know. Did you understand exactly what would happen to you if you got Aids?

The music played.

At this point somebody seemed to come to the glass door of the shop. It was difficult to make this out clearly, but there seemed to be a bulky shape in the door frame, like a heavily built man in a long coat and an old-fashioned homburg hat. He stood at the door for a few moments, then he turned around and simply walked away. He must have seen what was going on in there, there is no way he could have missed it, but he just walked away. He left you there.

Suddenly Davis was on you, punching you and kicking, pulling your hair back hard with a long knife at your throat. You flailed at him. There was a series of loud bangs and then I heard you scream just once. The sound drilled through me.

All four of them seemed to be attacking you then. I saw you being dragged across the screen, in and out of the picture, your fists lashing out at them. The film rattled a little, as though someone was shaking the camera. I heard a new voice, a deep gravelly voice, saying that he would rape you and then kill you if you did not help them. You said that you could not help, the till was broken now. Quinn pushed you. You grabbed a lemonade bottle from the counter and let Davis, the one with the deep voice, have it right in the face. You fell over and disappeared from the screen. There was another loud bang and then silence, except for the whine of the song on the radio. And then, after a moment, you started to plead with them not to kill you. Your voice could be heard quite clearly in the courtroom. Please don't kill me.

Take anything you want and go. But don't hurt me. I won't tell anyone. Please. I won't tell. I promise.

The film flickered and ended. The lights came back on in the courtroom. It was very quiet for a while. The judge was writing something down. Somebody coughed. An electronic watch started to bleep.

I raised my eyes to the three of them in the dock. They looked so pale and young. Davis was chewing gum and gazing at the ceiling. The other two stared blankly into the middle distance. Something went wrong with the tape as the court official tried to rewind it, and a high-pitched squeaking sound filled the room. Davis grinned. The other two kept staring.

Outside by the river that lunch-time I felt too sick to eat. I leaned on the wall and looked down at the grey water, desperately trying to steady myself. Seànie was starting to get on my nerves, droning on at me about not getting too bitter and turning the other cheek and all the rest of it. Did you ever hear of a more stupid unnatural thing in your life than turn the other cheek? At one point I wanted to grab him by the dog-collar and heft him over the wall into the fucking Liffey. Try turning the other cheek to that, Father.

'Bitterness isn't going to make anything better,' he said. 'And it'll do damn all for Maeve, you know that.'

'Don't talk to me about bitter,' I said. 'If it was up to me I'd string them up by their balls. Them and their fuckin' lawyers with them.'

'I understand, Liam,' he sighed. 'I'm only saying . . .'

'Fuckin' little liars,' I said. 'They'd swear a hole in an iron pot to get themselves off. Scumbags. They don't deserve a trial, Seànie, waste of taxpayers' money. And free legal aid, good Christ, when I think. It's my tax dollars goin' to pay for their fuckin' lies.'

We went across the river and had a coffee in a restaurant in Temple Bar. I do not think we said another word to each other for the rest of the day.

If I could have found Donal Quinn that night in Bray, I believe I would have killed him then and there.

The verdict finally came at the end of January, unanimous: all three were guilty on all the charges.

Just before the sentence was announced, Kelly's mother stood up and asked very quietly if she could speak to the judge. The court registrar made a shushing noise and shook his head, but the judge leaned down and said she could say a few brief words if she wanted. She moved out of her seat and went to go up to the bench; it was clear that she wanted to speak to him in private. But he held up his hand and told her to go to the witness box and take the oath. If she had something to say, the whole court could hear it.

She was a small, middle-aged woman, slightly built and very stressed-looking, with pallid lips and thin grey hair. She reminded me of a woman we used to know who lived down on Hope Street in Ringsend, a poor widow my mother used to help out from time to time, not that she ever had much herself. She gaped around the courtroom for a moment with a frightened expression on her face. It was as though being given permission to speak had shocked her. She swallowed hard a few times, I noticed; for a while she did not seem to know how to begin. Then she said that her son was not a bad person. He had been addicted to heroin since his early teens. He had fallen in with a bad crowd. She had tried many times to help him but he had never been able to stay off heroin for longer than a few weeks. It made him do terrible things. He had been out robbing since he was a boy. It was not his fault. In the part of Dublin where he had been brought up, heroin had been sold on every street corner for years. It was cheaper than alcohol. There were children half her son's age who were completely addicted to heroin.

'The dogs in the street know who these pushers are,' she said, 'but nobody ever does a thing about it. They're going around like dukes, your Honour, they're in all the ordinary working-class areas now. And nobody does a thing.'

'We don't actually say "your Honour",' the judge said. '"My Lord" is the correct term. Or "your Lordship".'

'My Lord,' she nodded. 'I'm sorry. My Lord.'

There was no help for the addicts. There were only a handful of beds in the whole city for addicts who wanted to come off heroin. It was at the stage now where methadone was being sold on the black market, and the women in her area were buying it to wean their children off heroin. The local parents had tried to do something about the pushers. They had picketed their houses and flats, but had got no support from anyone except each other. The women in the neighbourhood had started taking up door-to-door collections so that private security guards could be hired to come in and kick out the drug pushers, because the police would not help. In fact, once, when the women made a collection to buy walkie-talkies so that they could patrol the area themselves, the police had said they were acting illegally and confiscated the money. The women had then built shacks made of cardboard boxes outside the pushers' flats and sat up all night watching, making detailed careful notes of who was coming to buy drugs. On one occasion she herself had seen four hundred pounds change hands in two minutes. Some of the parents had actually been arrested by the police for doing this and accused of being vigilantes. Her neighbour's husband had helped to organise an anti-heroin demonstration outside a convicted pusher's flat; it had been broken up by police officers in riot gear. The guards had brought Alsatians and batons that night and they had used them against her neighbours but had not gone near the pusher. In the end he had been thrown out by the local people, but he had recruited youngsters in the area to keep selling heroin for him. He was well known around town. There was talk in the flats that the IRA were after him. He was the pusher who had sold her son his first fix of heroin.

Her son was after doing a terrible thing, she could see that. He would have to face his God for it one day. But she could not bear the thought of him going to prison. She knew young people who had been jailed and they had come out much worse than when they went in. The boy's own father had spent most of his life in prison, in England and here at home. In the end he had died behind bars. His first cousin was in Wheatfield prison now. She had heard terrible stories about prisons and what went on in them, how all kinds of drugs were available, how young men were locked up most of the day without exercise, how they were raped and abused, how Aids was rampant. Sending a boy with a heroin problem to Mountjoy was like giving him a death sentence, she said, it would be kinder to take him out into the yard now and put a bullet in the back of his head.

She began to cry at this point, softly at first, and she held a clump of tissues to her face as she tried to compose herself.

When the judge asked if she wanted a glass of water she shook her head. The court stenographer, who was sitting in front of her, poured out a glass anyway. He placed it before her, but she didn't even touch it. She put her hand to her chest and tried to speak, but then suddenly she sobbed out loud, a terrible wrenching moan.

'Don't be upsetting yourself now, mam,' the judge said.

She swallowed hard and looked up at him. 'He has my heart broke, judge,' she wept. 'That's the truth.'

The judge said he appreciated this.

'But I'm asking you to give him a chance, your Honour – I mean, my Lord. I'm sorry. I'm pleading with you to give him one last chance. I swear before Christ in heaven, as God is my witness, I'll lock him in his room all night if I have to. I'll get him off the heroin myself. I'll get the methadone for him. There's plenty of other women near me doing the same thing.'

'I can't do that, missus, you know that now. You've heard yourself the facts of this case.'

'Please, your Lordship. I'm begging you to give him one last chance.'

'You must be able to see that I can't do that, Mrs Kelly.'

'My grandfather died for this country,' she said. 'He was gunned down in this very building, your Lordship, in the Civil War. And I swear to Christ Almighty I'd rather that happened my own son tomorrow morning than you sent him into Mountjoy jail.'

Sobbing again, she pointed one shaking finger towards the ceiling. 'That's the Irish tricolour flying on the roof of this place today, Your Lordship. That's the country he fought for. My country. And all I'm asking it for is mercy for that man's great-grandson. One last chance.'

The judge looked at her for a time. There was total silence in the court, I could actually hear him breathing. He sighed and wrote something in his notebook. Then he glanced down at her again and shook his head. He said that he had great respect for Irish mothers and the work they did to hold families together. In his many years on the bench he had seen what ordinary decent women did for their children, and noticed how it was almost always the woman who seemed to suffer most in a situation. But really, there was nothing he could do here, nothing at all. The youth had been before him several times in the past; in fact, he thought he could remember seeing him in the juvenile court some years ago and as far as he could recall he had given him a chance on that occasion and applied the probation act, even though it had been a serious enough matter. Nevertheless, he had given him the benefit of the doubt. As things had turned out, he could not now say that had been the correct decision. This had been a premeditated, horrific and violent crime, one of the most distressing he had ever come across. Justice would have to be done.

'No reflection on yourself,' he said, 'but this lad is after becoming a danger to people. You can see that.'

'But there's more to him than that, judge. He took a wrong turn in his life. He never had the chances.'

The judge nodded in my direction.

'That man's daughter is in a hospital bed today. I have to think of her too. Little enough mercy she got, after all. And what about her chances? A young woman with everything ahead of her. We don't know if she can ever have a normal life, a happy family life, children and so on. Probably she can't.'

'One last chance, my Lord, is all I'm asking for. I swear to you, I'll keep him straight from now on. Let him come home with me now and I'll lock him in the flat with me.'

'I'm sorry, mam,' he said. 'Truly I am. But I can't do that, it wouldn't be right.'

'Judge, please, I'm sorry for what he done on that poor girl. I can't rest at night for thinking of it. If there was any help could be given her, God knows I'd give it.'

'No,' he said. 'Could you take your seat now please.'

'Your Honour . . . ?'

'Sit down, Mrs Kelly,' he ordered. 'I'm after hearing you out now, you can't fairly say I didn't.'

She went and sat back down, and a teenage girl who was beside her put an arm around her shoulder. But the woman was inconsolable by now. She shook with tears as the judge began to read out the sentence. Malone was given ten years. Davis got twelve, because it had emerged that he was the one who had planned the robbery and enticed the others to do it. When the judge came to the third name, Kelly's mother put her hands to her ears and began to whimper. 'Ten years,' the judge said. The woman's head sank forward until it rested on the bench in front of her. Her hands were trembling badly. A woman guard brought her a beaker of water but she pushed her away and continued to weep.

Her son did not even look at her once as he was taken

away with the other two and led down the stairs to the cells. He was absolutely white in the face and seemed to be limping badly.

The tipstaff opened the side door. The judge stood up and left. And then suddenly the whole thing was over. Even before the three of them had disappeared into the tunnel the courtroom started to empty. Everything went eerily quiet, except for the sound of shuffling feet and the occasional cough.

Up at the front I saw the lawyers from both sides begin to chat to each other. They all shook hands and laughed, one of them clapped another on the back. It was as though a game of tennis had just ended. It occurred to me then that any one of them could have argued any side of the case, it was just a professional thing to them and no more. They were like salesmen. That's all. Nothing more.

A good salesman can sell anything.

By the time Seánie and I got out to the lobby, Lizzie was speaking to a reporter. Duignan was being interviewed by someone from the television news. From where I was standing I could hear what he was saying. No, happy wasn't the word he would use in a case as tragic as this, but he felt that justice had been served today. No, he had no comment at all on the escape of Donal Quinn at the moment. Yes, of course, he and his men had strong personal views on the matter but he was not prepared to discuss same in public.

Seánie went over to talk to Lizzie and Franklin. I watched as he put his arms around them and ruffled Lizzie's hair. An old man I did not know shook my hand and said he was sorry for my troubles. I remember looking down the river in the direction of the Phoenix Park and wishing I was somewhere – anywhere – else. I found myself thinking about Donal Quinn, wondering what he was doing at that moment. I had a sudden sharp mental picture of him listening to the verdict on the radio news and laughing; perhaps, later on in the evening, he would be in a warm pub when he would glance up over the bar and see on the television screen the picture which was now being filmed in front of me. He would order himself another drink. He would laugh at his good fortune. He would walk home and sleep in a safe bed.

A few cold drops of rain fell on my face. I realised that I had left my coat on the bench in the courtroom. When I went back inside, the room was almost empty except for an old cleaning lady who was down on her knees in front of the judge's bench, scrubbing the floor and humming 'Boolavogue', an old tune that my father used often to sing when he was blind drunk. And Kelly's mother was still sitting where I had seen her last, her boney shoulders shaking as she cried into a handkerchief.

After I had found the raincoat I went over and tapped her on the arm. She stiffened.

'Mrs Kelly,' I said.

'Leave me alone,' she said, without turning around.

'It's Billy Sweeney here.'

She said nothing.

'Listen, love,' I said, 'are you all right? Do you've anyone here to see you home?'

'Please. Just leave me in peace.'

'Well look, I've a car outside with me, love. I could drop you off somewhere if you like.'

She shook her head and said nothing. I saw the whiteness of her knuckles as she gripped on to the seat.

Outside on the steps Seánie was reading out the statement we had written together during the lunch break. The reporters clamoured around pushing their microphones and lenses into his face. The statement said that we wanted to be left alone now, that there was absolutely no point in the press following us or contacting us at home because we would not be saying anything else. We had taken enough, we wanted some peace. We had nothing at all to say.

It was a cold dark afternoon and a light rain was falling steadily. Across the river, crowds of people were streaming out of the offices and going home for the night. Lizzie and Franklin left straight away, along with Dominic and his parents. Seánie and I walked up to the Quill Bar with Duignan and a few of the guards. The pub was dark and warm. There was a football match on the television. Seánie and I sat in one of the alcoves by the window; the guards all stood talking quietly in a semicircle by the bar. I saw Duignan pull a few banknotes from his wallet and hand them to one of the older policemen, nodding across in my direction.

The guard came over and took off his cap.

'Excuse me, Mr Sweeney, do you take a drink at all?'

I thought about this. If there's one thing I would have liked that evening it was a drink.

'I don't, thanks,' I said.

He smiled. 'I'll be in fierce trouble with the boss if you don't. I'm under orders here.'

'I'll have a tonic water and ice if you insist.'

He nodded. 'And yourself, Father. Would you have something to keep the cold winter away?'

Seánie said he'd have a mineral water. The guard left us, returning a few minutes later with the drinks, also a pot of tea and a plate of ham sandwiches on a tray. The three of us ate and drank in silence; I could think of nothing to say. After a time some of the other guards came over and sat down.

I suppose we must have stayed there for half an hour, the guards and Seánie attempting conversation about the football match on the television. There was a studied casualness to what they were saying and this annoyed me. I did not want to be given a reassuring hug or a kiss exactly, but I did not want them to pretend that this was all normal either, and that any evening of the week myself and Father Seán Ronan could be found sat in a pub on the quays talking football with a squad of policemen. Duignan walked over and announced it was time to get back to the station. The guards all stood up and shook hands with us. Duignan asked if he could have a private word so we went down the back of the bar together.

'Listen, I'm sorry we didn't nail the other fella,' he sighed. 'There'll be another day, though. That's one little gouger can't stay away from mischief long. Next time his arse won't touch the ground before he's up in the Joy.'

'That'd make my day right enough,' I said.

He took out his wallet and gave me a card. 'If there's anything we can do for you in the meantime, that's where we are.'

I think I might actually have laughed here. 'Like what?' I said. 'What exactly do you think you could do for me, Superintendent?'

Something flickered in his dark eyes. 'Occasionally people find counselling a help, that's all I meant. We've leaflets about Victim Support above in the station. I could drop a few of them out to you one of the nights if you like. I'm often out your way at night.'

'I don't have much time for that type of thing,' I said.

He nodded. 'Well, you know where we are anyway.'

We went back up to the front, then Duignan left along with the last of the guards.

After they had gone, Seánie realised that he was late for an appointment so he went upstairs to make a phone call. It was the first time all day that I had been completely alone. The barman lit the fire in the grate. I took off my tie and unbuttoned my collar. It felt good not to have to make conversation any more. I watched the office workers rushing in out of the rain and shaking their wet hair and ordering drinks. The television was switched off and a jukebox started to play Frank Sinatra. 'I'm Gonna Sit Right Down And Write Myself A Letter'. A girl came in selling raffle tickets. I watched her move around the bar. She would have been about your age. I put my hand in my pocket to get some change, in case she came near me. I wanted to have the change at the ready, so that I would not have to talk to her. I thought I would break down if I had to talk to her.

I felt Duignan's card in my pocket and took it out. Just at that moment the sound of wild laughter filled the bar. On the back of the card I noticed some words scribbled in red biro:

Christ Jesus, grant me the serenity to accept the things I cannot change, the courage to change the things I can and the wisdom to know the difference.

With best regards and prayers from a brother in recovery, Detective John Duignan, Store Street

Chapter Six

Some weeks after the end of the trial, Lizzie wrote me a long letter from Sydney to say that she and Franklin had finally made up their minds. They were coming to Ireland in the summer, and for good this time. She had missed home more than she thought. She did not like living in Australia any more. ('Try as I might, Billy, I just can't learn to say *Hawaii-yah* instead of hello.') Franklin understood and was ready to make the move.

It would be better for Conal and Erin too, they felt, to grow up in Ireland. I suppose that this news should have been a source of happiness, but to be absolutely honest with you, I had other things to think about. I don't think I even finished reading the letter.

I knew by then where he was staying, a small deserted-looking corporation house in a cul-de-sac parallel to the sea front, to which I had followed him one cold night in early February. I had some idea of certain of his haunts. I knew that there was a pub near the harbour which he frequented, and sometimes I would park the car there and wait for him. It was often a long wait. Some nights he would not show up at all. I got into the habit of trying somehow to slow down my mind so that I could deal with the tedium of waiting. I would think about work or the garden, some small thing – one of the many – that needed to be done in the house. I would watch the sea birds and try to remember what they were called. Other birds, too, I would try to name. I began to keep a notebook in which I would write down the names of whatever species of birds I saw on those nights in Bray. I would compose long letters to famous people in history on my dictaphone machine. ('Dear Lee Harvey Oswald, I wonder if you remember where *you* were when JFK was shot?') I would listen to the car radio. And often, to occupy myself during those endless hours, I would find myself thinking about your mother.

About three years after I had gone to London to try and find her, I was walking one hot afternoon through Stephen's Green with a girl called Bernadette French who I was seeing at the time, a nice girl from Donegal town who was a stewardess with Aer Lingus.

We had been strolling along by the duck pond when suddenly I saw a beautiful young woman crossing the little hump-back bridge, pushing a stroller which contained a laughing toddler. She stopped just a few feet from me and got down on her hunkers beside the child. Then she took a bag of breadcrumbs from her pocket and began tossing them into the water, cooing into the stroller and stroking the child's head.

'Hello, stranger,' I said.

She looked up at me as though she did not know who I was. Then she shaded her eyes with her palm.

'My God, is it Billy Sweeney?' she said.

She held out her hand, which surprised me a little, and felt strange, but we shook hands anyway. She appeared well and happy, older beyond the years which had passed since I had last seen her. She looked like an adult now. Her face was fuller and she was wearing dark lipstick. Her hair was cut into a boyish bob style; I had the idea that she might have dyed it. She was dressed fashionably – I can't remember how, exactly – but there was a touch of Jackie Kennedy about her smartly tailored clothes. She had on a pillbox hat. She certainly stood out from the crowd.

I introduced Bernadette and they shook hands. I noticed that Grace was wearing black leather gloves. Bernadette looked down at the stroller, where the baby was clucking with mirth and waving its arms. She laughed at the baby and stroked its plump face.

'Oh, yes, and this is Lizzie,' Grace said. 'Elizabeth the First. Always looking for attention, aren't you, pet? Always wants to be the centre of everything.' She grinned at me. 'Just like her auldwan,' she said.

The baby opened her mouth and yawned. When your mother took off the glove on her left hand, I noticed that she was not wearing a wedding band, and in fact still had on a silver claddagh ring I had once given her as a birthday present.

'Oh, isn't she a little dote?' Bernadette said.

'Not always,' Grace laughed, and she changed the subject back to me.

She asked me about work. I told her it was going all right, I was still in the shop, but had started studying at night for the UCD entrance exams. A few months earlier I had applied for a Dublin Corporation scholarship to go to college and won it. I was going to study English and History, if I could.

Her face lit up. 'Billy,' she said, 'oh, that's wonderful. Really, I'm so pleased for you.'

'Yes,' I said, 'well, I haven't got in yet.'

She clicked her tongue. 'Sure why wouldn't you get in?' she said, and she smiled at Bernadette. 'This fella's trippin' over himself with brains. He's wasted in that old shop.'

'I know,' laughed Bernadette. 'He's more interested in books than real life. That's what I'm always telling him.'

'And your mother must be so thrilled, Billy,' said Grace.

'You'd want to see her,' I said. 'You'd swear I was master of Trinity College the way she goes on. But I suppose we wouldn't get too many scholars down Ringsend way.'

All the time this conversation was going on I could scarcely take my eyes off the child. At first I was not absolutely sure whether or not she was Grace's, and because Bernadette was there I did not want to ask straight out.

Lizzie was an unusual name for a baby at that time in Ireland. I wondered if she might be a niece from England, where I knew your mother had relations, or even the child of some friend. But when the baby started to cry and your mother sighed softly and lifted her out of the stroller I could see by the way she held her and kissed her that this was her daughter. I think I might even have persuaded myself that I saw a resemblance.

We talked for a few minutes more. She was back in Dublin, living at her parents' house. Things were good, though looking after Lizzie was sometimes a handful. She'd had ups and downs but she was happy to be home. Her mother and father were a great help, they had the baby spoilt, they were completely in love with her. No, she wasn't intending to go back and finish her degree, that was all in the past now. She was doing a secretarial course and had a part-time office job at the Abbey Theatre, which meant she often got free tickets for plays and poetry readings. 'If you ever need passes for anything,' she said, and glanced at Bernadette, 'you must give me a shout and I'll fix you up.' We spoke about my sisters and various mutual friends. No, she hadn't seen much of the old crowd since she'd got back. She'd lost touch with most of them and to be honest was not that upset to let them go. She seemed shocked when I told her the news about Seánie.

'Seánie Ronan gone into a seminary?' she laughed. 'Well good God, I've heard everything now.'

'Yes,' I said, 'he surprised us all. My mother was delighted as you can imagine. Insisted she'd always known, of course. Offering up novenas for him by the day.'

The baby was getting bored and restless by now and had managed to work off one of her tiny woollen mittens. She threw it on the ground with a squeak of delight.

'Oh, she'll be trouble in a few years, won't she?' Bernadette laughed, as she picked up the glove and handed it to Grace.

'If she's like her mother she will,' Grace agreed. 'You're a little madam, aren't you, pet? A right little vixen.'

Lizzie put the mitten into her mouth and started to chew it. Your mother took it and put it in her pocket.

'She has me tormented,' she laughed. 'She'd eat the leg of the Lamb of God, wouldn't you, sweetheart? Wouldn't you now? Yes, that's right, you would, you'd eat the fingernails off my hand.'

Bernadette looked at her watch and said she didn't mean to be rude but she was late getting back for work. Your mother shrugged and said that it had been nice to see me again after all this time. She added, with a smile, that Bernadette was obviously looking after me very well. We said our goodbyes and shook hands again. Then she headed away towards Grafton Street, and myself and Bernadette set off in the other direction, towards the bandstand. I wanted to turn around and look at your mother once more but I did not dare.

'Who's your friend?' Bernadette asked me.

'Just someone I used to know,' I said.

She squeezed my arm and laughed.

'Aren't you a great man for the ladies right enough? I don't know how I'm going to hang on to you at all.'

'It wasn't like that,' I told her. 'I used to knock about with her a bit years ago. It was only a kids' thing. She used to sometimes come and see the band play when I was in it.'

'She's lovely looking, isn't she?' Bernadette said. 'She's the spit of Audrey Hepburn.'

Spring came, and in those awful sleepless months after the end of the trial one of the few things that gave me comfort was to go swimming in the mornings. I would park the car in the narrow lane beside Sandycove beach and stare out at the scene like a dead man. That early the bay would be almost empty, except for the gulls and herons, the graceful cormorants, perhaps the odd smoke plume from a steamer chugging out towards Howth. I found the emptiness comforting.

The coldness of the water would envelop me with a stinging shock; there would be an icy explosion and a roar in my ears. I loved the sensation of utter weightlessness which followed – it brought to mind the way I flew in my dreams. Apart from that and the intense raw physicality of the aching cold, I would feel nothing at all, and in those days feeling nothing was a relief.

I would swim out hard past the rocks, then dog-paddle around so that I faced the shore. I would watch the pink streetlights go out one by one, the long trucks trundling along the sea front in the direction of the port, the frumpy old town beginning to shake itself awake. It became a small routine to me.

A salesman finds routine comforting.

Sometimes I felt so alone that it frightened me. Other times I thought – I was certain – that I was going mad with despair. But going mad would not have been the end of the world. The way I felt around that time, even the end of the world would not have been the end of the world.

One morning, while swimming, I began to feel very ill. I had not been sleeping properly for weeks, nor had I been eating much. The night before, in the car out in Bray, I had smoked almost a whole packet of cigarettes – perhaps that was what did it. I do not know. But suddenly I felt as I swam that I was going to pass out. I managed to make it back to the shore and clamber out on to the rocks, where I vomited. My head seemed to howl with pain and my hands were trembling.

On my way back up to the car I saw a milk float clinking slowly along the lane, its engine surging and gently whining. The van stopped and a milkman got out. I had noticed him before, a well-built, muscular youngfella, maybe late twenties, with a skinhead haircut and a goatee beard. He had on dirty-looking black leather trousers under the white coat of his uniform. When I got closer to him I could see that he had a Swiss Army knife dangling from his belt; also, that his face was a mass of eczema scars.

'Excuse me,' I said, and he turned.

'Ah,' he went, like he knew me. 'How's the hard man?'

'Any chance I could buy a bottle of milk off you?'

He eyed me as though I had said something strange.

'I'm not supposed to,' he replied. 'I'm not allowed deal with cash.'

'Oh.'

'Cash is a different department,' he told me.

I looked at his pock-marked face. Another wave of silvery dizziness hit me. Everything shimmered.

'Are y'all right there, scout?' he asked.

I told him that I was feeling faint. 'And thirsty. I don't know. I might have eaten something off.'

'Yeah,' he nodded. 'Y'look a bit green around the aul' gills right enough.'

I sat down on the path and put my head in my hands. My stomach felt like it was twisted into a knot, I quickly became nauseous again and unbelievably hot. I remember breathing deeply through my nose to try and prevent myself vomiting. When I looked up he was staring at me. On the front of his torn green T-shirt was a cartoon of a naked woman with huge feathered wings.

'Ah here,' he sighed. 'Sure, we'll be a long time dead, wha'?'

He reached into a crate and took out a small carton of milk which he threw to me. From another crate he pulled a bottle of orange juice for himself. I got to my feet. We stood beside the van, the two of us, me swigging from the milk carton and your man throwing back the juice.

'Well?' he said. 'Are you feelin' better?'

'Yes,' I told him.

'Musta been out on the gargle last night,' he laughed. 'Musta got a bad pint, did yeh?'

'Maybe that's it,' I said. I did not like his laugh. I did not like his broken teeth. He had a mouth like a thunderstruck graveyard.

He looked out at the sea and went quiet. I felt that I should say something to him. The silence between us was making me nervous.

'Well,' I said, 'y'don't have much power there.'

'How d'y'mean?'

'In your van, I'm saying. They're slow old things, I know. My father was a coalman for years in Dublin. I didn't know those old things were still on the road. What kind of power would she have anyway?'

He shook his head and spat on the ground. 'Don't make me laugh,' he said. I certainly was not going to do that. I had seen it before and did not want to see it again.

'There wouldn't be the power in that shit-heap to power yer mott's dildo,' he said.

He nodded at the sea. 'Were y'in?'

I told him yes.

'D'say yeh got the bollix freezed off yeh.'

I tried to summon up a chuckle. 'It was cold right enough.'

'That's what I thought.' He took another slurp of his juice. 'Not goin' to work today, no?'

'Afraid so. I'm in sales. I sell satellite dishes.'

'D'say there's big shekels in that, is there?'

'Well,' I said. 'It's a living. They're popular enough these days. Specially for the sports.'

'I've a sister loves the telly,' he said. 'She's into things about the olden days. Jane Austen, is it? Charles Dickens. All that auld English shite. I like the American Gladiators meself. That one Jet, wha'? Nipples on her like football studs. I'd prefer her to Jane fuckin' Austen any day.'

Again I did my best to laugh. 'I read all those old things years ago. I don't like watching them on the box. I always feel they're not as good as the books.'

'Never gave a shite about books m'self. In school I mean. Course we'd a right psycho teachin' us English. Father Dalton. Head on him like a billiard ball. Prick-head Dalton, we used to call him, with him bein' so bald. PHD for short. Fuckin' psycho. Used to bite yeh if y'got a question wrong.'

'Bite you?'

'Fuckin' sure he would. Make y'stand up the front of the class and bend y'over he would. And bite yeh. In the arse. Swear to Christ, he'd take a bite out of yer arse y'wouldn't fit into yer hat. Redemptorist Father he was . . . Redemptorist cunt more like.'

I was not sure exactly what to say at this point. 'I taught English myself for a while actually, years ago. Before I got into the sales game.'

But he wasn't listening to me. 'It's like maths,' he said. 'I never gave a flyin' fiddler's mickey about maths either. I mean why the fuck d'y'want to know how long it takes to go from Dublin to Limerick on a train doin' fifty miles an hour?'

'How d'you mean?'

He took a deep drag on his cigarette. 'I mean I never been to bleedin' Limerick, sweat, and I'm not goin' neither.'

'Yes,' I said. 'Well.'

'I met him afterwards y'know.'

'Who?'

'Prick-head. I met him afterwards. Walkin' down the street like. One night in town, few scoops on me. I was with a pal of mine, big lad, he's a bouncer. Remember the night of Ireland versus England in Stuttgart? One nil? That night. Shapin' down Grafton Street he was, aul PHD, some dame with him, dress up to her fanny. Fuckin' bladdered he was, ossified. Couldn't believe the luck, so I couldn't. I told me pal to hang around, there'd be some right fun in a minute.'

'So what did you do?'

A thin smile spread across his blistered face.

'We fuckinwell decked him,' he said. 'We danced him into the cobblestones, that's what we did. We gave him one goin' over he won't forget in a hurry. He was old, y'know, there wasn't much he could do about it. He was squeakin' out of him like a little stuck pig when we left him there.'

He giggled into his juice. I began to feel very nervous.

'We milled him,' he said.

'You're a well-built man too,' I said, 'you look like an athlete.'

He scoffed. 'I dunno about athlete. But I can look after m'self OK. That's for sure.'

'I'd say that's right.'

'That is bleedin' right. Me and my pals, we know how t'look after each other. Anyone wrecks my head, they know what they're gonna get.'

I noticed the little steamer out in the bay again, the smoke rising in a thin blue plume and being coaxed back towards the land.

'How much for the milk?'

'You can owe me,' he grinned. 'Sure fuck them, wha'?'

Chapter Seven

Whenn I check my recollection against my diary I
see that I drove out to Bray as usual on the evening
of 10 May last, expecting nothing much out of the
ordinary. I remember a warm spring evening, airy and
pleasant, there was a mossy smell in the air and the journey
had been brightened by the cherry blossoms all along the
central island of the dual carriageway being in full, glorious
bloom. Arriving into the town I found him very quickly. He
was loitering just outside the church on the main street,
where he often was at that time of night, specially when
the weather was particularly fine. Yes indeed, of course
he was there, staring up at the stained-glass windows and
nervously clapping his hands. I congratulated myself on
anticipating him so accurately. I had even guessed correctly
which clothes he would have on; his faded blue jeans, his
docksider shoes, his Barcelona FC T-shirt, light hound's-
tooth sports jacket

A good salesman has an instinct for anticipation.

I parked the car further down the street, hoping not to
lose him. I got out and put on my hat – I had taken to
wearing one of those fishermen's hats with a low flopping
brim to cover the top third of my face. He was still there
when I looked, still hanging around in front of the church,
his hands thrust deep into his jeans pockets. I pretended to
stare into a shop window.

Before very long, a track-suited boy of about fifteen
approached him. I saw them exchange a few quick words.
The boy gave him some money. Quinn glanced up and down

the street several times before reaching into his jacket and pulling out an envelope. The boy took it, shoved it down the back of his track pants and strolled quickly away. Quinn lit a cigarette.

A couple of minutes later – no, four and a half minutes, the diary tells me – he walked down Quinsboro Road and went into a snooker hall. I crossed to the far side of the street and stood in a doorway, wondering what to do. I did not like being indoors with him, it made me feel panicky and a little out of control. Still, I was just about to go in after him when suddenly he came storming back out, walking very quickly down in the direction of the sea. I waited until he was maybe thirty yards ahead of me and then I began to follow. Something told me we were in for a surprise tonight.

About half-way down the esplanade an attractive girl of nineteen or twenty was waiting for him outside a pub. She had on a short red skirt and black tights. They kissed for a long time. This confused me, I have to admit it. I had not seen her before. He put his hand up the side of her sweater. She laughed and pulled back from him. They turned and walked away from me, down the sea front. I followed. They stopped at a stall and bought sticks of candyfloss. He took a bite out of his, but then threw it away almost immediately. She laughed again.

I remember thinking that she would not have quite so much to laugh about soon.

I waited outside the ghost train while they took a ride. Three minutes and forty seconds later, their carriage shot back out through the black doors. The girl got out, tottering on her high heels, making a great show of pretending to faint. Quinn caught her in his arms and kissed her hard on the mouth. They left the arcade. At this stage, naturally, I was expecting them to head back up in the direction of the town. But they did not. They turned and went to the right, down towards the very end of the esplanade. I crept along behind them, wondering where they were going now. There are no pubs that far down the sea front. This really was a departure.

For a moment or two they almost had me confounded. But then suddenly I realised precisely what they were doing. Of course. They were going to walk up to Bray Head. This was surprising. This *was* new. Once again, I told myself, I had been correct.

But then a good salesman will expect the unexpected.

The path up the Head was very steep and winding. On my left was the sea, on my right a low wall, then thick woods and long scrubgrass. Far above me I could see the cross at the top of the hill. I climbed up on the wall and got in behind a clump of thorn bushes. I waited for seventeen minutes. I remember lighting up a cigarette and promising myself that I would know what to do by the time it was finished. But in fact, when it was gone, I lit another on the end. After another quarter of an hour there was still no sign of them coming back. I got down from the wall and continued walking up the lane towards the summit. Snatches of music from the sea front drifted up on the wind, the crazy waltz of hurdy-gurdies, the thud and smash of heavy rock.

I walked slowly and quietly, keeping in as close to the wall as I could. This was risky, I did not want to meet them there in the lane. But then if I heard them coming, I told myself, I could jump back over the wall and disappear into the thick trees again. As I walked further, the music seemed to die away. There was no sound at all now, except for the swish of the waves down below me. I climbed over the wall again and waited. After forty-one minutes there was still no sign of them. I clambered down and walked up the path a bit more, the brim of my hat well down over my eyes.

Before long I came to a clearing in the woods on my right. In the moonlight I could see the girl standing under a tree. Her jumper was up around her neck and he was mauling her, his thigh between her thighs, his mouth on her breasts.

Her hands were above her head, her fingers grasping at the low branches of the tree. I could hear her moaning out a name as he shuddered against her. 'Niall. Oh, Niall.' The deceitful bastard hadn't even told her his real name.

I turned and headed back down the hill. The sea was a strange shade of purple. Far out towards Howth I saw a huge black cargo tanker, the size of a building, moving very slowly.

Suddenly I saw two men striding quickly up the hill in my direction. Two men in dark donkey jackets and heavy-looking boots. One of them scuffed his boot on the path and sparks flew from it. He had a knife in his hand, I could see it quite clearly, a long thick knife like a machete. I felt my heart thud. I looked around. The wall was too high for me to climb, I was stuck there in the laneway. There was nothing for it except to walk on. I stared out at the sea as though I was preoccupied. They came closer. I could hear them straining and panting with the effort of the hill. I looked out at that sea, love, like I was expecting it to fuckingwell talk to me. I could see them staring at me as they passed me by.

I drove home fast with the radio on loud. I wrote in my diary for a while.

That night, once again, I had the most terrible nightmares – your mother and yourself trapped inside the ghost train and pitifully calling out for me to come and find you. I woke up clawing at the air. It must have been half-four in the morning when I went out to the garden. I remember looking up at the sky through the trees, the feel of the grass under my bare feet. It was a beautiful clear night, a real balmy spring night. The flowers seemed to fidget in the breeze, it was almost as though they were alive. I walked right down to the back wall where the ground was moist and springy from the stream. In the moonlight I saw forget-me-nots, knitbone, honeysuckle, white bindweed, yellow bryonies, all swishing in a tangled mess. For some reason, it felt important to recall their names. I remember saying their names out loud.

The moon slid behind a cloud. Inside the aviary the swing perches creaked in the breeze. Then silence fell down on the garden, a silence so intense it was as though it had been caused by some act of shocking violence. Everything around me was dark. Even the flowers stopped moving. Suddenly I began to have a strong sensation of being watched. I was sure that there was someone in the garden, looking at me. I thought that I could smell cigarette smoke and hear breathing. I felt my heart throb.

I turned and walked quickly back up towards the house, terrified now, absolutely certain that I was being observed or even pursued. I broke into a run, stumbled into that thick blackthorn bush by the rockery. I felt the thorns gash me and rip my pyjamas. Every time I moved the pain was worse, it was as though the bush had come to life and was attacking me. When eventually I managed to get inside there was thin watery blood all over my face and hands, and the soles of my feet were badly cut.

I was half-way up the stairs when suddenly everything became clear to me.

I was still awake at dawn, my head actually buzzing with pain, my throat and pulsing adenoids shot from all the smoking I had done the night before. Although a dribble from my lips had somehow moistened the sleeve of my pyjamas, my mouth felt completely parched. I got up and took a long cold shower to steady my nerves. I threw on some clothes, got into the car and drove down to Sandycove. Everything was quiet. I swam for a while and dried myself in the early sun. Then I walked up and down the lane for a while, looking at the dewy gardens. I remember for some reason their wonderful smells, fresh crisp salad, moist warm hay, somehow so poignant that early in the morning. Truly, those aromas brought me close to tears.

When the milkman turned up in his float I waved to him. After a moment he waved back.

'Sorry, pal, didn't see y'there for a sec.'

'You look rough,' I told him.

'I feel rough as a bear's arse,' he laughed. 'Was out on the pull last night.'

'And? Were you lucky?'

He grinned. 'Lucky enough. But sure one swallow doesn't make a summer, wha'?'

I did my best to laugh.

'Anyways,' he went, 'what can I do yeh for?'

Here it was. 'I was wondering if I could talk to you about something?'

'It's a free country,' he said. 'Isn't it? Thanks to Michael Collins and all them cunts?'

His narrow ruined face looked as if his eczema scars might have been bleeding in the night.

'It isn't strictly legal,' I said.

He smirked and licked his lips. He glanced over his shoulder and then back at me, an expression of malevolent delight in his eyes.

'I thought *you*'d be well set up for that,' he said. 'In your line of work?'

'How d'you mean?'

He laughed. 'Well, is it the videos?'

'The videos?'

'Don't gimme the babes-in-the-wood routine, head. D'y'not know what I mean, no?'

'No,' I said.

He beckoned me closer to the driver's cab, where I saw a plump black sports bag sitting on the floor. He threw another suspicious glance around the laneway, unzipped the holdall and pulled out a handful of videos, all with lurid colour-photostat covers of naked women being penetrated by engorged, tomato-red penises. These he showed me with the reverent silence of a jeweller displaying precious gems.

'The brother-in-law does them for me. Gets them on

the satellite and tapes them. Has it rigged up special like. I thought y'mighta heard. I do a rake of them around here.'

'Around here?'

'Yeah, yeah, bleedin' sure I do. They do go mad for a bit of filth down here. And they've the readies to get it too.' He snickered. 'There's an auld English judge lives above in Glenageary there, you'd want to see what he gets off me. D'turn your stomach.'

He picked one out and offered it to me.

'That's good one there now,' he said. 'Dutch. There's a mott in it with a mickey. Serio. Fuckin' langer on her the size of yer own. Hung like a hoover hose. Lovely-lookin' bird though, I'll say that for her, knockers on her like the mountains of fuckin' Mourne.'

He took out another and peered at it.

'And there's a cracker there. Bloke in it can suck his own cock. Not jokin' yeh. Strides down, head down, nob in the gob, gobblin' away till he nearly gets shaggin' lockjaw.' He peered dreamily out at the sea, shaking his head and sighing. 'Jesus sake, if I could do that I'd never leave the fuckin' house, would you?'

'No,' I told him. 'It isn't those I was interested in.'

He scrutinised me for a moment. 'I do the gay as well,' he said, then. 'Twenty pound each, two for thirty-five.'

I shook my head. I suppose at this stage that there was at least *some* doubt in my mind, I have to admit it. But I mean, what was the very worst thing that could have happened? He could have laughed, I suppose, or thought I was joking. Well, that would have been fine, I had considered this possibility, I would simply have told him yes, that's right, I was only joking. He could have said no and told me to take a hike. Big deal, no loss really. And what then? What if he involved the authorities. If he went to the guards, I told myself, they would never believe him over me. Would they? Realistically? Him over me? Not a chance. And anyway, I felt sure he would never go to the guards. It was simply not in his face.

A good salesman can read a face.

'You know,' I said, 'what you told me a while back? About how you gave that fella a good going-over? The priest you met in Grafton Street that time?'

'Yeah. What about it?'

I turned and glanced at the beach. Suddenly there were three women up to their fleshy thighs in the water. I felt a shudder ripple down my back.

'Well,' I told him, 'I've been thinking, there's a certain fella I'd like to get a good going-over too. The thing is, he's a bit younger than me. I couldn't really manage it myself.'

Behind me, I heard the women laugh and shout.

'I don't know, if you were able to help me out at all, I'd make it worth your while.'

He stared at me. He climbed out of the van with a weird look on his face. For one long moment I actually thought that he was going to hit me. I found myself stepping back from him and feeling for the steak knife in my pocket. But then he just reached into his coat, pulled out a pack of cigarettes and offered me one. I took it.

When he offered me the cigarette I knew that he had bitten. I had closed him. Always be closing that's what they say. A good salesman will *always be closing*. A good salesman knows what ABC *really* stands for.

'Who might that be?'

'Just this little get who's coming between me and my sleep. It's a long story. It's about my daughter.'

He reached out his lighter. 'What about her?'

I sucked at the flame.

'I find it hard to go into the details. Let's just say he's after causing her problems.'

The seagulls screamed in the air.

'So I'd like to cause a few for him,' I said.

He lit his own cigarette and exhaled a mouthful of smoke. 'Is he what? One of them perverts or something?'

I nodded. He pursed his lips and whistled.

'Christ,' he said, quietly, 'I couldn't get involved in that, pal. Tell you the truth now'm under probation at the moment. I've a good bit of previous, y'know?'

The wind rushed in fresh and crisp off the water. Out by a line of grey–green, flat seaweedy rocks two of the women were efficiently swimming. A third, the youngest, was up to her waist, splashing her shoulders and face.

'I'd be willing to pay good money,' I told him. 'Believe me, I'd make it *very* well worth your while. If you could see your way clear to doing me a favour.'

'How much?' he went.

'Well, how much would you need? To give a fella a good fright?'

He took a deep drag on his cigarette and peered up behind me in the direction of the Martello tower. High on the parapet a faded Irish tricolour was wrapped hard around the mast. He put his hand over his eyes and stared out at the horizon.

'Are you serious now, or messin' with me?'

'I'm serious.'

'Because I don't like people pullin' me wire about this kind of thing.'

'I'm not.'

He nodded. 'If I was able to find someone to help y'out, it'd cost.'

'Well, amn't I asking you what'd be needed?'

He walked up and down for a few moments sucking on the cigarette, then came back to me.

'Five,' he said. He moved very close to me and lowered his voice. 'I know a fella drinks up my way might be interested, but he'd need five ton. To hurt him like.'

'To hurt him.'

He sniffed. 'For five,' he said, 'this bloke'd plaster the

walls of a jacks with him. Yeah. If that's what y'wanted. Now he couldn't do much more than that. If y'wanted more than that done, this head couldn't help y'himself. But he'd know a few that could.'

'What does that mean exactly?'

By now the three women were drying themselves on the beach. 'Well, put it this way. If y'wanted to be sure y'wouldn't hear from yer friend again, this fella could introduce y'to a few lads he knows in town. Mad lads, y'know? Fuckin' space cadets. They'd fix him good and final like. If it's more than a few good digs y'want him to get.'

'No,' I said. 'I wouldn't want anything more than that. To hurt him is all I'd want.'

He chuckled. 'So he wouldn't exactly be goin' out line-dancin' for a while?'

'Exactly.'

'Well five, so. I b'lieve he always looks for five.'

'I could manage that,' I told him. 'I could definitely manage five.'

'He'd need it in cash. I b'lieve his rate's half beforehand and the other half when the job's done. Cash on delivery, I suppose you'd say.'

'I understand that,' I said. 'Like I told you before, I'm in sales.'

He laughed. 'Sales. That's lovely. This fucker's some salesman, right enough.'

That was when I turned to look at the three women again, I was startled to see that they were wearing long black habits and cream-coloured veils.

'Look, there's one other thing,' I said.

'What?'

'I'd have to come with him when he does it. I wouldn't get involved but I'd have to be there to see it. I don't know if he'd've a problem with that.'

He nodded his head. 'They nearly always want t'come

103

with him. Watch whoever it is gettin' the dig. Sometimes give a dig themselves. And check they're gettin' value for money, wha'?'

I felt myself laughing a little too loud. 'That'd do me good, all right. That'd make it a good summer for me, I can tell you.'

'That's gameball so,' he said. 'I'm playin' pool up his way tonight. I'll see what's the story.'

He held out his hand. 'The name's Nap,' he said.

'Nap, right,' I said. 'I'm Lawrence. Lawrence Grace.'

'As in Larry?'

'As in Larry, yes. If you like.'

He wanted me to meet him next morning with half the money. Then, he told me, we could make a proper arrangement.

'And listen, pal, y'better understand, if anyone else heard about this, there'd be consequences. Big problems, Larry, y'know?'

'Oh yes, I know. It's strictly between us. I wouldn't cause your pal any problems.'

He sneered. 'I wasn't talkin' about him, Larry. I was talking about you. Anyone else heard about this, believe you me, you'd end up singin' soprano pretty fuckin' fast.'

The three nuns passed us by in the lane, the youngest one now carrying her veil in her hand. Her hair was still wet and stuck in long strands to her lovely face. She glanced at me and smiled.

'Nobody's going to hear,' I said. 'That's a promise.'

'Sound,' he said. 'Now I better make tracks.'

Later that day in Kildare town I was having lunch in a hotel after making a delivery when a short, stocky young man in a black leather jacket strolled into the dining-room. And I was convinced it was him, totally sure of it. I actually burnt my mouth on the soup, I was so shocked. But when he turned in my direction it was not him after all.

Out in the street a sudden hard shower of rain started. Everyone in the room stopped eating.

We all looked out at the rain.

On Hallowe'en night 1967, a couple of months after I had run into your mother in St Stephen's Green, I had a date with Bernadette French. She and I had planned to go to a blues session in some coffee bar in town with two other couples she knew from her work. Instead, when she arrived outside Trinity still in her Aer Lingus uniform to meet me I told her that I wanted to go and have a drink, even though we were already ten minutes late for her friends.

She looked at her watch. 'The others'll wonder what's up,' she said.

'Well, I'm going for a drink anyway,' I told her. 'You needn't come if don't want.'

Her face took on an expression of surprise.

'That's a bit bloody sharp, Billy,' she said.

I told her I was sorry. She stared at me.

'You've no call to talk to me like that,' she said. 'I just thought it'd be nice for us not to go to the pub for one night, that's all. We spend half our lives in bloody old pubs.'

I stood there saying nothing, but feeling my face throb with embarrassment.

'Is there something up with you tonight?' she asked me, and I nodded and said there was.

'Jesus, all right,' she sighed. 'Come on then. The other thing wasn't definite anyway.'

We walked up Grafton Street and around to O'Donoghue's pub on Merrion Row. I ordered a large whiskey for myself, a vodka and orange for Bernadette.

'And so,' she said, when I got back with the drinks, 'what's eating you then?'

I told her that I reckoned we had been getting too serious about each other and thought we should take a break. She raised her eyebrows and opened her mouth a little. She looked far more shocked than I had anticipated as she slowly placed her glass back on the table.

'I thought that was what you wanted, Billy.'

'No, I think we need to cool things off a bit. We could see how we both feel after a while.'

She laughed lightly, though I could see now that she was upset. 'You needn't bother saying that to me, Mac. You're not going to dangle a sword over my head, thanks very much.'

We drank in silence for a while. I remember the barman came around and handed out cardboard witches' hats for Hallowe'en, winking and leaving two on our table.

'So when did this terrific revelation come to you, so? About how we're too serious?'

'I don't know,' I told her.

She nodded.

'It's to do with that girl we met in the Green that day, isn't it?'

'Not really,' I said. 'Although I suppose that's part of it, yes.'

She hung her head for a moment. 'I knew it was. Have you been with her, Billy?'

'What do you mean, with her?'

'You know well what I mean, don't play the baby. Have you?'

'No.'

'But you've been seeing her, though?'

'I told you before, we used to pal around years ago.'

'Billy, I know well by your manner you've been seeing her. Don't lie to me.'

'I might have met her for a drink. So what?'

'Are you in love with her, then?'

'Don't be ridiculous,' I said. 'What does that mean, anyway? In love?'

She scoffed. 'Funny how men always say that when they want the easy way out.'

'I wasn't talking about men. I was talking about myself.'

'Oh, that's a new development all right,' she said.

She looked at me for a while.

'And do you really not know what being in love means, no?'

'No,' I told her.

Tears welled up in her eyes. 'That's very hurtful, Billy,' she said. 'That's a really lousy thing to say. I thought you did know, from the way you spoke to me sometimes. Did you not mean all those things you'd say to me?'

'I don't know,' I said. 'I'm sorry if I led you on.'

'Led me on,' she laughed. 'Listen to it, you sound like a Reverend Mother.' She shook her head and stared in front of herself. 'Well, don't be sorry, anyway. It's me that's sorry for you, Billy, truly, if you don't know what it is to be in love. You that's never done reading about it in books.'

'I'll live,' I told her.

'And are you going to marry her then? That girl.'

'No,' I scoffed, 'of course not.'

She peered into her glass. I remember she put her finger into it and stirred the ice-cubes around. 'I sometimes thought that you and me might have been headed that way. I used to think about it and imagine it. That we'd have a life together, Billy. Isn't that funny?'

A gang of cackling boisterous students in fancy dress came bustling into the pub. Bernadette looked up at them and tried to smile, though her face was pale and trembling.

'So that's it then?' she said.

'Yes. I'm sorry.'

'I suppose you'd better give me back the key, so. To the flat.'

I took it out of my pocket and put it on the table. She nodded, fingering the key for a moment before putting it into her purse.

'And do I get an invite to the wedding?' she asked me.

'I told you already there's no wedding. And if it comes to it, how do you know she isn't married already?'

'Sure it's a small town, Billy. One of the girls in work knows her. Or knows her brother. I think she was doing a line with him for a while.'

'You've little enough to talk about in work,' I said.

'Oh, for Christ's sake, her name came up one day over coffee, that's all, Billy. I know all about her, thank you very much.'

'What's that supposed to mean?'

'Just I know all about her, that's all. She's quite the reputation, your little girlfriend.'

'She isn't that,' I said.

Bernadette picked up one of the paper hats and played with the orange crépe frill around the brim.

'Anyways, it doesn't much matter now, does it?'

'No. I suppose not.'

'No. Still, I can't help wishing you'd've let me know how you felt before this. I don't think you've been very fair to me, Billy.'

When I told her I didn't know what she meant, she laughed.

'You know damn well. Don't play the gom.'

I did know. Bernadette and I had been sleeping together for some time. She had a small flat just off the South Circular Road where we had taken to spending whole weekends. On a Friday afternoon when lectures were over I would walk out from town and let myself in. Sometimes I would be so tired that I would get straight into her single bed and sleep for a few hours before she came home. It was a strange time in my life. What I remember most about those days is the sensation of being tired always. This had started in the months after your mother went away to England, a constant crushing physical tiredness, a frightening feeling of utter listlessness, punctuated only by flickers of terrible anxiety and a kind of resounding guilt. When I met Bernadette I suppose things improved. For a while I had thrown myself into studying for the university entrance exams but after I had passed, and particularly after I had left work and started attending college, the old feeling of exhaustion and depression quickly began to return.

In university I often felt stupid and gauche. I found it difficult to make conversation with my tutors and the other students. I was a few years older than everyone else in the class, painfully conscious of my accent and my address; even my clothes, which were those I had worn to work in the shop, old-fashioned and ill-fitting, I felt marked me out. I hated being asked questions in seminars and lectures; to read an essay aloud filled me with terror. There were times when I would become almost speechless with embarrassment. I coped with all this by cracking jokes and being as self-consciously shocking as possible, Jimmy Porter meets Brendan Behan, the working-class fool playing to the court, bitterly mocking the courtiers as a means of begging to be accepted by them.

The only person I felt easy around was Bernadette. Our weekends together became the only sources of anything like happiness in my life. When she would arrive back at the flat, I'd get up feeling dazed with tiredness. She would change out of her uniform and take a bath – sometimes we would bathe together – then we would go down to Rathmines or Ranelagh for a few drinks and something to eat. More often we just had the drinks. I was already in very serious trouble with my drinking if the truth be told, but it was relatively easy for a young man in Ireland to dress up serious trouble as *joie de vivre*, and I imagine it is still easy enough to do this now. At closing time I would insist on buying as many bottles of beer or cheap wine as we could afford. We would stagger back to the flat where we would drink for hours and furiously argue and dance to Radio Luxembourg as a prelude to drunkenly making love.

On a Saturday morning we would wake up wrapped in

each other's arms. I would get out of bed and stack up her record player with five or six discs. Then I would make breakfast, light the fire, get back into bed for the whole day, we'd only get up when it was getting dark and it was time to think about going out again. I remember the colours of that time as a black and amber blur of night and streetlights. They had been happy and comfortable enough times, I thought, and if I am honest, which I want to be now, they were little more than that for me. I had been inconsolable when your mother left. All lives have periods of radical and absolutely fundamental change which are not at all obvious as that while being endured. Thinking back now, I believe that I became a different person in those months, a person who talked endlessly about the importance of good times and fun and laughed a lot: every single photograph of me taken in those days shows me laughing. I fell in love with gaiety, which any drunk can tell you is only the shape grief takes on the good day, the day you don't want to scream with pain. Most alcoholics I have met have been wonderful company. It is because they have to be. They've built themselves that way, it is like putting on a coat for them. Outside his house, my father was the funniest man in Ringsend. Only at home would he become the shaking fulminating wreck I have sometimes seen when I have glanced in mirrors. He was a great actor; I have often thought he would have made one hell of a salesman.

At the age of twenty-three I already thought I had his act down to a fine art. I had convinced myself so thoroughly, it simply would never have occurred to me that somebody who cared for me might not have been fooled also. Looking at Bernadette in the pub that Hallowe'en night I suppose I must have been able to sense something of how wrong I was. Is it actually possible that I did not know those times had been more than a distraction to her? Certainly, I do not remember any such realisation. She was the first person in my life that I ever truly hurt, yet, to this day, all I really remember about her hurt is how inconvenient it was to me. I'm not proud of it. But it's true.

She sat beside me in the pub that evening looking limp with disbelief. Around us young people were laughing. Music was playing. Everyone was happy, just the way I liked the people around me to be in those days.

'All those things you'd say to me when we were together at the flat, Billy. Good God, you must have thought you'd found a right little fool. And you weren't wrong, were you?'

'I never told you a lie, Bernadette,' I said.

There were fresh tears in her eyes but she blinked them away. She put her finger into her glass once more and stirred the ice-cubes around. 'You never told me anything else, Billy,' she said.

Up at the bar, the students started to sing a loud rebel song. One of them, a plump, gleeful girl who was dressed as a squaw, threw a torn white eiderdown over her head and flapped her arms like a ghost while the others howled and laughed and clapped along with the singing.

So wrap the green flag round me boys;
To die were far more sweet,
With Erin's noble emblem boys,
To be my winding sheet.

'Well, you're free to go, Mac,' Bernadette said. 'Don't worry.'

'If you're upset I'll see you home,' I said.

'No, no, I'd better get on and meet the others.' She glanced at her watch. 'They'll think I'm after running away somewhere.'

'I could get you a taxi,' I said. 'If you're upset.'

'Don't bloody flatter yourself,' she told me.

She put her cigarettes into her handbag. I went to touch her arm but she pulled away. The last thing she ever said to me, I have never forgotten. She turned – I can still see her dusty blue eyes, the dry flesh of her lips – and looked right into my face.

'You're a dangerous man, Billy. I can see that about you now. You've some lovely qualities but you're dangerous. You should do something about it. You're going to cause a lot of hurt otherwise, to people who don't deserve it.'

She got up and left. I sat by myself in the pub until closing time, drinking, smoking, drinking more, watching everyone around me be happy.

Chapter Eight

On 28 October 1968, my twenty-fourth birthday, Father Seán Ronan married your mother and me in the University Chapel on Stephen's Green. We were his first wedding, he nervously told the congregation, and he hoped the same was true for the happy couple.

Your mother insisted that we get married in the Catholic Church. I had expected bitter arguments with her parents about it, but they never materialised. Not that I would have given a damn where the ceremony took place myself; by then I had lost any last shred of religious feeling. But I think your mother saw it as some kind of fresh start. Also, she was probably the most emotionally generous and spiritually wise person I have ever met; she knew it would have been important to my own parents for their grandchildren to be brought up Catholic.

Lizzie was your mother's flower girl. You have seen the photographs, you know how beautiful she looked as she tottered up the aisle in crinoline and lace. Although I stayed sober enough, for some reason I do not remember very many details of the day. There were police in the streets outside the chapel because of a protest march about the North. Our reception was in the Hibernian Hotel on Dawson Street. Your Uncle Jimmy was best man. The hems of his bell-bottom trousers were so large that they completely covered his platform shoes. Late in the evening he almost caused a punch-up when he told my father that he had to go and pay 'the priest and the other entertainers.'

As the gift of Grace's parents we went to Barcelona for

our honeymoon. It was the first time either of us had been on an aeroplane. I did not like the city much, so full of shadowy, narrow streets and the incessant sound of metal shutters slamming. But I loved the bars and the wonderful Latin music. One night we went dancing in an battered old dancehall where the tango band played until dawn. Your mother had on a very short green dress. She looked magnificent. We drank sweet white wine – it was only a few shillings a bottle – and walked back to the hotel at seven in the morning, hand in hand, exhausted, our feet raw and sore from dancing.

When we came home we moved into the small basement flat we had rented in Rathmines, just beside the canal. It was dark and a little damp, but it was cheap and clean and owned by a landlord who did not mind Lizzie being there. We liked the feel of the house. In the attic was a group of country girls who were nursing students. Below them lived an elderly woman who had spent time in Chicago and Boston and was full of stories. A couple of the other flats seemed to be inhabited by whole gangs of labourers, and these were sometimes noisy at night, but mostly your mother seemed to find that reassuring, or even amusing.

I was finishing my studies and teaching a few hours in a school in Ranelagh as part of my qualification. Your mother continued working part-time at the Abbey, writing press releases, organising interviews with the actors, compiling first-night invitation lists. We ate a lot of tins of beans. Lizzie did not get brought out much. I suppose we must have thought that things would get better somehow. Thinking that things would get better somehow had replaced hurling as the national sport in Ireland around that time, and after a while your mother and I got to be champions.

You were born on 20 September 1970, which my father pointed out to us was the anniversary of the execution of Robert Emmet by the English. Had you been a boy I would have quite liked to call you Emmet Sweeney, because that was the kind of fucking rubbish I believed in back then, just like everyone else in the country. It was just before the North really got going again.

It was a hard and long labour, and in the end you were breech born, which my mother used to say was one of the reasons that you and Grace were so close. The obstetrician who delivered you was some kind of relation of Éamon de Valera. I remember him once telling me proudly that his hands and surgical instruments had been blessed by the Pope.

As you grew up I noticed several strange things about you. Where Lizzie was gregarious and mischievously funny and used to bounce around the flat like a ball-bearing in a pinball machine, you seemed serious, almost solemn. I saw it in the curl of your mouth, the way you held yourself, the shockingly dark shapes and muddy colours in your drawings, the words you sometimes cried out in your dreams. Thinking back now, I suppose that your seriousness should not have been a surprise. Serious things were beginning to go on around you.

In 1971 I got a job teaching English in Dun Laoghaire Senior College. A year later, just before seven in the evening of your second birthday, I was arrested on the way home and charged with drink-driving. Shortly after this I was lifted again, on Talbot Street in town, not drunk this time but badly in the horrors, gibbering, seeing visions and swaying all over the road. I had three children from the school in the back of the car; I had been driving them home from a music lesson. I lost my job and was hospitalised for the first time.

I only ended up at St Ronan Finn's because the Dublin hospitals were all full. A riot had broken out after a demonstration at the British Embassy and the casualty departments around the whole city were crammed. Despite the horrendous state of mind I was in, some small details of the long journey down to County Carlow have stayed with me. At one point the ambulance took a wrong turn and got lost down a side road; I remember still how the sound of the low branches tapping on the roof filled me with utter screaming dread.

I believe that things have changed a great deal in St Ronan Finn's since my first stay there. It was, as you know only too well, the first of many such stays; in those days, once an addict had attended a particular hospital for addiction treatment he had to continue to attend the same one in future. What the neighbours referred to as your Daddy's business trips down the country were to become regular events. Sometimes I think that I only became a travelling salesman in order to publicly justify and legitimise such absences. In any case, Ronan Finn's now has a separate section for the specific treatment of alcoholism. An enlightened, humane woman professor runs the department, the staff in the unit are well trained, the therapeutic regime is designed to help patients reconstruct something of their lives. I have been told by people in AA that these days St Ronan Finn's is considered the Ritz Hotel of addiction treatment. Twenty years ago things were different.

For a start, the alcoholics were simply lumped in with everyone else in the mental ward. This was not a great idea. You can imagine, I am sure, how it felt to go out on a binge on a Friday night and wake up Monday morning with your arm in a sling, your nerves in shreds, your veins full of liquid tranquillizers and a Carlow schizophrenic in the next bed shrieking about his seemingly gentle grey-haired Mammy actually being the devil incarnate. Half the patients seemed to have delusions of grandeur, half the psychiatrists far more worrying delusions of adequacy. Their approach was to smash what was left of your personality to minuscule fragments and build it again in their own image. If you were not a chronic alcoholic already, St Ronan Finn's, in those days, would have turned you into one pretty damn quick.

The treatment was harsh and sometimes even cruel.

During various stays there over the years I heard stories of patients being force-fed alcohol until they vomited as a crude form of aversion therapy. There were tales of long-term residents – the Happy Gang, we occasional visitors called them – receiving regular electric-shock therapy without anaesthetic. The nuns who ran the place were mostly decent enough, but there were two or three sadistic hatchet-faced bitches who specialised in humiliation and the exacerbation of guilt. I can still recall the plangent cheer that went up in the day-room the morning a young idealistic Indian psychiatrist threatened to have the Mother Superior slapped into a strait-jacket and committed.

When I was released from my first stay I was very relieved to find your mother and you two still at home when I got there. I was grateful, too, and full of the best intentions, but it was a terrible time. I was on social security for almost six months. Finding another teaching job seemed to be absolutely out of the question. Even after one of the nuns from Ronan Finn's wrote me a good reference, it was a useless struggle. Sometimes I would get as far as the interview, but then the full truth about how I had lost my first job would emerge and there would follow embarrassed euphemisms, bowed heads, evasions, worst of all, long silences.

Things were not easy at home. Money was short, bills went unpaid, more than once we could not even afford a coin for the electricity meter; if it were not for Grace's parents I do not know what we would have done. There was endless talk about moving down the country, or even emigrating to London, but somehow we never got around to it. Still, the talking was something; it filled in the space that was growing between your mother and me, a torrent of words, aspirations, promises I think we must have known even then would never be fulfilled. In films and novels, I have noticed that those drifting apart are often shown in silent scenes. But it is my experience that when people are in trouble they talk with a kind of frantic and restless energy.

After some time I found work doing grinds, correcting the Inter and Leaving Cert exam papers, teaching English to foreign students. I even wrote a few articles for newspapers about the poets and novelists on the different school courses. Money came in slowly but at least it came. Your mother and I began to put together the pieces of a shared life.

Central to that effort were Lizzie and you. You were the absolute hub of that life, the force you exerted to keep us together felt stronger than gravity. There were times when I thought that it would be better and more merciful to leave, but I simply could not do it. Eventually, without my noticing, leaving simply ceased to be an option, and when that was accepted, consolation came, as it often does, I have learned, when your choices become limited. I felt healed by you. The expression on your face when you came in from school once and found your mother and me in an embrace, the sound of a stifled laugh from your room late at night, the heart-stopping excitement of watching you run in a school sports-day race or listening to you sing as I walked you to the bus in the mornings: these would fill me with a bubbling ebb of miraculous joy which I simply could not explain.

You were the most just child I ever saw. You could not pass a beggar in the street without giving him money, if you had it. We had to be careful about what you watched on the television: if you saw people hungry or lonely, refugees in Africa, or victims of the violence that was by then part of the everyday in Belfast and Derry, it would distress you in some fundamental way for hours at a time. One night I found you in tears on your bedroom floor. You had heard a radio interview with an elderly Derry woman who had been burnt out of her home by a drunken Loyalist mob. You clung to me, shaking with grief, asked me why the world was like this. I buried my face in your hair and tried to think of something to say.

I think that you were about ten when you first got into trouble at school. There was a plan for the girls from Mill Hill to put on a play with some of the boys from Blackrock College. You told the head nun that you would not take part. The South African rugby team were about to tour Ireland that year, and most of the players on the Irish team were members of the Blackrock College senior club. You had thought this over and decided that you would not have anything to do with Blackrock College.

The head nun was furious about this. There were letters and phone calls home to say that these plays had been produced and performed for years; you were embarassing the whole school with your over-idealistic nonsense, you were confusing the other girls and fomenting dissension. I tried for a while to talk you into it, but your mother was adamant that we should not force you. She insisted that I come with her to the school to discuss the situation.

'I admire Maeve for taking a stand,' your mother told the old nun. 'There's very serious things going on in South Africa, sister.'

'I've lived in Africa, Mrs Sweeney,' the nun sighed. 'I don't need lectures about Africans, let me assure you. I was seven years in Africa on the missions.'

'Well then,' Grace said, 'all the more reason you should support the child. There's terrible oppression going on over there, after all. Those poor people are being walked on. Don't you ever open a newspaper?'

The nun laughed here, which was always a big mistake with your mother. 'And what would a child that age know about oppression, as you call it? And really and truly, what would we here in Ireland know about it either? Especially those of us who haven't been there to see for ourselves.'

'Maeve's great-grandfather died in Auschwitz, sister. I never met my own grandfather because he was murdered by the Nazis in the gas chamber. Emmanuel Michael Lorenz was his name, if you want to remember him next time you're saying a prayer. He and two of his brothers. One of them was fourteen years old. So I think I know what I'm talking about, thank you. And so does Maeve.'

The nun was silent for a while. 'Well, God bless us,' she said, then. 'I don't know why a person would tell an impressionable child an awful thing like that.'

'I don't know why a person wouldn't,' Grace said. 'So we'll just agree to differ there.'

'Mrs Sweeney, you listen to me now. Maeve is looking for attention. Mark my words, you'll rue the day you gave that girl her own way. It's a stage girls go through, I've seen it before, I know girls. They can be an awful handful.'

'Like Africans,' Grace said.

The nun peered at Grace in an odd sidelong way. 'I'm sure you know very well what I mean. The things that can happen to girls that age when they're given too much attention.'

'And she can have all the attention she wants from me, let me tell you that. I'm her mother. That's my job, isn't it, to give her love and attention?'

Dots of dark red appeared on the nun's cheeks. 'It wouldn't be up to me to tell you what your job is, of course. You'd know a lot more about motherhood, now, than I would.'

'That's right, sister, I damn well would. And I'll thank you to remember that in future.'

'Yes. Some of us would know quite a lot about motherhood, right enough. A little more than we'd like to know, maybe. And some of it learnt the hard way.'

Grace stood up, breathing through her nose. 'My God, sister, do you know what it is you need?'

'No, Mrs Sweeney. What do I need?'

'A bloody good session in bed with a man,' she said. 'It might shift that dried-up old scowl off your face.'

After that, Grace and I agreed not to force you. The night of the school play you sat at home in the flat watching the television with us. When you were going to bed your mother told you how proud of you we were and said you were always to do what you felt was right, no matter what anyone else felt about it. You rushed over and hugged us both hard. A few weeks later, on the afternoon of the rugby international, you and Lizzie took the bus into town and went on the anti-apartheid picket outside Landsdown Road. You came home in a T-shirt that said: 'No Scrum with the Racist Scum'. This had been given to you by a boy at the demonstration, you explained, a very nice boy called Leper, who had leather bondage trousers and three steel rings through his nose.

'Look here, Miss,' Grace said. 'I hope you're not telling me you took off your blouse and changed into that thing in front of any boy, never mind a boy with a ring through his nose.'

'Oh I did, Ma,' you said. 'I gave him a good try-out. He was only great. Then Lizzie hopped on this other one and rid him till his eyes crossed, didn't you, Lee? He was a fine thing, Ma.'

You and Lizzie laughed. Grace turned to me.

'Don't we have two lovely daughters, Sweeney?' she said.

I wish I could stop thinking about you in the past tense.

Around that time I received a letter from the Department of Education telling me that they had considered my case and reached the decision that I could never teach in Ireland again. I wrote back and appealed for them to change their minds but they said no, they had sympathy for me and wished me all the best with what they called my difficulty, but there was absolutely nothing that they could do about the situation. I continued for a while with the grinds and the private English lessons but soon it became clear that I would have to find something else. We were flat broke. Very simply, we needed to make more money.

So I became a salesman, a job for which no qualifications are needed except a willingness to work hard and some ability to talk, a way of life which in many ways suits a man with a past. My first job was selling bibles and encyclopedias door to door around the housing estates of Dublin. Then I moved to electrical goods, transistor radios, tape recorders, small kitchen items, vacuum cleaners. This was a little better, there was a small basic salary as well as a commission, the job involved visiting shops around the city, there was no dry calling around the corporation schemes to busy housewives and furious unemployed men. I did well at this work and was soon offered promotion. My employers wrote several times to the garda traffic department and the court to say that I needed my driving licence back. When I got it, they provided me with a car and I began to travel the country.

I remember one incident around that time when I was down in Galway on a selling trip – you can imagine, I am sure, just how much I looked forward to overnight stays. I had spent most of the afternoon browsing in Kenny's bookshop and the whole night drinking in a rough bar down on the docks. It was long after closing time when I left the pub and I was badly drunk. Everything down by the sea seemed to be muddy and dark blue. I must have had what is known as a blackout, because I remember absolutely nothing from the time I was standing on the quayside looking into the swirling water to a good few hours later. God knows what I did. In the middle of the night, anyway, I found myself in the centre of the town, outside a shop that sold religious articles. The window was full of plaster saints and rosary beads and holy water bottles shaped like the Virgin Mary. I stared in at this stuff trying to sober myself up, but after a while I began to imagine that the statues were coming to life, that the tiny martyrs were actually bleeding before my eyes, that the foot-high St Francis was beckoning to the miniature nightingales painted on the canopy behind him. I stepped back from the window feeling nauseous with horror. The picture of Christ seemed to close and then open its eyes. I thought I was going insane, although, of course, I could not have really thought that, because you do not think in those terms when you have an attack of delirium. You think you are functioning normally. That's what is so frightening about it.

I never found the hotel I was supposed to stay in that night. I am sure you remember Galway, love, you know the way the centre of the town is a medieval warren of tiny, curling streets. It is a maze. It is comparatively easy to get lost in Galway even when you are stone-cold sober but when you are drunk it is almost inevitable. All I remember is stumbling around the dark wet lanes for what seemed like hours and then, I think, running hard for a time, as fast as I could. Then the speckled sweep of the stars behind the navy blue silhouettes of treetops. And then nothing.

The next morning I woke up on the grass in Eyre Square. It was very early and there was nobody at all around. I stood up and tried to find my balance. My head was reeling and I could see patches of shimmering blackness. I think I managed to totter a few steps and then I fell. I lay on the ground looking up at the clouds. After a while I realised I had soiled myself in the night.

I went in behind a bush and took off my trousers and underpants. I do not mind telling you, love, that I was actually crying with shame at that point. I think I tried my best to clean myself with grass and leaves but it was little enough use. I threw my underpants away and put my trousers back on.

Then I think I must have fallen asleep again, I cannot really remember. The next thing I do recall is startlingly bright golden sunlight, and two tourists standing over me looking worried. They were a young Italian couple, students I suppose, or backpackers. They offered me money. When I would not take it, the girl took a packet of sweets from her rucksack and offered me those. I think they must have thought that I was a tramp sleeping rough. They helped me up on to a bench and asked if I was OK. 'OK' was the only English word they seemed to know and they just kept repeating it – OK? – OK? – and I nodded until they went away.

That was when the paranoia started to bite. I remember being absolutely terrified that some passer-by would see me and call the police, or somehow telephone Grace. That's how nuts I was. I went into the filthy public toilet in Eyre Square and cleaned myself up a bit. Then I started thinking that a policeman would come into the public toilet and see me there, and I remember running into one of the stinking cubicles and locking the door. I do not know how long I stayed there. When I came out I felt a little better. I decided to go for a walk. Soon I found myself back in front of the window of the shop where I had been frightened by the living picture of Christ. I saw with some relief that the picture was actually designed like that; it was one of those optical illusion things which change their image when you look at them from a different angle.

I walked back to the hotel where I had left my bags the lunch-time before and rang Grace. She was worried and had been awake most of the night. She had telephoned the hotel around midnight and found that I was not in my room. We had a bad argument over the phone. I think it was the first time that she ever accused me of infidelity.

I got into the car and drove the four hours home to Dublin. You were at the kitchen table drinking orange juice when I came in. I will never forget your expression. I went to give you a kiss but you pulled a face and told me I smelled horrible.

'Mammy says you don't care about us any more,' you said. 'Do you?'

'Of course I do,' I said.

Grace came into the kitchen and saw me. She was wearing

a blue dressing-gown. Her face was white and she looked very tired. She went to the cooker, put on the kettle, rinsed out some cups. She looked at you and asked what was wrong.

'You know well.'

'I don't.'

'You said Daddy didn't care about us. You said you were going to go away.'

'Well, I didn't mean that, pet,' Grace sighed. 'I was only play-acting.'

'You weren't.'

'I was a bit upset, love. I'm sorry. We all say silly things when we're upset.'

She poured you another glass of orange juice and sent you inside to do some homework.

'Are you all right?' she asked me, and I nodded.

She sat down at the table and looked at me.

'Is there anything you want to tell me, Billy? About where you were?'

'No,' I said. 'I just walked around for the night. I was in a funny mood.'

'Were you drinking again?'

'No.'

'You weren't drinking?'

'I suppose I might have had a few.'

Her eyes darkened. 'You must think I'm some damn fool,' she said.

'What does that mean, Grace?'

She laughed bitterly. 'Is that the truth? You walked around Galway all bloody night? Since when were you so fond of walking, Billy?'

'That's what happened,' I told her. 'It's all the same to me what you believe.'

For a while I think we said nothing much. Your mother made tea, we sat there drinking it. She asked if she could have one of my cigarettes and I nodded for her to take it.

She smoked the whole thing in silence. Then she asked if I wanted something to eat. I shook my head.

'Please talk to me, Billy,' she said. 'You can tell me anything.'

'There's nothing I want to tell you.'

She sighed. 'Billy, look, don't sulk with me. I'm sorry if you thought I made a fuss this morning. I suppose I just got a bit of a shock when you weren't at the hotel.'

'Well, I didn't fucking think you'd be checking up on me,' I said.

Her lips started to quiver and her weary eyes flooded with tears.

'I only wanted to talk to you, Billy,' she told me. 'I missed you and wanted to hear your voice.'

Your mother was crying, love. She was crying like a child, in great breathy gulps. I went and put my arms around her and told her I was sorry. She said nothing but just cried harder. I remember that after a while she took my hand in hers and kissed it and squeezed it hard.

'Oh Christ, I love you so much, Billy. I love you. Please, you wouldn't ever leave me, would you? Or cheat on me?'

'Course I wouldn't,' I said. 'Jesus, Grace. I'm sorry. Don't be talking like that, sweetheart.'

'I get so afraid that you'll leave me sometimes. That I make you unhappy some way. My head, Billy. It just fills up with all kinds of things. I think I must be going mad half the time.'

'You're not going mad, love. I'm sorry I wasn't there when you rang. Really I am.'

'I just wanted so much to talk to you. I was missing you. I get so lonely when you're away. I wanted to hear your voice and say good-night. I love to hear your voice before I go to sleep. You remember the way you always used to ring me at night, Billy, when you went on the road first? It used to make me feel so safe. That's stupid, I know.'

'It isn't,' I told her. 'Grace, please, I'm sorry.'

'And anyway, I wanted to tell you about something.'

'Well, can't you tell me now, love?' I said.

She wiped the tears away from her eyes and peered at me. 'I'm going to have another baby, Billy,' she sobbed. 'I went down to the doctor yesterday. I'm two months gone.'

As long as I live, darling, I will never forget the look on your mother's face that morning. Never. It was a look of the most pure, undisguised fear.

After that day I tried to give up alcohol again, but could not do it. If anything my drinking got worse. Soon I found that I could not go out anywhere socially without drinking a quarter of a bottle of whiskey beforehand. Before too long Grace noticed this. For a while I got very good at fobbing her off. I would lie to her, sweetheart. Or I would tell her she was paranoid or nagging. I began brushing my teeth more often to hide the smell on my breath. I would brush my teeth fifteen times a day sometimes, and buy the strongest mints or mouthwash I could find. Then I discovered one particular cough medicine that had a strong smell of aniseed and let me tell you, love, for a while your old man got more serious coughs than poor old Keats did in the bad years. There was even a ludicrous occasion when your mother made me go see a doctor, thinking I must have TB or bronchitis, and I actually had chest X-rays in St Stephen's hospital, where you are now, and went along with all the pretence of that like a merciless bastard. And then I discovered vodka somehow, which has hardly any smell at all, or so the drunk will tell himself, and this seemed to me a very good thing. No more coughs. No more colds. For a while your mother was happy and so was I.

I started regularly drinking at lunch-time. Salesmen drink, that wasn't a big deal. For a salesman, drinking is a way of keeping up with the competition, finding company, counteracting the loneliness of the job for a short time, maybe picking up tips. But I would also drink on my way home from work. I would drink late at night, down in the kitchen by myself. And then, darling, after a time I found that I could not go out to work in the mornings if I had not had a drink. I would always have a bottle in the car, under the driver's seat or in the boot, where your mother would not come across it. This is the biggest mistake made about people like me; everyone thinks we drink to get drunk. But the true alcoholic drinks to feel normal, to function, to hold down a job, to be able to make love and experience the truth of that. Of course, he also goes blind screaming crazy from time to time and drinks to escape his demons. But mostly he does it just to stay on some kind of level, just to get back up to zero. It is the strangest thing in the world, but pretty soon it became everyday to me.

I hid bottles in the back garden of the house, I put them in plastic bags and dug them into the flower-beds, I would stick them into the bushes and the branches of the trees. The garden behind our flat was the only one in Ireland that grew brandy and beer. I would go out there last thing at night for a walk, and sit in the grass swigging down as much as I could in a few minutes. I began to take drink into the flat or the house shortly after this. I had various hiding places where I knew Grace and you kids would never look. Under a loose floorboard in the cupboard beneath the stairs, inside the toilet cistern, inside the toolbox I kept in the spare room. I found a way of screwing off the side panel of the bath, behind which I could put two or three naggin bottles of vodka at a time.

Whenever I thought about it – which was not very often in those days, believe you me – all of this surprised me because I did not like the taste of alcohol. I found it unpleasant and harsh and vaguely nauseating, except for sweet dessert wine or sweet sherry, but that made me sick to my stomach after only a few. I spent a lot of time and effort in my early thirties trying to find a drink that I liked to taste. I never succeeded. But I kept going anyway. You would be very surprised indeed, love, by the number of alcoholics who cannot actually stand the taste. Or perhaps you wouldn't, I don't know.

It is a thing that always surprised me.

Chapter Nine

S everal weeks after I had given the first of the money to the milkman, he still had no news for me about what we had agreed. I would drive down to Sandycove around dawn, swim for a while to the sound of frenetic birdsong, watch the sky turn gold and green, get dressed on the rocks, wait for him to show up. It was always the same story. He had not seen his friend, he would say; nobody in the area had seen him recently, there was talk that he was in England or down the country. One morning I was told that his friend had been spotted in a rough pub on the northside the night before, the next that he had been put into Mountjoy for a week following a fight outside a dance-club in Temple Bar during which a man had lost an eye. I began to get impatient. He reassured me, everything would be fine in a while, he had left a message for his friend at a certain place. Often, when I went silent, he would laughingly begin to relate his friend's exploits and adventures to me, long stories of what his friend had done to the people who had crossed him, how marvellously skilled his friend was in the art of knowing exactly which bones to break, how expert his friend was at fractures, how his friend could beat a man in such a way as to leave no marks, if that was required, or beat him to make him look half dead if necessary. He would always finish by telling me that I would have to bide my time. Maybe there would be some news soon from his friend.

I continued with my own preparations. Spring began to yield to the early summer, the dawns came earlier and more swimmers appeared down at the Forty Foot. Every night I went out to Bray after work to watch for Quinn. I got to know all his haunts, his habits and associates. I bought a thick notebook and began to note down even more precise details of his movements, times, dates, sketches of the street plan around his house, various addresses, an estimate of his body weight: ten stone five or six. No detail was too small for me to note. I dug out the newspaper articles and photographs I had collected at the time of the trial and the escape: some of these I pasted into the notebook also.

Most nights I would find him quite quickly and easily enough and be able to follow him for a while. I grew confident enough to be able to take a half-hour break, go for a coffee or a Coke and then be able to catch him up again, whenever I liked. But then there were the occasional evenings when I would stalk the neon-lit streets of Bray for hours at a time, lost in the growing crowds of wide-eyed, half-drunk, savagely tanned night strollers, and not see him anywhere. Those nights, I need not tell you, were more than a little annoying.

But then a good salesman thrives on the changing challenge.

In work, Hopper and Liam were convinced that I had met a woman. They would tease me about it, ask me why I was so busy these nights. They would laugh knowingly at my clumsy lies and evasions. One lunch-time Liam took me to one side and told me how happy he was for me, how great it was that I was managing to put the past behind me now, how he and Teresa would love to have the two of us over to dinner when I felt that the time was right. It was definitely what Grace would have wanted, he added, I was not to feel guilty or ashamed, Grace would not have wished me to be alone, she would have wanted the world to turn. I went along with their suppositions; in time I even added to them. Whenever they would invite me for a game of pool after work I would say the same thing. I can't, lads. You know I can't. I have a hot date tonight.

I suppose, in a way, it was true.

A strange event I remember from that time: late one night I was walking that part of the Bray sea front which is used by gay men as a meeting place when I saw someone I recognised. There he was, hands deep in his pockets, and staring out at the water. It was Seánie, wearing ragged old jeans and a denim jacket. He looked distracted, as though something complicated was on his mind. His feet kicked at the rails in a desultory way as he took long slow drags on his cigarette. When I called out his name he did not hear me at first. I shouted again. He turned and appeared absolutely shocked. Then he tried to smile, but I could see from his expression that he was not at all happy to see me.

'Liam, Jesus. What are you doing here?'

'I was going to ask you the same thing, Father.'

He shrugged. 'Ah, just hadn't been to Bray in years. I'd nothing on tonight so I wandered out on the Dart. I'd some thinking to do.' He nodded in the direction of the amusement arcades. 'Changed a bit, hasn't it?'

It was after midnight, so I knew that the last Dart would have left and the train station would be closed. When I told him this, he accepted my offer of a lift home. I walked up to the town with him, profoundly aware all the time that he was behaving as though I had caught him out in something. In the car he was very quiet. I tried to make conversation, told him that I had heard from Lizzie and Franklin recently, that they were thinking of moving to Ireland with the twins. He nodded and stared out the window. It was unlike him to be so silent and uninterested; for ten whole minutes he said nothing at all. After a while I asked straight out if there was something worrying him. He confessed that working in Dun Laoghaire was becoming difficult, getting him down. There was too much administration, too much organising sales of work, coffee mornings, bloody table-tennis tournaments in the youth club. It depressed him that so many people would come when he said mass, but hardly a soul would show up for anything else. He had tried to start up a prayer group, a centre for battered women, a soup run for the homeless but the parish priest had not been keen on any of his ideas. They had quarrelled badly. A summer vacancy had since come up in Lourdes, for an Irish priest to minister to those of the pilgrims who were terminally ill. He was thinking of applying. I told him it sounded a fine idea. He seemed strangely gratified – even *relieved* – to be encouraged.

'Sure if I get it, Liam, you might come over for a fortnight. Bit of a break?'

I laughed. 'I don't know about that, Seánie. It doesn't sound like much of a holiday. Not that I'm in holiday humour anyway these days.'

'Don't be such a dry shite, will you. Lourdes is gas at night, all the Irish bars.'

'Well, I'm not supposed to be frequenting Irish bars, am I?'

He slapped my arm. 'You know what I mean. We'll have the crack over there. You and me, what? Nice to spend a bit of time. Like the old days, what? I'm going in July if I get it.'

I told him I couldn't. Lizzie and Franklin's last letter had said that they planned to come home around then, if they were coming at all, and they might want me to help them find a flat.

It was almost one in the morning by the time we got to the presbytery in Dun Laoghaire and I was very tired. At first Seánie did not seem to want to leave the car. He asked if we could smoke another cigarette together before he went in. All the time he smoked he kept staring up at one of the upper windows of the house, which he explained was the parish priest's bedroom. He wanted to wait for the light to be switched off, he said. Yet when the room finally did darken he seemed disappointed that he would have to go in now. He thanked me for the lift and told me he was sorry if he had seemed a little offhand. It was just that he had things on his mind. He had not been himself lately. He had so many things to think about.

'Anyways,' he said. 'I'm only boring you. And sufficient unto the day is the evil thereof, what?' He went to open the door.

'Listen, Seánie,' I said. 'Can I ask y'something?'

'Shoot.'

'Where you were tonight. That bit of the sea front. You know it's where the gay fellas go? That's what I'm told. To meet each other.'

'So?'

'So. You're not gay are you?'

He took a long last drag on his cigarette, allowing the smoke to drift from his mouth and nostrils.

'Gay in Bray,' he said. 'Why? D'y'fancy me, Liam?'

'No.'

He smiled and threw his cigarette end out the window. 'No,' he laughed. 'Well I'm not gay, no, so it's just as well you said that, isn't it?'

It was only when he got out that I realised he had been sitting on my notebook.

After your mother lost the child, things between us started to change. This happened quite quickly. There was a new distance between us which would express itself in small enough ways at first; she would seem uneasy when I went to kiss her in the mornings, for example, on my way out to work. She often seemed preoccupied and silent when I was in the room, yet as soon as I would leave I would hear her laughing with you or Lizzie. The understood glances and elisions by which, I now know, a marriage telegraphs itself as still being something alive became less frequent. Sometimes at the weekend, it would seem to me that a whole day would pass without Grace actually looking at me at all. Her comments about my weight, which had started some years earlier as a joke, and had then become more barbed for a while, simply stopped. For some reason this bothered me. Around that time I remember noticing that whenever I tried to bring up the subject of my lack of fitness in some playful or irreverent way, she would look away or shrug and say nothing. She grew thinner herself, and you know your mother, she was always so slight anyway, she did not have much to lose. The fatter I grew, the lighter she became; sometimes it occurred to me that if someone had weighed the two of us at any point in the marriage our combined weight would always have been the same. Her face took on a gaunt hungry look. There were often grey circles around her eyes. One night she was undressing in the bedroom, or perhaps just sitting in her underwear at the dressing-table and combing her hair, and I remember noticing with a shock just how thin she had become.

Her view of me seemed to have changed fundamentally, for good reason as I can now see, but I sensed that she was troubled by other things than me too. Your mother became a woman who was marked by pain. A faint redolence of winter followed her around like a delicate perfume. Though she still played and laughed with Lizzie and yourself, and was never less than loving to you, I began to intuit for the first time that this was all an increasing effort for her. She lost interest in concerts or plays. She gave up reading poetry. She became withdrawn and very silent. There was hardly ever any music in the flat any more.

I think it was her father who told us first about the house in Dalkey. I remember laughing out loud at the advertisement he had cut out of the *Irish Times* and sent to us – I still have it somewhere, but the last time I came across it, the silverfish had nibbled it to lace. There was absolutely no way that we could afford the house. It was a solid square turn-of-the-century building, in very poor condition, but with a large garden, trees, even a ruined old stone stable block. It was owned by the Church of Ireland but they did not need it any more, there were too few Protestants left in Dalkey now, the rector and his wife were about to move to the North. The advertisement made it clear that it would be an unusual sale. The Church of Ireland elders were concerned that the house should go to people who needed it. It had always been a family home, the text explained, it was not a piece of real-estate investment to be sold to a developer; they intended it to be a safe home for a family who would benefit from it but could not afford the market price. To be considered eligible to bid for Glen Bolcain it was necessary to write a letter and say why you needed the house.

I remember that we were invited out to see it on an autumn Sunday afternoon. It was so difficult to find, pushed back like that into the cul-de-sac off the avenue, that I drove right past it several times without even noticing those two frowning stone eagles on the pillar, one with the chipped beak, which the rector had told me to look out for, and which you would always dislike. Finally, after asking directions from several mystified locals we found the house; there was the name on a terracotta plaque screwed to the huge black gates. Glen Bolcain. A winding driveway of potholed gravel and deep ruts badly overgrown with snipegrass and edged with clumps of nettles. A granite bird table on a small leaning plinth. A wooden-shuttered, damp-stained house that looked as though it was about to fall to its knees like a tottering drunk. You said the whole place looked haunted.

There was something very poignant about that sepia-coloured September afternoon. The rector and his wife had already packed up to go: I remember plastic crates and foil-lined tea chests all stuffed full of beautiful old leatherbound gold-tooled books. They had made soup for us, they gave you and Lizzie plums from the trees in the garden. They had loved the garden, they told us in their gentle Northern accents, as they led us around showing us the shrubs and flowers, telling you the names of some of the trees – oak, alder, yew, holly, birch, aspen. The rector was worried about the apple tree. It was a very good Bramley and it would need to be crowned soon. It had been planted by one of his predecessors almost eighty years earlier. I remember that he blushed with pleasure when your mother told him how beautiful the tea roses were. Oh, these too were the responsibility of a predecessor, he explained, the true credit belonged to another man.

'History is all around us, Mr Sweeney, isn't that right? And every garden tells its own story, of course.'

He asked me if I had ever read George Herbert. I said that I had once written an essay on him at university but it had been quite a long time ago.

'Do you know his poem on the garden at all, Mr Sweeney?'

'Is it stumbling on melons I fall on grass?'

'Oh dear, no,' he said. 'I think you'll find that's Mr Andrew Marvell, isn't it? A beautiful writer, yes, but I had in mind Mr George Herbert. For me, I must say, there are few to approach old George as I call him.' He smiled at me. 'He was a vicar too, of course.'

He reached out, caressed one of the roses, murmured a few lines of poetry:

> *If then all that worldlings prize*
> *Be contracted to a rose;*
> *Sweetly there indeed it lies,*
> *But it biteth in the close.*

When I looked at him closely I thought that I could see tears in his old eyes. 'It biteth in the close, Mr Sweeney. Aye, that it does.'

Perhaps a month later, the Church elders wrote to say that we had been chosen for Glen Bolcain. Grace's father gave us the deposit and we moved in almost immediately. On our first night we asked all four of your grandparents out to visit. Seánie said a mass in the living-room. To please Grace's parents we had also invited their rabbi, a tall, solemn, barrel-chested man who sang an ancient Hebrew blessing 'for the planting of new trees'. I remember how beautifully strange the singing sounded in the small room where I am now writing, how moving and dark those elongated, throaty vowels. It was the last time we were to see Seánie for a couple of years. He was about to leave for the Sudan, where he would be working in a poor parish so far out in the desert that his occasional letters would only arrive several months after they had been written.

Your mother loved the house. She seemed to want to be in the house all the time; the furthest she would happily go would be down to Dalkey village to the shops, or sometimes for a walk along Coliemore Road by the sea, which always seemed so extraordinarily waveless there, in the short stretch between the harbour and Dalkey Island, despite its infamously treacherous undercurrents. She began to smoke more and changed from light to full-tar cigarettes. When we got the colour television she took a huge interest in that, I noticed, but particularly in old black and white films and ancient, obscure documentaries on Irish history. Every other programme on *Telefís Eireann* back in those days seemed to have at least one flickering newsreel clip from the 1916 Rising or the War of Independence, Black and Tan soldiers marching up boreens, Pearse and the other rebel commanders being led hands high from the smouldering ruin of the GPO, walking quickly, comically, like silent movie stars, the fluttering green, white and orange flag behind them translated by the screen to black, cream and grey. Often I wondered what was the point of having colour at all, when your mother only seemed to like black and white. But whenever I tried to joke about it, she'd just ignore me or look away or shrug, as though the answers to my teasing questions were utterly obvious. She would sit and watch the screen with a closed-down look on her face, like some ancient sage scrutinising a mystic fire. Large things were happening in her heart, I am sure, and that would have frightened your mother. Though she had a temper, as you know, in truth she had no real facility for melodrama, she never liked the large things of life. An argument would exhaust her for days. But it is the small things I still carry with me from that time. One night you tottered into the living-room in ballet pumps and irritatedly asked your mother to show you how to dance. She laughed and stroked your face but said that she knew nothing about dancing. That amazed me. Your mother used to love dancing so much.

And then, around that time I would often wake up in the middle of the night to find that your mother was not beside me in the bed. The first time it happened I was convinced that she had left me. I remember getting up and walking around the house, looking for her. It even occurred to me to telephone her parents, although it must have been after two in the morning. Finally I found her in the garden, sitting on the grass under the apple tree and smoking a cigarette. Her feet were under her and she had pulled her yellow nightdress into a sack over her knees. When she saw me approaching, she asked where I had been the night before and who I had been drinking with. I was touched in a way, because these were questions that she had stopped bothering to put some time before. I sat down in the damp grass beside her and held her hand. She was so pale and delicate, she looked like an illustration of a wan ghost in a sad old storybook. She told me in a very quiet voice that she loved me and wanted to make me happy. I told her that I loved her too and she smiled and looked away. After a while she asked me to pick her up and carry her into the house. I thought she was joking, but she said no, she was not. I lifted her in my arms and did what she had asked. Then she made tea and we sat in the kitchen for a while saying nothing at all, your mother sitting on my knees, one hand on my face and the other holding my own hand very tightly. From time to time she would kiss my face and I would kiss her hair, but we did not say a word, just sat there in silence drinking tea, the two of us wrapped in an old coat, our shaking fingers intertwined like the wild flowers in the garden. I believe that was the last night we ever said aloud that we loved each other.

In the following weeks I would often find your mother down in the kitchen late at night, with the door of the Aga open; she would be sitting cross-legged on the floor and staring disconsolately into the flames. At other times I would be woken at three and four in the morning by the smell of meat cooking; she would be down in the kitchen again, cooking up stews and casseroles which she would then put into lunch-boxes and freeze. Shortly after this she started to stay in bed late, which was fine, although it surprised me a little because Grace had always loved the mornings. When we were first married she would always rise before I did. But in the months after she miscarried that was to change. At first I was not worried by this. I understood that she needed to rest, and actually liked it when she would not get up before me. Rest and sleep were what the doctors said she needed, and I truly believed that rest and sleep would give her the things she could not get from me. We evolved a kind of routine. I would get up and make you two your breakfasts, then bring your mother up toast and a pot of tea in bed. We would sit there and talk a bit, about nothing at all, oddly formal conversations about unimportant subjects; which new films were due to come to the cinema in Dun Laoghaire, the latest headline-grabbing speech by some absurd politician. Although she would be tired, she seemed a little easier in herself in the mornings. The haunted look would have faded from her features. Her eyes would be bright and clear. I have pleasant enough memories of those mornings, the two of us in the bedroom upstairs, her dark thick hair spread out on the pillow, the smell of tea, and the delicate sunlight making the filmsy curtains glow.

But then one day around that time I came home early from work. It was about four in the afternoon when I got in and your mother was in bed. When I walked into the bedroom she was wide awake and staring at the window. She seemed shocked when she saw me. She was like a child caught out in some domestic crime. She told me nervously that she had just come upstairs for a lie-down, but then you kids let slip later that she had been in bed all day, and that this had been the steady pattern of things for the last several months. You would arrive in from school to find your mother in bed; she would only get up at tea time when she thought that I was due home. She had asked you both not to tell me about this. It had become a kind of game, an enjoyable conspiracy, not telling me what was going on with your mother.

I did not know what to do. I was afraid to talk to her about it: perhaps, I think now, my not doing so was a way of refusing to acknowledge what was happening, and perhaps the same could be said of her also. Anyone who has ever been in a dying marriage – and I suppose that is what ours was by then – knows that not putting words on unhappiness is the moral equivalent of leaving the lights out so that you cannot see the monsters coming. But after this incident I began to find excuses to return home earlier from work. Sometimes, if I was passing during the afternoon, I would drop into the house to see how she was getting on. I got into the habit of coming home for lunch, but always at irregular times which she would not be able to predict. I could not bear the thought of her lying in bed all day. I suppose the truth is that her doing this would fill me with a kind of dread, because it reminded me of what my father would do during the times when his own depression would get the better of him. I wondered how best I could prevent it. Of course the solution was clear. For a brief period I did manage to give up drinking, or at least, drinking outside the house, in pubs. I tried to be at home every night with your mother, even if being at home just meant watching the television for hours on end, the two of us silently smoking until the living-room was cloudy with smoke. And that did work, actually; your mother was in some ways a woman who was very easy to please. Loss had come into our lives and had shaped the way we saw love. But when I think about Grace now, it often occurs to me that all she ever truly wanted in her heart was not even love, but companionship. It is shocking to learn the littleness of the things for which most of us will settle if ultimately necessary – and more shocking that we so often deny even those small mercies to each other. Well, perhaps that sentence is just one more evasion on my part, another way of hiding my personal culpability. Certainly, if I have learned anything at all – if I have one thing to bequeath to you – it is that every single statement on the subject of human morality that contains the word 'we' is a lie.

One day when I got home my mother was in the kitchen with Grace. I was surprised to see her. She was in poor health by then and did not often venture out to Dalkey. There was no reason at all for her visit, she told me, she just fancied it, she had come out in a taxi. Grace looked as though she had been crying. It was obvious from the quality of the silence in the room that I had interrupted a conversation, although my mother denied this and laughed lightly and told me not to be flattering myself, she and Grace had more to be talking about than the likes of me. I drove her home to Ringsend that night, and when we got there she asked me to come into the house for a while.

It was late and I was tired and so I told her no, I did not want to. We sat in the car on Joy Street and talked for a while. She told me plainly that I would never know the grief Grace was going through now, and that I would have to do a lot more to support her. To lose a child was the most awful thing that could ever happen to a woman. Everything else in my life would have to be put in second place to Grace now, she said. Everything else. She looked at me and touched my hand and asked if I knew what she meant by the words 'everything else' and I told her yes, I did know.

'You're at a crossroads, son,' she sighed. 'I prayed you never would be. But you are now.'

That conversation must have taken place in the autumn, because our wedding anniversary was coming up. As a surprise for Grace, I borrowed some money from the credit union and arranged for us to go to Paris for the weekend. She seemed pleased enough when I told her about it, but not quite as pleased as I had thought she would be, and in the days immediately leading up to the trip she was if anything more preoccupied than ever.

We stayed in a small and cheap hotel on the Place St Sulpice, a beautiful little square with a mighty old church and a preposterously gorgeous fountain. The first day was pleasant. We went to Notre Dame and the Louvre, we walked the Champs-Elysées and looked in the windows of all the elegant shops. But that night I got drunk on red wine and somehow got involved in a disagreement with an English couple in a restaurant. The following day your mother was furious with me, though she tried her best to hide it. We walked around Paris hardly saying a word, trying to find the Hotel Des Beaux Arts, where Oscar Wilde died. We never did. It was a hot, exhausting afternoon and we kept getting lost in the narrow, serpentine streets around Montmartre. We were on a tight budget and everything was so astoundingly expensive; for some reason I still remember being maddened by the price of two small glasses of orange juice. Later in the evening we had an argument because she wanted an early night and I had booked a meal for us on a bateau-mouche. She said that if I wanted to go that much I should go by myself. I suppose I must have lost my temper. Things were said by both of us that should not have been said. We spent the night of our anniversary not speaking.

The next morning we went for breakfast in a café on the

square. Your mother was wearing a pair of stylish sunglasses which she had bought the day before from a stall on the Quai des Contes. I gave her the present I had got for her in Dublin, a cheap brooch made of imitation emeralds and shaped like a bird on a twig. A haughty black waiter brought two enormous bowls of coffee, I remember, and I laughed because they were so big but Grace did not laugh back. She did not even smile. We sat and drank our coffee, and after a while your mother took a parcel from her handbag and gave it to me.

'You may as well have this,' she said.

I opened the package. Inside was a silver signet ring with our initials engraved on the inside and the words 'Happy Anniversary'. Underneath this, in tiny Celtic script, was the date of our wedding, 28 October 1968.

When I went to kiss her, she pulled sharply away. 'Don't, Billy,' she said.

I asked her could we not make up our row but she shook her head. She was very close to tears for a while, but managed to swallow them back. I remember her staring away from me across the square. A bell was ringing in the church steeple. People were going to mass. There were fat larks and pigeons splashing in the fountain and whirling around in the air. An old blind woman with a white stick was being helped up the steps by a gendarme in a beautiful, crisp-looking uniform. I remember the scene so clearly, all these things, and the warm, loamy smell of fresh bread rolls and coffee.

'I think we're on the slide, Billy,' she said, quietly. 'I think our marriage might be in trouble.'

I asked her what she meant.

She told me that a young woman had been telephoning the house during the day to speak to me. She would never say who she was or where she was from. All she ever wanted was to speak to me.

'You've been unfaithful to me, Billy,' your mother said,

in a quaking voice. 'You may as well tell me the truth now, before I find out from somebody else.'

I had no idea who this woman was. I told your mother this and swore that I had never cheated on her and never would. This was the truth. I loved Grace, I truly did. To read some of what I have told you of those dark times will be to ask yourself how this could be true. And yet it was true, I loved her passionately. When I think back on those years I see your mother and me not as a disaster, but as an absurd concentrate of the coexistences and compromises that grow up over time in every marriage. Perhaps I am justifying yet again when I say this, but I do not think so. Our love began to turn itself inside out, but it still had the same shape and dimension, and something of the same force. Certainly, I loved her in a way that blessed me. Any flickering moment of humanity I had in those years I owe to her, and to the two of you. Any small shred of mercy or compassion in my life I borrowed – I stole – from her. Infidelity had never so much as entered my mind.

I did my best to tell her this. There had to be some innocent explanation for these phone calls. She kept telling me to stop lying and just let her know the truth. When she started to cry, right there in the café, when she took off those beautiful black sunglasses and let me see the tears streaming down her face, I swore on your life, darling, that I had never once cheated on her and never would. When I said this, I think she believed me.

'I just want you to know,' she said, 'that I couldn't ever forgive you for that. If you ever do that to me, Billy, it's over. I just couldn't. That kind of weakness I couldn't handle. Don't ever ask me to.'

'I won't, love,' I told her. 'Jesus, I wouldn't, I swear it.'

She nodded and let me take her hand.

'I know I've been weak sometimes, Grace,' I said. 'I know you can't stand weakness. That's because you're so strong.'

145

And I tried to laugh then. 'You're so strong and precious to me.'

'No, Billy. I can't stand weakness because I'm so weak. And I know that scares you half to death.'

Perhaps a month after we had got home I happened to ask where her anniversary brooch was. She confessed to me that she had lost it.

By the first week of June, I began to get the uneasy feeling that the milkman was trying to fool me. There was still no word of his elusive friend, though the seemingly endless stories of his past continued and became, if anything, more chilling. By now he had turned into *my* friend, for some reason. Nap would come trundling into the lane, peer out of his van in a childishly crestfallen manner and call, 'How's she cuttin' Larry, I've no news yet on yer friend.'

Every morning he would tell me that he had left a message or tried to call my friend on his mobile telephone, but without success. My friend was a very difficult person to track down; that was because he was so good at what he did. But really, when we thought about it, we were lucky even to know about my friend. He was a professional, my friend, he was not just any old hatchet man. He was an artist. While he was telling me this I would try to scan his face for evidence of lies or distortions but could see nothing. Again and again he would tell me to be patient. My friend would be in touch soon. I became convinced that he had not tried to find this man. I suspected he had simply taken my money and spent it on ecstasy tablets, the consumption of which, he had let slip one morning, was the nearest thing he had to what you might call a hobby. By midsummer's day, I began to wonder if my friend existed at all.

By now I had built up a very clear picture of Quinn's movements. I had watched him as my father used to watch the birds. I knew a great deal about him. He would leave his house around nine or half-nine at night, walk into the town,

146

hang around outside the church and wait for young people to approach him and buy whatever it was he was selling – I assumed it was not holy pictures. When he had finished at the church, there were three or four bars he frequented; I got to know them all. He would drink for an hour or so – he drank lager, always – but would never get drunk. When he left the pub he would go to the snooker hall on Quinnsboro Road or one of the kebab shops or hysterically-coloured ice-cream parlours on the sea front; he was a good snooker player, he had once made a break of a hundred and four. He smoked Rothmann's and chewed gum. Occasionally he would walk the promenade or the path up to Bray Head. At the weekends he usually went to a late show at the cinema on the main street; he liked horror films. After that he would go to the nightclub in the Starlight Hotel. He would always be sober when he left. Sometimes, if he had met a girl, he would take her back to his house. He seemed to be living alone, although from time to time other men of his own age would come to stay, and when this happened he would take the girls down an alleyway near the harbour. He was never short of female company. Women seemed to like him.

I began to think in a more focused way about the best way of killing him. I had two plans, one which involved the milkman's friend – my friend – softening him up first, and another more awkward set of arrangements which I would use if I had to do the whole thing myself. I asked myself if I could really attack someone with a knife. One night I got the hunting knife I had bought out of the car and simply looked at it for a while. I found the thought of its serrated blade penetrating flesh sickening and almost unimaginable. But then could I hit a man with a hammer? At one in the morning I walked down to the apple tree and took a few good swings at the trunk with the hammer from my toolbox. The sound drove the birds out of the bushes in fright. It would not be easy, I knew that.

I would rehearse killing him in my dreams and wake up

in the mornings saying the words 'knife' and 'hammer' out loud. I found these thoughts disgusting. For a while I even considered hitting him with my car and claiming it was an accident, but I knew that nobody would believe it.

There were many times when I had serious doubts that I could go through with it at all. One evening in particular, I was almost certain that I could not. I had watched a television documentary about capital punishment in America, poor black men rotting on death row, grim photographs of charred and still-smouldering bodies being hauled out of the electric chair. I was seized by the sheer enormity of ending a human life, the awesome finality of stamping out that minuscule spark for ever. To think of that tangle of so many millions of impulses, so many possibilities, and to say no, to answer the endless questions posed by another life with the ultimate negation. It appalled me. I listened to the turgid little Texan sheriff who had arrested several of these men saying that it was a relatively straightforward thing to make a murderer confess. Unless he was a psychopath it was easy once you got him into the interrogation room. Actually to end the existence of another human being was such a devastatingly unnatural action that the guilty almost always admitted it within minutes. 'So what's your technique?' the interviewer asked him. 'Well, sir, y'jus' sit the sumbitches down and ask 'em if they did it,' he grinned, 'and they sing like the goddamm birds. Pardon mah French.'

I felt cold panic deep in my throat. For the very first time it occurred to me that I might be caught. I had planned everything so carefully, but maybe something would go wrong. Perhaps it would be Duignan who would come for me – when Quinn's body was found would some switch trip on in his policeman's brain? And if nothing went wrong on the night itself, what about the next morning? How would I actually feel when I woke up at dawn the following day, having committed murder? I had not planned for that. Would this famous desire to scream and blurt out one's own guilt infect me too? Would I be able to keep silent, or would I run howling to the authorities and plead with them to punish me? Who would speak out for me? Who would tell *my* story? And if I was found guilty, as I almost certainly would be – as I would deserve to be – would I be sent to prison for the rest of my life, perhaps to the same jail, the very same cell for which Donal Quinn had been destined when his luck had changed? I felt physically sick with fear.

But the next morning that feeling had vanished. I remember getting out my notebook in the kitchen around sunrise and writing for a while. I would have to get out of the house after it was done, that much was absolutely clear to me. I would not want to be alone in the silent house, waiting for that poisonous coruscating wave of guilt to come. I tried to think over my options with some kind of clarity. Where could I go? For five whole minutes, my plan involved flying to Australia the morning after the killing – I can scarcely write the word – to visit Lizzie and Franklin. I had been promising to go for years but had never done it; now I was going to do it before they came home to live in Ireland. I actually got as far as finding the telephone directory and looking up the numbers of long-distance travel agents. But it was ridiculous. It was not the action of a rational man. Suddenly it occurred to me, what Seánie had said about Lourdes! That was it. Here was the solution. I would go to Lourdes the day after the deed, I would help Seánie with the sick pilgrims, I would purge whatever guilt I would inevitably feel by easing the terrible lot of those poor people half in love with death. It was all so laughably simple.

Around nine o'clock I drove down to Monkstown village, where nobody would know me, found a pharmacy and bought a long length of adhesive bandage. All I needed now were the plastic sacks, the fan belts and the handcuffs. I went into work and sold well.

The day after this, Nap did not show up in the lane. I

waited for almost half an hour – twenty-eight minutes, to precise – but there was still no sign. By now it was well over a month since I had given him the first of the money. When the milk float finally did appear there was a different milkman behind the wheel, a much older man with large, stupid eyes and a pointed chin. He did not know anything at all about Nap, he told me, had never even heard the name in his life. He had been given this route to do for a few weeks, he had not asked any questions, he was only temporary. If I was interested, he had heard that the regular milkman was away on his holidays. In Rimini. But he did not know for sure.

When he had gone I went down to the Forty Foot and had a quick swim. The water was cold and a little dirty. I visited you in the hospital and then headed in to work, arriving almost twenty minutes late. Hopper and Liam got on my nerves all that morning, arguing and sulking, I think it was the heat and the bad coffee and the fact that the air-conditioner had broken down. At lunch-time I slipped out to the car-parts warehouse down the street and bought two fan belts for a Mini, making a point of paying cash so that there would be no records.

I put the fan belts into the boot of the car, along with the hammer, the hunting knife and the bandage. I covered them all with a blanket.

When I got back to the office there was a message from Seánie about the trip to Lourdes. There was still a place for me if I wanted it. But he would have to know soon.

I found the phone book and looked up the number of the dairy. There it was. 'Hibernian Milk Ltd.' I rang the distribution depot and asked if I could speak to Nap.

'There's nobody works here by that name,' the voice said.

'He's a milkman,' I said.

A soft laugh. 'He isn't, I'm tellin' you. We've nobody here called that. Hold on.'

He came back a few moments later. 'Yeah. There was a lad called that right enough, but he's after leavin'.'

'Leaving?'

'Yeah. Jacked it in.'

'Where is he now?'

'Dunno. Are you a customer or what?'

That night, I could not sleep for thinking about him. I lay on my back, eyes wide open, staring at the ceiling with my hands behind my head. It was all I could seem to get fixed on: Nap, my money, the whole dirty business. I had thought that I could trust him but I had had been wrong. I got up and walked around the house for a while, feeling strange and dislocated. It was not the money exactly, but just the way he thought could get away with it. The knowledge of this really did bother me, love. It started to grow into me like a parasite.

I got out of bed and looked out the window for a while. Through the trees, the moon was casting long lines of pale light over the garden. I took a piece of paper from the drawer and wrote down the words 'hammer' and 'knife'. Then I drew a small doodle, the hanging man.

If I am looking for landmarks of the last days of our marriage, I see in an older diary that there was a christening party for your cousin Molly in February 1982. The date is the only thing I need to be reminded about, because the most important things about the night I can still remember very clearly. At some point that morning I recall that I felt nervous about the prospect of the party. I suppose I had never truthfully been what you might call sociable, in the way that your mother was once, but this was a new thing, a kind of vague tension eating at me. I do not know how I would describe it to you.

Imagine, if you can, two pieces of music being played at the same time, one softly melodic, the other even more quiet but ugly and discordant, and that might give you some idea of how I felt. On the way to your Uncle Stevie's house, anyway, I recall being snappy with your mother in the car.

Then, when we got there and went in, I remember feeling very hot, and realising that I was blushing, for no reason, which was a thing I had never done before. Whenever anyone spoke to me – and I knew most of the guests well – I would feel myself blushing hard. People kept asking me if I had been away because, they said, I seemed to have got myself a touch of the sun. The remains of a childhood stammer which I thought I had managed to supress seemed all of a sudden to come back also. After a time I seemed to be stuttering whenever I spoke. It was a very cold February day – I think there might even have been snow on the ground outside – but I was sweating heavily. At one point I went into the bathroom and took off my jacket. My shirt was completely wet through with sweat and dark under the armpits. I stared at myself in the mirror. I looked like a fat, sad oaf who had been beaten up, I thought, jowly and dark-eyed and weak and untrustworthy. I reminded myself of Richard Nixon. I was sure that I was coming down with some kind of flu. I wanted to go home and get into bed.

When I came out of the bathroom your mother was not around. I felt far too anxious to go and look for her or even ask anybody else where she was. That was my overwhelming sensation, just not wanting to attract attention. The room was full and hot and very smoky. I positioned myself at the back, near the door, still feeling shaky and uneasy. There was a bottle of Bushmills on a table near me. When I was sure that nobody was looking I poured out a glass and drank it quickly down. I had another glass and then I remember Stevie getting up to speak. He looked so proud and excited. He threw his arms around your Aunt Catriona and kissed her and everyone clapped. He said something about your mother and me, how he hoped that we too would be hearing the patter of tiny feet again soon. There were cheers. Before the speeches were over I had finished three-quarters of the bottle. Later there was a violent argument between me and a colleague of Stevie's, a tiny bandy-legged fellow who I was sure had insulted me in some way. I think I even threw a few punches; certainly, I remember sprawling on the landing floor with the contents of a glass all over me.

My face felt as though it was on fire. People around me were laughing. I managed to get to my feet and stumble downstairs. I still could not see your mother anywhere. I went to the kitchen to get a drink of water. My heart was thundering. Two young people with long hair were lying on the floor under the table, moaning softly as they kissed – I remember realising that I did not know which was the man and which the woman. I could not find a glass so I filled a cereal bowl with water and just drank it down. I leaned over the sink and dry-retched a few times. My temples and eyes were pounding with pain.

When I came back out I wandered around the rooms for a while, lost and very hot. It was just a standard family house but for some reason it felt huge. And yet, despite that, I felt claustrophobic and exhausted, badly in need of more drink. Finally I turned a corner and saw your mother. She was standing in the corridor talking to a pretty young man with round glasses and raggedy hair. He had on a smock, which made him look like some kind of Russian peasant. His face was very close to your mother's. She was laughing softly, I remember, as he spoke to her, and gazing right into his eyes. She was laughing, the way she once used to do when I spoke to her, the way I had not seen her laugh for years.

I said her name. The young man peered over at me as though he did not like me. Your mother's eyes darkened. She introduced me as her husband – she did not use my name – and the youngfella nodded and muttered a slurred hello before slinking off down the corridor trailing his hands against the walls.

'D'y'know where there's any more drink?' I asked her.

'Don't you think we should go?' she said.

'I was going to get another drink.'

'You've had enough, Billy,' she said. 'Please.'

'Grace,' I said. 'I don't feel well. I need a fuckin' drink.'

Suddenly your Uncle Jimmy and two heavy men who I did not know were in the corridor staring at us. They seemed to be listening to the conversation and giggling. When Grace saw them her face went red.

'I'll be outside,' she said, loudly. 'I'm just going to say good-night to Catriona, then I'll see you outside in a minute. And we'll get a taxi back, Billy, you're too drunk to drive.'

She pushed past Jimmy and the other two and went up the stairs.

One of the men stared after her and whistled though his teeth. Jimmy grinned at me. 'By Christ,' he said, and he swigged from his beer bottle. 'I see you're on the short fuckin' leash anyway, soldier.'

He laughed at this. And I made myself laugh too. I could think of nothing at all to say, so I stumbled off through the corridors trying to find my coat.

Outside in the street your mother seemed very angry. She stood bolt upright with her arms folded hard around herself while we waited for a taxi. For a while she would not tell me what was wrong.

I went to embrace her.

'Don't you dare touch me,' she said, and nudged me away.

'Grace,' I said. 'Please? What is it?'

She whipped around to face me. 'Don't you know? You fall around the place like a fool. You let them all make a holy show of you. I hope you're proud. That . . . that dirty little knacker, your brother, laughing at you like that. Making personal remarks. I didn't know where to look.'

I said that he had only been joking.

'He's a little pup, that's what, and a tinker. You could have said something, but of course you didn't. I can't believe how bloody weak you are sometimes. It's the thing I hate most about you.'

A taxi pulled up beside us. I opened the back door and got

in, your mother climbed into the front. She did not speak to me all the way home, except to ask for some money to pay the babysitter. When the neighbour's girl had gone we sat in the kitchen for a while. I opened a bottle of beer I had in the fridge and started into it. Your mother was still fuming and waiting for an argument to start. For a time I was too drunk to fight with her. I wish that's the way things had stayed.

'Do you have to drink that?' she said after a while.

'It's only a beer.'

'Haven't you had enough tonight? You must have had ten beers.'

I told her I hadn't realised she'd been counting. This, by now, was a familiar line in our arguments. When she heard it coming out again, she just sighed and stood up.

'I'm going to bed,' she told me.

'Grace, look, I'm sorry if you're upset.'

Her cheeks were like blood drops in snow. 'You're sorry, good Christ. You bloody disgraced me and disgraced yourself and you're sorry. I had to apologise to Catriona. I didn't know where to look. Is that the way you were brought up, to behave like that in front of your wife? What do you think your mother'd've said if she'd seen you?'

She turned away from me and went to the stove. There was a pot on one of the hobs and she began to stir it. That was all she did. Stirred it around with a wooden spoon and ignored me when I asked her to stop. Something in what she was doing completely enraged me, I can't explain why. To this day, when I think about the events of that evening, which I do very often, I wish I had just gone to bed as soon as we got home, or even that I had fallen down senselessly drunk in the street, or on the floor of Stevie and Catriona's house. But I didn't. Instead, I came home and just let the rage come. I felt it, deep down in my stomach, like a drug. I sensed it flooding the walls of my veins. I looked at your mother's long straight back. I took a drag on my cigarette.

'You're one to preach, all the same, Grace.'

'What?' she said, in a quiet hoarse voice.

'Who was that effort you were talkin, to in the hall? When I came out?'

'What do you mean?'

'That fuckin' longhair you were talkin' to. Who was he, anyway?'

'I don't know who he was.'

I laughed. 'An old friend, maybe.'

She turned around slowly, a glass of water in her hand. 'What does that mean?'

I looked at her. I felt out of control now. The room was spinning and full of strange light. My tongue felt like a slab of soap. 'But sure, come on, that's where you met him, isn't it? Lizzie's auldfella. At a party? Full of poets and artists, wasn't that it? No knacker Sweeneys there, like my brother. No tinkers. No commoners. Just Grace Lawrence's intellectual friends that the likes of fuckin' me was never good enough to meet.'

Her body sank back against the stove and she put her fingers to her forehead. Still I continued. I do not think I could have stopped. It was that cold stage of drunkenness when a parody of rationality takes over and you will say anything you have to in order to hurt.

'Maybe that was him tonight, was it? Maybe it was him. Would've been nice to meet him after all this time. Yeah, lovely, shake his hand. Buy him a fuckin' drink. Let him know how his kid is gettin' along. His bastard kid I'm payin' the bills for. And you're going to lecture me about fuckin' shame, Grace. You hypocrite.'

Your mother hung her head low for a while. She took a sip of water and ran her fingers through her hair. When she raised her eyes to me again there was a look I had never seen before on her face, an expression of absolute white-hot loathing.

'What did you say to me?'

'You heard me.'

'Say it again.'

'Fuck you, Grace.'

'Billy Sweeney,' she said, 'I curse the day I met you.'

I laughed at her then. 'Sweetheart, that makes two of us.'

Her cheeks were flushed, her eyes narrow and glimmering. She took a step forward and threw the water in my face. She dropped the glass and it shattered on the tiles. I stood up shaking with fury. I remember being aware that I had clenched my fists.

'Go on,' she screamed. 'If you're man enough, go on. It'll be the last fucking thing you'll ever do, you whore's melt.'

I staggered to the sink and got a towel.

'You low dirty cur,' she said. 'I hope you die tonight.'

'So do I,' I said.

'I'm glad I lost your child,' she said. 'Christ help me, I'm glad.'

'If it was mine,' I said.

She put her hands into the pockets of her jacket and dashed from the room.

'That's it,' I bawled after her. 'Run, Grace. Oh, you're good at that, all right. Always were. You just run, baby, that's the fuckin' style.'

I heard her feet on the stairs and the sound of the bedroom door slamming hard. Shortly after this I heard the sound of your bedroom door opening. There were voices upstairs. I heard the ting of the telephone being picked up and quickly replaced. I remember hearing the toilet flush. I listened to the pipes for a while, as they gurgled in the wall. I remember looking at the plaque which the old rector had screwed up in the kitchen: 'Man does not live by bread alone'.

I went into the boxroom where I was sleeping at the time on a camp bed. I lay down. Everything was quiet. The room seemed to be somersaulting, spinning on several axes, but I felt fine. I felt happy. I felt so good that I wanted another drink. So after a while I got up again and crawled on my hands and knees back into the kitchen where I had hidden a large bottle of vodka down behind the fridge. I opened it and drank all of it.

I believe it was Lizzie who found me on the kitchen floor when she came down for her breakfast the next morning. I believe it was you, love, who called the ambulance. I vaguely remember the sound of you shouting into the telephone that the house was hard to find and had a strange name.

Glen Bolcain. Glen Bolcain. Glen Bolcain.

They had to pump my stomach and put me on sedatives. Your mother never once came to see me in the hospital. The day I was finally released I was driven all the way home from Carlow in a taxi. Even then, she and I did not speak one solitary word to each other for almost three months. It was a hell of a night, love, your cousin Molly's christening. If the truth is told – and why not tell it now – I do not think we ever got over it.

Chapter Ten

Finally.

I was at my desk in the office one morning in the middle of July when the telephone rang. I had just asked Hopper to give me the precise address of a sex shop he knew in the city centre, so I was laughing like a drain when I picked it up. There was a crackling, distorted voice, like it was a bad mobile connection.

'That Bill?'

'Yeah.'

'Bill Sweeney?'

'The same. Who's this?'

'It's Nap here. The milkman of human fuckin' kindness.'

I almost dropped the phone with shock.

'How did you find out my real name?'

'I've a pal a guard, Billyboy. Got him to check out the reg on yer car.'

'Where are you? How did you get my number?'

'Y'd be amazed, Billyboy. Now listen to me, I've only a minute, right. That thing y'talked to me about, it's on for Monday night.'

'It's on?'

'Yeah. I'm after talkin' to yer friend and it's on. He'll do it for y'Monday night.'

'You sure?'

'Course I'm bleedin' sure, man, what, y'think I'm guessin'? Only thing is, he'll need six.'

'Six.'

'Six ton, yeah.'

'That's not what we agreed.'

'Well lookat, it's all the same to me. I'm only tellin' y'what I was told.'

The line bleeped a few times. 'All right,' I said, 'I can manage six. But no more.'

'We're laughin' so,' he said. 'We're laughin', Larry.'

But I did not really feel like laughing at all, to tell you the truth, when I hung up the phone. My mind was racing. I went to the toilet and bathed my face with cold water. I smoked a couple of cigarettes. I knew it was important to try to think clearly now. I got out my notebook and jotted down a few details It was absolutely vital not to panic, not even to show any excitement. I went back to the office and sat at the desk.

I switched on the computer and pretended to do some work, my fingers so sweaty that they kept slipping on the keyboard. Gradually managed to calm down. I picked up the phone, rang Seánie and told him that I would come to Lourdes with him after all. He was leaving the next Tuesday morning; I would travel on the same flight if I could get a ticket. He sounded delighted. Then I went into O'Keeffe's office and told him that I would be taking two weeks' holidays from Monday. I was going to Lourdes. He looked up at me blankly.

'Monday?'

'Yeah.'

'Lourdes?'

'Yeah.'

'You?'

'That's right.'

'As in Virgin Mary Lourdes?'

'No, Hugh. As in Billy J. Kramer and the Dakotas Lourdes.'

'Jesus. Thanks for all the notice, Billy.'

'It only just came up, Hugh. We're quiet enough at the moment, anyway. The lads can manage.'

His face changed then. He started to do his understanding expression that he learnt on the staff-relations training course he had attended the previous summer. I always find this upsetting. To me the sudden appearance of O'Keeffe's understanding expression is like bumping into someone in an alley who is wearing black tights and a mask and lightly swinging an executioner's axe.

'So I suppose the new love is coming with you?'

'I don't know, Hugh,' I said. 'Maybe. She's busy just now.'

He sighed, nodded, wrote something in his note pad.

'Well listen, I'm thrilled skinny for you, Bill. We all are. I was just saying the other day how well you're looking lately. Because you didn't seem yourself for a while there.'

'Yes, Hugh,' I said.

'Everyone needs someone, don't they?'

'That's true, Hugh.'

He laughed. 'You're a dark bloody horse, Bill. Anyway, have a good time over there, the pair of you.'

I went to leave. Just as I got to the door he called out my name. When I turned around his face was dark and serious.

'You know the really gas thing about Lourdes, Bill?'

'What's that?'

He grinned. 'They say the only virgin in the whole town is the one in the bloody grotto.'

Back at my desk I found it hard to focus on anything much. Hopper's mobile kept ringing, which drove me crazy, I wished he'd switch the damn thing off. The computer was printing out some long complicated-looking document whining and straining and rattling from side to side as it tried to deal with the graphs and pie-charts. After a while I could not stand it any more. I got my keys and told them that I was going out. Hopper grunted. Liam ignored me. What a surprise. You could tell that pair you had just grown a ten-foot tail where your coccyx used to be and Hopper would grunt and Liam would ignore you.

I headed into town and got parking on Ormonde Quay. The sex shop Hopper told me about was just where he said, in a tiny laneway off Bachelor's Walk. Out front there were stainless-steel shutters splashed with graffiti warning drug pushers to get out of the area. Inside was a long narrow fluorescent-lit room stuffed with racks of dirty magazines and books.

Down the back was a row of three tall glass cases full of headless dummies in different uniforms. There was a nurse's outfit, an air hostess's suit, Jesus Christ, there was a nun's habit done out in white leather and black lace, complete with rubber veil and stockings. On a shelf beside this sat a collection of blow-up dolls in boxes. The illustration on one of these boxes grabbed my attention because this particular doll looked exactly like Mrs Thatcher. It was actually a bit frightening, the resemblance, but it was there all the same, the same candyfloss hairstyle and fearsome glint. The doll was anatomically correct, the box announced in day-glo green letters. She certainly did not look it to me, I must say, but then neither did Mrs Thatcher, at least not very often, and in any case I had no intention of checking. On the wall by the counter there were long rows of vibrators and false penises and vaginas made of plastic. Underneath this were cardboard boxes of playing cards with pornographic pictures on them, tubs of lubricants, chocolate nipples, candles shaped like breasts, fruit-flavoured condoms. They have kiwi-fruit-flavoured condoms nowadays, for Jesus' sake; when I was a kid they did not even have kiwi-fruit-flavoured fucking kiwi fruits. And handcuffs. There they were. Hopper had been right, after all. I picked up a set and gave them to the long-nosed youngfella behind the counter.

'Want any videos or mags?' he asked. I told him no.

'Do you a good deal, no? Summer sale.'

'No, no. Just these.'

He nodded and smiled not at all unpleasantly. He looked a bit like an unambitious junior civil servant, I thought, as he put the handcuffs into a bag and sellotaped it up.

'How much anyway?' I said, taking out my wallet.

He peered up at the ceiling and scratched his head. 'Ah, I'll take ten off you. I'm in good humour today. Must be the nice weather, what?'

Back in the car I got the handcuffs out of the box and tried them on. They were fine. They had a little pink fake-fur lining on them, 'for comfort', the instructions explained. Not that Quinn would be wearing them very fucking long, I told myself, but at least he would be comfortable for his last few minutes on earth. This thought amused me. I sat in the car and laughed out loud for a while. I laughed so much that a couple of snotty-looking kids on skateboards stopped to gawp in at me.

I took a spin out to the hardware shop in Sallynoggin and bought a thick roll of refuse sacks, good strong tough ones that would not leak – it actually said 'Leakage Resistant' on the packet, which was reassuring in the circumstances. Once again I paid cash and made absolutely sure that the girl at the checkout did not get a good straight-on look at my face. Now I had everything I needed. There it all was, in the boot, laid out neatly under the blanket.

Next morning I gunned it down to the bank in Dalkey to collect the French francs I had ordered for the trip to Lourdes, along with the 1,950 in punts I knew I would need for the plan. The girl behind the counter asked me to say a prayer at the grotto for her mother who had lymph cancer, and I assured her that I certainly would. Just as I was leaving, the manager, Ronnie McDermott, ambled out of his office and saw me.

'Ah, Billy,' he said. 'How's tricks?' He put his hand on my shoulder. It felt like a spanner.

What I was thinking was: Hello there, Ronnie, I'll tell you exactly how tricks are, Ronnie. Outside in the back of the motor I have a hunting knife, a hammer, a fan belt, leakage-resistant plastic rubbish bags, a pair of handcuffs and a gag. You feel like taking a stroll out to see, Ronnie, do you? Ah come on, Ronnie, I could do with a bit of practice actually, Ronnie, you crawling Cork shit-heap, and it couldn't happen to a nicer guy. 'Mon out to the car park with me, Ronnie, I can't wait to thank you for all your fuckin' support over the years.

But what I said was: 'Fine, Ronnie. Sound as a pound. Yourself?'

'Never better, Billy. And I hear you're off on the holliers.'

'Lourdes,' I said.

'I know all about it,' he laughed. 'Father Seán was in earlier and told me.'

He raised his hand and carved a crucifix in the air.

'*Dominus vobiscum*,' he crooned.

That night I was excited but managed to sleep for a while with the radio on.

My mother died in June 1982, three months after Grace left the house with you and Lizzie and moved back into your grandparents' place in Harrington Street. The morning of the funeral the papers arrived from her lawyer, telling me that she was taking me to court for a legal separation and custody. The envelope was on the mat when I came down the stairs in my black suit.

It bothered me what happened at the funeral. There was no need for her to turn up like that, with her father and all her brothers in tow like I was some kind of animal who could not be trusted. It upset me too that she had not arranged for you and Lizzie to come home from your school trip at least for the few days. It would not have hurt to do that much. Whatever about me, but it would have meant a lot to my dad.

The separation hearing was fixed for September in the family law court. When I told my own solicitor that I wanted to contest it and apply in a counter-claim for custody, he said I was absolutely crazy. I was wasting my time and money, he insisted, but the more he did this, the more determined I became, until finally he backed down and grudgingly said all right, whatever I wanted.

'I mean, if I were you,' I remember him sighing, 'I wouldn't want all that responsibility anyway. But maybe that's just me.'

'Yeah, maybe it is,' I said. 'Maybe if your fuckin' wife took your kids away and didn't let you see them for a few months you'd feel a bit different.'

On the third or fourth afternoon of the case your mother was called to give evidence. When she came up to the witness box I noticed she was wearing the dark glasses that she had bought on our anniversary trip to Paris. Her voice was very quiet as she took the oath. When she answered the first question, the sound of a fire-brigade siren came suddenly pealing in from an open window and the judge motioned to one of the court attendants to go and close it.

She began to talk about our marriage in a way I did not recognise, or certainly did not want to. She had found me distant in the last few years. She had found me very secretive and dishonest, at times I had appeared as though I hated her. At first she had not been able to understand this. She had thought that it was some problem of her own, that I had not been able to trust her for some reason, probably to do with the circumstances in which she had had her first child. She had often blamed herself for this, had often thought that our agreement not to discuss those circumstances was unrealistic and cruel, that I could not get over my deep-rooted resentment of her. But then she had come to realise that this was simply the way I was. I was cold and emotionally violent. I was adept at using silence as a form of bullying. She had suspected me often of having affairs and once or twice, she still felt, she had been correct to suspect this. This had hurt her very much. There had been violent arguments in the house for many years. No, she could not say they were all my fault, not in truth, not on every occasion, but certainly we would not have argued so much had it not been for my drinking.

'Did you ever feel fear of your husband?' her solicitor asked her.

'There would have been times when I was afraid of him, yes.'

'And would the girls have been afraid of him, Mrs Sweeney?'

She put her hands on the rail of the witness box and bowed her head for a second. 'Lizzie and Maeve love Billy a lot,' she said, 'but yes, sometimes they were frightened of him. When he was drunk or hungover. I'd be dishonest if I told you otherwise.'

'Mrs Sweeney, can I ask you now, how was your intimate life with your husband?'

Your mother was silent for a moment. Then she cleared her throat. 'There was very little affection between us for some time,' she said.

The judge leaned down and said he realised that this was a delicate matter, but he would have to ask the defendant to be a little more specific in her answer.

Your mother took a sip of water and stared at the ceiling. Then she took off her sunglasses for a moment and wiped her eyes with the back of her hand. She put the glasses back on and bowed her head so that it seemed she was looking at the floor. 'My Lord,' she said, 'I blame myself completely for this.'

'Mrs Sweeney, with respect, that isn't what I asked you.'

She nodded. 'Well, my husband has not been inside the four walls of my bedroom for over five years now. For any reason.'

'Thank you, Mrs Sweeney,' he said.

She nodded and took a long drink of water.

'And would that have been a difficulty for you, Mrs Sweeney?' her solicitor asked.

Her lips trembled a little. 'I very much missed the closeness and the company, yes,' she said, and her voice began to crack. 'That aspect of our marriage was always very special to me. When it started to go I was heartbroken.'

'Mrs Sweeney, do you have anything to say to your husband now?'

She shook her head. 'Just that I'm sorry,' she said. 'I'm truly sorry for hurting him whatever way I did. To make him hate me so much.'

At that point I stood up and left the court. I simply could not bear to hear any more. My solicitor followed and pleaded with me to stay but I told him no, I would come back at the end, for the judgement. He told me that he did not want to cross-examine your mother if I wasn't in the room. I said I did not want him to cross-examine her anyway. I had made up my mind. He was not to ask her any questions at all, I told him; when she was finished giving her own evidence he was just to let her sit down. I did not want her put through any more.

In the end she won the case which was not much of a surprise. In his summing-up, the judge said it would be very difficult indeed for a father to win a custody hearing in any circumstances, but particularly when one of the children was a female step-child. As things stood, Lizzie was almost sixteen and therefore would soon become old enough to be beyond the reaches of a custody order. But in an event, it had been clear to him very early in the case that the girls' best interests would be served by living with their mother.

Grace left immediately, without speaking to me. It took me five minutes in one of the conference rooms to get calm enough even to think about getting into the car. I drove out of town on my own. All I could think was that there was no drink in the house. I stopped in at McDonagh's pub in Dalkey, where I bought a half-bottle of whiskey and forty cigarettes. I went home and took a long shower.

When I had finished showering, I poured out two large glasses of whiskey and drank them back, one after the other, as fast as I could. Then I walked down the garden, stepped ankle-deep right into the stream and threw the half-empty bottle over the back wall, into the travellers' field. I came back into the house, took four sleeping pills and went to bed. From that day on I never had a drink.

Until this summer, when I decided to murder Donal Quinn.

The first Saturday morning after the custody case I called to your mother's place just after nine o'clock. You will remember, I am sure, that forbidding black security gate out the front and the way they were always changing the access number without telling anybody, or maybe it was just me that never got told. Anyway, I certainly did not know it that first morning, so I had to park out on the road and go in on foot.

I liked the look of the place, the clean new cars sparkling in their bays, the modern red brickwork, the neat little communal garden laid out with trees and shrubs and well-tended flower-beds. It made Glen Bolcain seem even more old and unkempt.

I found the apartment and rang the bell. Your mother's voice came over the intercom. She asked me to stay where I was for a minute, there was something she wanted to talk to me about. She came down in the lift and appeared in the doorway, wearing a light blue dressing-gown and slippers. She looked tired. In a cautious tone she asked how I was. I told her I was OK. I gave her an envelope in which was a maintenance cheque and also a set of keys to the bank box in which we had put the small amount of jewellery and personal stuff she had inherited from her mother. She took the envelope and peered at it.

'This feels funny,' she said.

'Yeah,' I told her, 'well it wasn't my choice.'

'Let's not go over it,' she said.

I asked what she wanted to talk to me about.

'Billy,' she said, 'I think it's best if you don't come here in future. To the flat, I mean. I've been mulling it over a bit and I think we should meet on neutral territory from now on.'

In the argument that began, she kept using this phrase. Neutral territory. We stood in the front doorway fighting, while people pushed in and out past us.

'Neutral territory?' I remember saying, at one point. 'What Grace, it's a fuckin' war now, is it?'

'No Billy, it isn't,' she said. 'Not any more. So you'd better get used to it.'

You both came came down in the lift, then, and climbed into the car with me. You were dressed up like you were meeting some ancient maiden aunt and not your father. The feeling between us was strained, you did not seem to want to talk much, I noticed that you were both avoiding my eyes. We went to the zoo and walked around for a while in the drizzle, then back into town for lunch in McDonalds. On the way down Grafton Street later we met some of your school friends. They all looked at me in an accusing way, as though they knew secret things about me.

It was very hard dropping you home that first time. There were a lot of tears. You wanted me to come up to the flat for a cup of coffee, but I had to tell you that I did not think your mother would want this. I remember you asking me if I thought that she would ever change her mind. I was not sure what you were asking. I did not know whether you meant change her mind about allowing me into the flat or change her mind about something else. So I just said no, I did not think she would. Which covered all the possibilities, I suppose.

An incident which has stayed with me from around that

time: a few months after the custody case I arrived early on Saturday morning at the Royal Marine Hotel. I walked up and down the car park for a while. You all turned up ten minutes later in that battered little red Fiat your mother had bought. She pulled into a space on the far side of the car park, it was as though she was deliberately parking as far away from me as possible. The two of you got out of the car and walked towards me looking like a pair of hostages about to be swapped for a spy. You got into my car and kissed me. Grace did not even wave. She jumped back into the Fiat and drove away fast.

You each had your book lists for school that day, so we went into town to Fred Hanna's and got your books. You wanted to go to Captain America's for lunch. Then the three of us drove back out to Booterstown Field where the Fossett's circus was on. I had got tickets one evening during the week while I was passing on the way home from work, but all that Saturday morning I had kept it as a surprise. I thought you would both be absolutely thrilled when we pulled up outside the big top. But your faces took on a kind of horrified scowl when I told you where we were going.

'Dad, we're too old for the circus,' you informed me, nose in the air.

'Is that right?' I said.

'Yes.'

I sighed. 'Well so am I, pet, if you want to know the fuckin' truth.'

'Circuses are for kids,' Lizzie added.

I considered the situation. 'Well, what would you be doing today if you weren't with me?' You both laughed a bit and asked me if I really wanted to know. I said yes, of course, and you told me. We drove back into town again, to that place, McGonagle's, on Anne Street. I had somehow heard that this kip was rough enough at night, but that summer they were organising punk rock concerts for teenagers on Saturday afternoons. Lizzie knew some girl who sang in a group (the Blitzkriegs, as I recall – I told her not to mention the name to your mother) and the two of you wanted to go in and see her perform and meet your friends.

So that's what we did. I stood at the back swigging a tepid Coke and watched the pair of you as you danced around in your best clothes to the deafening noise of Belinda Bombs and the Blitzkriegs. I felt more than a little old, I can tell you, although there were one or two other parents there, skulking about and doing a lot of staring at their shoes. Anyway, at one point I was coming back from the toilet when I saw a very strange thing. There you were, Maeve, in a murky corner kissing some boy. Not just any boy, but a boy with a purple mohican haircut and a tartan vest and tight leather trousers that looked like some kind of wild dog had been let loose on them. This amazed me. That was my feeling about it, sheer amazement. There was our little Maeve, kissing someone. You were only thirteen. I did not know what to do about this. It was when he put his hands on your backside that I thought I would wander over and start saying loudly how good I thought the music was.

This was Hugh Gormley Jones, I was told. He was in a band also. His band used to be called the Spanish Inquisition but now they were called the Vatican Two. I was glad, I told Hugh, that my daughter had friends who were so religious. He did not get the joke. Hugh Gormley Jones's conversation seemed to be limited to a variety of bleatings, gruntings, suggestive barkings and incoherent gurgles. The smell of drink off him would have felled a docker. After a while he tottered over to the dance floor and started leaping about – 'pogoing', I believe you told me it was called, or 'moshing' – which is still the nearest dance I have ever seen to actual physical violence. He jumped up and down in one place, flailing his arms and jerking his head back and forth as though heading an invisible football. He then lurched up to the front of the stage and began copiously spitting at the bass guitarist. This, you explained, was a sign of appreciation.

'It's like those parrots, Billser,' you said. 'Aren't there parrots like that in South America, who puke on each other as a mating thing?'

'Yes, love,' I told you. 'Parrots and Irishmen. Two wonderfully expressive species.'

I asked you if this boy was someone special to you and you scoffed.

'I was only gettin' off with him, Dad. Actually I think he's a bit of a wuss.'

'Maeve, you're a young woman now. You're not a girl any more. You have to be careful who you hang around with.'

You sighed and threw your eyes to the ceiling. 'Listen,' you said, 'you needn't give me the period talk, Billser, and the facts of life. I've had all that from Ma till it's coming out my ears.'

'I'm just saying, I know what boys are like. It wasn't that long ago your auldfella was a boy himself, you know.'

'Yeah, right,' you said. 'Back in the Pleistocene era.'

'Everyone thinks boys and girls are the same these days. But they're not. They're made differently.'

'Jesus Dad, go on. Are they?'

'I mean the way they think. The way they behave themselves.'

'Yeah, this spazzo of a priest told us all about it at the Christmas retreat last year.' You squinted your face into a hideous leer and began to jabber in a mock rural accent. 'Now girls, de wimmen are like irons and de men are loik lightbulbs. It takes de wimmen a bit of a whoile to heat up like, but de men do switch on just loik dat.'

I couldn't help laughing.

'He was a dirty old patronisin' bastard,' you said. 'It wasn't one bit funny. You'd want to hear the things he was askin' us in confession.'

'Maeve,' I said.

'Father Danker was his name,' you said. 'I told everyone it was rhymin' slang.'

'My Jesus, the world's changed a good bit since I was a kid.'

'Yeah, well it's had enough time, Billser, God knows.'

Hugh Gormley Jones and Lizzie were up on the stage now, arms around each other and howling into a microphone. According to you it was a song about smashing society. Just as you had commenced to parse the rather arresting text for my benefit, a thick hail of beer cans came raining down on the stage. This was not what took my attention. What did take my attention, what truly impressed me in fact, was the way Belinda Bombs, who seemed to be dressed in a bin-liner and stilettos, began bouncing up and down and heading them back into the audience. No wonder the Raytown Rhythm Kings never made it big. In my day, we just didn't have that level of commitment.

By the end of the first year or so, the access arrangements had become tolerable, if only just. You would turn up ten minutes late at the Royal Marine, cross the hotel car park, get into my car. Grace would never stop to say hello but would rush away as soon as possible. Some kind of diversion would be found for five or six hours and then I would leave you back to the hotel where your mother would collect you. This became the routine of our Saturdays, and I suppose like all routines it had its comforts, even if they were not many.

Another thing that gave me solace around that time was the fact that I was not alone. Indeed, after a while, I found I could spot them and pick them out of a crowd, the Saturday fathers, whose ranks I had now joined. No matter where we went, you and Lizzie and I, to burger bars or ice-cream parlours, to cinemas or parks, there they would be, vaguely crumpled in ill-fitting suits and five-o'clock shadows but trying to look cheerful all the same, middle-aged men with children and sins and lost expectations and beer guts. They seemed to carry their pasts around with them like ghosts or physical weights. I mean this literally, you could often identify them from the crushed-down way that they had of walking. And they would have a haunted and guilty look, these men, as they tried to laugh loudly and make jokes and talk about pop songs about which they knew nothing to bewildered and frightened children under whose feet the ground had just opened up. After a time I even got to distinguish different kinds of expressions of guilt on the faces of these men. There was the kind of guilt which has turned inwards and is eating up the heart like some kind of vicious carnivorous worm. There was also the guilt which has taken the shape of suppressed rage. And then there was the kind of guilt which leaves nothing except an odd suppurating blankness behind the eyes. I got to know all these expressions on those Saturday afternoons with you two. Sometimes in those days, passing a shop window or glancing into the car mirror, I would see those expressions on my own face.

Sometimes I even thought – though it may have been my imagination – that these men recognised me also, that they could mark me out by some kind of moral radar, that there would be a certain sidelong glance of understanding as we would brush past each other, middle-aged men in a punk-rock record shop or busy boutique, arms full of clothes that looked like banners of war. This would seem to me a look that implied something was known and noted fundamentally about what you were enduring yourself; for that little, or that much, I was grateful.

After a time I fancied that I could spot the children too, the children of separated parents. These were the children with many presents and big bags of shopping; they would be weighed down with computer games and expensive toys, every week like Christmas week. I have since found out that this is a thing separated fathers do, they buy their children presents. Men in these situations get good at buying presents. It is a silent way of apologising, I suppose, and of saying other things which may not be easily

174

said in language, or even things for which there can never be any real language. It is a thing I did myself for a time, until Grace wrote to me one week, a cursory note, saying that she did not want the girls to be spoilt. She understood that I wanted to be generous, she wrote, but the girls would have to work for the things they wanted. The note was on headed paper. I noticed that she'd had it printed with her maiden name. She was Grace Lawrence again.

It was very late one night around the time of your four-teenth birthday when I was awoken by a knock on the front door. On my way down the stairs the knock came again, much louder this time; it sounded like someone was kicking at the door. The hall was dark, I remember, the bulbs had gone recently and I had not got around to replacing them. The banging rang through the house once more. I looked at my watch. It was just after four in the morning. I ran back upstairs and got out an old torch. Then I came slowly down and shone the beam through the glass panels at the side of the front door. There was nobody there.

I heard footsteps walking quickly around the house and the clank of the side gate being repeatedly tried. I was scared now. The gate must have been locked because I heard the sound of someone climbing over and then the crunch of feet hitting the gravel on the other side.

I went into the kitchen and stood in the darkness looking through the window. For a moment or two I could see nothing, and then suddenly, there it was, a black-clothed body moving around in the darkness. The body came up the path and as far as the back door. The handle was tried. There was more loud knocking, then I heard a few deep sighs. I glanced around the kitchen for something sharp.

'Dad,' a voice hollered out.

I could feel the adrenalin pumping through me as I opened the back door to let you in. Your eyes were streaked with mascara and you were crying. My first terrible thought was that you had been attacked or assaulted in some way.

You stumbled into the kitchen, mumbling, hugging me. I sat you down and held you in my arms.

After a few minutes I got it out of you. You'd had an argument with your mother, you told me, and so now you had made up your mind that you wanted to come and live with me.

I think I might have started to laugh and tell you this was silly. But then you began wailing and pulling at my sleeve.

'Please Dad,' you said, 'please. Don't send me away.'

I just did not have the heart to give out to you then.

'Don't be dense, love,' I told you. 'You're welcome here any time, you know that. Why the blazes would I send you away? Sure I'm always delighted to see you. Though I'd prefer it wasn't nearly dawn, Maeve.'

I made you tea and a sandwich and we sat in the kitchen for a while just talking. I remember being shocked when you wondered aloud if there was any drink in the house; you wanted to have a drink. I said no, there was no drink and at first you did not believe me. You asked me what about all the drink that I used to hide around the place and I felt embarrassed then, because of course I had never realised that you knew about this. But you laughed and told me that you did know, and indeed, that you and Lizzie had often drunk a quarter of one of my bottles of vodka before filling it up again with water. 'And you can't read me the riot act about it,' you said 'After all, Billser, that probably saved your bacon a few times.'

Your mother had met a man, you told me. She had been going to Al-Anon, the support organisation for the families of alcoholics. I was surprised to hear this, it was news to me. But Grace had been going to these meetings for some time, more or less from the week she had moved out of Dalkey, and apparently had met a man at one of the meetings whose wife was an alcoholic. 'Like you, Dad.' She had begun to see him socially, they had been to the cinema a few times. You thought they might even have been out to dinner.

I was surprised by the surge of jealousy I felt. But then, I told myself, I had no right to such feelings any more.

'Well, going out for a meal isn't a criminal offence,' I said to you. 'Your mother needs company, that's all. She's a very sociable person. Like you.'

'I came home tonight and he was there in the apartment.'

'Look, Maeve . . .'

'And he was kissin' her on the sofa. He had his hand practically right on her tit. And he's been staying the night, Dad.'

I told you then that I thought it would be better if we talked about all this in the morning. You said that there was nothing to talk about, you had it all figured out, you were coming to live with me, and Lizzie could stay with Grace. It was only fair, you said, that each of us should have one of you. You had been thinking it over for ages. It just was not right, me living here in the house by myself.

By now it was almost five o'clock, so I did up the bed in your old room and made you go up and get into it. I waited until I was sure you were asleep, then I wrote you a note telling you not to worry about anything which I pinned to your door. I threw on some clothes, got into the car and drove down to your mother's place.

When I rang the doorbell, a moment or two went by before her voice, sounding very angry, came over the intercom. She said your name. I told her no, it was me. She sounded surprised then, and let me in. I came up in the lift. A long-faced streak of ugly misery in striped pyjamas opened the door of the apartment. He was taller than me and ten years younger. His face had an odd, slightly concave shape, as though he had recently tried to head a football that had turned out to be made of cement. I told him my name and that I was Maeve's father. He nodded and said he knew who I was. The way he said it made it clear that I was not welcome. He brought me in without speaking another word.

In the small neat living-room your mother was sitting on the sofa with her head in her hands. She was wearing a nightdress. There was a bottle of red wine on the floor with two glasses. When she looked up at me her face had a frightened expression.

'Don't tell me it's Maeve,' she said. 'Jesus, Billy, don't tell me anything's happened.'

No, I told her, you were fine.

'So where is she?'

'She's with me,' I said. 'She's above in the house.'

'What? In Dalkey?'

'No, Grace,' I said. 'On Mars. Where the fuck else except in Dalkey? I nearly bottled her an hour ago. I heard her prowlin' around the place. I thought she was a burglar.'

She jumped up and left the room. Head-the-Ball sat silently gaping into the fireplace and picking his teeth with a match. A minute later Grace stormed back in wearing training shoes, and a raincoat over her nightdress. I asked her what she thought she was doing.

'She'll have to come home,' she said, and turned to him. 'Phil, you can drive me up to get her.'

'I'm drunk, honey,' he said.

'Well, I'll go myself then.'

'Grace,' I said. 'You're not going near her tonight. And that's that.'

'She'll come home tonight,' she said. 'This is her home.'

I grabbed her arm to stop her leaving. 'She's asleep,' I said. 'And you've been drinking. You're not all right to drive.'

'Take your hands off me, Billy.'

'You won't take her away tonight, Grace. I won't allow you to do that, I'm telling you.'

'The day you'll order me's long gone, Billy.'

I opened my mouth and bawled. 'You won't take her, Grace. End of story. Do you seriously think for one single minute I'd let you do that? Don't you know there's no way in the world I'd allow you do that, Grace?'

She went to slap me in the face but I grabbed her wrists and pushed her away from me. Your man came over then and put his hands on my arm. I turned to him. He looked pale and very nervous. The skin on his lips was cracked, his small eyes bleary and moist. I stared down at his hands.

'I'm going to count to five,' I told him, quietly, 'If you're still touchin' me when I get there, I'll rip your fuckin' head off, Phil.'

'I don't want trouble,' he said.

'I'll beat you to fuckin' death, Phil, I swear it, if you're still touchin' me in five seconds.'

He took his hands away.

'Thank you, Phil,' I said.

Your mother was back on the sofa and crying. 'We can talk about this again,' I told her. 'I didn't come here looking for a scene, I'm sorry. I just thought you should know she was safe. I'm going home now. Good-night.'

'You lousy bastard,' she said.

'Yeah, good-night, Grace. And listen, thanks again for all your help.'

It was good and kind of your mother to let you stay here with me. I always admired her for that. I know all too well what it is to live without your children, it cannot have been easy for her. But she knew you were unhappy and knew too that you loved the old house almost as much as Lizzie hated it. She would not give up legal custody, she said, but as an experiment you could stay with me in Glen Bolcain for a while. But she asked me then not to bring Lizzie to the house any more. She told me that Lizzie was having nightmares about the house and did not want to see it again.

After we agreed to you coming back I thought things might calm down for you. But I was wrong. You were at a difficult age anyway. Not that there is ever an easy age.

Maybe I was too strict with you, I don't know. I suppose I must have been aware that your mother would drag me back into court at the first sign of you getting into trouble. But you did not care. You seemed to like trouble. Before too long, you seemed to be seeking it out.

You would stroll blithely in on a Saturday afternoon from town with your face daubed in white or yellow make-up, hard black triangles of eyeliner around your eyes, black lipstick smeared across your mouth like a scar, your hair thick with gel or glue. I could never make myself understand why you would want to do that to yourself. We argued about it but you would never listen. I told you that you were immature, that you were still dressing up to play, like a child would. 'I'm fourteen now,' you'd say. 'I'm *fourteen*. I can do what I like, you fascist.'

I think I started by trying to bribe you out of it. I would drag you into town and buy you expensive, respectable clothes, but you would refuse to put them on. I would raid your room and fling out every scrap of make-up I could find. You would throw tantrums and accuse me of invading your privacy, but I did not care, I did not want my teenage daughter looking like a low-grade Commanche hooker. You told me I could trash your clothes and make-up if I wanted, it did not matter, you would get more. I warned you not to threaten me, pointed out that it was my house, you would have to do what I said while you lived there.

'Oh, very mature,' you sneered. 'Daddy's little dictatorship.'

As you grew taller you became more evasive. I would ask where you were going, you would say 'Out', if you answered me at all. Then I would say 'Out where?' and you would do that infuriating shrug and sigh deeply 'Just out', or 'Nowhere'. If I was foolish enough to continue and wonder aloud who you would be with, you would reply 'Nobody', and if pressed, 'Nobody *you*'d know'. It got to be almost a game we played, a catechism of frustration.

You began to wear your outlandish clothes into school until the head nun called me down and said that something would have to be done about this. There was a uniform, she said, this was not some working-class area after all, this was Dalkey. I told her I was from a working-class area myself, if she didn't mind. No, she said, she didn't mind in the least. But this was still Dalkey. And there was still a uniform.

You had come into the school wearing pyjamas recently, the nun told me. When you were ordered to go home immediately and change, you did. You arrived back in class an hour and a half later wearing a different pair of pyjamas. This simply could not go on.

I told you to wear the uniform, which you did for a while, albeit reluctantly. But then I noticed that you were altering it. You would cover the lapels of the fifty-quid crested blazer with row upon row of metal badges, safety pins, bits of chain; you'd clank around the house like a sleepwalking medieval knight. One morning you went into school wearing a swastika armband which you absolutely refused to remove. There were ructions, one poor nun practically had to be hospitalised. I had to get off work and come home early and give you a good lecture on some of the finer points of your family history. This you sat through, chewing gum, blowing bubbles and staring at the wall. The very next night I caught you in the kitchen cutting several inches off the hem of your school skirt with a garden shears.

One Saturday morning not long after this I was out in the garden looking at the birds when I noticed that the door of the old stable had been forced open. When I went in, I found piles of clothes, records, expensive art books, whole boxes of make-up, all of them brand new. Slung in a ball on the floor was a red leather evening dress with the price tag still attached: it was more than I was earning in a week. I brought all the stuff up to the house – it took almost an hour – and simply left it lying on the living-room floor. When you got home from town you had a pal with you,

Josephine Ryan, that blousy little brasser from Monkstown Farm who smoked in front of me. I told her to go home and asked you about the things I had found in the stable. At first you pretended not to know what I was talking about. I brought you into the living-room and showed you the pile. You absolutely denied knowing anything about the stolen stuff, you were adamant, you swore and promised, it just drove me demented. I lost my temper with you in a way I don't think I had ever lost it before. I felt rage with you, love, I really did. I could not believe that you would lie to me like that. I warned you that I would have to telephone Grace and make her come over immediately to sort this out. You pleaded with me not to do this. You confessed that you and your mates had been spending your spare time down in Dun Laoghaire shopping mall, stealing as a dare. It was some sort of game between you, to see who could pull off the most audacious theft; Josephine Ryan had once managed to steal a new bicycle straight out of the shop. I swear I still do not know how I managed not to hit you. I bawled and roared until I was hoarse, I'm sure the language must have been choice. I told you about Seánie's brother Frank who stole a pound of butter when he was fifteen, got sent to Letterfrack Borstal and progressed to burgling houses.

You rolled your eyes. 'Oh, here we go again,' you sighed. 'Life in proletarian Dublin.'

I warned you to listen or I would stop your pocket money for a month.

'I don't give a flyin' fuck about Seánie's brother Frank,' you yelled, 'and neither do you, so don't pretend.'

'The reason I'm working my arse off every day is so you don't have to steal. Can you not get that into your head, Maeve? I was brought up without a thing and none of us stole.'

Your expression reminded me of Grace then. You promised that you would never do it again.

Shortly after this I allowed you to have a party. You

persuaded me to go and stay with Jimmy for the night. Lizzie would be coming, you said. Lizzie would make sure there were no problems. I told you I was surprised to hear that Lizzie would be coming, since she had told her mother she did not want to visit the house any more. But you swore it was true. Next morning when I got home, I was kicking around in the long grass down by the back wall when I found a packet of condoms. When I opened it I saw that three or four were missing. I stormed up to your room and pulled open the curtains.

It was the first time I had been inside your room in some months. It looked as though it was inhabited by some kind of rabid animal. I could not actually see one square inch of the carpet for clothes. The inside of the door had been daubed with thick streaks of black and red gloss paint. The words 'Yeats is dead' had been scrawled in thick green marker across the ceiling. The place reeked of incense and dirty socks. There was a pint glass of brown water on your bedside locker with the stinking remains of dozens of cigarette butts in it. There were beer cans on the window-sill. The walls were covered with twelve-inch records, the edges of which had been melted and twisted out of shape. When I saw these it annoyed me even more. I could not believe that anyone would do that to records.

I threw the pack of condoms on the bed.

'What do you think they are?' I shouted.

You yawned up at me. 'Balloons?'

'Smart aren't you, Maeve? If you were half as clever in school you'd be away in a hack. Are they yours?'

You said nothing, just rolled around to face the wall.

'I'm very disappointed with you,' I said.

'Well, aren't you glad I used them? And didn't end up like Ma?'

'What's that supposed to mean?'

You scoffed. 'You know well.'

'I don't.'

'You bloody do so. Mammy the dirty whore.'

'How dare you talk about your mother like that.'

'I heard you do it often enough,' you shouted. 'You came out with a thing or two about her in your time. You've forgotten that maybe. Like you forget everything that doesn't suit you.'

'You're one right little bitch when you want to be.'

'Oh, I know, I know, I know. Just like Mammy.'

'That's right, love. Just like her.'

'Yeah, look, change the fuckin' record, Billser, all right?'

'You're so like her I don't know why you don't just shag off back to her.'

You sat up in bed with your eyes flaring. 'I remember you well,' you roared. 'Christ, don't think I don't, I remember what you were like, the fuckin' state of you. Who the fuck d'y'think you are to lecture me, anyway?'

'I'm your father, that's who.'

'Are you really? And how do y'even know that?'

'It's just as well you're a girl,' I told you, then. 'I'd take a fuckin' strap to you otherwise.'

'Sure c'mon, don't let that stop you. It never stopped you with her.'

'I never laid a finger on your mother, that's a dirty lie.'

'Great, great, you didn't beat her around the place. What do you want, a medal for bein' the perfect fuckin' husband now? Daddy dearest?'

I left your room in a red-hot rage and went out for a long drive.

A couple of nights later I was half-asleep when you knocked on the bedroom door and came in with a cup of tea for me. You sat on the edge of the bed and we talked for a while. You apologised for what had happened; I did too. We agreed to try again. I threw on a dressing-gown and we went down to the kitchen together where we wrote out some rules on the back of an envelope. You would not have your friends in without telling me, I would not shout at you when I lost my temper. You would not lie to me and I would not lie to you. I would allow you to stay out one night a week in a girlfriend's house, if you cleaned your room regularly, and if I knew exactly where you were. And we would both – this was your idea – we'd both try to mind our language in future.

'Because sometimes your language is fuckin' atrocious, Billser,' you said. 'You're settin' me a fierce bad example.'

Around that time things at work began to suffer: I had realised by then that I simply could not be away on the road as much as I had in the old days. I began to come home early so that I could be there when you got in from school. As a result my wage packet would often be well down, and in any event, there was rarely a whole lot to spare after I had made the monthly payments to Grace. The arguments between you and me certainly did not stop overnight; in fact, you may as well know, love, there were many times when I really did think it might be better for you to go back to your mother. But eventually things seemed to calm down a bit. When you took up the acting again in school you were like a different girl. Sometimes I would find you actually reading a book or doing homework. The situation between your mother and yourself improved a little. In time I think you even looked forward to seeing her at the weekends.

Slowly Grace and I began to talk to each other again. Sometimes when she dropped Lizzie down to the hotel on a Saturday she would stay and make conversation for a minute or two before you and she would drive away. One morning you suggested that all four of us could go into the hotel and have coffee together. It wasn't great but it was something. After that day your mother and I agreed to stop communicating through the lawyers: she would telephone the house whenever there was a problem. She made it clear that I was to feel welcome to phone her too, although I do not think I ever did unless it was absolutely necessary. We began to meet once a month, when I would hand over the maintenance cheque instead of posting it. We attended a couple of parent–teacher meetings together and one of your plays in school. After Phil the Failure disappeared off to England, there was even a brief period when she and I would occasionally go out to dinner on a weekend night to talk about you and Lizzie. This, too, felt like progress of a sort.

One of these nights you should know about. You were away on a class trip to Stratford, your mother and I had been to a play at the Gate and we had gone to supper afterwards in La Stampa. We'd had a good chat – I think we were talking mainly about Lizzie's plans to attend art college, or possibly your own to go to UCD. Time slipped by. Before we knew it, we were the last customers in the restaurant. The waiters were putting the chairs up on the tables and switching on the lights. It was time to go home.

For some reason your mother was driving the two of us that night. When she dropped me back to Dalkey, I invited her up to the house for a cup of tea. Of course she did not want to come in at first, but in the end I persuaded her. I said that I knew she had loved the house and did not want her to feel that she could never set foot inside it again; if we wanted to make an effort for you and Lizzie, this might be a good way to start.

She seemed uneasy as she walked around the house; at first she did not want to take off her coat. In the living-room I tried to make a joke about the untidiness – I had finally got the builders in to begin fixing the place up a bit after all those years – but she did not laugh. She stared at the pictures on the walls as though she had never seen them before. I had an old photograph on top of the television, of you and Lizzie in Hallowe'en outfits – Arab head-dresses and fun furs of heart-attack pink. She picked this up and looked at it for a long time, rubbing the dust off the glass with the back of her hand. I remember going upstairs to the toilet and then, when I returned, finding her still looking at the picture.

I made tea and we went for a walk in the garden. It looked a mess because the builders had dug a long, deep drainage trench all the way down to the back wall, and they had not yet put up the aviary, which was still lying in its flat crates under the apple tree. She looked at the photograph of the aviary on the side of one of the boxes and teased me that it looked like a prison cell. The newspapers had said that there would be a comet that night – in fact, a comet shower – but the sky was a little too bright to see it. We strolled around and talked about the plants. It must have been summer, because the garden was full of wild flowers. We talked about the names of the flowers, how beautiful they were: silverweed and ling, harebell and wild orchid, heart's-ease, meadowsweet, cranesbill, feverfew. I told her that was a job I'd like for myself, being the man who thought up the names for wild flowers. She laughed.

'It's so lovely and quiet here,' she said. 'You could be in the country.'

'Yes,' I said. 'The Residents' Association finally blocked the sale of the back field.'

'Our place is so small,' she said. 'If you let a good roar all the neighbours know. Not like here.'

'Well, we don't do that much roaring any more,' I said.

She looked around. 'I don't know how you find the time to look after the garden so well, especially now Madam Maeve's in residence. If I buy a pot plant it keels over.'

'Not me with the green fingers, I'm sorry to say. One of the old travellers from the back field comes in to me once a fortnight. Knows damn all about gardening, the poor chap, but he needs the dough. He's kids to feed.'

She reached out and stroked the leaves of a lovely tall purple fern that was growing around the trunk of the apple tree, its thick fronds digging into the bark. 'You're such a generous person, Billy,' she murmured.

'Indeed I'm not,' I said. 'I'm not long giving him a good roasting when he needs it, believe you me.'

'No,' she said, 'you are. It's a lovely thing about you.'
She turned to me then and stared at me.

'Jesus, Billy,' she whispered, 'what happened to us?'
I was taken aback. 'I thought you knew that,' I told her.
'We had some lovely times though, didn't we?'
I nodded. 'Yes, we did.'
'What I miss most is being able to talk to you,' she said.
'Well, I miss that too, Grace,' I said.

We were standing very close to each other. She had on a
dark short-sleeved silk dress, and I could see the tiny white
hairs on her arms. She stared at the flowers again. I found
myself reaching out and taking her fingers in mine.

'Don't, Billy,' she said, but although she turned away she
did not let go of my hand. With my other hand I touched
her face.

Your mother turned back and looked into my eyes. I
began to kiss her. I suppose it is not quite true to say that I
could not help it. But I did not want to help it. She kissed
me back very gently. I remember touching her hair, the sweet
winey smell of her hair. We kissed for a few minutes more.
Then she pulled away from me and walked up and down the
garden for a time, knotting her fingers, rubbing the nape of
her neck. She looked weak with anxiety. I was just about to
tell her that everything was all right, and that she was not to
worry, and I was sorry for touching her like that, when she
came back over and put her arms around me and kissed me
very hard on the lips.

We went upstairs and into our old bedroom where we
took off some of our clothes and kissed again for a while.
After a time she asked me to turn out the light and I did.
In the darkness I could hear her removing the rest of her
clothes. She asked me to do the same. We embraced for
a few moments, I was trembling. She asked if anyone else
had been in this bed with me and I said no, nobody had,
which was the truth. We slid under the sheets together and
made love very gently. I remember – and you may as well

know this too, love – that afterwards we just lay in the dark, holding each other for a long time and crying.

Next morning when I woke up your mother was gone. There was an earring on the table beside the bed. I threw it away.

It never happened again. Less than a year later she was dead.

Chapter Eleven

On the evening of Monday 1 July 1994, I left the house at seven o'clock and drove down to Dun Laoghaire, where I parked the car on Marine Road, just outside the entrance to the Royal Marine Hotel like the milkman and I had agreed, and simply sat and waited. I knew what to look for. My friend would be about twenty-five years old, wearing tight black jeans and a black Chicago Bulls bomber jacket, a stocky lad, built like a body-builder, with big muscles and a skinhead hairdo.

Unfortunately, this is a description that applies to approximately half of the citizens of Dun Laoghaire at any given time, or it did that night at any rate. The town looked as though a shipload of aspiring neo-Nazis had recently pulled into the harbour. Several times I was right on the point of giving the two hoots on the horn we had agreed or even opening up the car door to smilingly invite in some passing psychopathic degenerate when I realised at the last minute that I was wrong, and it was not him after all. Clearly I would have to be a little more cautious. The idea was for Quinn to get killed this evening, after all, and not myself.

Finally I saw my friend, shaping up Marine Road from the direction of the Dart station with a holdall in his hand. I knew it was him because he looked a little out of place, as if he did not know where he was exactly and wasn't familiar with the area. He sat down on the low wall outside the church and lit a cigarette. He was big all right. He looked like a nightclub bouncer or a boxing instructor about to get struck off by the authorities. He took a tabloid newspaper out of his jacket pocket and started to read it. I knew he really *was* reading it because I could see his lips moving. I hit the horn twice. He looked up and saw me. He pointed to himself and raised his eyebrows. I say eyebrows, although in reality he had just one long eyebrow which stretched all the way across his forehead, making him look a bit like a thuggish muppet. I hit the horn again. He leapt up and crossed the street to where I was parked.

He opened the passenger door and bent down. 'Billy, is it?' he said, and I nodded.

'Pony,' he said. 'Pony Sheehan.'

He climbed into the car, reached down to adjust the seat, nodded and coughed. He smelt of carbolic soap. 'Have you three and a half for me?'

I opened the glove compartment, took out the seven fifties and gave them to him. He counted the money twice, lifted his backside and slid the notes into his jeans pocket.

'Right. Let's get a move on.'

On the drive out to Bray he was very quiet. His eyes were shining brightly and he was chain-smoking. The smoking surprised me because he looked like a health fiend. By the time we got to Shankill the car was so full of smoke that I wanted to ask him to stop, but I did not do this; instead I just rolled down the window. There were all kinds of things I would have liked to ask him. I realised this as we drove along, that I was curious about him and wanted to know something about his life. But it was difficult to know where we might start, and after a while I began to think maybe it was a bad idea anyway.

'Nice motors these,' he said.

'Yes.'

'New model, aren't they?'

'Yes.'

He slapped the dashboard. 'Nice finish in them.'

'They're a good solid car,' I said. 'Very dependable in the mornings.'

'I heard that,' he nodded. 'Have to hand it to the Japs all the same.'

'Do you drive yourself?' I tried.

'Well I do, yeah. But I've no motor just now.'

'That's a pity. A car's handy to have.'

'It is, yeah.'

'When you're mobile you're laughing.'

'I lost the licence a while back there,' he said. 'Bit of bother with the coppers.'

We were coming through Shankill village now, past the church at the fork in the road and on towards Bray. He raised his massive head and sniffed.

'I love the smell of a new car,' he said.

'Well yes, it isn't that new actually.'

'Y'keep it nice,' he said. 'It smells new to me.'

'I'm a salesman,' I said. 'A good salesman looks after his car.'

Out on the street a skinny lad in a tuxedo and a girl in a pink evening dress were having an argument. He looked out at them and snickered. We drove on. He seemed to be staring at me.

'And he's small, I hear?'

'Who?'

'The Pope, man, who do y'think?'

'Well, he's not big,' I said. 'You couldn't say that about him.'

It was stiflingly hot in the car. But it surprised me how contented and calm I felt. I thought about getting up the next morning, how pleasant it would be to rise early and maybe take a walk in the damp garden before putting my case into the car and driving out to meet Seánie at the airport. Arriving tired in Lourdes around lunch-time, a sandwich in the hotel, one of those long French cheese sandwiches and a strong coffee, then maybe a short nap or a walk down to the basilica. And then a long deep sleep. To know that I had finally dealt with Donal Quinn, that he simply would not be there to torment me any more.

'He looks like a jockey,' I laughed. 'That's how you'll know him.'

'No, no,' he said. 'I'll know him when you point him out to me, sweat. That's how I work. You put the finger on him. I don't want any fuck-ups.'

He reached out his shovel-like hand and switched on the radio. It was playing a mournful old folk song with a plaintive melody. He seemed to know it. He joined in with the words, singing softly through his teeth

> *Through field and town we'd roam around*
> *In search of the droleen;*
> *We'd search for birds in every furze*
> *From Lifford to Dooneen.*
> *The same boys who fought the auxies,*
> *And who braved the Black and Tans,*
> *Were the boys of Bar na Stráide*
> *Who hunted for the wren.*

As we came into Bray he reached his bomber jacket and pulled out a gnarled grey lump of metal welded to a set of metal rings which fitted neatly over the fingers of his right hand. From another pocket he yanked a crumpled khaki balaclava. The knuckleduster and the mask were not what worried me so much. It was what happened then. He thrust his hand into the holdall and took out a shotgun.

I had gone hunting once or twice with Liam from the office but I had never seen a gun like this before. It was maybe nine inches long with a squat handle covered in thick layers of black masking tape; the barrels had been roughly sawn off. It looked like something home-made. I wondered was this possible. Next he produced one of those old-fashioned tobacco tins from his jacket and flipped it open. I saw that there were four cartridges inside. He took out two and loaded the gun.

'You don't think that's a bit much?' I said.

'Not takin' any chances,' he said. 'Some of these small lads are tough enough.'

'I didn't hear anything about a gun,' I say.

'It's a last resort,' he said. 'It's insurance. Way it is, I don't work without it.' He grinned at me. 'I mean there's a lot of fuckin' crime around these days.'

I was bothered now. I tried to think straight as I drove on. I certainly did not want him killing anybody. It had to be me who did it, that much was clear. No way did I want him to do it, not after all I had been through.

'The only thing is, right,' he went. 'If things go arseways and if I have to use this – I'm not sayin' they will, but – if I do though, then you'll have to buy it off me. It'll cost you four hundred.'

'What?'

'That's the deal I have. It's only rented. There's a geezer in town rents them to me. Fifty notes to rent it for the night, I cover that out of what you're after givin' me. But if the job goes baw-ways and I have to use it, then it's traceable so it has to disappear a while. So you have to stump up for it. Four ton.'

'That's not what Nap told me.'

'Well see, I'm not fuckin' askin' you what anyone told you, pal, *I'm* tellin' you that's the score or we don't do it.'

'OK, OK.'

'Are y'game ball then?' he said. 'Y'can run me back to the borough right now if yer not. 'S'all the same to me.'

'All right,' I said. 'All right, yes. Four if you have to use it.'

'Sound,' he nodded. We drove on. He turned up the radio.

'I love this one,' he said.

194

In a dreary British prison, where an Irish rebel lay,
At his side a priest was standing, as his soul did pass away;
Tell me this, oh gentle father, so that I may understand,
Tell me this, before your blessing,
Shall my soul pass through Ireland?

At this point he seemed to be overcome by emotion. Perhaps it was the song, I don't know. In any case, he put his head in his hands and made some kind of strange snorting noise. He did this a few times, his stertorous porcine grunts filling the car. I remember wondering if I should offer him a handkerchief or, at the very least, my sleeve. He drummed his fingers on the dashboard. After a few minutes he sighed.

'Listen, about what I said earlier, don't be shittin' bricks. I've done this before. Only gobshites take a chance, is what I'm sayin'. That's why I've the heater with me.'

I felt droplets of sweat on my forehead. 'OK, OK. I understand. Thanks.'

'Are y'all right?'

'I'm fine.'

He put his hand on my thigh and squeezed. 'Don't worry,' he said. 'It'll all be over soon.'

> *'Twas for loving dear old Ireland*
> *I am now condemned to die.*
> *'Twas for loving dear old Ireland*
> *In this foreign land I lie.*

We got to Quinsboro Road and swung down left in the direction of the sea. Right turn along the front, then another right, one more and a left and suddenly we were there in the small quiet cul-de-sac. I pointed out the house, then drove slowly past, did a U-turn, came back down and parked. He scanned the scene, swivelling, peering, nodding to himself. 'OK,' he kept saying. 'OK, OK.' We got out of the car. A television was on in Quinn's house, I could hear canned laughter and loud applause. Sheehan walked up to the end of the street and looked around a bit more, then he came quickly back down in my direction. Half-way along on my right, just across from the house, there was a little laneway, maybe six feet wide. He disappeared down there for a few minutes, then emerged again and came quickly back to me. He had a cigarette in his enormous mouth.

'What time d'y'say he comes out?'

'Between nine and nine-thirty. Always.'

'And does he know yeh?'

'How do you mean?'

'Well, would he know y'to see, like?'

'I don't know. I don't think so.'

He shrugged. 'Suppose we'll have to chance it.'

'Chance what?'

But he did not seem to be listening to me now. He raised a finger and thumb to his nostrils and exhaled, sharply, several times into his hand. He stared at his palm for a moment, his elongated eyebrow going up and down, then wiped his hand on his jeans and sighed.

'Here's what'll happen,' he said. 'We'll get him down that laneway. There's a little bit of a field there, an auld dump just, at the back of them houses, it'll be quieter. When he comes out, you'll be fixin' your car some way. Just get his attention for a minute. Because if I just take him from the front or the back he'll hear me comin'. That's no use because Christ knows what he might have, a knife or a piece or any bleedin' thing. So you just get his mind on yeh, just for a second, like. Just two shakes. And then bang. Good-night Vienna, what? We can all go home.'

'You want me to attract his attention?'

'Well, I don't mean send up fuckin' flares. Just, y'know, take his eye off the ball for a sec.'

'Are you serious?'

'Yeah, yeah. And listen, did you bring anythin' for yerself?'

'Like what?'

'Jesus,' he said. 'I thought you wanted to get involved yerself. Give him a dig when I get him down. So Nap told me. Did y'bring anythin'?'

'No,' I said.

'So what are y'gonna use then? To give him the dig?'

I thought about this for a moment. 'Well, I've a golf club in the boot.'

'Give us a dekko at it.'

I opened the boot carefully because I did not want him to see the other stuff in there. I took out the golf club and showed it to him. It was Liam's from work, a driver, beautiful wood, solid handle. I could not actually remember why it was in my car.

He took it in his hands, leaned over it, made an invisible putt down the cul-de-sac.

'That'll do grand,' he said. 'I'll give y'a few good swings at him when he's down, don't worry. Put it on the deck under the motor.'

It started to rain but very softly. The rain was actually warm to the touch. We got back into the car for a few minutes. He insisted that we switch on the radio again. When the rain stopped we got out once more. It was five to nine. I went down on my knees by the right front wheel, which is what we had agreed. He slipped across the street and slid well in behind a rusty Hiace van which was sitting up on four concrete blocks. From where I was kneeling I could just about see him shifting his weight from foot to foot. Sometimes he would come out from behind the van and stroll up and down. Most of the time he waited in the shadow, just doing that little dance of his, jumping lightly from side to side and softly humming. After ten minutes my knees were aching. I had to stand up and massage them. He motioned for me to get down again. Another ten minutes, then another. No sign of Quinn.

From time to time people passed up or down the street,

walking dogs or just by themselves. I made absolutely sure that they did not get any kind of look at me. The time crawled. I look at my watch, certain that another fifteen minutes had passed, but in fact it was only five. Up in the sky I saw the trace of a jet. I found myself wondering whether it was the one I would be on the next morning. I do not know why I should have thought that, but thinking it was oddly comforting.

Behind the van I could see him getting restless, softly kicking the bricks and scratching at a bit of rust with his fingernail. Another five minutes. No sign. I saw him glaring at his watch. I was sure that he was about to come over and tell me he wanted to call it off. And then, suddenly, at twenty minutes to ten, Quinn's front door opened.

Yellow light spilled out on to the street. A milk bottle clinked. Somewhere a dog began a repeated two-note bark. Come on out, I thought, come on out to your Uncle Billy. A pause. A scrape of feet. The door clicked closed. Quinn walked slowly down his footpath.

He opened the gate, stepped out with a rucksack on his back. I could see him peering up and down the cul-de-sac. He clocked me kneeling on the ground by the car, then he glanced back at his doorway for a moment. Looked at his watch. Whistled softly. For a moment I thought he was going to turn and go back inside. I found myself hoping that he would.

He didn't. He turned right and began to stroll down the street in my direction. His boots clicked on the pavement. He trailed his right hand in the hedges of the front gardens. Behind the van I saw Sheehan pulling on thick leather motorbike gloves.

'I'm sorry,' I said, 'you don't know anything about cars?'

He stopped and peered down at me. I slid my hand in under the car to where I could reach the golf club. For a moment I thought I saw a flicker of recognition in his face. But then it vanished. He went to walk on and ignore me.

198

'I'm stuck here,' I laughed. 'I'm in an awful hurry. My wife is after having a baby down in Cork.'

Again he started to walk. 'Look,' I said, 'there's a few bob in it for you. I wouldn't trouble you, honestly, only I'm badly stuck.'

Always be closing. Always be closing.

'I'm sure you're in a hurry,' I told him, 'but I could pay you for your time.'

He sighed and cursed under his breath.

'What's up with her anyway?'

The first words he ever spoke to me.

'I don't know, she has me bloody tormented. Some fuel thing maybe. She's surging badly on me when I get her up to third. And then in fourth she's losing power. She's not getting enough juice some way.'

'And what are y'at down there?'

'The fuel pump's under here, I think. I was goin' to have a look what's the story.'

'Y'sure the pump's under there, yeah?'

'Yeah, I'm after checkin' the manual. It's definitely some fuel thing. I can't even get her up to thirty without her shakin' all over the place like a mad thing.'

He nodded, pursed his lips, moved a little closer. 'Shouldn't be happenin' in that motor. Sure, that's a fuckin' flying machine. You've a problem there, right enough.'

He put his rucksack on the roof of the car and got down on the ground. Right in front of me, his head bowed low, he looked under the car. His nose was practically touching the tarmacadam. He was so close to me that I could smell beer on his breath and see the label inside the collar of his shirt. Sheehan stepped out from behind the van. He sprinted across the road with the knuckleduster in one hand and his other first clenched. Quinn turned, seeming to hear the footsteps, swivelled his neck around just as Sheehan got to him.

They stared at each other for a second. Quinn looked up at me. I smiled.

'Hello,' I said.

Sheehan pounced, tried to hit him in the face with the lump of metal. Quinn jerked away and the knuckleduster grazed his ear. He tried to get up but Sheehan kneed him in the chest. He went down, expelling the air from his lungs with a harsh gushing sound. He panted hard now, in through his nose, out through his mouth. He reached up and grabbed the handle of the car door. Sheehan peeled his fingers away.

Quinn opened his mouth. 'Rory?' he screamed. 'Fuckin' *Rory?* Are you there?'

Sheehan clamped his gloved hand across Quinn's mouth and pummelled the back of his head. Suddenly they were on the ground beside the car rolling, pucking, squirming desperately in a tangle of limbs. Quinn got the driver's door open and hit the horn hard. Sheehan dragged him back out and flung him to the ground. He grabbed him around the neck, began dragging him down the laneway and towards the field, Quinn's hobnailed boots scraping on the concrete, kicking against the pebble-dashed walls. I ran ahead of them. Across the field was a battered doorless coach, spray-painted with IRA graffiti, surrounded by mounds of old tyres and dumped fridges. Sheehan hissed for me to get out of the way. Quinn's arms flailed, his terrified eyes were bulging. Sheehan kneed him in the ribs a few times, flung him head down into a puddle of muck, sat on his lower back and began to work him over, slowly now, methodically, without emotion, like a man doing a job.

I ran back to the car and got the refuse sacks out of the boot, along with the hammer and hunting knife, the handcuffs, the elastoplast and the two fan belts. I put the hammer and knife in the deep pockets of my anorak, got the club from under the car. Back in the field, Sheehan was still pounding him, hitting efficient punches to the spine and neck, the gun in the grass beside him. Quinn gasped, rolled over, jolting Sheehan to the ground. Sheehan flailed out, punched him in the head, knocked him to the ground, crawled on to him, twisted his arm around his neck, sat him up.

'Is this the right man?' he panted.

I nodded.

'Are y'sure? I thought Nap said his name was Donie Quinn.'

'It is.'

He shrugged. 'I must a been thinkin' of a different Quinn. I thought from what Nap said I'd met him once up in the Joy. The Quinn I knew was in the army until they fucked him out for robbin'. But I don't think this is him.'

'It's him, don't worry.'

He shook his head. 'I don't think it is. He looks different to me, pal.'

'It's him,' I said.

'Well go on then,' he grinned. 'Say hello properly.'

My hands were so wet that I could hardly hold the club. I swung it, felt it connect with the base of Quinn's neck. He fell forward on to his face.

'You bastard,' I heard myself say. I opened my mouth so wide that it felt as though my lips were tearing at the edges. A sound I had never heard before came out of my mouth. I kicked him, lashed out with the club, brought it down hard in the middle of his back. He put his hands up to protect his head.

'You bastard,' I said, 'I'll teach you something now.'

'Me name isn't Quinn,' he cried. I hit him again. Several times.

'Take it easy now, sweat,' Sheehan said. 'Don't go spare altogether on me.'

Quinn rolled over and made for the bushes. In a second Sheehan was on him, elbowing him in the face and pulling hard on his hair until he sank back limp into the muck. His jeans were ripped up one seam to the thigh and he had lost one of his boots. I went for him again with the club.

'That's enough,' Sheehan panted, grabbing my arm. 'He's had enough, pal, he's finished.'

I turned to him, breathless and boiling. 'Beat it,' I said. 'Go on, fuck off out of here.'

I took off my belt and tied it around Quinn's knees, pulling the strap as tight as I could.

'Me name is Niall Conroy,' he gurgled. 'Who the fuck are you?'

'Find his boot,' I shouted.

Sheehan's eyes widened. 'What are y'doin' to him?'

From my pocket I grabbed one of the fan belts and twisted it round his ankles. 'Find his boot I said!'

He began groping around in the grass. I got the cuffs on to Quinn. I pulled out a handkerchief and shoved it hard into his mouth. I ran the elastoplast strip around the lower part of his head a few times, until it looked like the head of a mummy. I took two sacks and put them over him. Then I got out the second fan belt and squeezed it down over his head until it contracted around his neck, just tight enough to hold the sacks over him. He wriggled his torso and moaned. I stood up and hit him in the calf with the club.

Sheehan had found the boot now and was dangling it by its lace.

'What the fuck are you doin' to him?' he said.

'Nothing.'

Suddenly, he groped at his belt.

'Me knife,' he said. 'I'm after losin' me Swiss Army knife. It's got me name on it, pal. We shouldn't leave it here.'

I ignored him. I turned the club upside down and held it like a spear. I jabbed at Quinn's back a few times. Sheehan rushed over and hauled me away, trying to lock my arms behind my back.

'Give over,' he shouted. 'That's enough, I said.'

He gave me a shove that almost sent me to the ground.

'Since when are you the bloody law, Sheehan?'

I moved towards Quinn again. Sheehan grabbed my wrists and held me hard. I struggled to get out of his grip, but his fingers were like blunt pincers.

'Leave it, y'fuckin' spacer. You'll kill the cunt. Is that what you want?'

Somehow I managed to yank away from him. Heart pounding, I reached into my pocket and took out the wad of bank notes I had prepared. I held it up. I saw him looking at it.

Always be selling. Always be selling.

'There's seventeen hundred pound cash there,' I said. 'Just leave the gun and I don't want to see you again. I don't know you. Never met you. Goodbye.'

His long arms were hanging down by his side. His voice was quiet. 'You're a fuckin' psycho, you are. Y'know that? Y'need help, pal.'

I held out my hand. He sighed and gave me the gun. It felt heavy. He took the roll, snapped off the rubber bands and counted it. He looked at me for a while.

'That's not Donie Quinn,' he said.

'Goodbye, Mr Sheehan.'

'Listen, man, if that's Donie Quinn I'm Mother fuckin' Teresa.'

'Goodbye,' I said.

He turned, shot a glance at Quinn on the ground, shoved the money down the front of his jeans and walked quickly down the laneway. A high-pitched, frightened sound came from Quinn then. It was as if he was trying to scream.

I got out the hammer and the hunting knife and put them on the ground. I found the safety catch on the shotgun and took it off. Shaking and breathless, I pointed the gun at the plastic-wrapped globe of his head. I cocked it. From down on the sea front I could hear the screech of the ghost-train siren. I could not hold the gun in one hand, I was trembling so much. I changed my grip and tried to keep it steady with both hands.

I nudged him with the toe of my boot. 'I'm going to shoot you now,' I told him. He made no sound.

'I'm warning you,' I said, 'I'm going to shoot you. Get ready.'

Still he said nothing at all. The siren sound came again, ebbing and receding on the wind. Twenty feet away from me I saw the red eyes of a squat scared fox glaring at me, like the tips of cigarettes.

I put my finger on the trigger. My mouth tasted sour. I thought of what he did to you. I felt the coldness of the metal against my finger as I tried to pull.

I could not do it.

I closed my eyes for a second and saw you lying in your hospital bed, your skin and lips so pale, the plastic tubes running into your thin white arms. I thought my head was going to crack in two. I saw your naked feet.

And still I could not bring myself to do it.

I just couldn't. No matter how I tried.

I heard a muffled throaty sound coming from inside the sacks. It was the sound of him laughing.

I kicked him hard in the stomach. He rolled over and laughed even louder.

PART II

Chapter Twelve

Tuesday 12 July 1994

194–172
Week 28
14th Week in Ordinary Time

VESTMENTS Green. Green/White
HOURS   Psalter Week 2.
MASS   Of choice

Gen. 49: 29–32, 50: 15–26; Ps. 104; Mt. 10: 24–33
Saving events and significant realities which have found their fulfilment in the mystery of Christ.

Anniversary of the epsicopal ordination of Most Revd Thomas Finnegan, 12 July 1987

HOLIDAY (N. Ireland)

Patron: *St Killian.*
Thought for the day: *A friend in need is a friend indeed.*

Late last night it occurred to me again: what a pleasant drive it is from Bray back in towards the city. It is a journey

I have always liked, a good long straight road paid for by EC money, the surface as smooth as a politician's lies. You leave Bray, passing the Solus light-bulb factory on your right – that giant black and white light-bulb wrapper on the roof, M always used to laugh at it – and you pass by Woodbrook Golf Club, and then before you even know it you're on the dual carriageway where you can really open the throttle and give it some stick. All along the carriageway the bright orange sodium lights and concrete flyovers, the direction signs the size of gable walls, the cats' eyes so new and clean they nearly jump out at you when your headlights catch them. Makes you feel modern to drive that road. Makes you feel European. Giant green banners and tricolour flags hanging from the bridges, last night too, because of the world cup being on. One sign: 'Big Jack Charlton for President!'

Police car came speeding towards Bray on the far side of the carriageway. Blue light flashing and the siren was on. When I see this, get scared it's me they're after. Reach down to the floor and pick up the shotgun. But no, flew past me and kept on going. Left the gun there on my lap, just in case.

Ripped along doing seventy. Could hear him kicking away like mad inside the boot. After a short while this begins to get on my nerves. So what I do from then on, every time he kicks, I jam hard on the brakes and swerve a little. Just a bit. Then remembered something I noticed one night delivering a dish. Pulled off the carriageway and up into Markievicz Estate where I know there are speed bumps. Hit them one after another doing maybe thirty. He gets the message pretty fucking quickly. Back out to the dualler again.

At Loughlinstown hospital turned up right towards Killiney. Bad memories of Loughlinstown, that Saturday morning I'd been out jogging. When I got back to the house M was waiting for me, sitting in the driveway. UCD scarf around her neck. Face white as paper. The way she stood up and ran towards me when she saw me coming. Came towards me with her eyes half-closed and her hands held out. Like we were attached by some invisible thread. Knew whatever had happened must have been something terrible. It's Mum, Billser.

G's car had hit a lamp-post on the Rock Road. She'd been driving L into art college and was on the way home when she hit the black ice and went into the skid.

Remember the sharp smell of formaldehyde in the hospital morgue. Had put her into a white paper shroud and an old priest was giving her the last rites. Had to interrupt him to say G was Jewish; for some reason seemed important to make this clear at that moment. Asked me if I'd like him to say a prayer anyway and I told him yes. The two of us knelt down on the hard floor and said a decade of the rosary. Was halfway through when I started to cry and he took my hand and squeezed it while he kept on praying. Very conscious of the sound I was making as I cried, echoing in the tiled clean room, and I tried to stop but couldn't. When we finished the prayer he murmured something about trying to find a rabbi later – or perhaps Father Ronan – he had telephoned him. There was G, her face bruised, her lips swollen. The priest had his hand on my shoulder. Kept saying 'I know, I know' in a soft voice. But he didn't know. He didn't fucking know. How could he know?

After a while asked him to leave us be for a few moments. Nodded and said he would. I stood beside G for a while – suppose I must have said another prayer or two. I took her hand in my hand and kissed it. Dried blood on her fingernails. Noticed she was still wearing her wedding ring. Thick scar around it, raised flesh on her knuckle. I folded her arms across her chest. More tears. Remember touching her face and feeling how cold she was. Brushed a few strands of hair from her forehead. And found I wanted to tell her that I was sorry for everything. I mean that I actually wanted to say this out loud, right there in the white tiled room, just to say her name again, Grace Lawrence, and tell her I was sorry and thank her. But for whatever reason, I could not do this.

By the time I left the morgue, Seánie had arrived. In the corridor with his arms around M. Both crying. Something about this appalled me, had never in my life seen S crying before. Unimaginable. Looked over at me with tears in his eyes and held out his hand. I took it. He put his other hand on the back of my neck. Held me close to him.

—Billy. Billy. Jesus, I'm so sorry. Funny. Because he usually calls me Liam, like when we were kids in Irish class. No Irish for Grace.

Loughlinstown hospital. St Colmcille's.

Driving through a rough part of Ballybrack then. Q gave another few kicks – I jerked the wheel from side to side. Foot down hard. Two kids painting graffiti on the side wall of a house. Republic of Ireland shirts. 'Tommo is a –'. Wondered what exactly Tommo was. Bonfire smouldering on a patch of waste ground. Young girls swinging on a rope. Travellers' caravans. Turned off at the roundabout by the Graduate, took Avondale Road, past the convent, then down the hill into Barnhill Road, the brakes squealing a little because the hill is so steep. Long arch of dark thick beech trees along the road so beautiful, with the gold and white of the streetlights winking through. Then into Dalkey village, round the one way, up Dalkey Avenue and home.

Pulled into the drive and stopped, screeching the tyres on the gravel as hard as I could. Got out, closed the gate behind me. Q kicking again. Another sound in the boot now, a repeated dull metallic clunk. Ignored him and back into the car. Gunned it up the drive, swerving a bit just to give him something to kick about, and stamped on the brake around by the side of the house. Cloud of gravel dust.

Climbed slowly out, reached in, got the golf club from the back seat and put it on the roof. Then got the shotgun and jammed it under my elbow. Opened the boot. Stepped back. Q lying there not moving, legs twisted, head and torso still covered by the plastic sacks and his hands in the cuffs. Wrists bleeding quite badly. So much for fucking comfort. Heard him breathing through his nose.

—Sit up.

He still doesn't move. For a moment I think he's losing consciousness. Feel my mouth getting dry.

—Sit up, I say, or I'll shoot you right there like the animal you are.

Very still for a bit but then rolled over and sat up slowly in the boot. Could see his trousers were soaked around the crotch. He was breathing even harder now, snuffing in the air through his nose. He stirred. Black sacks had a zigzag tear in them, shirt stained with dull blood.

—Stand up.

Managed to get to his feet. Behind him in the boot I saw the wheel brace which he's somehow worked out of its slot beside the spare wheel. Stretched in and took it out. Threw it on the gravel. Left him standing there for a minute. Then pushed him hard. Fell backways into the boot, banging his head on the panel. High-pitched gurgling sound coming from under the sacks. Listened to it for a while. Then grabbed him hard by the ankles and pulled him out. Much heavier than I thought. Sacks caught on the lock and ripped more. Heave and strain. He fell out backwards on to the gravel. Moan of pain. Hauled him round to the front of the car, left him on the ground. Went and turned on the full headlights. Back to him. Down on my knees and got the fan belt off from around his ankles. Unlaced his boot and pulled it off. Got his socks off. Opened the driver's door. Got the club from the roof and leaned it on the side of the car. Stood behind the door with one hand pointing the gun right at him.

Told him to sit up straight. Reached out and tore the sacks off his head. Pulled the tape off his chin and jaw. He winces with pain, spits out the handkerchief. Face and forehead very bloodied and dirty, upper lip crusted with blood, dyed hair tangled and matted. He throws back his head and sucks at the air, chest heaving. Speak to him.

—How's she cuttin', Mr Quinn?

Eyes very wide in the car headlights. Kept the gun pointed right at his head, with both hands now. He licked his lips.

—That's not me name.

Swallowed hard a few times, gawped up at me. Then did his head-jerk I'd seen him do so many times.

—No? Your name's not Quinn? Donal Michael Quinn, formerly of Michael Collins Buildings, Dublin 1?'

—No.

—Really?

—Me name is Conroy. Niall Conroy.

—Is it? Jesus.

—I swear to Christ, pal. You've the wrong man.

—Oh my God. That's awful. I'm sorry.

—Lemme go.

—I couldn't. You might hurt me.

—Lemme go. I swear to fuck, I won't go near yeh.

—Really? Honestly? Would you do that? You wouldn't hurt me?

—Course I wouldn't. I swear.

—That'd be very good of you in the circumstances. Could I really trust you though, not to hurt me? Considering everything.

—I swear to Christ. Just lemme go, man. Me name is Niall Conroy. I won't touch yeh.

—That's so nice of you. Really.

Put the gun on the car roof and picked up the club.

—Do you know what you are?

Gaped up at me.

—No. How d'y'mean? Look, just lemme go.

Lashed out with the club and caught him bang right on the wrist.

—You're a lying little bastard, Mr Quinn. That's what you are.

—I swear, man. That isn't me name. I'm *Conroy*. Niall Conroy.

He tried to stand but toppled right down on his backside. Laughed at him. With the gun still on him, went to get the refuse sacks. Down on my knees beside him, ready to put the sacks back over his head. Suddenly sucked in his breath and spat into my face. I dropped the gun. He let a scream and jumped to his feet. Hurled himself towards me, tried to butt me in the stomach but I grabbed his head in a lock. Bit my hand. Hard, still sore now, cramping up around knuckle of thumb, difficult to write. Tried to get my hand out of his mouth but he wouldn't let go. Growling like a dog. Punched the back of his head but still, biting me hard, wriggling his head from side to side. Managed to get him stood up and lashed out with my foot and caught him slap between the legs.

Sank down moaning. Grabbed him by the shirt and started dragging him up the path towards the house. When he saw the back door seemed to panic, absolutely wild. No, don't, don't. Wriggled and squirmed and tried to kick me. Very strong. Tried for maybe a full minute to get him in through the door, but just couldn't seem to do it. Finally got him back down on the ground and sacks over his head again. This time tied them with my belt, nice and tight around his neck.

Got him up on his feet. His black toenails like claws. Let himself go limp in my arms and then suddenly started flailing at the air with his feet. Grabbed the belt and pulled it tighter. Warned him. One more move and I'll fucking strangle you. OK, OK. Was just about to make him go in when it occurred to me.

No.

I don't want this scumbag in here. I don't want this piece of shit inside my own house. I know what I'll do with him.

Yes. I know.

Turned around and looked down the garden. There it was. The aviary.

Grabbed him by the head and dragged him down the steps by the rockery. Stumbled into M's old bicycle still lying there in the uncut grass. Made him stand and started hauling him down the length of the garden. Security light on the back of the house clicked on. Blazing whiteness. Startled birds whistling and fluttering in the trees.

Old song came into my mind. *'Twas early early, all in the spring, When the young birds did whistle, and sweetly sing. Changing their notes all from tree to tree. And the song they sang was old Ireland free.*

Found myself singing the song. *As I was climbing the scaffold high, My own dear father was standing by. But my own dear father did me deny. And the name he gave me was the Croppy Boy.*

Garden full of rustling, scrabbling sounds. Somewhere up above, that old pheasant croaking. Dull beating of wings. I felt good. More drunk than anything else. Q tottered from side to side, bumping against the trunks of the beech trees. Lurched into the flower beds and I hauled him out. Stumbled to his knees and I kicked him in the back. Snatched at his hair through the sack and pulled him up to his feet. Walked forward, right into that low bough of the apple tree. Told him to stand up and stand still.

Opened the metal gate of the aviary and managed to push him through it. Hit the floor with a clanging metal sound. Breathing quick and very hard. Lay on the floor and said sweet fuck all for a while. Slammed the door closed and looked in at him. Strange bird.

Blood pumping through my temples. Locked the gate. Seemed that I could actually *hear* the palpitations of my heart. Straining to keep me alive.

Reached my hand in through the bars and undid belt around his neck. Then ripped the refuse sacks off him.

—Well now. Welcome home, son.

His head darted from side to side. Twitching. Got up on his knees and looked himself, saying nothing at all. Looked at him. Suddenly felt very thirsty. Back up to the car and got the gun.

When I returned Q had his back to me. Pointed the barrels in between the bars. He heard the sound of me clicking the safety catch. Could tell this, because suddenly his shoulders stopped moving. Told him to turn around and face me but he didn't.

—Get on with it, he says, if you're gonna do it.

—I told you to turn around. Or believe you me, I'll let you have one in the leg first.

Swivelled around to face me, head low.

—Not so brave now, are you, Quinn? Not such a hardchaw now.

—Please. Listen. Me name is Niall Conroy, I swear. Look here in me wallet.

—You make me sick, Quinn. You make me puke my ring up. I'm going to go over there into the dark for a while and just watch you, Quinn. If you make a single sound I'll come back here and shoot you in the leg. And then every time you make another sound I'll come back and shoot you again some other place. Now, turn around and sit down.

He did this. I left him there.

Sky like a bowl of navy and fiery light. Walked up the garden, looking at the stars. Yellow satellite tracing long straight line across the northern sky. Two aeroplanes trailing white smoke. Venus winking, brilliant puncture in the sky.

Came in here, locked all the doors and unplugged the telephone. Looked at Sky News. Riots up North the last few nights. Orangemen marching. Nationalists under curfew. RUC threatening rubber bullets and tear-gas.

Amazes me how well I slept.

Strange dream. Old English car we bought once with GB sticker. Kids wrote 'race' and 'illy' after the G and the B, whole thing in a heart.

Half-five this morning the alarm went off with a sound like shattering glass. Got up and went to the window. Grass moist. Steaming. Lying on his side on the aviary floor, with his back to the house.

Went down and rang the presbytery in Dun Laoghaire. Rang for a long time and then some old man answered. Parish priest? Told him I needed to speak to Seánie. Started on at me about the time and I say it's urgent. Another long wait. S came on the line, coughing and yawning. Pinched my nose hard while I talked to him. I'm feeling awful, just dreadful. It doesn't look like I'll be coming to Lourdes after all, you see I've come down with some terrible bug in the night, I've been puking and sneezing and running to the toilet.

—Billy, Jesus, sure you have to come. It's booked.

I can't, I'm absolutely dying. Silence on the line for a moment. Could hear him breathing.

—Billy, God, this is terrible luck. Are you sure?

Yes, yes. Actually I think I might need to go down to the hospital in a while. There's something seriously up with me. I've been passing blood. I'm in pain. Did a bit of groaning and sighing. Christ, yes, he says, I seem to be in a bad way all right. Funny, he's been thinking how run down I've looked the last few times he's seen me. Yes, I tell him, badly run down. Well, he goes, then maybe it's just for the best. Makes me promise to get myself down to the hospital.

S says he'd better get going. Taxi for the airport is calling in half an hour. Am I sure I'm going to be OK? Do I want him to send somebody up? Yes, yes, he knows I'm a big boy now. Well look, he'll say a prayer for me over there.

He should do that, I laugh. He should say a rake of prayers. That way, maybe I'll get a miracle.

Last thing. – Billy, did I leave my diary in your place last time I was up there? A big thick thing with black covers, ecclesiastical diary? Gold cross on the front.

—I don't know, Seánie.

He yawned. – I did I think. On top of your telly. But sure keep it. I won't need it where I'm going.

—I'll use it to write in.

—Yes. Why not. Use it to write in, Billy.

And spent this morning in bed, feeling strange and heavy. From time to time up and went to the window to take a quick look out at him. I suppose some small part of me maybe even hoping he's escaped, because let's face it, it isn't an easy situation here. But he hasn't escaped. Every time I looked he was there, still lying on his side, with his back to me in the cage. Noon by the time I got out of bed properly.

Why didn't I have the nerve to do it? One pull on the trigger. A couple of stabs with the knife. *Why* not?

Very bright today and ferociously hot. Radio news said it's a record summer. Water running short in the reservoirs. Strange plants blooming up in the botanic gardens. Department of Health warning about sunstroke and melanoma. Nothing about his disappearance on any of the bulletins.

Maybe lunch-time when I picked up the gun and went down the garden to see him. Looked dreadful. Face coming up in yellow and navy bruises. Pus. Discoloration around the eye sockets. His mouth crooked with pain. When he got to his feet noticed he was limping badly.

—Are you gonna lemme out?

—What do you think?

—Just lemme out and I'll go, I swear. There won't be any trouble.

Told him I couldn't do that.

Looked like he genuinely didn't understand this.

—Why not, for Jesus' sake?

It wouldn't make me happy to let him go, is what I say. That's all there is to it.

Leaned his face against the bars so they pressed hard

against his cheeks. Stayed like that for a while with his eyes on the ground. Then he looked at me.

—I've money, he says. If it's readies you're after I can get them. Lemme outta here, and we'll go and get readies right now.

—Fuck you and your money.

Blank stare.

—Then tell me why I'm here at least.

—You just have a think about that. You just have a good sit and think about that.

He looked up at the sky.

—Where are we?

—Guess.

Clocked him peering around the garden, at the stable and the broken wall behind him. Perhaps he hears the chuckling of the water in the stream, although it has grown faint since this hot spell began.

—Is it in the countryside?

—Yeah. It's miles away from anywhere. So you can roar and scream all you like, son, because there's no one out here to hear you.

—What bit of the countryside?

—We're in Wicklow. Near Glendalough. The nearest town is ten miles away.

Sat down on the floor of the cage. Soles of his feet all blackened with dirt.

—Listen, I swear to Christ, man, y're after makin' some and mistake here. Me name is Niall Conroy. Lemme out and I won't do anythin'. I'll walk out of here and leave y'alone.

I laughed.

—No. You won't do that. You won't leave me alone.

—Y'need help, pal. Y'don't look well. Y're not well in the head. I hope y'know that.

—No. That's true. I'm not well in the head. I get a bit mad sometimes. I don't think you'd like me much when I get like that. I get very unpredictable. I can do dangerous things.

—Y'need a doctor, pal, I'm telling yeh. Would y'not go and phone a doctor?

—I've loads of doctors, Quinn. But they can't figure out what's wrong with me.

—Why d'y'keep callin' me that, man? That isn't me fuckin' name.

Sat there on the grass and looked at him for a while. Time passed. Allowed the dreaminess of the hot day to come down over me so I'm half-asleep. Thought about Seánie in Lourdes, Lizzie, Franklin and the twins down in Australia, Hopper and O'Keeffe at loggerheads in the office, M in the hospital, me here in Glen Bolcain. Found myself trying to imagine all the people who have been in this garden over the years, all those who have passed through the house for different reasons, all shadows now, all shades. Like Grace.

Next thing I know he's standing up, face right against the bars.

—Any chance y'd gimme a glass of water? I'm parched.

—There's water there, nodding at the trough.

He looked at it.

—There's no cup.

Shrugged.

—Don't be a bollocks. Gimme a cup, for fuck's sake?

—No.

Crawled over and put his head down into the trough like the pig he is. Sucking sounds when he drinks. Don't like the sounds, warned him to stop making them. Ignored me. I screamed a bit and that shut him up all right.

Up to the house later to get a chair. Brought it down the garden, placed it in front of the aviary. Just sat and watched him for a long time, thinking all sorts of strange things. Seánie in Lourdes again; in a white shirt, leading a section of the torchlight procession down to the grotto. What a creepy place that grotto, with the wheelchairs and crutches left behind by people cured. The bells of the angelus are calling us to pray, *Ave, Ave, Ave, Maria.* Kind of eerie. M and Li hated it, the one time we took them. G amazed by the stone wall, worn down to the smoothness of silk. All the millions of hands. Incredible coldness of the holy water baths.

Kept my eyes on him. Sometimes he drinks water, other times puts his head into the feed tank and gets a mouthful of birdseed. Every now and then asks me to stop watching him, but only makes me want to watch him even more.

More time drifts. Now he's asking me to take off his handcuffs and I tell him no, I can't do that, can't do that, can't do that.

Tells me he needs to go to the toilet. So go. Asks if I really want him to go to the toilet in his trousers. I don't care where he goes to the toilet. Tell him where he goes to the toilet, on a scale of one to ten, is a pretty firm zero in my general view of things.

Looked at me for a while, through the bars. Looked back at him. Asked me to turn around for a minute. I did. When I turned back he was lying on his stomach with his face turned away from me. Wrists very raw from the handcuffs. Might have been crying but I don't know. And I don't care. Turned his face to me.

—Please, mister. Me name is Niall Conroy. As true as Christ.

—Say that again and I'll shoot you, Quinn.

—But it *is*. That's the truth, pal.

—I'm warning you not to say that once more.

Just kept watching. Hours went. Couldn't believe some of the things going through my head. Almost dark when I came in here and up the stairs.

Into bed with S's diary and started to write.

This.

195–171
Week 28
14th Week in Ordinary Time

VESTMENTS Green
HOURS   Proper: Psalter week 2
MASS   Proper

Amos 7: 12–15; Ps. 84; Eph. 1: 3–14; Mk. 6: 7–13.
'He chose us in Christ to be holy and spotless.'

Patron: *St Henry.*
Thought For The Day: *A smile costs nothing.*

Fuck. Fuck.

Just before dawn now. Woodpigeons and starlings shrieking out the back. Am hot. Fingers sweating on the paper as I write, damp bedsheet wrapped hard around my limbs. Tongue feels like it needs to be scrubbed clean with a nailbrush.

Wondering whether what happened with Q was a dream or flashback of delirium, which I've had more than just once or twice since the old days. A lie. I know it is real. Look at my hands. That's my way of telling. They're not shaking so I know I'm sober.

Thirst like a fucking dredger. Want a drink. Will write more later.

Another hot morning today. Sky full of haze. Light painful to look at.

Lying face down on the floor of the aviary when I came out to him. I think that is thy grave for thou liest in it. Seemed

221

to be asleep but of course very hard to be absolutely sure. Cunning enough to try anything.

Had managed to peel back a corner of one of the sheets of wire mesh in the night. But metal bars far too narrow for him to get out.

Kicked the wall of the aviary. Didn't move. Kicked it again a few times. He stirred, rolled over, looked at me.

—So, Mr Quinn. And how's the hardchaw this morning?

—Take the cuffs off me.

I tell him no.

—Please, man? For Jesus' sake.

—No.

—The pains in me shoulders are killin' me, pal. And I've a terrible pain across me chest. Please. I'm after havin' the cuffs on too fuckin' long now. I can hardly breathe.

Shook my head.

Looked around himself like he was getting desperate, which is a good thing, because I'd like him to feel a little desperation. Would like him just to feel what that's like, to be in a situation you can't control. Bruises on his face have got worse now. Flecked with dots of blood and pus. Skin around his nose thick with crusted blood too. Stared at me.

—Who the fuck are yeh?

—Maybe you're dead, Quinn. You're dead and gone to heaven.

Laughed.

—Fuck off.

—No, no, I could be your guardian angel, Quinn. Your guardian angel's going to look after you really well. Don't worry yourself.

—Me name isn't Quinn. It's Niall Conroy.

Looked scared and sick. Hair stuck to his scalp with sweat. Noticed the dye has begun to fade. Red roots. Light rusty beard.

—Would you like a razor, Mr Quinn? Or are you thinking of growing your moustache again?

He stared at the ground for a while.

—What do y'want with me? How do y'know me name?

Voice badly slurred, like his mouth full of mush.

—Don't you recognise me, Quinn?

—I never seen you before in me life, man, I've told yeh.

Went right up close to the aviary. Told him I wanted him to look at me very carefully.

—There's shite in me eyes. Take the cuffs off and let me clean meself a bit.

Told him he could see me perfectly well. Managed to get on to his knees, swaying a little as he stared at me.

—You don't notice a family resemblance, Quinn, do you?

Looked at me for a while.

—No.

—Ah, you do.

Shook his head. Wide innocent green eyes like a baby. Colour of Heineken bottles.

—You do, Quinn. Look hard.

—I don't know what y'mean. Why don't y'just tell me what y'mean? Or what y'want with me? Am I after doin' somethin' on yeh?

Left him there. If he wants to be like that, fine. I have all the time I need.

Came into the house and rang the office. Hopper picked up, surprised to hear me. No, I told him, didn't make it to Lourdes, came down with the summer flu. Yes, it's getting a lot better. But going to stay out for the two weeks, I've decided, just going to stay in bed and get myself better. Hopper agrees with me that this is a good idea. Things are quiet in the office anyway. O'Keeffe acting the prick, as usual. Came in yesterday with new hairdo which Hopper says is like a madwoman's armpit. Male menopause, Hopper's theory. Wants to hire full-time secretary. Issued memo to head office saying we *need* full-time secretary. Agree with Hopper about menopause.

223

After I'd finished on the phone, into the car, drove down to Dalkey. Sat in the church car park for a while looking at the kids kicking a football. Then into the Dukes. Bought a bottle of whiskey, a half of gin, a couple of bottles of wine and some crisps and nuts. Man behind the counter as fat as a beach-ball on legs. Gaped for just a second when I asked for the whiskey and gin. Small town. Knows me well and remembers me of old. Glanced into my eyes for a second, like he was going to be stupid and try to talk me out of it, but then I got out the cash and put it on the counter and he nodded and turned and took the bottles down from the shelf. Starts on at me about his water rates bill and his gay son and the horrors of being married to a woman who's mean. She'd peel a fuckin' orange without takin' it out of her pocket, Mr Sweeney, and that's the gospel truth. It *is* Mr Sweeney, isn't it?

—Yes, it is.

—From Glen Bolcain, isn't it? Up the hill?

—Yes.

—I thought it was. We were all very sorry about your news that time. Last year.

—Thank you.

—How is she, anyway? Your poor daughter.

—Well, she's the same.

—Dear, dear, Mr Sweeney, that's an awful cross for you.

—Is there any change?

—I'm sorry, Mr Sweeney?

—I said is there any change?

—Well, isn't that what I'm after asking you, Mr Sweeney? But you said she's the same.

—I meant is there any change from the fifty I gave you.

—Oh, of course. Sorry, Mr Sweeney. I'd forget me head if it wasn't screwed on.

Started up then about the will of God. Words were bouncing away from me. Didn't care what he was saying.

Knew I was going to drink when I got home, for the first time in nearly thirteen years.

Home to find the telephone ringing. Let the machine answer it. Hopper again, wanted to know something about an order. Waited for him to finish talking, then plugged out the phone. In the living-room put the whiskey and the gin sitting on top of the television. Put the bottles of wine under the sink. Put on a record. Spanish music. Tango.

Sat on the back steps in the sun, opened the peanuts and ate them. Should have been feeling worried but I wasn't, just felt resigned to something. Came inside, opened the bottle of whiskey and poured out a full glass, almost up to the brim. Left the glass on the television for a while. Tried to find some programme to watch but nothing much on. More bloody world cup. Big deal. Got the glass and sniffed the whiskey. Sour mashy odour of rot. Can still smell it from my skin now.

Started to drink it down.

Stung my gums and made my eyes water. Swilled it around my mouth and had more. Finished the glass, poured another. Then another. Drank about half the bottle in fifteen minutes. Managed to get up here and lay on the bed. Room spun and lurched. Felt it seep slowly through me. Soaking into me like a sponge, a hard-baked garden parched for the want of rain.

It felt good then, but doesn't now.

Must have fallen asleep for a while. Woke up a few hours ago with my head pounding. Not sure where I was. Took a few moments for me to steady myself. Up, went to the window and looked out. There he was in the aviary, standing now, but still with his back to me. Had another small drink and more peanuts.

Have just come in from the garden where I brought down a length of chain and a padlock. Looks very distressed and malicious now. Know he's been charging hard at the aviary gate because I heard him earlier as he battered into it.

Perhaps he thinks I'm deaf. I said nothing. Just wrapped the chain through the gate and padlocked it.

—Gimme a glass of water.

—Oh right. Would you like that?

—Yes.

—Well then, I'm not going to do it.

Noticed that he had been been crying. White lines through the muck and grime and dried blood on his cheeks.

—Please. Tell me why yer doin' this to me? Please?

So OK. I mean fair is fair. I don't want to be unreasonable, after all, I wouldn't give him that to say about me.

Pulled up the chair and sat down with my arms folded. Sun in my eyes. Shielded them with my hand.

—I'm doing this to you because last August you robbed a petrol station in Stillorgan, you little scumbag. Do you remember now? Last August? My daughter worked there. Maeve Sweeney, yes, think hard, I'm sure that does ring a bell. Well I'll remind you. You and your pals took a syringe full of your filthy blood and threatened to stick it into her. Then you battered her with an iron bar. She begged you to stop but you didn't. You wouldn't. So that's why I'm doing this to you, Quinn. Only I haven't started doing anything yet. I've big fucking plans for you, son.

Silence. Face showed maybe the first flicker of real fear.

—I dunno what yer talkin' about.

I grabbed the bars and rattled them hard. He fell over on his back, whimpered with pain. Rattled the bars again.

—Do you like birds, Quinn?

Panting. He did look scared then, definitely fear in his face. If his hands weren't cuffed I'm sure they'd've been shaking.

—What d'y'mean, do I like birds?

—It's a simple question, son. Do you like birds?

Thought about this.

—Well, I'm not a bleedin' queer or anythin'.

—I mean proper birds. With feathers and beaks.

Stammering then.

—No. Or I d-d-don't know. What do y'mean? I'm con-fused.

—Me, I like birds, Quinn. I'm something of an orni-thologist actually. Used to win prizes for it as a kiddie. And tonight, in a little while actually, do you know what I'm going to do? I'm going to go out and buy meself a sparrowhawk. Big hungry bastard, the sparrowhawk is. Eats flesh. Carrion. Rotten flesh, it actually prefers to good stuff. Not fussy what. Doesn't care what little pox-ridden hoor's flesh it eats. There's one lives in the back field. I was going to try and trap it, but it's too tame. Not fierce enough because the knackers feed it. So I've ordered one from a guy I know breeds them for hunters. I've ordered it and everything. I've the licence for it up in the house. You'd want to see what a sparrowhawk's beak can do, Mr Big Man Quinn, 'specially when he's hungry. Oh Jesus, he'd take the eyes out of your head. Seriously. Like pluckin' a grape. And its claws, dear oh dear, its little claws. They're like knives. You'd be interested in that, I know, you take a keen interest in knives. And all I have to do is collect it. And then, of course, it'll need somewhere to live, won't it?

—Will it?

—Oh it will, Mr Quinn. So I was wondering might you've any ideas for me? About where it might live?

Turned around and walked up the garden. Heard him rattling around the cage and shrieking like a mad thing. Made me laugh out loud.

There it is again.

Thursday 14 July 1994

196–170
Week 28
14th Week in Ordinary Time

VESTMENTS Green. White
HOURS   Psalter Week 3
MASS   Of choice

Ex. 1: 8–14, 22; Ps. 123; Mt. 10: 34–39
The people of Israel are oppressed by Pharaoh and cry to God for deliverance.

HOLIDAY (France)

Patron: *St Camillus de Lellis (1550–1614).*
Thought For The Day: *Can I help another to carry his cross?*

Stayed in the house all morning. Drank the wine, then the last of the gin.

After that felt tired and hot and had to rest. Perhaps the lie I told Hopper about the summer flu is turning out to be unlucky. Feel feverish and nauseous. Shirt is sticking to my back, even now, though the evening is cool enough and the window is open.

A few minutes ago in the bathroom I took off my clothes. Skin stinging me. Naked, standing sideways in the mirror, I looked pregnant. Held my stomach in my hands. Then touched my breasts. Turned to look head on in the mirror.

Held my penis and testicles and pushed them far back between my legs, then crossed my legs so my genitals couldn't be seen.

I am a woman now.

Man delights me not, nor woman neither.

Turned on the bath taps. Clanks and gurgles but nothing came out, except for a thin black trickle. Pipe blocked? Ballcock gone again? Tank burst? Can't be bothered to find out. Had quick wash at kitchen sink. Felt no better.

At about four this afternoon went down the garden to play with him again. Realised half-way down that I was still a bit drunk. He was sitting cross-legged on the ground, breathing in and out very deeply and looking like he was asleep. Something of the maharishi about him, except, of course, that he's in handcuffs. But then I suppose the real maharishi has spent time in handcuffs too when you think. Said his name. Slowly opened his eyes and looked up at me.

—I remember y'now. I saw y'in the court that time. The screws pointed y'out to me.

—Is that right?

—Yeah. And lookat, I meant to go over and say sorry. About your daughter and that. And what happened to her. I was gutted about it. Straight up.

Some bird I didn't recognise made a fluting noise in the ditch. Nightingale? No, only sings in June. Warbler maybe. Rare anyway. Fat yellowhammer hopping along the grass.

—Well, that would've made a huge difference all right. I always like that, when some little cur threatens to rape my daughter and puts her in hospital, I always like it when he apologises to me.

Shook his head.

—The thing at the garage wasn't my idea. I was forced into it. I swear. I was scared into it. I'd no choice. And I never laid a hand on her, that's true as Christ.

Laughed then.

—You're a fuckin' little liar, Quinn. I can't believe what a liar you are. And what a gobshite you must take me for.

For some reason I still don't understand he tried to smile then.

—It's as true as I'm in here. If it wasn't for me she'd've

229

got worse, I'll tell yeh. And a lot worse, I'd say. Them fellas with me were psychos. Animals, I swear.

—Oh right, well look, can I just thank you, Mr Quinn, on behalf of the family, for all your efforts? Of course she'd thank you herself only she's in a coma, as you know.

He said nothing for a while. Head lolling on his neck. Chin heavy with growth and dirt.

—Y'should let me out of here, man. Please. I'm not well.

—Neither am I. Neither is my daughter.

Wiped his nose on his shoulder and licked his lips.

—Look, I'm on smack. I'm on heroin, pal. Don't do this t'me. I go spare if I don't get a turn on, I go fuckin' crazy altogether.

—It's tough all over, son. Isn't that the nineties for you. Long, tough and cruel, huh?

—Don't bleedin' do this to me? Please?

Too late. Was already on my way back up here and making a point of ignoring the little liar.

197–169
Week 28
14th week in ordinary time.

VESTMENTS White
HOURS   Psalter Week 3
MASS   Of choice

Ex. 2:1–15; Ps. 68; Mt. 11: 20–24
In Christ is the new Israel and the new Moses.

Patron: *St Bonaventure (1221–74).*
Thought for the Day: *If at first you don't succeed, pray and try again!*

Low. Stayed in bed till after twelve.

Didn't go near him today. Sometimes heard him pacing up and down in the cage and rattling the bars. Just closed the windows and laced into the drink. Only time I left the house was to get more. Whiskey and beer, gin, wine. You must be having a party, Mr Sweeney.

There's something badly wrong.

G used to say I was weak. Unmanly, when we argued. Wasn't she right?

The more I drink the worse it's getting, it won't go away. Am in big trouble. Danger. Very scared. Should have just let Sheehan beat him stupid. Beginning to feel even that was a terrible mistake. What *possessed* me to bring him here? Should I just let him go?

Afraid he'd kill me after what I'd done to him, either now or later. Sorry now I ever arranged things the way I did.

Have just gone over and closed the window. Do not want to hear him any more.

Do not even want to know if he is still out there.

Sunday 17 July 1994

The Fifteenth Sunday in Ordinary Time
199–167
Week 28

VESTMENTS Green+
HOURS   Proper: Te Deum; Psalter Week 3
MASS   Proper: Gloria; Creed; Preface: Sundays, 29–36

Amos 7: 12–15; Ps 84; Eph. 1: 3–14; Mk. 6: 7–13
He began to send them out . . . to preach repentance.

No masses for the dead, except funeral masses, are permitted today.

Anniversary of the episcopal ordination of His Eminence Cathal Cardinal
Daly, 16 July 1967

Patron: *St Declan.*
Thought for the Day: *If you can say nothing good, say nothing.*

Very tired all day. Again, didn't go out to him. Heard the
phone ring a few times downstairs. Answering machine
seems to be broken. Didn't pick it up. Stayed in bed.

Once it rang for over five minutes.

Monday 18 July 1994

200–166
Week 29
15th Week in Ordinary Time

VESTMENTS Green
HOURS   Psalter Week 3
MASS   Of choice

Ex. 11:10–12, 14; Ps. 115; Mt. 12: 1–8
The meaning of the Eucharist in the Christian life.

Patron: *St Monnie of Killeavy.*
Thought for the Day: *All things are possible with prayer.*

And what happened tonight.

Six hours ago, at about half-five, was watching a children's programme on BBC 2 with a large neat vodka in my hand and another three or four in my stomach. Feeling very uptight. Suddenly heard loud shouts coming from the garden.

When I got out there he was on his back with his legs up against the bars. Naked feet sticking through them. Breath coming quick and fast through his nose. Groaning.

—Me legs. I can't feel me fuckin' legs, man. Help me.

Looked at him. His hair is two-tone now, red and black. Thick dirty beard.

—Stop it, Quinn.

—I'm a junkie pal, I'm tellin' you. I'm in bits here, *I can't feel me legs*!

Horrible low moan started in his throat, followed by a screech of pain. Started rolling from side to side on the floor of the aviary, kicking hard at the bars. I didn't

233

like this. Know I shouldn't care, but I mean, if anything were to happen to him in there. His face dark red and completely soaked with sweat. Again the gurgling moan. His eyes screwed shut.

—What do you take me for, Quinn? Cut it out.

—I swear to Jesus, pal. I'm in bits. Help me.

—Cut it out. Or I'll give you something to moan about.

—I'm on smack, I told you. I haven't had a turn-on in days.

This wasn't in the plan. Unpredictable. I don't know what is going to happen here.

—We wouldn't be in this situation, Quinn, if it wasn't for you.

—Shut up for a second, he says. Please. Just say nothin'.

Fell to his knees and started to shake. Looked like he was beginning to lose control of his movements. Dry-retching again and again. After a while began to cry.

—At least take the bleedin' cuffs off me. Please, man.

Got the handcuff keys out of my pocket.

—Come over to the bars. And keep your back to me, I'm warning you.

On his backside and hunkers he manoeuvred himself over to the bars. Unlocked the handcuffs and took them off him. He winced with the pain, massaged his bloodied wrists. Then opened his mouth wide and pushed his fingers down his throat. Leaned forward and retched again.

—Do you want water?

Shook his head, started sneezing uncontrollably. All he did for a couple of minutes, just sneezed, great violent sneezes that jerked his head back and forward.

—There's water there in the trough.

He started to sway from side to side. Hands to his temples. Looked up at me.

—You'll have to get me some gear, he says, please?

—What are you talking about? I can't do that.

A tremor seemed to run through him. He collapsed. Legs

twitching and thrashing more violently. He looked terrified. Eyes and nose streaming badly. His arms jerking. Pulled his trousers down. Diarrhoea.

Started sobbing.

—Please. Look please, man. If yer gonna keep me here, y'll have to get me some skag or some methadone. I'll tell y'where to go. I'll fuckin' die if y' don't help me. Please. Don't let me die, pal. I'm sorry for what I done on you.

Fell in a heap and retched again. Reached his hand out through the bars.

—Just don't let me die, man. I'm beggin' you. Please. I'm sorry.

Red and black hair, red tortured eyes, streaming nose, smell of shit. Looked like some creature out of hell. His fingers grasping at my shirt.

—Help me, man. For Jesus' sake, man. Help me.

Felt something inside me cave in.

Ran up here and got him a blanket and a change of clothes. Pushed them in through the bars. He took the blanket, wrapped it around himself, still shaking and retching. Teeth chattering. Lay down on the floor of the aviary. Muttering.

—Please man, help me, I'm beggin' you. I'll tell y'where to go.

—I can't do that. You know I can't.

Another tremor in his upper chest. Terrified bloodshot eyes. Opens his mouth and screams in pain.

Next thing I know I'm downstairs in the kitchen with my head under the tap, pouring coffee into myself to try to sober up enough to drive. Emptied all the opened bottles down the sink. Shaking. Scared.

Truth is he reminded me of myself.

I must be mad, I know that. Know I am stone mad now but don't care any more. Knew that already. Billy Sweeney, you are mad.

Parked the car on Parnell Square. Walked over to O'Connell

Street and down Sheriff Street, like he told me. Young guy in a wheelchair outside the rear entrance to the Savoy cinema, pushing himself backwards and forwards. Purple wine-stain mark all around his mouth. That was him. Went over. Watched me coming.

—I want to buy some methadone.

Looked at me. Fish's dead eyes.

—You don't look like the type.

—It's for my son.

—Fuck away off and don't be annoyin' would yeh?

—He's in college. We've only just found out about all this. This drugs business. We don't want to be going through the official channels.

Always be closing. Always be closing. Good salesman only as good as his last sale.

—You couldn't just swill methadone into him like lemonade. It's dangerous.

—My wife is a doctor.

—Then why the fuck don't you get it off her?

—She's a heart specialist. What's this anyway, twenty questions? I've got the money.

Down at the far corner children playing tag. Squeals of pleasure and excitement. Apart from that, the street is empty.

—Gimme your wallet.

—I can't do that.

Parts his lips and lets a piercing whistle through his teeth. Two men jump the wall and over to us. One of them with a wheel brace. Looks like a slab of meat with mittens on. The other takes a short fat cosh out of his pocket.

He reaches into my jacket and takes out my wallet. Opens it and flicks through. Looks at my driver's licence and my business card. Gives them to your man in the chair.

—I thought you might be drug squad.

—I'm sure they wouldn't be that stupid. Sending someone like me.

—You'd be surprised how stupid some people are.

—I said I'd get methadone. Can you help me?

Looks into my eyes. – I'd say now you say more than your fuckin' prayers, pal, do you?

—I need methadone.

He opens the wallet again. – I'm takin thirty.

—Where's the methadone?

—You'll be all right. Gwon back to your motor.

—Well look, I can't go without the methadone. Please.

—There's ways of doing things. Gwon back to your motor and don't be annoyin' me. It'll be there.

—How will you know my car?

Looks up at the sky and grins. – Silver grey Suzuki Baleno, 93D54961, car phone, stereo, scratch on the driver's door. Parked over on the square. Needs a good bleedin' wash.

—How did you know that?

—I told yeh. There's ways of doin' things.

Young kid waiting for me when I got back to the car. T-shirt that said 'Power Rangers'. Like Erin and Conal.

—Mister, I've a message for you.

Reaches inside his trousers and pulls out a medicine bottle. Dark glass. Puts it on the ground beside the back left wheel. Turns and runs up the street.

Drove home as quickly as I can. Q asleep when I went down to him but still mumbling to himself. Woke him up. Gave give him in the bottle through the bars. Also, a cup of water and some bread rolls. Put the bottle to his mouth and swallowed fast.

—Are you all right?

He nodded, choking a bit.

—I thought you said we were in Glendalough.

—We are.

—We couldn't be. Y'got in and out of town too fast.

—Never mind that.

—Lemme out of here.

Told him I couldn't do that.

—Y'don't have to lemme go. Just lemme out for a few minutes. To walk around the garden.

Got the hammer from downstairs. Then back out to him.

—Hold out your hands, Quinn.

Passed him in the cuffs, through the gap where he peeled back the wire mesh, told him to put them on himself and close them. Reached in through the bars and checked they were on him properly. Opened the gate. Started to climb out. Helped him. He fell to the grass. Helped him move his leg down.

Showed him the hammer. —If you try anything I'll have to hurt you.

Shook his head. —I won't, man. I won't.

Up on his feet. Took a few steps and his knees buckled a bit, but then managed to steady himself. Tottered around the garden and I followed close with the hammer in my hand.

He looked up at the house.

—What d'y'do up there every night?

—Nothing.

—Y'must do somethin'.

—I write in my diary. Now shut up.

After five minutes: —Can I have a piss, man?

—Go on.

—Me fly's closed. Could y'open it for me?

Reached down and opened his fly.

—I need a bit more help, man. I'm sorry.

Put my hand down and took it out for him. Went over to the blackthorn and pissed into it, groaning. When he'd finished, jumped up and down a bit, on the spot.

—Could y'put it back in for me? I'm sorry t'ask. I know I'm stinkin'.

—When I put you back inside I'll take the cuffs off you again. You can do it yourself then.

—OK, man. Thanks.

—And I'll bring you down underwear tomorrow.

—That'd be great. If y'could.

Did a few circuits of the garden. He took tiny steps, sometimes wincing when his bare feet would tread on a stone. Seemed completely exhausted. Started to get dark. Took him back in the direction of the aviary. Now we're at the gate. He pauses. Looks down at his penis, hanging out the front of his trousers.

—Get in, I tell him.

—Please, man. Just let me go.

—Get back in. I said.

Starts to whinge again. – Please? I'm sorry.

—No. Get back in and I'll let you out again tomorrow.

Clambered in and dropped to the floor. I locked the gate, reached in and undid the cuffs. He stuffed his penis back into his jeans. Then, before I know it, the little fucker's lunged and grabbed my hand. Pulling hard at it, forcing my face closer to the bars. He's gnawing his lip as he strains on my arm. He moves his face closer to mine. Through the bars he tries to bite my nose. I stab at his knuckles with the handle of the hammer and he lets me go.

Crying bitterly now. – Please. For Jesus' sake, let me out. I'm crackin' up, man. Please.

—You wouldn't be here now if it wasn't for what you did.

—You're sick. You need a doctor, I'm tellin' yeh. You're after flippin' your fuckin' lid some way, man. *Listen to me.* For Christ's sake listen to me.

—No, I don't want to listen to you any more. I trusted you and you let me down. After what I did for you tonight, you let me down, Quinn. And you'll pay for that I can tell you.

—Please.

Excuse me. Have to stop writing now. Going downstairs to turn the record up very loud. Drown out the noise of his screaming.

Tuesday 19 July 1994

201–165
Week 29
15th Week in Ordinary Time

VESTMENTS Green, White/Green
HOURS   Psalter Week 3
MASS   Of choice

Ex. 12–37–42; Ps. 135; Mt. 12: 14–21
Night of the church's bridal, night of new birth in baptism.

Patron: *Maelruain (Maolruain).*
Thought for the Day: *Suffer the little children to come unto me.*

Bad night last night, terrible dreams. M in coffin, triangles of mascara around her eyes. Up at dawn and down the garden to see him. Seemed to be sleeping soundly. Curled up under the blanket with his thumb in his mouth. Not sweating as much.

Went down again a few hours later with coffee and bread. Took them in through the bars with a sullen nod. Not a word. Has put on the clean clothes I gave him. Asked him to hand me out the dirty ones. Put them in a plastic bag, stepped through the stream and flung them over the back wall.

Spent the morning watching children's programmes on the television, cartoons, puppets, things about aliens, flying superheros.

Later in the day went back down to him. Something changed about him now. Prowling up and down the cage looking strange, in control.

—I was just thinkin' about yer daughter.

—Were you now?

—I remember her now.

—I'd say you do.

Walking up and down in the cage, like I say, not looking at me. Hands on his hips. Noticed he had torn strips out of his shirt and wrapped them around his wrists. Brown stains of blood.

Nice-lookin' girl, he says. Lovely lookin'.

Suddenly stops prowling and glares at me. —Must take after her mother, does she?

—You're funny, Quinn. Real comedian.

—Yeah. Must take after her auldwan. Couldn't take after yerself anyways. You've a face that'd stop a fuckin' clock.

Wondered what he was at. Did not understand the new light in his eyes, casually surly expression which he looked like he'd been practising. I don't like one bit.

—Nice attractive girl. Nice body. Lovely mouth.

—Shut up.

—Lovely arse on her.

—I'm warning you, Quinn.

—Y'know what we did to her after we bet her round the place? Laughs.

—Shutup, Quinn.

—One after the other. We took turns. And she loved it too. Oh man, beggin' us not to stop she was. Course they love a bit of the rough stuff, these posh girls, Homer. Jesus, I thought she was gonna faint on me, she came so much.

I look around in the grass for the hammer. I pick it up, fumble in my pocket for the key. I get it out. About to tear the door open and go for him when I see what he has in his hands. I stop. Now I understand.

—You better give me that out now, Quinn, or I swear to Christ I'll leave you in there for a week.

He holds up the Swiss Army knife and grins at me. Points to the name carved on the handle. Pony Sheehan.

—Very careless lad, the Pony. Shite for brains, Homer. Y'wouldn't think he'd leave this just lyin' around in the grass for anyone to pick up. I mean, you give someone a hidin', you don't leave a knife there for them to grab. And Jesus, y'd think y'd've searched me before you got me in here, Homer. Y'fuckin' gobshite.

—That's not my name.

—What? Homer or gobshite?

He stabs the knife hard into the long wooden perch, then pulls it out again.

—Throw it out here now, I'm warning you. Or I swear you'll get no water for a week.

Smiles.

—Come on in and get it off me, Homer. 'Mon in here and take it, y'cunt.

—You better believe me, son. You've hardly any water left in there. I swear to Christ you won't get another drop till you give me that out.

Looks at me for a minute. Could happily kill me right now. Sighs and throws the knife through the bars.

—You're a clever lad, Quinn.

Pick up the knife and pocket it. Stand there for a while listening to him laugh at me. Then:

—So you do know Sheehan then?

—Course I do, Homer. Met him above in the Joy.

—So how come he didn't recognise you?

—Brains wouldn't be the Pony's strong point, Homer, y'know? Couldn't find his own arse in a darkroom. Bit like yerself that way. Thick as a bucket of shite.

Cackles again, long and loud. Stalks up and down the cage like a lion in the zoo.

—You brought all this on yourself, I tell him.

—Yeah, well it don't matter now anyway, Homer.

—Why's that?

Horrible smile creeps over his face. Takes a few steps and grabs hold of the bars.

—Because I'll get outta here, Homer. I've it all figured out how I'm gonna do it now. I've gotten outta worse than this before. That's right. And when I do get out d'y'know what I'm gonna do? I'm gonna batter seven shades of shite out of yeh, Homer.

He yawns.

—It's the only thing keepin' me goin', just the thought of it, the thought of the sound of your neck snappin' under my boot, Homer. That's gonna happen very soon.

He lashes out with his fist and punches hard at the bars.

—Snap, he says.

Doubles up with laughter.

—You keep talking, Quinn. The more you talk, the longer you'll be in there.

—No, Homer. I'll be outta here very soon, don't you worry. And we'll see who's fuckin' clever then, Homer. Because I'm gonna burst yeh. Y'll be beggin' me to kill y'by the time I'm finished with yeh.

—You couldn't do anything to me, you fuckin' junkie.

Throws back his head and cracks up.

—The state of yeh, man. The way you swallowed that. Poor little lad, sure, sure isn't he only a junkie? Like all them poor inner-city lads these days.

Points his finger at me and howls with laughter.

—Y'bleedin' thick. I only wanted you out of the house for a few hours so's I could try and get outta this.

—You're not on heroin?

—I am in me arse. You guessed it, Homer. Pullin' your wire. Haven't been on it in five years. Haven't touched it. But I remember the symptoms good, y'know? Good auld act, wasn't it? D'yeh think I'll get the Oscar this year?

He raises his eyebrows a few times, then he winks.

—Yer windy, Homer. Know what that means where I'm from? Means yer fuckin' yellow. You're scared. I can see it in that ugly auld mug of yours. Because y'know what I'm gonna do t'yeh. Y'll be dreamin' about it tonight. So lock up the auld doors, Homer. Because y'just never know where I'm gonna jump out of.

—You'll do nothing to me, Quinn. And you know what you said about my daughter? What you did to her? You'll pay dearly for that, son.

—Yer a windy, jumped-up, fat little loser, Homer. And y'll soon rue the day y'ever laid a finger on me. Because I'm gonna slit yer throat for yeh.

Have been up here since. The bedroom door is locked. Won't go down again tonight.

Wednesday 20 July 1994

202–164
Week 29
15th Week in Ordinary Time

VESTMENTS Green
HOURS   Psalter Week 3
MASS   Of choice

Jer. 23: 1–6; Ps. 22; Eph. 2: 13–18; Mk. 6: 30–34
They were like sheep without a shepherd.

Patron: St Anthony Zachariah.
Thought for the Day: Be slow to anger.

Around nine this morning went down to see M in the hospital. The nurse looked shocked when she saw me, but I told her I'm OK, I just haven't been sleeping. M's had a bad night, the nurse tells me, she seems to have been dreaming. Unusual, she says. Maybe a good sign.

It's the first time this has occurred to me, that she might still dream. Frightens me, for some reason. Terrifies me.

Had a sudden feeling of the most awful helplessness. Later, on the way home past the police station in Dun Laoghaire stopped the car. Just sat there for a while, smoking.

Almost went in and told them everything.

Still nothing about him on the radio or in the newspapers. Why?

How can a human being disappear like that and nobody care enough even to call the police?

Jesus Christ, how can that *happen*?

203–163
Week 29
15th Week in Ordinary Time

VESTMENTS Green. White
HOURS   Psalter Week 3.
MASS   Of choice

Ex. 14: 5–18; Ps. 27 Ex. 15: 1–6; Mt. 12: 38–42.
The Israelites pursued are in fear but God answers the prayer of Moses.

Patron: St Lawrence of Brindisi (1559–1619)
Thought for the Day: Blessed are they who hunger for justice.

This afternoon I take a chair from the kitchen and go down the garden to the aviary. He is squatting on the floor with his back to me and won't turn around. I put the chair down in the grass and sit on it. He knows damn well I'm here but won't say anything to me.

—Quinn. Do you want something to eat?

He starts to whistle.

—Do you want anything?

No reply. Just keeps right on whistling, bobbing his head from side to side in time to the music.

—Do you want me to let you have a walk?

He stops the whistling and begins to softly sing.

Down in the willow garden, where me and me love did meet
She passed the willow garden, with little snow white feet
I had a bottle of burgundy wine
Me love she didn't know.
So I did murder that dear girl, all on the banks below.

—Lookat, Quinn. Do you want to have a walk or not I said?

He raises his fingers in the air and begins conducting.

I drew me sabre through her, oh it was a bloody sight
I threw her in the river, it was a dreadful night
Me father'd often told me that gold would set me free
If I did murder that dear girl, whose name was Rose Connolly.

—I asked you if you wanted a walk, Quinn.

He manoeuvres himself around to look at me. Small devilish face set in a sickening leer.

—But I'm after been out for a walk already today, Homer. I'd a grand stroll around the gaff while you were out earlier.

He laughs – Look at the mug on yeh.

—Bullshit, I said.

—Take a dekko up in the kitchen if y'don't believe me. I took two cans of yer Coke out of the fridge. Very nice. Lovely and cold. I like them cold. Long, tall and fuckin cold. Like me women, Homer.

He turns away from me again and continues singing. I look at the gate of the cage. It's definitely locked. There's no way he's telling the truth, is there? Is it possible he got out some way while I was down in the village? No. I sit and stare at his back. I take out a cigarette and smoke it. Surely he couldn't really have got out, could he? After a while I get up and go to leave. He calls out 'hey' and I turn. He is grinning.

—Can I tell y'somethin', Homer?'

—What's that?

He points at me.

—Y're gonna be sorry for all this, pal. Y're gonna be one sorry yellow fucker when I decide t'let meself outta here again. I might do it later tonight. Y'never know.

—You'll get out when I'm good and ready to let you out.

—We'll see about that. I'd lock them doors if I was you, Homer. Because I'm gonna come up and visit later, Homer. And that's a promise for y'now. Don't forget that. Go on now, you just shag away off with yerself and I'll see y'in a little while for me supper.

Came up here and into the living-room. Switched on the television. Nothing much to watch. What he said was bothering me. Flicked around the channels. Some documentary about people climbing mountains in Russia. Twenty minutes ago I heard a twig snap just outside the window and jumped up. Just a blackbird, pecking around in the briars. Sat back down. Watched a man on the screen dangling over a precipice from a rope attached to his waist. He swayed in the breeze, twisting his knee around the rope. Then went into the kitchen and opened the fridge. He's bloody lying, of course. The six cans of Coke I had are all still there. But he made me look, that's the thing. He made me look. Took out the ice tray and held it to my forehead. So cold it stuck to my skin.

Came up here and smoked a cigarette. Through the open window I can hear him singing again now, loud and strong.

Me race is run beneath the sun
The scaffold now waits for me.
For I did murder that dear little girl
Whose name was Rose Connolly.

I wish to Christ Jesus he would stop singing and let me sleep.

Why can't he just leave me alone?

Friday 22 July 1994

204–162
Week 29
15th Week in Ordinary Time

VESTMENTS White
HOURS   Proper; Psalter Week 4 at Day Hour
MASS   Of the memorial

Cant. 3: 1–4 or 2 Cpr. 5: 14–17; Ps. 62; Jn. 20: 1–2, 11–18
'She stood by his cross.'

Patron: St Mary Magdalene.*
Thought for the Day: The two words Jesus said most often were
'fear not'.

** NB: The gospels give no warrant for identifying her with the 'woman who
was a sinner' who anointed Christ's feet (Lk. 7: 37) or with Mary the sister
of Martha who also anointed Him (Jn. 12: 3).*

Newspapers say it's one of the hottest summers in Ireland
since records began. Tomorrow will be the hottest day of
the year. Government warning the farmers to be careful.
Conditions absolutely perfect for potato blight. Some people
in Ireland would actually *like* this, of course. Yet more
tragedy and self-pity. Fed up to the back teeth reading
articles about how the Great sodding Famine still important
in Irish psyche. Some foreign director making a fucking film
about it now. Hope it's a comedy, myself. *Carry On Starving*.
Nothing about Q in any of the papers, searched from cover
to cover.

This afternoon when I brought him down bread and water
he was doing push-ups on the aviary floor. I put the bread
rolls and the glass of water on the ground close to the aviary.

Where he can reach them if he wants. He can't say I'm not being decent. But he doesn't take them. Doesn't even look at them. Just keeps at the push-ups. Stand there and watch. Just keeps on going, pushing himself up and down very fast, and grunting. After a while I tell him to stop but he ignores me. Could see the tendons in his neck and temples straining as though they're going to pop.

—Cut it out, Quinn.

But he doesn't. If anything he speeds up. Panting.

—Just keepin' meself right, pal. Just stayin' strong so's I can split y'in two when I get outta this.

Pushes up now and while his arms are fully extended he claps his hands together before slamming them to the floor again and lowering his weight. Groans and does this a few more times. Sweat running in sticky rivulets down his arms. Bloody bandages on his wrists soaked through. Turns over and gets on his back. Jams his feet between the bars, puts his hands behind his head and starts to do sit-ups. Grunts every time he sits up. Throws himself up and down with such force that the whole cage creaks. Closes his eyes and yelps like an animal. Face purple and completely drenched with sweat but he just keeps going.

—I said cut it out.

He gasps, spits on the floor.

—I'll cut yer heart out, Homer, when I get outta here.

—If you don't stop I'll give you no food or water.

Keeps going, pushing himself up and down, fingers clasped to the side of his head.

—Yeah, well I don't want anythin' from you, Homer. I don't *need* anythin' from you.

Flips over on to his side and stares at me, his chest heaving. Licks the sweat from his upper lip. Taps the side of his head.

—Y'don't know how strong I am in here, Homer. Y've no idea. Thought you'd screw me up, didn't yeh? But y're after backin' the wrong bleedin' horse, Homer.

—Why are you calling me that?

—What? Homer? Because that's what y'look like. Homer Simpson. A fat stupid gormless twat. A fuckin' loser. Look at yerself, man. Pathetic. Getting your kicks are yeh? Lookin' at me in here, Homer?

He giggles.

—Well, yeh'll get your kicks all right, when I get out.

Stand and go to the cage.

—Give me back that blanket, Quinn.

Big ugly grin. Yellow teeth.

—Come in and get it off me, Homer. Just come on in if you fancy yer chances. I'll tear the fuckin' head off yeh. And you know what I'll do then?

—What?

Smiles, puts his hands on his hips, starts thrusting his pelvis.

—I'll do what y'want me to do, Homer. I'll give y'the ride of yer life, don't worry.

I leave him and come up here.

Spent the afternoon sleeping and listening to records. Bedroom door locked and barricaded. Hunting knife under the pillow. From time to time heard the cage creaking again, or thought I heard it, and then I knew he was doing his push-ups.

Of course he would love me to go down to him again, I know, so's he could try to freak me and frighten me. But I'm not going to. Intend to stay up here in the bedroom.

Went downstairs an hour ago. Won't be intimidated in my own house. Turned on the television and looked at some stupid sitcom. The kind of American family where the teenagers have their own telephone and the fucking dog has had orthodontistry.

The moon is full tonight and the sky is very clear. When I went to close the curtains saw him hanging on to the roof bars, pulling his body up and down, and grunting. Loud chant.

Watched him doing this for a while. Pulled the curtains closed.

—I can *see* you, Homer.

Singsong voice.

—I can *see* yeh, Homer. Lookin' down at me. Don't hide, Homer. I can *see* yeh.

What am I going to do?

205–161
Week 29
15th Week in Ordinary Time

VESTMENTS Green. White
HOURS   Psalter Week 4
MASS   Of choice

Ex. 16: 1–5, 9–15; Ps. 77; Mt. 13: 1–9
'The Lord gave them bread from heaven, mere men ate the bread
of angels.'

Saturday Mass of the Blessed Virgin Mary

Patron: St Bridget of Sweden (1303–73).
Thought for the Day: In work is human dignity.

Letter from Lizzie today. Coming home next month.

Postcard from Erin in the envelope. Asking after M.
Poor kid.

L's letter says 'The Sleeping Beauty' is Erin's favourite
story now. One night recently Franklin asked her why.

'Because it reminds me of Aunty Maeve.'

Came up here to the attic a while ago. Safe up here,
nesting among the oak beams. Will never think of looking
up here.

The Sixteenth Sunday in Ordinary Time
206–160
Week 29

VESTMENTS Green+
HOURS   Proper: Psalter Week 3
MASS   Proper: Gloria: Creed: Preface: Sundays, 29–36

Ex. 19: 1–2, 9–11, 16–20: Ps. Dan. 3; Mt. 13: 10–17
Moses is called to the mountain.

No masses for the dead, except funeral masses, are permitted today.

Anniversary of the episcopal ordination of Most Revd William Lee, Waterford and Lismore, 25 July 1993

Patron: St Declan.
Thought for the Day: Even the Lord fell three times.

Attic. Have pushed tea chests of books over the trapdoor so he can't open it. Appalling heat up here. Found stinking dead rat under rafter.

Funny the heat. Fibreglass insulation looks like dirty old snow.

Monday 25 July 1994

The Feast of St James the Apostle
207–159
Week 30
16th Week in Ordinary Time

VESTMENTS Red
HOURS   Proper: Te Deum: Psalter Week 4 at day hour
MASS   Proper: Gloria: Preface: Apostles 64–65

2 Cor. 4 4: 7–15; Ps. 125; Mt. 20: 20–28
The first of the apostles to die for Christ.

No masses for the dead. except funeral masses, are permitted today.

Patron: *St James.*
Thought for the Day: *You'll always hurt the one you love.*

This morning there were three rabbits down the back, snuffling around in the hollyhocks. Watched them from the kitchen window while I waited for the kettle to boil.

Went out to the garden. When they heard me coming they froze and then darted away into the thicket. I looked down at him. Had his feet and calves wedged through the bars on the roof – hanging there. Actually *hanging upside down* with his arms folded. Not moving at all. Just hanging there like some weird bat.

Inside again I walked around the house for a while. Feel cooped. Place has been getting on my nerves so much the last few days. When all this is over – will it be over? how will it be over? – have to get someone back here to fix the place up. Or maybe I'll just sell after all.

NB: That day last winter the estate agent came to the door saying he had a client looking for a house just like this.

An American? Told him no, but he made me take his card anyway. Said he always had buyers for places like this.

Decided to get out for a while. Walked down to Dalkey feeling thirsty. Bad case of the shakes. Got some food and a few bottles of wine.

Wonderful to get out of the house. On the way down the avenue the smell of mown grass. Buzzing bees everywhere. Gust of wind came billowing down the railway cutting, carrying dust and soot. Outside the vintage car shop a beautiful slim Beamer being polished by an athletic-looking youngfella in boxers and a vest. The tar on the road melting in the sun. Could feel the heat through the soles of my sandals.

In the supermarket the air-conditioning on at full blast. The place so cool and pleasant, I could have stayed there for ever. Got a trolley and began to stock up. Young women everywhere, in tight shorts and T-shirts and bikini tops. I'm wandering around when something odd happens. I notice this guy I think I know from the old days. I don't quite remember him at first. He's certainly aged a bit and his hair is quite thin, but I definitely know him.

There he was, poking through the cold meats in the delicatessen section, looking grubby and tired. Walking with a limp. Turned around and headed in the other direction.

Walked around the fruit and vegetable section looking at all the strange fruits they have. Kumquat and mango, star fruit and pawpaw. A yowling kid sat in a rocking train engine, turning the wheel like he was trying to twist it off. Two shop girls chatting and laughing by the biscuits. Kept thinking about the man I saw in the aisle. Started to bother me. Was about to go and look for him when it occurred to me – probably just some sad bastard I got drunk with once. Big deal. Just another drinking companion, probably wouldn't even remember me anyway. Went and got some Cokes, a fat litre bottle of 7-Up, one of mineral water, three bottles of white wine, a naggin of vodka. Ten minutes later pushing my trolley around a corner by a pyramid of fruit cans when I practically bumped into him. Stared at me, looking startled.

—*Bill*, isn't it? Bill Sweeney?

—Billy, actually.

—It's Phil. Phil Fortune. I was a friend of Grace's. We met once or twice.

—I know who you are.

Held out his hand. Thought about this for a moment before taking it.

—Well, this is . . . How's life treating you, Bill?

Told him fine.

He smelled of drink and stale cigarette smoke. The collar of his shirt dirty. Grubby tie with parrots on it. Saw then that his shopping basket was almost full of that cut-price own-brand beer. He'd put an *Irish Times* over the top, but I could see there must have been two dozen cans. It was just after eleven in the morning.

Metallic bong sound and a woman's voice came over the crackling loudspeaker. Special offer on ice-cream. Then the tinny music starts up again.

—And the girls? They're keeping well too, are they?

—Maeve isn't, no.

—Oh well yes, yes, of course. Any change there, Bill?

—No. No change.

—I meant to drop in and see her a few times. Never got round to it. She's still down in St Stephen's, is she?

—It's like I told you already, Phil. There's no change.

Shook his head and did a bit of tongue clicking.

—Well, things are great for me, Bill. Well, I say great. Up and down, you know. I was in England for a while. Things didn't work out for me businesswise. I was into the property thing over there for a while. Got the old fingers burnt a bit though. Negative equity.

—Really.

—But I'm living up in Ballybrack now. Knackeragua, you

know. HA HA HA HA, ah no, it's not too bad. With my sister. I don't think I'll be there for long though. I've got plans. I was thinking of getting into this internet thing. Selling it. I reckon it could be big over here, you know the way the Irish love to talk? I mean, on that damn thing you get to talk to people all over the world. You're a salesman, aren't you, Bill?

—Yes.

He tried to laugh.

—Well, I might have to look you up for a few tips. On selling. I'm sure you'd be able to help out a novice like me.

—I sell satellite dishes. That's what I know. Not much else.

His lips worked against each other.

—Yeah. But that's technology too, isn't it? And selling's selling, isn't it? You see, *my* thing's people, Bill, I can see that now. And selling's all about *people*, Bill, isn't it, really? Selling's all about making people happy?

Clearly more fucking drunk than I thought.

—No, Phil. It isn't. It's all about selling things.

Whites of his eyes flecked with thin broken veins.

—Yes. Well. And listen, how's the golf, Bill? Going around under a hundred these days?

—I don't play golf.

Confused gawp.

—Don't you play golf, Bill?

—No, Phil. I've never played golf once in my whole life.

His face a deep shade of pink. – I thought one of the girls told me you played golf, no? I could have sworn one of them said the old man was never off the green, no? I was going to invite . . . I was just thinking, maybe some time, that you and me . . . I mean, I thought the girls once said . . .

Shook my head and interrupted him.

—Wrong girls. But then I suppose you must meet a lot of girls on your travels.

He looked at the floor and nodded.

—Oh well, never mind then, Bill. See you around some time then.

—Not if I see you first, you prick.

Laughs. —What? What do you mean, Bill?

Went up close to him.

—Fuck you, Phil. That's what I mean.

Sighs and looks into his basket.

Turned around and left him there, staring at his beer cans and surrounded by whole shoals of shrink-wrapped smoked salmon.

'Bong' went the bell over the speaker.

Bong. Bong. Bloody bloody bong.

Came home and straight up here but didn't have the heart to start into the drink.

Enough for now. Going up to sleep in the attic. Goodnight. Over and out.

Bong

PART III

Chapter Thirteen

Maeve, when I think back now on those dreadful days, those seemingly endless nights of roosting like a mad bird in the sweltering attic, I hardly even recognise myself. Certainly, when I read over what I wrote at that time, the sensation is one of scrutinising the posthumously discovered confessions of some depraved monster who, in another time, would have been led lurching through the streets in chains for the horrified amusement of the innocent. Although only four months have passed, those scrawled chaotic pages seem to come from another life. I mean this literally, by the way; I do not exaggerate at all when I tell you that I read them now as though they were written by somebody else. And yet they were not. They were not. There is my handwriting, there are the inky smudges of my own fingerprints on the pages. To deny them would be like denying my own child. What happened over those two weeks in July I set before you now, real and unchangeable, a collection of actions and choices that are as much a part of me as the poisoned blood in my veins.

The morning after I wrote that last page, I remember waking late in the dark attic, with the weird confluence of the wood's sweet aroma and the chemical stench of fibreglass all around me. I was very hot. I climbed down. In the kitchen I tried to shave, although it was difficult to hold the razor steady. The windows were open and the room was flooded with clean light. I remember that I happened to glance out and notice that the rabbits I referred to in my diary were back in the garden. I let a roar and they hopped away, down towards the stream. I filled the kettle. What then? I suppose I must have opened the fridge and begun to unpack the shopping which was still in its bags from the day before.

That was when I saw it. There, on the kitchen table, was a Polaroid snap. Leaning against the teapot with the image turned away from me so that I could not see it. I was curious. I tried to figure out how it could have got there. Your Instamatic was still up in your room, I could have sworn it. I picked up the snap. It was wet and grey. As I held it in my fingers, an image started to form.

It was him. Quinn. Naked, his eyes wide, his protuberant canine teeth grimacing up at me. I ran to the window and looked down at the aviary. I saw the rabbits under the apple tree. From behind, a gloved hand clamped across my mouth.

'Homer,' he whispered. 'Are you comin' out to play?'

In a split second he was on me, punching me hard in the small of the back, swift, efficient jabs at the bottom of the spine. He hooked his arm around my neck and said nothing at all as he began to choke me, breathing very hard, kneeing me in the backs of the legs. I felt the air being squeezed out of my lungs. He got his hand around the front of my crotch and tried to rip open my trousers, flung me face down on the floor, stamped on my back. I must have managed to turn myself around then, because I saw his stubbled, purple face above me. He was panting harder. He had your hockey stick in his hands.

'Any last requests, Homer? Before I brain yeh?'

I lunged at his legs and tried to knock him over. He staggered backwards against the stove, then ran at me, kicked out at my chest, sending me sprawling over the floor again. I hit my head on the leg of the table and knocked off my glasses. When I tried to take a breath I was sure that he had broken my windpipe. He looked blurry and shapeless, out of focus.

Then I heard my own voice as though it belonged to someone else. It sounded weak and frightened.'Fuck off then,' I croaked. 'Go on. You win.'

He took a step forward and kicked me hard in the side. A bolt of pain shot through my chest.

'What did y'say to me?'

'I said go. Just go on. Get out.'

He laughed out loud and wiped the sweat off his face. 'But y'don't realise, Homer,' he said. 'I'm grand here.'

He threw down the hockey stick and his eyes ranged around the kitchen. 'I like it here, Homer. This is great. Lovely place y'have.'

He started to walk around the bright room then, pressing switches, trying the knobs on the Aga, turning the taps on and off. He opened the cupboard under the sink and took out the toaster. He put it on the kitchen table.

'You're nicely set up here, Homer. I'll give y'that much.'

He picked up the hockey stick and began battering into the toaster with it, thumping again and again until the screws shot out and it lay in a mangled heap.

'Was that guaranteed, Homer?'

I said nothing. He took a swing at me. My vision flashed as the stick connected with my kneecap.

'Answer me, Homer. Was that guaranteed?'

'I don't know,' I said, gripping on to my knee now, mouth dry with agony.

'Why don't yeh?'

'I just don't. I mean I can't think.'

He stood in front of me then, trying to balance the stick on one finger, all the time watching it, jerking his arm from side to side as it threatened to topple. 'Homer can't think. Homer can't think.' He let the stick fall into his hands. He grinned at me.

'Well I'm gonna give y'somethin' to think about in a minute, Homer.'

He jerked open the cupboard beside the chimney of the

265

Aga and began to pull out the stacks of crockery. The plates and dishes shattered on the tiles. When he started frenziedly stamping on the broken pieces I saw that he was wearing a pair of my shoes. He jumped up and down, smashing the wine glasses and tumblers. He took the hockey stick and battered wildly around himself until the perspiration was streaming down his neck.

'I fuckin' like it here, Homer,' he panted. 'This is fuckin' Disneyland.'

He put the stick on the table, pulled out a chair, swivelled it around and sat, arms on the backrest. He stared down at me then with a kind of stony fury.

'What d'y'say now, Homer?'

'I told you. Go on, just go. I won't call the cops if you leave.'

He screwed up his face and simpered. 'I won't call the cops if y'weave, I won't call the cops if y'weave.' Then he grinned. 'Yer pathetic, Homer. Y'know that? And yer borin'.'

He turned away from me and went to the sink. He ran the tap and splashed water over his face. 'Homer can't think. Homer can't think. Well dear dear, boys and girls, isn't that a good one now.' I tried to get up and make for the door but he ran and kicked my legs from under me. He stood on my hand, grinding his foot from side to side until I howled with pain. I yelped and pleaded with him to stop. Finally, when I was almost in tears, he got off me and stood chuckling with his hands on his hips.

'Please just go,' I said.

He shook his head. 'But I'm not goin' anywhere, Homer. I told yeh, I like it here. So I'm gonna stay. Isn't that nice?'

I could not speak, the pain in my hand was so bad. He picked up the hockey stick and shouldered it, like a soldier on parade. His turned his face to the warm light which was pouring through the kitchen window.

'I've a few things to tell y'now, Homer. Make yerself

comfortable there. Right so, let's see. Well now, the night y'nabbed me, I was on me way down to get a taxi to Dun Laoghaire, Homer, and wait for the boat to England. That's why I'd me clothes with me. I was headin' to London. And d'y'know why I was doin' that, Homer?'

'Why?'

His voice came breathless. 'Because the local hardchaws were after tellin' me to split, Homer. The RA, out in Bray. The boys of the old brigade thrown me out. Found out who I was. I mean, there I was a few weeks ago, Homer, up Bray Head one night with the mott, gettin' dug into each other, and anyways, up they come, the two Provos and they're open for bleedin' business, Homer, if y'get me meanin'. Talk about coitus fuckin' interruptus.

'Told me the Irish fuckin' Republican Army was puttin' me outta the country. An expulsion order, they call it. Heard I was dealin' smack. And they don't like that, Homer, the laughin' boys, don't like it at all. Told me I'd two days to leave the shamrock fuckin' shore, Homer, or they'd stiff me.'

He laughed. 'In fact that time you and Flynn jumped me, I thought you was them. Some RA-heads, youse two, what? Some pair of fuckin' desperadoes, Homer. Like bein' mugged by Laurel and Hardy.'

'Who wanted you out? Who did you say?'

'The Provies, Homer. The local RA out in Bray.'

'What are you talking about?' I said. 'They don't have the IRA out in Bray.'

He raised his eyebrows. 'Oh do they not? Right so. Homer's the expert.'

He put the hockey stick on the table and jerked up the front of his T-shirt. A thick purple X-shaped welt was slashed across his chest. Down the slender abdomen and around his hairy navel there were more scars, criss-crossed patterns of cuts and jags.

'See that, Homer? Well, that's where I got the visit that

night. Told me I'd get more if I wasn't out of Ireland by the end of the week. Stanley knives, Homer. Y'ever been cut with a Stanley knife?'

I said nothing. He kicked me hard in the shin.

'Fuckin' answer me, Homer, when I'm talkin'. Y'ever been cut with a Stanley knife, y'know, them little knives they have for cuttin' up wallpaper?'

'No.'

'No,' he said. 'Well it hurts, Homer. Believe you me, it hurts.'

'Anyways, when they've finished cuttin' me they pull out a blade the size of yer cock, Homer. They show it to me and and then they tell me again to get out. And I said I would. Pronto. Because y'don't fuck around with the RA, Homer. They shot me brother dead two years ago, did y'know that? Yeah. Comin' out of a pub in town. And bang. Back of the head, Homer. Three inches behind the ear. Undertakers had to take his fuckin' head to the morgue in a plastic bag. So I know what I'm talkin' about here.'

'Yes, boys, right enough, says I. I'll shag away off t'England. But then didn't you step in, Homer. And now here I am. In Homer Simpson's gaff. Sure it suits me grand. They don't know I'm here and neither does anyone else. Perfect. So the long and the short is yer stuck with me, Homer. I'm stayin' here as long as I fancy it.'

'You certainly aren't. Get out of here before I call the police.'

He strode over and punched me just once in the side of the head. The room danced. He sat on my chest, his knees pinning my arms to the floor. His face was bright red and his teeth were gritted. 'Listen to me, yeh gunner-eyed prick yeh' – he put his hands around my throat and began to squeeze hard on my windpipe – 'if y'start, I'll go straight to the pigs meself, I swear to fuck, and I'll say y'picked me up in on the quays and brung me out here and molested me. I'll put one hand on any bible and swear yer the biggest perverted queer in Ireland.'

He squeezed harder. Black spots loomed up in my eyes.

'I'll say y'took the clothes off me and touched me up. And then bet me round the place for yer kicks. That's happened me before, Homer. I know all about that kind of shite.'

'All right,' I managed to croak. 'OK then.'

He climbed off me and went to get the hockey stick. While his back was still turned, I half got up and tried, bent double, to make another move for the hall. Just as I made it to the doorway he turned and leapt on my back, his hands on my neck again. I fell over. He dragged me to my feet and shoved me into the middle of the kitchen again. I was so weak now that I could barely stand.

'I feel like a bite of lunch now,' he said.

He grabbed me by the hair and hauled me over to the fridge. He opened the door, tore out the top shelf and flung it and its contents across the room into the sink. He grabbed up a saucepan and started smashing at the inside of the fridge with it. When he had finished he glared across at me.

'Make us a sandwich, Homer.'

I got the bread out of the bread bin. He went to the sink, fished around for a moment and pulled out a few slices of ham, which he sniffed before handing to me. I opened the drawer and went to pick up a knife.

'Don't be a comedian, Homer. Use a bleedin' spoon if you don't want that between yer shoulderblades.'

My hands were shaking. I picked out a teaspoon, spread butter on the bread and made him a sandwich. He tore it in two and started to devour it, his eyes wild now as he swallowed.

'Very nice too,' he said. 'But you can have this half, Homer.'

I told him I didn't want it.

'I said fuckin' have it before I burst yeh.'

He lifted the top slice of bread, loudly cleared his throat and spat into the sandwich.

'Now, eat it.'

'No.'

'You'll eat that, Homer,' he smiled.

'I won't.'

He sighed and stared at me while he slowly chewed. He finished his half. He licked his fingers one by one. Then he strolled over to me, his fist clenched, and thrust his forearm up in the air as though about to hit me. I put my hands over my head. He grabbed me by the balls and squeezed hard. I opened my mouth and screamed. He started pushing bits of the sandwich into my mouth. I slumped over the table and threw up. He stood watching me, with his arms folded. He took my cigarettes from my pocket and lit one up.

'Now, Homer. Say grace after meals.'

He held the lit cigarette in front of my wet eyes and stared at me.

'I said, say grace after meals, Homer.'

My throat felt raw. 'Bless us o Lord . . .'

He slapped my face hard.

'That's grace *before* meals, y'fuckin' Protestant. Grace after meals. Y'do know it, don't yeh? We give thee thanks.'

'We give thee thanks, almighty God.'

He waggled his finger at me. 'No, no. On your knees, Homer. Show some respect.'

I went down on my knees.

'We give thee thanks, almighty God, for all thy benefits, who livest and reignest, for ever and ever.'

'Amen,' he smiled.

His face darkened. He reached behind himself and pulled my hammer out of his belt.

He ordered me to stand and turn around. I tried again for the door but he was too quick. He yanked me back by my shirt with such force that the buttons ripped off and shot across the room. He elbowed me hard in the side and I doubled up. 'You're one contrary little get, Homer, y'know that?' He dragged me from the kitchen, out through the back door, down the steps. I stumbled and fell sideways into the rockery. He took a hold on my calves and began dragging me over the stones and then down the garden, my back sliding on the grass. He hauled me right through the drainage trench without stopping. I heard my shirt and trousers rip, tried to to kick at him but it was no use, he got up speed, he was actually running now, cantering along backwards as he dragged me past the apple tree.

He dropped my legs and opened the aviary gate. His chest was heaving. He told me to stand.

'Get in there, Homer,' he said.

My knees felt liquid with fear. I told him no.

'Get in, Homer.'

'No.'

He sighed and looked around himself.

'I'll bleedin' kill yeh with me bare hands. I've done it before now. I was in the army. I was in the Lebanon, Homer. Didn't know that about me, did yeh?'

He saluted. 'Private Donal Quinn, engineer's corps.'

He took a sudden stagger backwards and glared up at the sky. 'Christ, man, what's that?'

I looked up.

He lunged forward and head-butted me hard, right in the forehead. I sank to my knees, head reeling. When I opened my eyes I saw splashes of blood on my palms. I put my fingers to my nose and looked up. He was holding the hammer in his right hand and slapping it against his hip while he laughed.

'I don't fuckin believe it. Homer the halfwit, he fell for the auld look-up.'

I lay back trembling in the grass. For a while he just stared at me, nodding, like he was thinking about something. And then suddenly his face went solemn with fury. He pointed the hammer at me.

'I know what it is to kill someone,' he said, in a quiet voice. 'It doesn't bother me. I'd worry more about pickin' me nose. So I swear to Christ, you're gettin' into that thing, pal, or I'll split your scalp down to your arse right now and burn this place to the ground and no one'll ever even know I was here.'

I stood up, my stomach boiling, and started to climb into the aviary. My vision was cloudy, my left eye was begining to close. Half-way in I thought I was about to faint. He grabbed my thighs and pushed me. I fell in forward and banged my head on the metal floor. It smelt of shit. He slammed the gate shut behind me and chuckled gently as he locked it.

'Poor Homer,' he said, and he bashed the thick steel mesh with the hammer. 'Poor auld Homer's all lonesome now.'

He pointed at the sky and howled with laughter. 'Look up, Homer,' he cackled. 'You just keep lookin' up now. Here's one little junkie's gonna make sure y'see the fuckin' stars.'

He walked the length of the garden and went into the house.

I lay on my back and tried to get my breath. I felt the acrid, metallic taste of blood in the back of my throat. My arms and legs were trembling badly. Across the ditch I thought I could hear the distant sound of an old car being revved up and driven around the back field by the travellers.

I got to my knees and tried the gate but could not open it.

I sat back down and looked out through the bars. My left ankle was throbbing with sharp, insistent pain. I tried to concentrate. See things clearly. I tried to run back over what happened in the kitchen, get it straight. Every time I had turned my back to him he had hit me. I told myself that I would have to remember this, when he let me out, not to turn my back to him. Look at him head on. That way I might have some chance.

I knew that I had to think about something, focus fast on something – anything – to stop myself panicking. In my head

I began to list out all the towns you go through on the drive from Dublin to Galway, then I did Dublin to Belfast, after that Dublin to Cork. Stations on the Dart line, the names of all my first cousins, all the cars I had ever owned, the names of the weather stations in the meteorological report on the radio at night – Malin Head, Fair Isle, Rockall – the seven deadly sins, the surnames of the neighbours who lived on the street in Ringsend, the ten gifts of the Holy Spirit, all the states in America. I forced my mind to keep going, just making lists. The names of your friends. The names of Lizzie's friends. It seemed to work, somehow it stopped the fear biting into me completely. After a while I even felt it subside a little.

When I looked at my watch it said quarter to five. That confused me. I thought it must be later than that. Names of the kings and queens of England, the thirty-two counties of Ireland in alphabetical order, all the shops on my patch. But when I next glanced at the watch, it was still reading quarter to five; it had stopped or been broken in the fight. I had no idea how much time had passed.

Then panic started to well up again. My head was aching, I could think of no more lists to make. For some reason it frightened me to the core that I was not in a position to know how much time was passing. I stared at the ground outside the cage and tried to focus my eyes on something small. I started trying to count the number of daisies I could see but quickly got lost. I focused even smaller. A spider's web glistened in the bars of the cage. A line of fleas crawled along one of the perches. Outside, a ladybird was scuttling along the spine of a broad leaf of snipegrass. I followed it with my eyes. Suddenly I saw a nail. Just lying there in a tuft of dock leaves, a rusty bent nail, I told myself the builders must have dropped it when they were working in the garden. I stretched my hand out through the bars, but could not reach the nail no matter how hard I tried. I rolled up my sleeve and tried again. I pushed harder, until I could

feel the skin on my arms being torn by the bars. With the
very tips of my fingers I managed to brush the nail and roll
it backways towards me, until I could grip it between my
middle and index fingers. I moved my arm as slowly as I
could so as not to drop the nail into the grass. In it came,
in through the bars. I pushed it into the eye of the lock and
rotated it. I jiggled it and pulled it, I tried just inserting the
point and gently working the body of the nail. I do not know
how long I did this, my clammy fingers just moving the nail
around as softly as I could in the lock, thrown half-glances
all the time at the house. But nothing happened. The sky
began to turn orange and gold.

I noticed lights going on in the upper windows. I hid the
nail in my pocket and lay down, pretending to be asleep.
I saw him up in my bedroom. He had the wardrobe open
and seemed to be pulling clothes out of it, throwing shirts
and pullovers and slacks over his shoulder. After a while
he disappeared from view and the light went off. A few
moments later I hear loud thudding sounds from the house,
a wrenching sound like wood being broken. And then I
could see that he had gone into your room.

I jumped to my feet. 'Get out of that room,' I screamed.
'Get out of there.'

But either he did not hear or did not care. I could clearly
see him moving around your room, a black silhouette against
the dull yellow glow of the blind. I saw from his shadow that
he was swigging a bottle and eating something. Moments
later he peeled off his shirt. I heard the sound of glass
shattering and then another loud, solid thud, as though
something heavy had hit the floor. The light in your room
went out.

As the sun continued to fade, the garden grew noisier.
I remember chaffinches and flycatchers whistling in the
bushes, the old pheasant croaking up there in the apple
tree, the call of a cuckoo in the travellers' field, from the
sky the sharp, clear screech of a blackcap. Wind rustled in

the rushes. The crickets began to chirp. I listened hard for the stream but could not hear it.

Darkness came down slowly over the garden. The stars began to appear. It was clear on that night, so cloudless that soon I could distinguish the different colours of the stars. This helped me, simply because it occurred to me before too long that I could list these too. There was the Plough, there was Cygnus and Hercules. There was Cassiopeia, Ursa Minor, there was Pegasus. I tried to recognise as many of the constellations as I could and give them their names. Then I tried to recall others. I trawled through my memory. Cepheus. Tucana. Corona Borealis, whenever I remembered a name I would say it aloud. It became a victory to remember another name. I thought of Stevie and me in the back yard as children, having slipped out on to the coal-house roof after your grandparents were asleep, his trembling finger pointing out the stars and constellations, his soft hesitant voice just whispering their names, with awe, almost with fear, as though if the stars were to hear him they might somehow take fright and disappear.

Aquila.
Delphinus.
Andromeda.
Vulpecula.
Arcturs.
Draco.
Castor.
Ophiuchus.

Chapter Fourteen

Some time later that night I woke up shuddering. My neck was aching, my throat dry as hot sand. My ankle felt like a blunt spike of pure pain had been knocked through it. It took a minute or two for my eyes to adjust to the thick, velvety darkness of the garden. A small rat was nuzzling the wire just by my hand. I lurched away and it scampered into the bushes.

Over by the stable block I saw the glow of his cigarette. He flicked it through the air.

'Well, well, girls, would y'look at our big hero now.'

He stepped out from behind the apple tree. It was too dark to see his features but I could make out the shape of his wiry body. He was drinking from one of my bottles of wine. He slurped at it and wiped his mouth with the back of his hand.

'Take a dekko at John Wayne now, ladies and gentlemen.'

He sounded drunk. A torch sprang on. He shone it up into his own face.

'Together again, Homer. Like the cheeks of me arse.'

'Let me out.'

'Comfortable in there, isn't it, Homer? Like the Ritz fuckin' Hotel in there.'

'Let me out,' I said. 'I have a heart condition.' My tongue was badly swollen. I must have bitten into it earlier when he had forced me to eat the sandwich.

'Oh, I see. Homer has a heart now. It's lately it happened him.'

'Let me out.'

'Say please, Homer.'

'Please.'

He put his hand to his ear. 'I didn't hear that, Homer.'

'Please.'

'I'm gone a bit deaf, Homer.'

'Please.'

'Please what, Homer?'

'Please let me out.'

He stared at me. He flicked the torch on and off a few times.

'Fuck yeh, Homer,' he said, and he strolled up the garden.

After he left I must have slept again, because I remember having a dreadful dream. I was walking alone through a sloping, wet, green field near the sea shore. Some kind of battle was going on there but I could not see it. I could only hear it. Around me rose the deafening screams of men and animals, the sound of iron clashing on iron, the thundering of horses' hooves on the earth. Someone kept roaring my name, but still I could see nothing except the trees in the field, the light blue sky, in the distance the white tips of the waves. Suddenly I saw myself as though from above. I was wearing a suit and carrying a briefcase. And then the noise began to grow even louder. Before long I could stand it no longer. I sank to my knees in the mud, hands to my ears. A church bell rang. Seànie appeared before me, weeping, his priest's robes completely drenched with blood, the bell in one hand and a spear in the other. He seemed to be trying to speak to me, but the sounds around me were so loud and intense by now that I could not make out what he said.

I was awakened by the hysterical screaming of birds. The daylight was already bright white as salt. When I closed my eyes I saw rhythmic orange flashes. A faint echo of the awful noise from the dream seemed to sound. My back was stiff and sore, my neck was dully aching. For a moment or two I was not even sure where I was. Then I remember the sunlight glinting between the bars, dazzling me and forcing me to move my head, which made me groan with pain. I was so incredibly thirsty that I cannot describe it to you.

Quinn was sitting in the grass, chewing speculatively like a curious cow and staring in at me. His face was clean-shaven, he looked younger and healthier. He took out a match and began to pick his teeth with it.

'Cock-a-doodle-doo, Homer,' he said. 'Sleep well in there?'

I said nothing. When I moved I felt a spasm shoot across the top of my back. Then I noticed that the mobile phone from my car was lying in the grass beside him.

'Good. Well, I'd a grand night's sleep in your bed, Homer. The sheets were disgustin' though. The filth of them. Would y'not change yer sheets sometimes, Homer, no? You and the boyfriend?'

I got to my feet and tried to walk up and down the cage, but my calves and knees were pulsating with pain. When I tried to put weight on my left ankle, an excruciating pang bolted through my foot making me gasp.

'Don't feel like doin' the Macarena, Homer, no? Don't want me to come in there and give y'a dance.'

I eased myself down on to my backside and tried to not cry out.

'You've made your point,' I said. 'Let me out and just go, all right?'

He scoffed. 'I've no point to make, pal. I'm not inclined to make points.'

He spat in the grass, picked up the phone and dialled a number. Then he clamped it to his ear and leaped to his feet. 'Is that you, head?' he said. 'Yeah. It's me, y'fat bollocks, who do y'think? Yeah. Donie Quinn.' He looked at his watch.

'It's eight in the morning here. Serious. So listen, cm'ere to me, how's Australia treatin' yeh?'

He must have spent ten minutes jabbering into the phone. 'Any decent women over there, is there? I'd say that's the truth, all right. Y'did not. Y'dirty little . . . What? Two of them? . . . I'll give y'such a right batterin' the next time I see yeh . . .'

He came close to the cage, grinning so broadly that I could see his yellowed bicuspids. Then:

'Only messin' with yeh, Homer. I don't know his number.'

He held the phone to his ear again and rattled it from side to side. 'But I'd say they're handy enough things though, are they?'

I said nothing.

'Yeah,' he said 'That's right, Homer. Funny, I often thought to meself, one of them mobile phones'd come in handy. It's amazin' though, isn't it, when you think, like? What'll they invent next? Somethin' like that, I really would say that's fierce handy, is it?'

Still I said nothing.

'Are y'deaf, Homer? I'm after askin' y'a question. They come in handy or not?'

'Yes,' I said, 'they come in handy.'

He tossed it to the ground and stamped on it, again and again, grinding his foot into it. Then he took the hammer from his back pocket, squatted down on his hunkers and carefully, almost delicately, smashed what was left of the twisted phone to pieces. Every time he hit it, a small moan of almost sexual pleasure would come from him.

'Well, that one won't come in handy any more, Homer.' A grotesquely clownish smile. And then he went whistling back up to the house.

From over the wall I thought I could hear the sound of the travellers' old car again, a faint grind of gears, a mechanical surging thrum. I asked myself whether to call out or not. If I shouted, I thought he might come down and attack me. I tried to gauge the distance of the car and in what direction it was driving – but all the time I did this I knew I was fooling myself, it was clearly too far away for me to be heard even if I were to roar. I sat on the floor with my back against the bars and attempted to stay calm. I wondered what he was planning to do with me. If he wanted to attack me he would have to get into the cage himself. I knew I must expect that. If it happened, there could be no weakness this time. If he tried to climb in, I would have to be prepared to attack him with my bare hands in such a way as somehow to do him serious harm. How could I do this? Was there some way I could exploit the fact that he would have to be physically very close to me if he wanted to hurt me? Could I perhaps unscrew one of the perches and use it as a club? I felt a sudden icy hand of fear grip around my spine. It occurred to me that I did not know where Sheehan's shotgun was. Quinn could shoot me through the bars while I was sleeping. He could kill me without my even having any warning.

My stomach was in ruins by now and I was desperate to go to the toilet. I crawled into a corner of the aviary and dropped my trousers. My bowels opened as I squatted, a sickening stench rose from behind me. I plucked a handful of grass and leaves from outside and tried to clean myself. I felt like screaming with rage and despair. I lay down and closed my eyes. For some reason, my father came into my mind then, not as I remember him but as he must have looked when he was a young man, in one of those forties suits with very wide lapels and a spotted handkerchief in the breast pocket.

I took out the nail and began to work on the lock again. I did this for I do not know how long. But it was no use, a complete waste of time. I went to the back wall of the cage and tried as hard as I could to pull two of the bars apart. But I simply did not have the strength. I could not move them even a fraction of an inch.

I sat down feeling weak with depression. I knew I would have to be careful not to lose control now. I tried to think myself out of it. But slowly it began to creep up on me. I felt like a man beginning to sink. A story my mother used to tell came into my mind. When Cromwell came to Connemara, he chained a priest to a rock on Inishboffin strand – then he and his soldiers drank wine and simply watched while the tide came in, slowly, up the beach, until the priest was drowned. I felt terror now, raw, unadulterated dread. It started to dawn on me as a reality that I might never get out of there again, that even if he did not shoot me, he might simply disappear from the house and leave me in the cage. How long could I last before it would even occur to someone to come and look? What would they find?

I cried. That's all I remember then, weeping with anguish, my hands cradling my chafed face, my skin raw and smarting.

Some time later he came strolling down from the house with a can of beer in his hand. The sun was high, the shadowless garden seemed to be sucking the muggy heat into itself. He was wearing your UCD sweatshirt and had your red scarf tied around his head. He belched as he gazed in at me. He took a banana out of his pocket, peeled it and ate it in a couple of gulps. A small, important thing happened then. I happened to glance away from him and up at the sky. And I sensed irritation from him. A quick frown of annoyance. It faded in a couple of seconds and his expression returned to one of studied nonchalance. But what I had seen told me something. It told me that he wanted my attention. I suppose it gave me a weapon.

I resolved to try not to look at him directly. I half-turned myself so that I could only see him in the corner of my eye.

He took the key of the aviary gate out of his pocket and dangled it.

'Lookat what I've here, Homer.'

He reached it out towards the cage.

'Ask me for it.'

I said nothing. I stared at the ground.

'Go on, serious now, I'm not messin' with yeh. Ask me for it.'

My eyes felt puffy and swollen. 'Give me the key,' I said. 'Please.'

He took a few steps to his left so that he was behind me. Now I could not see him at all. Still I was determined not to turn. He must have stood in complete silence for maybe ten whole minutes until finally I had to swivel back around and look at him. He put his hand to his ear and raised his thick eyebrows in a question.

'What do y'say, Homer? D'y'want this or not?'

'Yes.'

'So ask me for it again. Nicely. That's all y'have to do, man, it's not much.'

'Please can I have the key?'

He stepped up and pushed his fingers in through the gap in the mesh. I could see the russet nicotine stains around his knuckles. He held the key out and dangled it against my cheek. 'Here, take it?' I did not move. He dropped it on the floor, walked slowly backwards, moved his hand behind his back and pulled my hunting knife out of his belt. He stared at it for a minute. He swivelled the blade so that it flashed as it caught the sunlight. Then he licked his finger and ran it along the edge.

'Let yerself out, Homer,' he grinned. 'If you've the bottle.'

'How do you mean?'

'What I say. I'll wait for y'here. You just let yerself out and we'll see what happens then. We'll see what's the fuckin' story then.'

I gazed at the key on the aviary floor.

'There it is. Gwon. Use it, why don't yeh?'

I picked it up and held it. I looked out at him. He snapped his fringe out of his eyes. He raised the knife and drew the blade across the palm of his left hand, without even wincing. Then slowly, methodically, he replaced the knife in his belt. He held up his open hand so that I could see it. The blood was pumping, tracking the lines of his palm, spilling down his wrist. He laughed. He rubbed his hand on the white sweatshirt, leaving startlingly bright red smears. He licked some of the blood from his palm and looked at me.

'Come on out here till we play, Homer.'

I put the key in my pocket and sat down on the aviary floor.

'I'll be waitin' up in the house. Whenever yer ready. Just let yerself out, Homer, whenever the mood strikes. And I'll be waitin'.'

Suddenly he yanked the knife out of his belt again and stabbed it into the trunk of the apple tree. He pulled it out and stabbed it in again with such force that he had to use both his hands and his whole weight to haul it back out.

He winked at me.

'Any time, Homer,' he said. 'Y'know where I'll be.'

Later in the day I think I must have fallen into a deep sleep. Certainly, I remember being awakened by a heavy shower of rain. I was wet, lightning was flickering in the sky. I heard long deep rolls of booming, cracking thunder, punctuating the soft sound of spattering on leaves. Before long my clothes were completely saturated. I took them off and tried to wash myself in the rain. When I had finished I covered myself with the blanket I had given him, which was now reeking and filthy. I examined the thick yellow and black bruises on my legs and arms. My ankle was swollen so badly that I thought it must be broken.

When the rain stopped the sun broke through the clouds. I sat naked in the aviary and allowed the heat to dry me. I think that a few hours must have passed. Next thing I clearly remember is seeing him come out of the house with these long thick canvas bags which he deposited in the middle of the garden, just beside a clump of dead hydrangeas, their crisp, brown, brittle flowers like rotten blasted globes. Then he went back inside, emerging a few moments later with a stack of bamboo poles. He emptied out the bags and placed the poles in a circle on the ground.

It took me some time to realise that he was putting up the wigwam. That's right, love, that old wigwam we got you in London when you were six or eight, somehow he had found it. I asked myself how he could possibly have done that. Even I would not have known where the wigwam was. Clearly he had been searching all over the house. I watched him walk around the laid-out poles, inclining his head and making shapes with his hands and muttering to himself as he began to assemble them. All the time he worked, he ignored me completely, just whistled and sang at the top of his voice.

> *Ah goodbye Mursheen Durcan,*
> *For I'm sick to death of workin'.*
> *No more I'll dig the praties.*
> *I will leave me native home.*
> *Now as sure as me name is Barney*
> *I'll be off to Californee,*
> *Where instead of diggin' praties*
> *I'll be shaggin' Sharon Stone!*

He must have sung it twenty times. And every single time he would get to the last line – he would screech it out in a horrible exaggerated Kerry accent, which he clearly thought was hilarious.

'*I'll be shaggin' Sharon Stone!*'

I did not like the way he hammered in the tent-pegs. The ground was sopping wet by then, there was no need to hit them so hard. I remember thinking, he's trying to get at me, look at him, whomping into them with the lump hammer like he's trying to win some prize at a funfair. Before long he had the poles up in a perfect cone. He went back into the house and got the stepladder from the boxroom so that he could climb up and drop the canvas covering with the dancing Indians and running buffaloes over the apex. He tied the guy-ropes to the pegs. He gave the pegs another good dramatic bashing with the hammer.

When the wigwam was done he stood back and lit a cigarette, every inch the satisfied artist just finished his masterpiece. He peered up and down at it for a while, cackling gleefully every now and again, for absolutely no reason that I could see. I turned away from him and began to put my still damp clothes back on. I heard a wolf-whistle and a slow hand-clap. By the time I had finished dressing he had gone back into the house. I could hear more loud hammering sounds, coming, I thought, from the kitchen. As if to confirm this, the back door suddenly opened and pieces of a wooden kitchen chair were flung out into the garden.

A few minutes later I noticed thick grey smoke coming from the chimney. I knew there was no coal. The fucker was breaking up the furniture and burning it.

I think that I waited for about half an hour and then I went to get the key from my trouser pocket. It was not there. I stood up and searched all my pockets but could not find it. I scanned the floor, but there was no sign of the key. I began to ask myself was I losing my mind. I walked slowly around the perimeter of the cage, my eyes fixed on the grass, wondering if it was somehow possible that I had dropped it outside, even though I knew all the time I walked, my fingers clutching the bars, the small muscles of my eyes straining to focus, that of course this was not possible. I began to look through my trouser pockets again. Just then I heard another shrill wolf-whistle from the house. When I looked up, I saw him standing in the window of your bedroom and waving the key in the air.

'Shouldna gone to sleep, Homer,' he called.

I turned away from him and sat down.

It was the middle of the afternoon. The heat seemed

to be pounding into the garden. The sunlight was bright, it was as though everything was bathed in a gorgeous simmering lacquer, I remember faint steam rising up from the still-damp grass. As time passed the temperature seemed to rise even higher. I climbed up on the perch, grabbed on to the roof bars and tried somehow to fix the blanket into them in order to block out the worst of the sun. But no matter what way I did this, the blanket kept falling down a few minutes later. The effort of climbing back up to try again quickly became too much, and from then on I just had to lie there baking in the dazzle, my forearms covering my eyes, my teeth gritted to block out the pain in my ankle. My stomach pulsated with hunger.

Time passed. Before long my mind began to race into panic again and I tried to stop it, to find something – anything – on which to focus.

Common Irish birds. *Ardea cinerea*, the grey heron. *Sturnus vulgaris*, the starling. *Anas platyrhynchos*, the mallard duck. *Corvus Monedula*, the jackdaw. *Phasianus colchicus*, the pheasant. *Gallinula chloropus*, the moorhen. *Columba palumbus*, the woodpigeon. *Pica Pica*, the magpie. *Accipiter nisus*.

The sparrowhawk.

Perhaps a couple of hours later he came down the garden with a greasy pint glass of water, which he handed in through the bars to me. Maeve, I would love to be able to tell you that I flung it in his sneering face but I did not. I took it and drank it half down in a few swallows.

'I'm after pissin' into that, by the way,' he said.

I glared at him.

'Jazus, look at the face on it. Yeh'd turn milk sour, Homer. Would y'relax, I'm only messin with yeh. I didn't.'

I drank more. He looked up at the sky, wrinkled his nose, shaded his eyes.

'Hot enough to melt snot this weather, isn't it? Got a grand summer in the end.'

I turned away and stared at the back wall.

'D'y'know any jokes, Homer?'

I drank more water.

'What do you call a Northsider in a suit, Homer?'

I finished the glass.

'The defendant,' he said. 'The defendant, Homer.'

It occurred to me then that I might be able to hide the glass in the cage, maybe break it later and somehow use the pieces to hurt him if he came close enough to me.

'And how d'y'know when a Northside mott has an orgasm, Homer?'

I lay down on the floor, still refusing to look at him.

'She drops her chips on the bus-shelter floor, Homer.'

He laughed.

'But you wouldn't know anythin' about Northside motts, would yeh, Homer?'

I heard the flare of a match and the sound of him exhaling a lungful.

'No, funny y'sayin' that actually Homer. Because neither would I, t'tell yeh the God's honest truth.'

I said nothing.

'So anyways, Homer, Paula Yates is at home one day and there's this knock on the door. When she opens it, who's outside, only the drug squad. This big copper says, "Howarya Paula, we're here lookin' for magic mushrooms" And Paula goes, "Well yiz'll have to come back later, lads, cos she's not home from fuckin' school yet."'

I said nothing.

He walked around the aviary and stood looking down at me, all the time softly whistling through his teeth. I noticed his small, precious hands, the fingernails dirty but the wrists peculiarly slender. After a moment he trudged down through the hollow of the stream, shinned up the back wall, peered over for a while. Quickly I slid the glass across the floor towards the piled-up blanket. He dropped into the ditch again and clambered out, sniffing at the air like a dog.

He whipped out the hunting knife and began cutting into the bark of that old ash down by the wall, repeated little stabs, deft scrapes. He picked off a few small bits of the bark, slipped one into his mouth, started to chew, then spat it out. He turned sidelong and began chipping at the tree again, cigarette drooping from his lip. With the end of my foot I gently nudged the glass into the blanket, coughing as deeply as I could to cover the sound. Still hacking into the trunk, he peered over at me.

'Well, this is some fuckin, mess we're in now, isn't it, Homer? Some mess all the same.'

'That isn't my name,' I told him.

'Yeah. This is a mess an' a half, Homer. Yer right there. Absolutely.'

He took a long drag on his cigarette and stared at me. He spat at the ground a few times in quick succession. The way he was spitting, it looked like he was trying to hit one particular blade of grass. He must have done this for a minute or two, a large, snuffling spit every few seconds. Finally the effort seemed to bore him. With his thumb and middle finger he flicked his cigarette end in my direction but it bounced off one of the bars.

'Y'know, it's a pity y'didn't laugh at me jokes, Homer. Because I made up me mind, up in the house there, sure, I'll give auld Homer one chance, I'll go on down and tell the poor auld miserable steamer a few good gags. And if he laughs even once I'll let him out.'

He shrugged. 'But y'didn't laugh, Homer.'

'No, I didn't.'

'That's right, y'didn't. So now I can't let y'out, can I?'

The travellers' car revved again in the distance. He turned towards the wall and cocked his head. Quickly, I managed to toe the glass into the blanket.

'Yes, true enough, yer absolutely correct there, Homer, I can't. And d'y'know what it is? Me heart pumps piss for yeh, Homer, it really does. I swear to God.'

He looked back in my direction and did another deep belch.

'Now chuck me out that glass, Homer, there's a good lad.'

'No,' I said.

The bullfinch, the rook, the black-hooded crow. His voice was calm and measured. 'If y'ever want to see me again, Sweeney, throw that bastardin' glass out here now. And quick.'

Still with my back to him, I tossed it through the bars. A waft of sticky, rich pine-sap scent drifted on the air. I could hear his soft whistle recede as he strolled up the garden. The back door clunked shut. A few minutes later the sound of loud punk rock started blasting from the house.

Corvus corone. The carrion crow.

He left me in there for two days and nights with nothing at all to eat except the birdseed in the trough and only an occasional cup of water. Before long the stomach pangs became unbelievable. I began to imagine that I could actually feel my intestine beginning to tie itself into a knot. Whenever I could not stand the hunger any more, or the thought of birdseed, I reached out through the hole in the mesh, pulled up a few handfuls of grass and dock leaves and ate those. I tried eating dandelions also but they tasted bitter and poisonous.

The attacks of diarrhoea grew terrible and completely unpredictable and by the third day I had soiled myself several times. My thighs and buttocks were so raw that it was becoming difficult to walk. Also, that was the morning I realised that despite my efforts to shade myself my head and arms had been badly burnt by the sun, and the back of my neck was heat-blistered. I remember being absolutely terrified that I would get sunstroke, there in the cage, with hardly anything to drink. I managed to tear a piece out of my shirt to cover my peeling, roasted scalp. I lay down on my front, so weak that I could barely move.

That night I stirred in my sleep and saw your mother sitting on the perch above me. A pink phosphorescent gleam seemed to surround her. She had a gaunt smile on her waxy face and her hands were stretched down in my direction.

On the fourth morning the sun climbed fast, bright and mercilessly hot. By eleven o'clock the sweltering garden seemed almost completely airless, and the stench from where I had gone to the toilet in the corner of the cage was appalling. There were maggots and bluebottles and crawling flies everywhere. My scorched mouth felt as though I had swallowed a cake of salt. My ankle was very bad, the insides of my thighs scalded with pain. When I tried to move I realised that the ache in my back had spread up my spine and into my shoulders.

Around what I thought must have been midday, he came down from the house with two cans of Coke. He was wearing a pair of clean white track pants – yours – and a grubby faded T-shirt which was mine, left over from some promotion we did in work, across the chest a washed-out, discoloured cartoon of a satellite orbiting the earth. He popped open one of the cans and rubbed it against his forehead.

'God now, that's lovely and cold.'

He took a long slug from the can and allowed it to gurgle in the back of his throat before swallowing. 'Straight out of the freezer, it's cold as a well-digger's arse, that is, Homer.'

Another slug, a long gargle and a gasp of pleasure. 'Would y'like one, Homer? Lookat, I've two here.'

I said nothing.

'I'm after bringin' one down for yeh. Would y'not like it, Homer, no?'

'Yes,' I said.

'Well, I'll give it in t'yeh so.'

And then he smiled.

'Gimme out that blanket and I'll give y'in one of these cans. That's fair exchange, isn't it?'

I thought about this for a moment. Then I gathered the blanket into a ball and pushed it out through the hole in the mesh.

He looked down at it, kicked at it. 'Jaze, the state of that.'

He laughed and shook his head. 'But yer some dozy shite; Homer, aren't you?'

'Why's that?'

'Well y'didn't really believe me, did yeh? Y'didn't seriously think I'd give y'in one of these lovely cold cans of Coke did yeh? For that stinkin' thing?'

'I don't know.'

'But why should I, Homer? When y'think?'

'I don't know.'

'That's right. Y'don't. And neither do I.'

He whipped around as though heading back up to the house. But then he turned again, strolled over slowly and handed me in one of the cans, a big toothy smile on his face. I opened it, drank it down as fast as I could. It was so cold that it stung the back of my throat but I did not care. It bubbled up through my nostrils and made me splutter and choke. He reached into his pockets and took out five or six bread rolls. These he threw in to me, one by one, and I caught them, a performing animal in a zoo. He would cheer softly whenever I managed to catch one. I devoured two and started on a third.

'If I was you, I'd keep a few,' he said. 'Y'won't be gettin' any more today.'

I put the rest of the rolls on the aviary floor.

'Give me a cigarette,' I said.

He folded his arms.

'I'm not sure I could do that.'

'Why not?'

'Cigarettes're fierce bad for people, Homer. That's why. It wouldn't be right. It'd be on me conscience.'

'Look, please.'

He sighed, took out a cigarette, sniffed it for a second, pushed it in through the bars to me.

He peered up at the sky. 'God forgimme,' he said.

'Have you a match?' I said.

'Your face and me arse, Homer.'

'Give me a light.'

'I don't have one.'

He pointed at me. 'But I gave y'a cigarette. So just don't say I did nothin' for yeh, Homer. When all this is over, just remember somethin'. When y'were hungry I fed yeh. When y'were thirsty I gave y'a drink. And then a cigarette. So I treated y'better than you fuckin' treated me.'

Falco Tinnunculus. Larus ridibundus. Streptopelia decaocto. Athene noctua.

Curk Coo. Oo-w-oo. Tek Twoo Coo. Kurruk. See-ee. Chack-chack. Whee-ew.

Swee-ney. Swee-ney. Ssssweeeeneeeeeyysss.

Next day – I suppose it must have been early in the morning – I awoke from another hideous nightmare with that same terrible susurration of birdsong still in my ears. Everything around me was shimmering as though bathed in some gruesome light. My head was so heavy that I could not lift it. The edges of my lips felt as though they had been smeared with glue. I was not even sure that I was conscious.

He is holding the bars and staring down at me. For a moment he seems to have black wings. When I blink and put my fingers to my caked eyes he vanishes.

Minutes later he appeared again, on his way down the garden now, carrying a holdall, also an apple and a banana which he handed in to me. I remember looking at the fruits and gently touching them to see if they were real.

I went to put them on the floor of the cage but he told me to eat them now, so I did. He handed me in a litre bottle of mineral water. He watched me eating and drinking. When

I had finished he threw me in a box of matches and a pack of cigarettes, but I felt too sick to be able to smoke.

'Drink more water,' he said.

I held the bottle to my mouth and sucked at it until it was almost empty. Gradually the sibilant sound in my head seemed to subside. I began to see things a little more clearly. And then I remember being suddenly aware of the black holdall as something dangerous, and wondering if he had the shotgun in there.

When I had finished the water he told me to stand and remove my clothes. When I asked him why, he answered that he was going to allow me to wash, which, he pointed out, was again more than I had allowed him. He reached into the bag, produced a bar of soap, clean pyjamas and a couple of towels – these he pushed through the bars, and I remember smelling the soap as though it was some precious flower. He went back up to the rockery, where, I saw then, he had connected the garden hose to the outside tap. He turned on the tap, coiled the hose around himself, waited for the water to come spurting, then dragged it down the garden.

He pushed it through the bars to me, the hose jerking and coiling like a snake in my trembling hands. Then he sprinted back up to the tap and turned it on full blast. I began by spraying the part of the floor where I had had to go to the toilet; next I attempted to clean myself. It was difficult to make the soap lather with the cold water, but still, I tried my best, spraying my scorched and peeling skin, so sunburnt and sore from the diarrhoea that even to twist my torso or raise my legs so that I could wash between them was an agony. All the while I did this he sat in the grass outside the cage, expressionless and munching on a fat red apple.

When I was done he took the hose back from me and wandered up the garden with it, pausing from time to time to spray some of the flowers and shrubs. Then up to the rockery and he turned off the tap. My flesh was far too sore to use the towels on myself, so I folded them over the perch, put on the pyjamas and sat down to smoke one of the cigarettes. I fully expected him to go back into the house at that point, that I would not see him again until the next day. But he turned and came slowly back down for a third time. There was a serious and concentrated expression on his face. He told me that he had made a decision. He picked up the holdall. When he did that I felt a nauseating wash of fear.

'Light yer cigarette,' he said. The first drag made me cough up a mouthful of sticky, dark green phlegm.

'I'm gonna let y'out now, Homer,' he said. 'Straight up and no tricks. But don't try anythin' smart or I'll fuckin' reef you round the gaff, I swear to Christ.'

I asked myself whether this was another of his games. But no, over he came and unlocked the gate. He stepped back. I did not move. For some reason, in my state of half-madness, I still wanted desperately to see what else he had inside the bag.

'Come on, come on. Just get out nice and quiet and I won't touch yeh. Swear to Christ.'

I got to my feet. Skin screaming with pain, I climbed out of the cage and fell face forward on to the grass, fully expecting him to be on me straight away, and – I think now – more than half-expecting that he was going to shoot me in the back right there. I could smell the earth, the loamy, bean-sprout aroma of the hot summer soil. I closed my eyes. I did not want to die. I felt myself start to weep.

'Stop cryin,' he said.

I could not for a while.

'Quit the fuckin' pussin', Homer, I'm tellin' yeh. Or I'll give you somethin' to whinge about.'

I tried to get to my feet but my legs were too weak and sore. He sighed loudly, grabbed the collar of my pyjama shirt and helped me to stand. He brushed a few strands of grass from my chest, went to the holdall and reached into it, pulling out slacks, a couple of T-shirts, some underpants, a pair of runners. These he threw at my feet. Then he jerked his head in the direction of the wigwam.

'You're to sleep in there.'

'What?'

'You're kippin' in the tent, Homer. I'll be up in the house. I'm gonna lock all the doors and the windows. I'll be in the room upstairs at the back, your room. Y'better not come near me. There's a bit of grub in the bag for y'there. Y'can let yourself in and outta the kitchen to get more grub when y'want and roam around the garden. But yer not to come near me. That's fair, isn't it? Y'can't say that's not fair, Homer.'

'Get out of here,' I said. My tongue felt as though I had bitten it again in my sleep.

'No,' he said. 'I'll be up in the house.'

'I'll call the police.'

He smiled. 'No y'won't. Y'won't do that, Homer.'

'Why won't I?'

'Because if y'do, I'll kill y'stone dead. And if I don't, there's others will.'

'But this is ridiculous,' I told him 'You'll have to go. Please.'

'I'm not goin' anywhere, Homer. I'm stayin' here, I told y'already.'

'You're not. I'll call the guards.'

He sighed and moved over close to me. I prepared myself to be struck.

'If you call the guards I'll kill yeh, Homer, I swear to Christ. Or me pals'll do it for me. And if they don't manage it and I don't, d'y'know what they'll do then?'

'What?'

'They'll go down to that hospital, Homer. Where yer girl is. And she'll get paid one little fuckin' visit now that won't be forgot in a hurry.'

He turned and walked towards the house. Half-way up he

stopped and plucked a few drooping dahlias. Then on, up the steps, into the kitchen. The back door closed.

I went into the wigwam and lay down in the shade. The warm air was heavy with the smell of damp canvas and straw. I curled up and fell asleep.

I dreamed that I was in a small church. You and Dominic were getting married. All your college friends were there, the rows of dark mahogany seats were completely full. Your mother was across the aisle from me, dressed from head to toe in black.

Chapter Fifteen

When I woke up again, my head was protruding from the tent and my nose was in the grass. I looked up and the first thing I saw was a line of dark shaggy treetops in the back field, moving gracefully in the pure breeze. The sky was shining like a blue lake. My face and arms were drenched with sweat. I remember actually being surprised to be still alive. I crawled over to the bushes, a scratchy wheezing sound coming from my throat, and went to the toilet.

When I had finished I sat in the shade for a while and asked myself what to do next. Wisps of clouds eased across the sky like ghost ships. I looked at my ankle. It was still very sore and throbbing, but the swelling had started to go down. I waited for some time, absolutely certain that he was watching me from the house and would be down any minute to plague me, now that I was awake. But after almost an hour he still had not appeared. I found myself wondering what would happen if I tried to get away. Cautiously I pulled on the slacks and shoes. I crawled out of the wigwam and went slowly, on all fours, up the garden. There was no sound at all coming from the house. I tiptoed down the driveway, terrified that the gravel would crunch and betray me. The front gates were closed, a length of locked chain wound through the bars. With great difficulty and pain I managed to climb up and over the gates.

My first thought was to hail a car but there were no cars. I began to limp down the hill towards Dalkey. At first it was an agony to walk, but before long I discovered that if I favoured one leg the pain was not quite so bad. At the bottom of the avenue a large hole had been dug into the tarmacadam. A bockety-looking cement mixer and a generator sat on either side of the hole like anxious parents guarding a cradle, but they were switched off and there was no sign of any workmen. On the far side, a yellow diamond-shaped sign had been nailed to a plank and shoved into an old barrel full of bits of old cement blocks. 'Closed for Repairs. No Through Road.'

The village was crammed with people. The summer festival had begun, a brass band was playing a pompous march on a makeshift stage in the church car park, the sweating, red-faced players all dressed in white sailor suits. Stalls selling food, souvenirs and cans of drink lined both sides of Castle Street. Long banners and Irish flags had been draped from the upstairs windows of the shops. An ice-cream van tinkled the melody of '*Frère Jacques*'. A collection of beauty queens in florid bathing suits sat smiling on a float made up like a medieval castle while a man in a tinselly pantomime dress serenaded them through a bull-horn. On the corner by the police station, children in Republic of Ireland football shirts were watching a puppet show and eating plump globes of candyfloss. A Teddy boy strode past me in drainpipes the colour of tangerines. I watched a young woman guard amble out of the station in her shirtsleeves, look up and down the street, wave and make a thumbs-up to someone I could not see before strolling desultorily back in. The puppets barked and whinnied. The children screamed with laughter.

I must have stood in front of the station for twenty minutes just thinking about what he had said to me – how he would kill me if I went to the police. Then I thought of what he had said would happen to you. The image of his face when he said it. She'll get paid one visit that won't be forgot in a hurry.

In the end, I could not go in. I turned around and limped all the way back up the hill to the house. The gates were open when I got there. He was sitting on the back steps and playing with a chessboard, an opened can of lager by his small, naked feet. He did not even look up at me.

'Good auld stroll, Homer?'

I said nothing.

'Yeah, it's nice to have a dander around in this nice weather, all right.' He slid a piece across the board and scowled. 'But I hope yer after bringin' me back a present, Homer.'

'I want to talk to you,' I said.

'Mutual, Homer.'

'Look, you'll really have to go. I can't allow this. This is my home. We'll have to work something out, I can't have you here like this.'

'What's that shack down there?' he said, nodding at the stable block.

'It's a stable.'

'Oh, right. And d'y've a horse, Homer?'

'No, I don't. Look, I was saying . . .'

'So why d'y've a stable?'

'The people who lived here before had horses. If it's any of your business.'

'I'd an auld horse once,' he said. 'Bought him in Smithfield market. Big stupid-lookin' black and white thing, he was. Awful lookin' ibex. Thick as a brick. Kept him in a dump down on the docks.'

'Listen, we were talking about you going,'

'D'y'like ridin', Homer? I'd say y'do. I'd say y'do, all right. I'd say y've a horn on yeh like a rhino, Homer, do yeh? When y'wake up in the mornings? I'd say yer a great ride altogether.'

'I'm saying you'll have to go.'

'D'want to see me when I wake up in the mornin', Homer. Hard as a knacker's boot I am. It'd scare the shite outta yeh.'

He stood up and opened his fly. 'Want t'see?'

'No.'

He zipped himself and sat back down to the chessboard. He peered scrupulously at it as he moved the pieces around, although after a short while I noticed that he was only moving the white ones.

'Now,' he said. 'What were we talkin' about?'

'You leaving.'

He nodded. 'Oh yeah. The stable, Homer, that's right. I remember now, yeah.'

'You'll have to go.'

He slid the white queen across the squares and flicked a bishop off the board. 'The thing is, Homer, I'm after makin' a place for meself down there. While y'were out strollin'.'

'What do you mean?'

'I'm after cleanin' it out a bit. See, I got to thinkin' about it and I don't want to be in your way up in the house. Fair's fair like. So I'll be grand down there. I'm after findin' a bit of a camp-bed up above and I brung that down for meself, and a few sheets and blankets.'

I noticed now that there were chairs and a coffee-table under the apple tree, along with a few cushions and the beanbag out of your room.

'What the fuck do you think you're playing at, Quinn?'

He laughed. 'Chess, Homer.'

A scabrous-looking blackbird scampered across the grass, darting its head at the ground.

'Look, you'll really have to get out of here. I don't want you here.'

'Yeah. And look, I'm after borrowin' a few of yer things and some food I found in the fridge. And I took a bottle of wine from under the sink. And a few auld magazines. I hope that's OK. Is that OK, Homer, yeah?'

'This is my house. Get out of it.'

'Thanks. And I took a few of yer shirts and knickers by the way. But when I split I'll send y'the dough for them, don't worry, Homer. And I'm after havin' a bath because

I was stinkin'. I managed to turn yer water back on in the bathroom by the way, yer stopcock was banjaxed. Always feel better after a scrub meself, Homer, do you? On them hot sticky days?'

'You get out of here now,' I said, 'before you regret it.'

'Yer a decent skin, Homer,' he said 'Anyone ever tell y'that, no?' He jumped up, grabbed the beer can – 'if there was more like you in the world, things'd be only fuckin' mighty' – and sauntered down the garden, into the stable.

I stood still, I suppose wondering what to do. He emerged after a few moments and peered around himself at the ground, irritatedly toeing the grass as though he was looking for something he had lost. Suddenly he saw it. He leaned down and picked up Sheehan's shotgun. He rubbed the barrel carefully with his sleeve and pointed it at the sky.

'Bang,' he roared.

Birds scattered out of the trees.

He turned around and pointed the gun at me. 'Bang, Homer,' he called. 'I like a good bang of a summer's evenin'. Do you?'

He went back into the stable and closed the door. I heard the thunk of bolts being drawn.

The following morning I woke up in my bed, but still thinking for a moment that I was in the cage. It took me a while to calm down. I turned over on my side and tried to go back to sleep but could not. The room was sweltering and airless. From somewhere in the distance I could hear the insistent drone of a lawnmower floating on the breeze. When I got up and opened the window the garden smelled of roses and phlox. Wasps were buzzing crazily around the flower-beds. Far off in the back field I could see the traveller women hanging laundry on lines strung between the caravans, a scrawny boy feeding a donkey, the bronzed men beefy and hot-looking as they lumbered around in suit trousers and string vests, kicking a football to each other.

I envied them.

I put on some clothes and went out to the landing. The floor was strewn with bits of broken wood from where he had burst down the door of your bedroom. Your dressing table looked as though it had vomited its contents. I noticed that the poster of James Joyce on the wall beside the window had a long, jagged tear all the way down the middle, also, that Dominic's guitar had been smashed in two and was lying on the floor in a crumpled tangle of strings. I went down to the ruined kitchen and made coffee. I sat at the table for a while trying to rehearse what I was going to say. There was a pack of cigarettes beside the sink and I smoked a few. For some reason, I could not stop thinking about the travellers. Something I had once read came into my mind, about how the travelling people are the true descendants of the Milesians, the ancient Irish who settled the land long centuries ago, only to be dispossessed during the oh-so-famous fucking Famine. I thought about the sleety winter morning one of them had come to the door selling heather – a middle-aged woman with dark, wrinkled, nutty skin and haughty Iberian eyes. She had been so cold that she was shivering in her tartan blanket. I had asked her if she wanted a hot drink but she said no. I told her that I had no use for heather but I would give her some money anyway. She shook her head very firmly. She could not take money for nothing, it was bad luck, but she would tell my palm if I wanted. I held out my hand.

'You're a travellin' man yourself, love,' she winced, her teeth set against the chill. 'I see fierce roads.'

I laughed and told her I was a salesman.

'There you are so,' she said. She held my hand lightly and nodded as she traced along it with her thumb. 'God will bless you on the roads if you ask His protection. An angel in heaven is waitin' to go before y'in the sky. No harm can be done you – the divine protection is there but must be asked for.' When I gave her the few pounds I had in my pocket she kissed her index finger three times and touched the frame of the door with it. 'May the devil never enter this house.'

I had watched her pad down the frosty driveway, clutching the rug hard around herself as the wet snow began to fall. This blazing summer morning four months ago I found myself wondering where she was now.

When I had finished the coffee I stuck my head under the cold tap for a minute, took a few deep breaths and headed out to the garden.

In front of the stable he was sitting on a deck-chair and reading a magazine. He had on my prescription sunglasses and a blue and white striped rugby shirt which I had seen both Dominic and yourself wear. Now the sleeves had been ripped from it. There was a beer glass half-full of red wine on the grass, beside a plate on which were the remains of a sandwich, a pear, a few plum stones. He let me just stand there for a while before finally he looked up at me.

'Mornin', JimBob,' he said.

'Listen, you'll have to leave,' I told him. 'I don't know what you're trying to prove, but you've proved it, all right? So go.'

He picked up the pear and bit into it, wiping the juice from his chin.

'I slept very well, thanks,' he gurgled. 'And yerself?'

'Will you go now?' I said.

He shrugged. 'You wanted me, Homer. Now y'have me.'

'Well, I want you to go now.'

'I didn't ask to be brung here.'

'Well, I didn't know you'd dig in like a tick.'

'Funny,' he said. 'Funny, Homer.' He flipped a page of the magazine.

'Will you go now?'

He held up the magazine so I could see the centre pages. A photograph of a gorgeous young black woman, sashaying along a tropical beach in a brief red bikini.

'Isn't she one beaut, Homer?' he said.

'Will you go now?'

He closed the magazine and shook his head. 'You're really startin' to fuckin' bore me, Homer. And y'know what happens me when I get bored?'

'What?'

Suddenly he's on his feet and clutching my arms so tight that I'm sore. His mouth is open wide. 'I GO FUCKIN' CRAZY HOMER,' he screams. 'FUCKIN CRAZY.' I get the warm sweet smell of wine on his breath. He shoves me hard away from him. I trip, fall backwards against the apple tree. He picks up the beer glass, rushes over and holds it in front of my eyes, brandishing it. Wine slops against my face. His eyes narrow to tiny slits.

'Leave me alone, Sweeney, I'm fuckin' warnin' yeh. Don't keep on tryin' to spoil everythin'. Or I swear to Jesus yeh'll be sorry.'

Round about tea-time I went down to him again. From inside the stable I could hear the crackle of the radio, an overexcited reporter commentating on a world cup match, the blare of horns, the swell of the cheering crowd in the stadium. I tried the door but it would not open. I kicked it hard a few times. The radio was turned down. The door opened and he peered out at me. His chin and cheeks were plastered with shaving foam and he had a disposable razor in his hand. I noticed that for some reason his fingers were heavily bandaged.

'Homer,' he said. 'What's up with yeh now?'

'I think it's only fair to tell you. I'm giving you ten minutes to get off my property and then I'm calling the guards.'

'Is that right?'

'That's right.'

He nodded. 'Well, I'll tell yeh what, Homer. I'll make yeh one promise. If y'call the pigs up t'me, by Christ it'll be the last thing y'ever do in yer life. Now go call them if you're callin' them. And I'll be in here waitin' when they arrive, OK?'

He slammed the door closed. I heard the radio again. The volume went up louder than before, so that the voice was distorted and the roar of the crowd seemed much nearer.

At half-past nine that night the radio was still on.

When I looked out the kitchen window, I saw that he had lit a fire under the apple tree. He seemed to be cooking something in a frying pan. He glanced up and saw me watching him. He stuck a fork into the pan and pulled out a slimy, fat sausage. He waved the sausage in the air and laughed.

At this stage I decided I had to get out for a walk.

I got into the car and drove down to Dun Laoghaire. There was nowhere to park on the sea front. I put it into the underground at the shopping mall and walked back down Marine Road to the pier.

The new night ferry had just left for Holyhead. It is a huge thing, the size of a football pitch, or so the radio advertisements have been saying. I watched it pull slowly away from the quay. It surged into the middle of the harbour, then did a three-point turn, sending six-foot washes breaking against the pier walls. It headed out past the lighthouse, churning up thick white waves behind it.

I started to walk the pier. It was very crowded that night, as it always is on a hot evening in summer. I remember young kids zooming around on roller-blades and skateboards, doing wheelies on their mountain bikes. Sweaty teenagers in leather. A ceilidh band playing jigs and reels on the old bandstand, girls dancing in tartan kilts and sashes, one with a head shaved smooth as an egg. All around in a semicircle old people in striped deck-chairs, clapping or lilting along with the music. Business types with jackets slung over their shoulders. Down past the lifeboat memorial, a trio of policemen awkwardly kicking around a football with some laughing Spanish girls, goalposts marked out with navy caps on the flagstones. The water so clear and bluey green. A line of teenage boys fishing for mackerel. I was sitting on the bench down at the end and looking out at the ferry, far off in the distance now, when I noticed a plump sleek seal break through the surface of a rolling wave, its broad large-eyed head bobbing back and forth in the fizzling foam. It had a silver fish in its mouth. The fish was wriggling hard and trying to escape but the seal had its jaws clamped shut.

For a few short seconds I felt something inside me relax. I closed my eyes and breathed in deep. The air smelt of salt and paraffin. I remember the sound of the ropes clanking on the yachts' masts. I love it down there on a summer's evening. I sometimes think that I could stay there for ever.

I was walking back up towards the town when suddenly I saw Dominic coming towards me, linking arms with a tall, slim girl who had short cropped hair dyed peroxide white. She was wearing a black leather miniskirt, a black bikini top and tartan tights and seemed to be talking quickly, her hand chopping her palm, her fingers counting off points. Dominic was listening so intently to her that he did not see me until I was right in front of them.

'Mr Sweeney,' he said, wide-eyed.

'Dominic, how's tricks?'

He was blushing now. 'Oh, not too bad, thanks. And you?'

'Grand, Dominic. Grand.'

'This is amazing. What a coincidence.'

'Isn't it? I had a dream about you, Dominic, the other night actually.'

'Really?'

'Yes.'

He looked at me as if he was expecting me to tell him all about it. When it became clear that I was not going to, he licked his lips a bit and stared at me.

'So all's good with you, Mr Sweeney, is it?'

'Yes, Dominic, never better. Results out yet?'

He shook his head. 'Any day,' he said. 'Fingies crossed.'

'*Fingies*?' I said. The girl laughed. He blushed even deeper. 'I mean fingers, sorry.'

Then he peered at me again. 'Are you sure you *are* all right? Because you don't actually look the best, Mr Sweeney. Speaking as a medical student, I mean.'

'I'm grand,' I told him.

'You look a bit strained or something, I don't know. A bit stressed out. You've lost some weight. And are those bruises on your face?'

I touched my cheek. 'Oh, I gave myself a bang in the head at home, that's all, Dominic. Walked slap into the freezer door like a fool. I meant to get a bit of steak to cure that shiner I have.'

I looked at the girl.

'Oh, this is Sinéad Caffrey,' he said. 'A friend from college. Sinéad, this is Maeve's dad.'

'Maeve?'

'Yes. Maeve Sweeney. You know, that I told you about?'

The girl seemed embarrassed as she shook my hand.

On the drive home I thought a bit about Dominic. He looked so shamefaced, poor kid, when I saw him with that girl. As if I had caught him committing adultery. I found myself thinking about what he had said to me early one morning in the hospital at the beginning of the summer, the two of us standing together beside your bed in awkward reverence.

There's always hope, Mr Sweeney.

Was that true then? Is it true now?

As I turned into the driveway a strange thing happened. I should explain that I had opened the car windows and sun-roof all the way because it was so hot that night – and I thought I could hear music coming from somewhere near. This disturbed me. You know that driveway, so completely silent and still as you move through the tunnel of overgrown trees. I told myself that I must be imagining things and drove on. But half-way up I realised that it was not my imagination. There was loud raucous Irish music blasting from the house.

I parked, got out of the car, took my briefcase from the boot, opened the hall door and went in. The music was so loud now that the old mirror on the wall was rattling. It was coming from the living-room. Slowly I opened the door. Quinn was in there with his back to me. The carpet had been rolled up. The television was on but the sound could not be heard over the roar of the stereo. All the furniture had been pushed into one corner. And he was dancing.

Arms straight down by his side. He skipped and jigged, lurched from side to side, clacking his feet against the floorboards. He clamped his hands to his hips and shimmied forward, as far as the wall, and then back to where he had started. He stamped and kicked to the caterwaul and clatter. And every now and then he let a great piercing whoop, like a rebel yell or an operatic scream. He wheeled around towards the door and saw me. He staggered backwards into the sofa.

He rushed to the stereo and switched it off. His face and the top of his neck were purple.

'Sorry,' he said. 'I was only dancin'. I was bored.'

I turned off the television and plugged it out.

'I did it in school,' he said. 'The ma made me do it. I was the only lad in the whole class did Irish dancin'. Had t'wear a kilt and all.' Here he let a soft chuckle. 'Sometimes I think that's what happened me, Homer.'

I remember that there was an extraordinary sunset that night. When I went to close the curtains, the light was fading down to ochre and deep orange. What can I tell you about it? Streaks of variegated green and rich purple were spread out in the sky, and the sun was a brilliant white disc on a field of mottled pinks. I looked at the sky for a moment or two – I couldn't recall a more beautiful sunset – before deciding to leave the curtains open. I switched on the wall lamps, went to the table and opened my briefcase. I could smell fresh, ripe sweat in the room.

'Jaze,' he said. 'I'm fuckin' scarlet now.'

'I thought we agreed,' I said. 'You stay out there in the stable and I stay in here. I thought we agreed that. If you have to be here at all.'

He sat on the sofa, crossed his legs and lit a cigarette.

'Sorry, Homer,' he said. 'I was bored outta me tits.'

I started getting my order forms and brochures ready.

'What's that yer doin'?'

'I'm going back to work in the morning,' I said. 'I've paperwork to do here.'

'Paperwork?'

'That's right.'

He looked closely at me and nodded understandingly, as though I had just let him in on some grave secret. The last of the dusk light faded in the bay window. He muttered the word 'paperwork' a few more times. He seemed to enjoy saying it. Stars appeared in the lower sky. He sat there for a while and smoked another cigarette. Then he brushed the ash from his knees, stood up and ostentatiously yawned. 'Well, I suppose I'll head on out,' he said. 'Goodnight so. I'll leave y'to do that paperwork.'

'Round the house and mind the dresser,' I told him.

Next morning, when I arrived into work, Hopper gaped up from his desk as though I had entered the room naked except for a crash-helmet and tutu. I admit that I had of course expected some reaction to the bruising and the grazes; and as if things were not bad enough, while shaving that morning my hands had been trembling and I had sliced open my lip and lower face, so that buds of toilet paper were attached to my cheeks and chin and I must have looked like something from the worst days of the Spanish Inquisition. But Hopper seemed absolutely horrified as I did my best to stroll casually in and get to the desk without him seeing me head on. He asked me was I all right. I told him I was absolutely fine. He asked me was I sure. I said yes. He wanted to know what had happened to me. I told him it was a long, complicated story. He nodded towards O'Keeffe's room.

'Someone to see you, Billy.'

'In there?'

'Yeah. Fuck-head's gone out. I showed your visitor into his lair. He said it was personal.'

A wave of shock rippled through my stomach as I opened the door. Inside the office, Superintendent Duignan was standing at the window and staring down at the street with one finger on the venetian blinds.

'Duignan,' I said. 'Something up?'

He turned. I saw him clocking my face. 'Not at all,' he smiled. 'Just passing. Thought I'd look in on you.'

I came in and closed the door. He sat down on the edge of the desk, offered me a cigarette, lit one himself. He smiled like a man who had learned to smile from a textbook. 'You look like you're after been in the wars there, Mr Sweeney.'

'I hopped my head off a door at home. And then cut myself shaving.'

He clicked his tongue and nodded. 'So tellus, how was your trip to Lourdes?'

'Oh, I didn't make it in the end. Came down with some bug.'

He glanced around the room as though looking for an ashtray. 'God, I don't believe you. After it was booked and everything?' He tapped his ash into his cupped palm.

'Yes.'

He clicked his tongue again. 'That's unfortunate, isn't it?'

'Yes,' it is.'

'You look a bit under the weather all right, now you mention it.'

'Yes. I haven't been the best.'

He pulled a wincing face. 'Well, I'd a touch of that bad auld thing myself there recently. Sweats and shakes. Nasty.

Touch of the runs.' The dead smile appeared again. 'After a few days I could have shat through the eye of a needle, if you pardon me.'

'Me too.'

'And the doctors are an awful waste of time and money, aren't they? Mine keeps telling me I'm to give up work and go live in the country.'

'That'd be good right enough.'

'The country,' he scoffed. 'Sure that'd finish me off for good, Mr Sweeney. I'm a city boy. Like yourself. Pure Liffey water flowing in the veins.'

A mobile phone rang in his jacket pocket. Without taking his eyes off me for even a moment, he took it out and switched it off. I felt my heart thud.

'And you've no news for me yourself, Mr Sweeney?'

'No. No news.'

'You sure?'

'Well, no.'

'Funny. I heard you did have a bit of news.'

'Well, I don't.'

He took a long drag on his cigarette and started blowing smoke-rings through the air. His jaw made a soft cracking sound as he did this. 'Come on now, Mr Sweeney. Are you not going to confess?'

'To what?'

He tapped the side of his nose. 'Just I heard you were keeping certain company these days. That correct?'

'How do you mean?'

'A little bird told me there was someone new in your life. A love interest.'

'Oh that. Well. I've met someone, yes.'

'Congrats,' he said. 'That's what I heard. Anyone I'd know?'

'I don't think so, no.'

'Ah well. That's great for you anyway. But sure, don't look so nervous about it.'

He went back to the window and stared down again into the street, craning his neck this time. 'And of course our mutual friend hasn't been seen around for a few weeks now. But sure you knew that already I think.'

I was not sure whether this was a statement or a question. I felt the muscles in my throat tighten.

'No, I didn't actually.'

He cocked his head. 'You haven't heard from him at all?'

'From Quinn? No. Why would I hear from him?'

He turned and stared at me. His face creased into a laugh.

'Oh no, I didn't mean Quinn. I meant Father Seán. I heard he was out of town.'

'You meant Seán?'

He nodded. 'Who else? That's gas you thinking I meant Quinn, isn't it? That's a good one now.' Yet again he turned to the window and peered out, chuckling gently to himself. 'No, no, Father asked me a while back if I'd drop down to the school and have a chat with the youngsters about drugs or some damn thing. But sure then when I phoned him about it, hadn't he bolted off to Lourdes. I was relieved, between you and me and the wall. I wouldn't be much use at public speaking.' He hummed a few notes of a tune that I half-recognised. 'You'd be good at that, I'd say.'

I tried to laugh. 'I don't know.'

'I'd say you would. You seem very good with words. Very *au fait*. Your training of course.'

'My training?'

'Well, your line of work I mean. I'd love to have that' – he paused and rubbed his middle finger against his thumb – 'I don't know, that confidence you have. I'd say now, you could sell snow to the eskimos, Mr Sweeney.'

He nodded a few times, his eyes still on the street.

'My problem is I get confused,' he shrugged. 'Sometimes I don't say exactly what I intend to say, you know?

But then I suppose even you must get confused sometimes.'

'I'm sure I do. Though a good salesman tries to keep a
clear mind.'

'Of course he does. Like a good policeman. But still, it's
gas you getting confused when I said our friend hadn't
been seen around for a few weeks. When I put it like that,
I mean.'

'Well, it's as you said. Seánie went off to Lourdes a few
weeks ago.'

'Yes. But the bould Quinn didn't go missing a few weeks
ago though, did he, Mr Sweeney? He went missing last
October, isn't that right? That's why I was surprised.'

Suddenly I began to have the definite sensation that he
was watching my reflection in the window. I felt his eyes
on me. My palms moistened. I plucked one of the knobs of
toilet paper from my chin and threw it into the bin. 'Well,
I don't know what I was thinking. I got mixed up.'

He sniffed and rubbed his nostrils. 'You see, I was right.
Even you get confused. Ah well, that could happen to a
bishop, I suppose. Or a young pope on his holidays, as
they say.'

'Superintendent Duignan,' I said. 'Do you mind me
asking why you're looking out that window?'

He turned to me and smiled again. 'Can you keep a secret,
Mr Sweeney?'

'I don't know. It depends.'

'I'd say you can. I'd say you're very discreet. Are you?'

'What should I be discreet about?'

He said nothing for a moment, just regarded me closely
with a sad, baggy expression. 'Well, y'see, I'm a fugitive
from justice, Mr Sweeney.'

His eyebrows went up and down. He reached into his
breast pocket, pulled out his car keys and dangled them.

'Double yellows,' he said. 'I'm illegally parked.'

After he had gone, and I had spent ten minutes calming

down in the bathroom, Hopper and Liam gleefully showed me the mountain of paperwork in my mail tray, also the exciting new screen saver which Hopper had put on my computer without my asking – a slightly nauseating illusion of moving at high speed through a cluster of stars. I did not like it much, but I sat down to the desk and managed to get through a surprising amount of work before O'Keeffe swanned in like the Prince of Darkness around half-past eleven and announced that it was good to have me back. I could not believe the new groovy hairstyle. For one awful moment I was certain he was wearing some kind of Afro wig. He took a long look at my face.

'So this new mott of yours is into a bit of S and M, Billy, is she?'

'You've a great sense of humour, Hugh,' I said. 'Anyone ever tell you that?'

'No,' he said.

'And so does your fuckin' hairdresser,' added Hopper, under his breath.

I spent the rest of the day doing the shops in town and taking orders. I sold well enough – we were doing special prices for the pre-Christmas buy-in – but the afternoon passed very slowly. I could not stop thinking about Duignan's visit to the office. What did it mean? What did he know? Around lunchtime, I went into Stephen's Green and sat for a while by the fountain. The fresh air helped me to think more clearly, my fear quickly faded. From then on, for the rest of the afternoon, whenever anyone in a shop asked how I had been lately, I kept getting this strange and strong compulsion to own up to exactly what had been going on. It occurred to me just how exquisitely pleasurable it would have been to see their amazed expressions, their startled, disbelieving gawps. No doubt they would all think that I was joking. But I did not tell them, of course, I just nodded like a fool and said everything was fine and couldn't be better and how's tricks with yourself. Like I could care.

314

I got home around six and found him in the living-room again. He had his feet up on the coffee-table and was watching some sitcom, a squat pyramid of empty beer cans on the floor beside him. The ashtray was so full of butts it looked like some terrible spiny creature from under the sea. He did not even raise his head when I came in.

'My husband mean?' exclaimed the middle-aged woman on the screen. 'He made me breastfeed the kids to save money.'

Quinn chortled lazily through his teeth.

'Make us a cup of tea there, Homer,' he said.

'What?'

'You heard me, Homer. Make us a cup of fuckin' tea.'

I put down my briefcase and looked at him. 'You could at least use the little word, couldn't you?'

'The little word?'

'Yes, Quinn. The little word.'

'Oh right. Make us a cup of tea, Homer. Now.'

I was not at all sure just how much longer this could go on.

Chapter Sixteen

In the middle of August, Lizzie, Franklin and the twins
arrived from Australia, but the way things worked out,
apart from one or two quick lunches in town, I think a
day out at the zoo, we did not spend much time together.
For a while they stayed with their friends down in Wicklow,
and then they were busy, finding a place to live in Dublin,
arranging schools, looking for work. Whenever I did see
Lizzie she would have pocketfuls of notes and scrawled
reminders, immigration forms, passport applications. She
got one or two portrait commissions. Franklin quickly found
a part-time job writing computer programmes while he
searched around for a band to join. There was one tense
enough moment, when Conal and Erin asked if they could
come out to the house some day soon. I told them yes, in
a little while. This worried me greatly for a short time, but
then, on reflection, I knew that Lizzie would not really want
to visit the house; she had not been there for several years
before she left for Australia; the night before going she had
got drunk and told me she hoped never to see it again, it held
nothing but painful memories for her. They rented one of
those new small apartments in the tax-incentive zone on the
south quays, with a good view of the river and the roofscape
of the north city. In small ways it was made clear that they
had a life which did not include me. I left them to it. I was
happy enough to stay at home.

Now that he was here and haunting the place I found that
I was spending most of my spare time in this room. I mean
the small room downstairs at the front, looking out on to the

drive, where we used to have the piano and the sideboard when you were kids. He did not come in here much, he seemed to prefer the living-room, I suppose because that had the television and the video machine. When the builders left last year I did not bother moving anything much back into the small room: I have scarcely anything but books in here now, also a stack of reclaimed oak planks the builders did not use, a box of leftover floorboards intended for the stairs, a few sacks of cement, a roll of fibreglass insulation. Sometimes it feels like living inside the ark.

I have always liked this room, love, although God knows it has seen a few things. It has a history. The day we moved into the house the old rector told me that it had been his meditation room, though little enough meditation ever got done in here by your mother or me. There on the ceiling you can still see the stains from thrown cups of coffee and glasses of beer. The window-sill is chipped from the time she flung a half-full bottle of gin at me. There are even a few drops of blood on the carpet over by the fireplace. A person with an eye for a story could learn a lot from looking around this room.

This is the room your mother and I were in when she finally told me she was leaving, and for good this time. The sun was shining hard through the blinds that afternoon. Your mother was wearing a smartly cut black dress that made her look very slim, and she had around her slender neck a small silver crucifix which I had bought for her on our first trip to Spain. When she moved as she spoke the sunlight seemed to catch the cross, or perhaps the chain, and it sent spangles of whiteness dancing across her breasts and face. And because of the glow of the sun behind her, there was a filigree-thin line of golden light all around her body, like a distended halo, or a mysterious force field in a science-fiction film. It was the strangest thing. Her dark eyes were shining also and her lips moved with ease as she told me in a calm and measured voice that she did not love me any more and that when she thought about it she was not completely sure if she had ever loved me. Certainly, she did not now. She had no feelings at all for me now. Our marriage was over.

She looked magnificent as she told me all this. I do not think I had never seen her so alive, so sure or self-possessed. There was an elegance about the way she spoke and moved; I kept thinking how appropriate her name was. It was over between us, she told me; she would not live like this any more. She actually offered me a cigarette.

I could hardly hold my fingers steady as I took it. I felt so scared by what she was saying that the feeling was almost pleasurable; so this is what happens, I found myself thinking. This is what happens when you finally drive away the person you love, this is what loss feels like. We were here now, we had arrived, as I suppose we must have known for a long time we would. It was not as actors often perform it. This was no punch in the lungs, no sudden inner scream. It came in rivulets or gentle cascades, this sensation, and as I smoked the cigarette I tried to let the feeling come to some kind of conclusion, but every time it did seem to bubble to an end, there was something else behind it.

'Don't leave me, Grace,' I said to her, brilliantly, and I think I took her hand. She gazed up at the ceiling as though she was expecting to read something written there.

'I swear we'll work things out, Grace. Just give me one more chance. Please.'

But she had already made up her mind. I could not believe it. I mean this literally, by the way. I could not – or did not – believe what she was saying to me. I thought that any minute she would change her mind and I would persuade her to stay, as I had succeeded in doing so many times before. I am a salesman, I remember thinking, even as she was carefully explaining the fact that she had at last decided to go. I am a salesman. I should be able to sell this.

But then she was suddenly talking about arrangements,

what would happen about the cars, what she had in mind about money for you and Lizzie, having an agreement drawn up for a legal separation. She had been to a solicitor in town; he had recommended a number of barristers. She had found a flat in Dun Laoghaire and intended to move in when the tenants left in a month. She would need me to help with the deposit. She wanted nothing from the house, she told me, nothing at all. In the meantime she would be at her father's. She would need some money for Lizzie and you immediately. I could send it on to Harrington Street, or she would ask her father to drive out and collect it some night. I felt the anger boil up inside me until I puked it out.

'Yes, I suppose you think I'm paying for Lizzie, do you? You'd like that all right. You must think I'm some prize eejit, Grace.'

'Thanks, Billy,' she said. 'If I had any last doubts, you just took them away.'

She walked out and closed the door. I heard her going up the stairs and then coming back down with you two, who were laughing lightly as I recall, as she led you outside. I do not know whether you realised what was happening. I was expecting the front door to slam closed, but it did not. I kept waiting for that thunderous slam, the sound which more than any other had punctuated our marriage, but it never came. I heard her car start up and then the noise of the tyres on the gravel.

The clock ticked on the wall. The pipes under the floor made that soft coughing sound as the central heating sputtered on. A few minutes later I went into the hall. The front door was open wide. The wind had whipped up; dry leaves and dust were blowing through the air. There was a black ragged dog I had never seen before in the driveway, lying on its side and wagging its tail. Three rooks were singing on the bird table. And Grace and you two were gone.

I closed the front door and came back into this room. I suppose that I thought she would be back before too long. I imagined her in the car – for some reason I had a sharp mental flash of her hands on the wheel – and I remember now, all this time later, that in my mind I saw the car as though from very far above, in miniature, moving further and further away from me across a crested and hilly landscape. I put on a record and then another. I thought about how I would behave when she got back. I began to plan out all the cutting things I would say.

A good salesman always plans out the things he will say. He can rarely afford the risk of spontaneity.

After a while I switched on the television. It must have been a Friday night, because *The Late Late Show* was on. I recall Gay Byrne moving around the studio with a hand-held microphone and a basket of giant jigsaw pieces, everybody laughing, the cameras gliding like graceful ships across the glossy-looking white floor, a soldier singing a romantic song to a blushing woman in the audience. When it was over I kept watching, until all the programmes had ended and the national anthem had been played and there was nothing on the screen except a grey matrix of lines and dots and no sound but for a high sibilant hiss which reminded me of the sea. Still I waited for her.

At three in the morning I went to the front door and opened it. The dog was still there in the driveway. I could hear bells tolling in the old church up the avenue.

I came back in here and put on another record. I did not come out again for the rest of the night.

By dawn it was clear that she was not coming back, so I locked the door, turned off the lights and went upstairs to bed.

One night near the end of August it rained heavily and I heard him slip in through the back door at about one in the morning, cursing and staggering into the furniture. He spent some time down in the kitchen – I heard the scrape of a chair on the tiles and then the sound of the taps running in the sink – then he came up the stairs and went down the landing into Lizzie's room. I do not think he left it at all for a couple of days. Before long he had abandoned the stable completely. He never even discussed it with me, just moved right into Lizzie's room, down the corridor from my own, bold as you like.

During the days he seemed to sleep for hours. One afternoon I had to come home from work to collect a file and his door was locked. I could hear him snoring inside, a soft light snore like a child's. He seemed to have the bloody radio on again, I could hear it playing in the room. He loved that radio.

Often I would hear him walking around downstairs in the middle of the night. He seemed to watch the television for hours on end, the rock video channels or the late films, quiz programmes, old sitcoms, American cop shows, any kind of junk the satellite dish could suck down from space, he did not seem too fussy. What drove me half-crazy was not just the noise but the way he insisted on continually flicking around from one channel to another. Some nights it was almost impossible to sleep, with the noise coming up through the floorboards.

Other times, when the television was off, I would hear him opening the fridge door or turning on the heat, looking in the cupboards or pulling out drawers. Often he would whistle or sing as he stalked the house like a ghost. It was usually close to dawn by the time he would come up the stairs and go to bed. I would hear his footsteps on the loose boards, he'd come padding down the landing, sometimes he would stop for a moment outside my room, before continuing down the passage and into his own. He would close the door and lock it. Sometimes he would jam a door against it. He would always – always – turn on the radio.

One evening around that time I arrived home hungry at about six and went straight to the kitchen. I noticed with some surprise that he had tidied the place up a bit. The dishes had been washed and put away, the Aga had been scraped clean, the tiles around it polished. For the first time in some years I could actually read the words on that little plaque on the wall behind the Aga, Man does not live by bread alone. He had draped an old tablecloth over that pile of concrete blocks the builders had left beside the sink. The floor tiles were gleaming and the windows were clean.

I prepared some food and came in here to eat it. Then I saw that he had clearly been in here also: the wooden planks had been stacked up in a neat pile by the wall, the bags of cement and plaster heaped into a corner, the carpet thoroughly hoovered.

After I had eaten, I sat at this table and began to write. I wrote for several hours, the very first of these pages for you. I listened to records while I tried to think of what to put down. I remember Bessie Smith and Beethoven.

On my way up to bed that night I went into the living-room to look for an old order book that I needed. He was sitting on the floor with the lights off, looking at the television, and he was barefoot. The cool blue light of the screen played across his face. He was drinking a can of beer and eating a plate of sausages. He sucked down the drink, his eyes on the screen, an American documentary programme about the background to the O. J. Simpson case. I could see by his movements that he was quite drunk.

'You should stop drinking so much,' I said.

He laughed without looking up at me. 'What the fuck would you know about it?'

'I'd know a lot about it, son. I'm an alcoholic. A drunk.'

He shrugged and kept staring at the television. 'Drink a little wine for the sake of thy stomach. Saint Paul said that, Homer.'

'So?'

'So we all get scuttered sometimes.'

'Well, I scuttered myself into the ground, son. I was a great lad altogether, just like you. A mad bastard. I went down to the floorboards and then I crawled in under them. I'd a wife and two kids until I pissed it all away.'

'Big deal, Homer. Now shut up, I'm watchin' this.'

His tone of voice irritated me. 'It is a big deal, yeah, when you wake up in a cell with your trousers plastered in piss and shit. A grown man. I've been dragged into hospital and pumped out more times than I care to remember. I've seen things crawling out of the walls at me and rats coming to get me in the middle of the night.'

'So bleedin' what?'

'So don't tell me I don't know anything about it, son. I'd have a wife and a family now if it wasn't for what I know about it.'

'Well, don't take it out on me, Homer.'

'I'm just saying, I know.'

He picked up the remote. 'Here Homer,' he said. 'I think you're makin' a mistake. I think you're after mixin' me up with someone else here.'

'With who?'

'With someone who gives a flyin' fuck about you. That's who. Now I told y'to leave me alone, I'm watchin' this.'

The next night when I got in I saw that he had fixed the stairs. Seriously, love. He had found those oak floorboards in here and nailed most of them into place on the staircase. I walked up and down a few times, testing them, until he appeared before me on the landing carrying a toolbox.

'Jesus, come up or go down, Homer,' he sighed. 'I need y'out of the bleedin' way there, I've to tack the carpet back down properly.'

In your bedroom a new door had been hung – he explained to me that he had taken it from the boxroom downstairs and found a set of hinges out in the stable. Up in the bathroom he had fixed the shower curtain back to its rail and cleaned the toilet. The carpets on the landing had been vacuumed. He had opened all the upstairs windows to let in clean air.

There was an ancient sheet of yellowed notepaper pinned to the door of my room. I read the letterhead: Reverend W. F. McCracken, MA, Glen Bolcain, Dalkey'. Underneath, in blue biro:

'Dear Homer, it is like a SHAGGING STY in there. You are ONLY AN ANIMAL. Do you want me to do it out for you?'

The weather was rainy and a bit cold that night, and in here it can get quite chilly anyway with the damp in the front wall, so I lit the fire in the grate over there and ate my dinner without taking off my jacket. I could hear the television blaring through the walls but I did not do anything about it. I was trying to concentrate on what I would write to you later and had no heart for a confrontation. Instead I closed the door and put on a record – I think it might have been Dave Brubeck – and when I had finished eating I began to write, as was my habit by then.

Around eleven I was reading back over a few pages and drinking a Coke when he knocked on the door. I was a little surprised by this, to tell you the truth; etiquette was never exactly his strong suit. But then he knocked again, more firmly but still politely. He came in with a cup of tea and a plate of biscuits which he put on the table beside me. He sat back against the stack of planks and lit a cigarette.

'What's that you're writin', Homer?'

'Nothing.'

'It's an awful lot of nothin' then. You're in here every night doin' it.'

'It's just something I'm doing for work.'

'Listen,' he said, 'I've somethin' t'say to you.'

'What's that?'

He blew a globe of smoke. 'I'm sorry about what happened your daughter.'

I put down my tea. The wind whistled in the chimney. The curtains moved in the draft.

'And were you sorry when your scumbag mate hit her with the iron bar?'

He stared at me. 'She gashed her head on the edge of the till, man, I swear to Christ. Nobody hit her.'

'Don't talk shite, Quinn.'

'Listen, I had to do the job. I'd no choice, man. I've a sister borrowed big dough from a bloke out in Tallaght, a shark, and he had to have it back. He threatened her kid otherwise. The kid's four years old. This toerag said he'd get him out of the school and fuckin' molest him if he didn't get his dough back and pronto.'

'So why didn't you say that in the court?'

He shrugged. 'Never got the chance. Anyway, what d'y'think he'd've done to the kid if I had? This guy's one sick, twisted fuck. The things he said he'd do to the kid, they'd turn your stomach over. I'd no choice.'

'Is that right? And what about my kid? What about her?'

'That's what I'm tryin' to explain.' He got up, went to the fireplace, peered into it. He picked up a log and threw it into the spitting flames. 'When we arrived into the place that night she saw us straight away. She tried to go for the alarm and we had to stop her doin' that. We had to. I didn't know about the syringe till Kelly pulled it out, I swear to Christ. I knew he was a psycho all right but I didn't know he'd pull a stroke like that.'

'I saw the security video in the court,' I told him. 'I heard what she was saying.'

'What?'

'You know damn well what.'

'I don't.'

'She was asking you to spare her life. She was begging. Don't tell me you don't remember that.'

He shook his head and brushed some dust off the mantelpiece. 'She was scared, that's all, man. She didn't know what she was sayin', the words were just . . . We weren't gonna touch her, that's the truth. I swear to Christ.'

He tossed his cigarette into the fire. 'I never hit a woman in me life, I swear to God. I wouldn't do that.'

'Oh right. Big man, aren't you? Gentleman Jim.'

'Well, lookat, I'm sorry anyway. All right?'

He came over and held out his hand.

'And I'm supposed to be impressed,' I said.

'Lookat, I'm tryin' to say I'm sorry, that's all. And I am.'

'Oh right. She's lying in a hospital bed for the rest of her life and you're sorry?'

He looked at the floor. I laughed.

'You know, Quinn, one thing I never took you for before is a gobshite. But all of a sudden I'm beginning to wonder.'

He stepped towards me, looking angry now. I found myself covering my writing with my hands.

'Look,' he snapped, 'do y'want me to be sorry or not, y'stupid prick?'

'I don't care any more,' I told him. 'And that's the truth.'

'It's a fuckin lie y'mean. I know your type, pal, I've met them before. Never happy unless they're miserable. Yeah. That's it. And y'won't be really happy till yer six foot under and feedin' the fuckin' worms.'

I sat back and folded my arms. 'Go on, son,' I said. 'That's it. You tell me all about myself.'

He pointed at me. 'Did nobody ever have to forgive you for anythin', no? What are you, pal, some fuckin' saint? St Homer. Well, for a saint I don't see too many people beatin' the door of this kip down to see how yer doin' these days.'

'Get out of my sight,' I shouted. And to my surprise, he did. After a moment the television was turned up loud again next door.

Around one in the morning he was sitting at the kitchen table when I went in for a glass of water. He was drinking a cup of tea and cutting pictures out of a magazine with a scissors. I emptied my leftovers into the bin and rinsed off my plate. When I went to get a glass I noticed that they had all been cleaned and dried and neatly put back into the cupboard. I got my water and drank it down. I remember the buzzing of the fridge. He reached to the floor and picked up a pile of magazines and newspapers. He began to look through them, cutting out more pictures and arranging them into small piles on the table.

'Look,' I found myself saying, 'I'm sorry for throwing the head with you earlier. I've been thinking about it and I'm sorry.'

'Well, y'can go shag yerself now. I've nothing else to say about it.'

'I wasn't there that night. I know that. And I believe you, what you said about the syringe.'

'Just leave it,' he said. 'And don't be annoyin' me.'

I poured myself a cup of tea from the pot and sat down at the table. I watched for a while as he cut the photographs out of the magazines. Outside in the garden I could hear the cry of an owl. The wind threw leaves against the kitchen window.

'Homer,' he said. 'I phoned the mother today.'

'You *what?*'

'Don't worry, I told her I was in London, didn't leave a number. She said it was just as well I was over there.'

'Why's that?'

'Someone in the flats is after tellin' her there's a contract out on me.'

'A contract?'

'I'm after fallin' out with these lads in town. Some dough from a big enough job went for a fuckin' walk a while back. The word's out it was me knocked it off.'

'And was it?'

'No. But I'm after gettin' the blame. The mother says they've been lookin' around town for me. She's astray in the fuckin' head about it. Five grand, Homer. That's what they're givin' for whoever does me.'

He laughed. 'Maybe y'should do me yourself.'

'I don't know why you don't go to England,' I said. 'You'd be safe over there, from whoever it is that's trying to get you. Nobody's going to do anything to you over there. You know that. And you know you can't stay here for ever.'

He was silent. Just snipped harder with the scissors.

'Look,' I said. 'I'll even give you money, all right. As much as you need. And I'll drive you myself down to the boat.'

He glared at me. 'Oh yeah, y'd like that, wouldn't you? Well, I'm stayin' here as long as I like, man, and there's fuck all y're gonna to do about it.'

I took a few swallows of tea and tried not to lose my temper. 'Listen, you give me all this stuff about the Provos being after you. And these merchants as well now. But the Provos aren't running around London, are they?'

'Oh right. No Provos in London. I can see you've been readin' the papers lately, Homer.'

'You know well what I mean. OK, there's a few Provos in London, but not like here.'

'I know, all right?'

'So why don't you just go to London then? I'll give you money.'

He turned a page of his magazine. 'Because I don't know anyone over there,' he said. 'Now. Are y'happy?'

'What do you mean, you don't know anyone?'

He glared across at me. 'Did y'never hear of fuckin' loneliness in your life, man, no?'

He got up and walked from the kitchen. I heard him storming up the stairs. He went into his room and slammed the door closed. A moment went by. He opened and slammed it again, so hard that the windows in the kitchen shook.

And then the radio went on.

Two or three days went by without a single word. And then one evening he was in the garden when I got home, up to his knees and digging with an old shovel in the drainage trench. He had taken off his shirt and was sweating heavily as he worked, a mound of wet black earth behind him. He grunted hard as he sliced the shovel into the ground. When he caught my eye he did a cautious nod.

'I thought I'd have a go at your sewer. I was bored.'

'There's really no need. I've decided to get the builders back in a while.'

'Well, I hope you're not gonna be thick enough t'get the same crowd from last time. Shower of useless cowboys. Shagged off without finishin' the job.'

'It wasn't their fault,' I told him. 'We had a row. It was just before the court case and my nerves were bad. I lost my temper with them. But you needn't be doing that. I'll get them back in the new year.'

He wiped his wet, tanned face. 'Yeah, well I was bored out of me skull anyway. And the jacks is gone baw-ways in there. I'm after flushin' up a breakfast y'must've had six months ago.'

He rummaged in his jeans pocket. 'Oh yeah, lookat. Little present for yeh, Homer.'

He handed me a wad of tissue paper. I opened it and stared inside. A small imitation emerald brooch shaped like a bird sitting on a twig. At first I did not even remember it. Just some cheap trinket someone once threw away, I told myself, some worthless bit of tawdry junk one of the travellers had flung in over the wall. And then, slowly, it began to down on me where I had seen it before.

'My Jesus,' I said. 'Where did you get this?'

'Was in your main sewer over there,' he said, nodding his head. 'Caked in shite and all. But I saw it glintin' up at me. Picked it out and washed it down under the tap. Thought it might be worth a few bob.'

'This belonged to my wife,' I told him. 'It was an anniversary present.'

He shrugged. 'Happy anniversary so. That's nice for you to have it back.'

He went back to work on the sewer, cutting deep into the earth, throwing shovelfuls over his shoulder.

PART IV

Chapter Seventeen

On the morning of 20 September, your twenty-fourth birthday, the Jewish feast of Tabernacles, I was on my way down the driveway when I noticed the chestnuts on the heavy sagging branches. Some had even fallen, I saw, green spiked bombs on the dark gravel. I knew then that the summer was well and truly over. For the last few weeks there had been fewer flycatchers and willow warblers in the garden. The chaffinches had started to flock together, the way they always do when the sharp weather is on its way. The night before a convoy of wild geese had flown honking in a V over the roof and in the direction of the South. The redwings would be here soon, I told myself. And there was still no sign of him going.

When I got down to the hospital that morning, I was surprised to find Seánie in the ward with you. He looked tired and stressed and a little run down, but he stood up and smiled when he saw me. I went to shake his hand. He pulled me to him, told me not to be such an anal Irish bastard, gave me a hug. The plastic curtains had been drawn around your bed. The nurse was inside, he explained, changing your clothes.

'So how was Lourdes?' I asked him.

'Great,' he said. 'It was really terrific. You should've come.'

We chatted for a while, about Lizzie and Franklin coming home, the heat of the summer months, the colourful behaviour of the pilgrims in Lourdes at night. I clocked him looking at me closely and trying to read my face. Seánie knows me well enough to know when things are bad. He kept up the smile, of course, there's always the smile with Seánie, but I could see his weary eyes flicking over me.

'Are you after losin' a few pounds?' he said. 'You look like a different man, Billy.'

'Yeah, I slimmed down a bit.'

'I've lost some hair,' he laughed. 'From my head, I mean. But I'm gettin' more in my nostrils.'

'It's an inverse proportion thing,' I said.

He nodded. 'I did a lot of thinkin' in France, Liam. Mullin' things over, you know. I took a bit of quiet time after the job. Did a retreat. Made a few decisions.'

'Oh yeah? Like what?'

'Ah well, I'm gettin' itchy feet again.' He looked at his fingernails and sighed. 'Look, I may as well tell you, keep it under your hat for the moment. But I'm after applyin' to go back on my travels. I've asked for Central America this time.'

The nurse opened the curtains and stepped out. She had a plastic basin in her hands and a blue nightdress folded over her wrist. Your face was shining like a new apple. You were wearing white pyjamas with a red heart on the breast pocket.

'Now,' she said. 'Isn't Miss looking well in her new attire?'

'Lovely, yes. Where did she get those?'

The nurse nodded towards Seánie and smiled. 'Father brought them.'

He was blushing. 'I just saw them in Dunnes Stores on my way down earlier. They had them on a model in the window.'

'God, Sean. Thanks. Did you know it was her birthday today?'

'No, no. Is it? That's a turn-up.'

'It's very decent of you, Seán.'

'Stop it, would you, Sweeney. It's little enough chance

I get to be buyin' women's clothes. Though I suppose the girls down in Dunnes'll think I'm a bit funny now.'

'Funny indeed,' the nurse said. 'They wouldn't be the first to think that, so.'

He grinned. 'Listen to this bad County Kerry rip, Liam. Breakin' my heart as usual.'

When the nurse had left, Seánie and I sat by your bed in silence for a while. In the corner of my eye I saw him peeping at me. I avoided his stare. Finally he did a bit of throat clearing and coughing, which as you're aware probably is Seánie's way of letting you know that he thinks something is up. In the end I had a pain in the neck from trying not to look at him, so I had to turn and face him then, if only to allow my circulation to keep going.

He did his understanding glance.

'And you Liam? Everything's been good with you, has it?'

'It's been great, Seánie. Everything's been just fabulous. You wouldn't believe how great everything has been.'

'You sure?'

'Course I'm sure.'

'OK,' he said, 'OK. Just asking.'

'Why?'

He shrugged. 'No, it's nothing. Just that I had a strange enough call last night from that copper, Duignan. Something I asked him to do a while back there. But I noticed he kept asking me were you all right.'

'Well, I'm fine.'

'Good, good.' He slapped me across the shoulders. 'So lookat, will I call up to you tonight for a proper chat?'

'No, Seán. Don't do that, if you don't mind. I've something on this evening actually.'

'Oh yeah, Duignan told me you're after meeting some bird. I'm always the last to hear all the good news, of course.'

'Well, I haven't. I did a while back, but it's over now.'

He nodded. A bit more coughing. A bit more throat clearing. A bit more staring at his fingernails.

Sometimes, love, I could happily wring that man's neck.

A few days later I was on my way back to the house after work when I decided to call into SuperNova Electrics down in Dalkey village. We'd just had our new catalogues delivered from the printer that afternoon and I wanted to look after the local shops well.

You can guess, of course, where a good salesman would stand on the issue of how to look after his local shops.

I got a space in the church car park and walked down Castle Street in the evening sunlight. The village looked lovely with the sun reflecting gold in the shop windows, but I was in a bad mood. Frankly, what with Quinn's absolute refusal to compromise on his nocturnal television extravaganzas, the sleep situation had got out of hand; by now I was only sleeping three or four hours a night, if I was lucky. Work was suffering too, I could not hide it any more; O'Keefe and I had had several big and so far unresolved rows. What bothered me more was that I had also argued badly with Liam that day. He and I had rarely crossed swords before.

When I got to the SuperNova shop, I did what the good salesman will always do, I went to check the window display first. They had our posters and cut-outs, fanned-out stills from the brochure and leaflets. They had even set up one of the new dishes on a little revolving plinth. It all looked wonderful. Then I happened to glance up through the window. I almost fainted. He was in the bloody shop. Quinn, I mean. I could see him through the window! He had a newspaper in his hand and was talking away nine to the dozen to the girl behind the till, leaning in close to her and laughing. For a second or two I stared at him. He was jabbering and cracking jokes. I ducked into the alley beside the supermarket. What the hell was he doing now?

336

When I emerged from the alley a minute later I saw him up ahead of me, walking slowly along the street. The little pup was casually strolling down the main street of Dalkey now, bold as brass, and wearing my overcoat! I followed for a while, but kept my distance. Just in front of him, two policemen came out of a shop. He walked boldly straight past them with his head held high.

Suddenly I noticed Mr Pollexfen from the residents' association bustling along the pavement towards me. He had on his serious expression and was walking as though he had a corn-cob stuck up his backside. I could tell that he wanted to talk to me. Your mother used to say that Mr Pollexfen geared up for a conversation the way an oil-tanker gears up to stop.

'Ah, Sweeney,' he said. 'How's tricks?'

'Sorry, Jack,' I said. 'I'm in an awful rush.'

'Yes, Sweeney, but lookit. Something will have to be done about those knackers up in the back field. They make more noise than an army.'

'Yes, Jack. Can we talk about it again?'

'One of them exposed himself to my mother the other week. It isn't right, Sweeney, I tell you, and it isn't decent. She's eighty-two years old.'

'Awful, Jack, I know, but listen . . .'

'They say they're down on their luck, but I notice they've damn plenty of money for drink all the same. Now look, I'll call up to you tonight to discuss it, shall I? With a few of us from the committee?'

'No,' I said. 'I mean, don't do that, Jack, if you don't mind. I'll call up to you.'

'They're only bloody animals, is what I say, Sweeney, really they . . .'

I walked off leaving him in mid-flow. Up ahead of me, Quinn passed the church car park and the Queen's pub and kept going. One of the policemen turned and stared after him, then said something to his colleague. I stopped dead. But after a moment they shrugged and simply walked on. They passed me by and both nodded a hello. Half-way down the main street, Quinn stopped and looked up at the castle tower, shading his eyes. I caught up with him and hissed his name.

'Ah Homer,' he said, 'how's she cuttin'?'

'What are you doing down here?' I dragged him into the castle doorway.

'Where in the name of holy fuck are we, Homer?'

'We're in Dalkey, all right? *Dalkey*. There. Now you know.'

'Dalkey? But y'told me we're down the countryside.'

'Yes. Well, I was lying. We're in Dalkey.'

'Where Bono lives? Out of U2?'

'Well, that's really Killiney,' I said. 'But yes. Basically.'

'Jaze,' he said, looking around. 'And I thought we were in some little kip down the country. It doesn't look like Dublin, does it? Bleedin' Dalkey.'

'And what were you doing in SuperNova, for Christ's sake?'

'Tryin' to find out where I was.'

'What?'

'Well, y'can't walk up to somebody and say sorry, darlin', have y'got the right town please? I'm after been lookin' around all the shops for a clue. But I couldn't see anythin'.'

'You asked that girl what town this was?'

'Yeah. And then I invited her up to the house later for a jockey's breakfast.'

'What's that?'

'The jockey's breakfast, Homer. A rasher and a ride.'

'You invited her up the house?'

'Course I did. Told her to bring a friend too. I mean, I'm after bein' cooped up for an age, Homer. A man has his needs, y'know.'

His face crumpled into laughter. 'Look at the mug on yeh, Homer. Of course I didn't. And of course I know where we are, y'dipstick. I saw it written on yer post weeks ago.'

'Smart, aren't you?'

He pointed to his feet.

'Down there for dancin', Homer'.

He tapped his head.

'And up here for everythin' else. Now come on, are we goin' home or what? It's nearly time for the tea. The girls'll be along up shortly.'

He stalked off quickly ahead of me, swinging his arms from side to side and softly singing to himself.

At half-past seven that evening we were in the kitchen making boiled eggs when the row broke out. I was simply trying to tell him that you don't put the eggs in the pot until *after* the water has boiled.

'Me hole,' he said. 'I know how to boil an egg, Homer.'

'You don't. You've put it in too early.'

'I didn't.'

'That's not how you boil an egg,' I told him. 'That's all I'm saying.'

'Leave off, Homer, will yeh? Don't be such an aul' woman.'

He poked me hard in the ribs and I pushed him back. He grabbed the soft part of my forearm and pinched hard at me, laughing, twisting his fingers until I yelped with pain, then he shoved me away from him with such force that I crashed into the table, upsetting the cups and the milk jug. He threw back his head and laughed again, louder this time.

'Were you born fuckin' stupid,' I say, 'or did you have to fuckin' practise it?'

His smile froze. His glistening face suddenly whitened with anger. He picked up the pot with the eggs and flung it across the kitchen into the sink. Then he turned and glared at me.

'You're one bollocks sometimes, Homer, do y'know that?'

'Well, at least I'm not stupid as well,' I said.

He snatched up a milk bottle and took a step in my direction. 'What did you call me?'

'You heard me.'

'Say that again, y'little fuckin' cunt.'

'No,' I said, 'I won't.'

He pointed the bottle at me. 'When are you goin' away again?'

'Tomorrow,' I said. 'To Galway.'

'Well, I'll be gone when y'get back. Don't worry.'

'Good,' I said.

He stormed out to the garden and I saw him through the window, kicking at the bushes.

Later that night I knocked on his bedroom door and went in. He was lying on the bed, reading a newspaper and smoking. Needless to say, the radio was on. I saw then what he had been doing with the photographs from the Sunday magazines. There they all were, sellotaped in rows to the walls. Pictures of skeletal supermodels pouting on catwalks, three or four of footballers embracing and laughing, another of a sioux chief with a feathered head-dress that reached all the way down to the desert ground. A white map of Ireland with the border marker in red. A diagram of the London tube system. A six-inch emerald shamrock cut out of an advertisement for Aer Lingus.

'Look,' I told him. 'If you need a place for a while, it's all right. You can stay.'

'No, it's fine. I'm goin' in the morning.'

'I said you can stay if you want.'

He whipped over a few pages of his newspaper. He reached into his breast pocket and took out a biro. He bit the lid off and began to do the crossword.

'I said you can stay,' I told him.

'Yer all fuckin' heart,' he said, and went back to the paper. I found myself staring up at the pictures once again. There in the middle of the wall was a black and white photograph of the Statue of Liberty with, I suppose, an emigrant family in the foreground, a mother and father in grey rags, arms around each other, a scrawny toddler sitting on a trunk and waving his hands in the air. I went to leave.

'Here, Homer,' he said. 'You know the difference between a raw egg and a good ride?'

'No. What?'

He never took his eyes off the newspaper. 'Y'can beat a raw egg,' he said.

A few nights later, at about ten o'clock, I was in the kitchen washing some dishes when a sudden movement out in the garden caught my eye. It was very dark that night and a few minutes earlier it had begun to rain quite heavily. But when I looked out I thought that I could see someone moving around in the shifting shadows down behind the apple tree. A stocky man dressed in black clothes. He seemed to be slowly circling the aviary and looking into it. I called out for Quinn, but quietly. I knocked on the wall of the living-room but he did not come. I knew then that he must have been upstairs.

I switched off the kitchen light and looked out again. The glass misted. But when I rubbed the steam away I could see him again, I was certain of it, directly beneath the apple tree now and staring into the grass. I crept to the back door and opened it as quietly as I could. The rain was falling hard. From above me I could hear water gurgling in the gutters. When I got out on to the steps I could not see him any more. I moved cautiously forward, down the steps, until I set off the security light. The blazing white beam flooded the garden. There was nobody there. I told myself that I must have been imagining it.

I went back inside, made some coffee and brought it in here, to the small room. I tried to write for a while, enjoying the sound of the rain sputtering against the window. By then, writing these words to you was the only thing that could give me relief, that could turn off the hot light inside my head and switch the cool light on. I would write every night for several hours, until my hand ached, and that seemed to melt away the tension of those mad days. But it bothered me that night, what I thought I had seen in the garden, I could not stop thinking about it. I went into the living-room where he was now watching the television.

'Were you out the back a while ago?' I asked him.

He shook his head.

'I saw someone in the garden. Definitely. Are you sure it wasn't you?'

'Course I bleedin' am. Jesus, Homer.'

'Well, I saw someone out there not half an hour ago, I'm telling you. A man.'

'Was it one of them knackers from the field?'

'I'd be surprised if it was. They never come in here.'

He shrugged and peered back at the television screen. 'Musta been a ghost, Homer. Y'must have a guilty conscience.'

'For God's sake,' I sighed. 'Do you have to call me that?'

'What?'

'Homer.'

'Oh yeah. Sorry,' he said. 'I meant Marge.'

'Who the blazes is Marge?'

'She's Homer Simpson's auld lady, y'dipstick. D'y'know nothin'?' He giggled. 'The gas thing about you, man, is y'look like Homer but y'act like Marge.'

As I went to leave I noticed something that struck me as odd. 'How come your hair is wet if you haven't been outside?' I asked him.

He touched his head. 'I had a shower,' he said. After a moment.

Every evening around that time I would come back from the office to find him hard at work, painting a patch of wall, heaving blocks about the place, nailing down loose

342

boards, varnishing doors. He fixed the toilet and made it flush properly, cleared out the kitchen drain, got the long ladder out of the stable and dug handfuls of rotting leaves from the gutters. One day he mixed up a mess of plaster on the back steps and filled the cracks in the concrete. The next morning he asked me to bring him home some special kind of textured paint for exterior stone which he had seen in a magazine. We spent four long hours painting the rockery steps that night, Quinn kneeling on the concrete, me making strong tea and toasted sandwiches, and walking up and down the garden to keep the security light clicking on after it had got dark.

What he did in the garden you would not believe. It is still not perfect by any means, love, but if you saw it now you would be amazed. In the space of a week he trimmed back the hedges, weeded out the flower-beds; he got the bamboo poles out of the old wigwam and sawed them into neat halves to trail the wild ivy. He mixed up more plaster, smashed a load of old bottles and fixed pieces of the glass into the top of the back wall. Then he dug the ditch a few feet deeper, so that if anyone did manage to climb in, they would at least not find it an easy stroll up to the house. And every night when he had finished working he would simply come up into the kitchen, eat a bit – either sausages or a mound of toast – watch the O. J. Simpson trial for a few hours and then go to bed, usually without having hardly said a word to me.

The day Liam insisted on giving me back some money I had loaned him for his daughter's wedding, I handed Quinn two hundred quid when I got home.

'What's that?' he said, staring at it.

'It's toilet paper,' I went. 'What do you think it is?'

'I don't want yer money, Marge.'

'Take it and don't be annoying me,' I told him. 'I'm not having you working here for nothing.'

I made him go down to the village and get himself some

clothes, warning him not to be conspicuous, and not to talk to anybody unless it was absolutely necessary. He landed back two hours later with a fluoresent yellow shell suit, a pair of doc martens, a bag of underwear, a T-shirt featuring the words 'Mad for it' and two green budgies in a small cage. He opened up the aviary gate and put in the budgies.

'For aul' time's sake, Marge,' he smirked. He seemed to think this was amusing.

And then, one Saturday morning, the toilet broke again. I was in the kitchen looking for the toolbox in the cupboard under the sink when I noticed something strange. The shotgun was not there, where I had hidden it away some weeks earlier. I went down on my knees and took everything out, the polythene bags, the mousetraps, the plastic bottles of disinfectant, but the gun was gone. I searched around in the other cupboards and then the drawers but there was no sign. I sat at the table for a while and wondered what exactly to do. In the end, I just went into the living-room and asked him straight out about it.

He told me it was definitely under the sink, he had seen it only a week ago, wrapped up tightly in a refuse sack. I told him it was not there now, I was certain. He looked worried then, and that worried me. 'Billy, man, I never went near it.'

I think it was the first time that he had ever used my name.

'Well, it's gone,' I said.

He scratched his head and frowned. He followed me back into the kitchen and looked in the cupboard himself. He too took out the pile of plastic bags and rummaged around. He spent an hour taking things methodically out of the kitchen cupboards and searching hard but it was nowhere to be seen. He glanced up at me.

'I never went near it, man,' he said. 'Honest.'

We spent the whole day looking around the house. We

344

practically took the place to pieces. We searched the living-room, the small room, the bathroom, everywhere. I even unlocked your bedroom and had a good long look in there. Then we did the garden, the stable, the heavy under-growth on either side of the drive. No policeman could have searched more carefully than me. But the gun was gone. I did not sleep very well that night, I can tell you.

All that Sunday I stayed in here, mentally trawling around the house for the gun. Every location I could think of, we had searched already. I found myself wondering if there was any way it could have got up to the attic, or even over the back wall. While he was making himself something to eat downstairs I slipped out and throughly checked the stable again. There was no sign. After a while I became absolutely convinced that he was lying to me about it. It was so obvious. He had simply taken it and hidden it, I don't know why I did not want to believe it. He was cunning enough to do it, it should not have surprised me. All that innocent act the evening before and again that morning, that's all it had been, another act, just as I had seen him do before. I started to see the situation more clearly. Maybe, I told myself, that explained all this strange, irrational business of his fixing up the house and working like a demon in the garden. It was all part of a clever preparation; it was a leading somewhere. He was trying to soften me up before retrieving the gun and coming in one night when I was not expecting him. He was going to rob me blind, I figured, before disappearing off to England. Or perhaps he was going to kill me after all.

I felt terror then. I could see that the time for secrecy was over; I would have to talk to somebody about it. Late on the Sunday afternoon I barricaded myself into the bedroom and made up my mind: that night, after he had gone to bed, I would sneak out and go tell Seánie. Just tell him the truth. Or at least, part of the truth. It was the only thing to do now. I would say that I had been secretly drinking when the whole insane plan had first occurred to me, that I had gone out and tracked him down, that I must have had a blackout and gone crazy in some way, and that when I had woken up again he was here in the house. Stranger things have happened, Seánie knows that, I mean, they've happened to me. Once when I was in the horrors of drink I started thinking I was actually Don Vito Corleone, the old Mafia leader in *The Godfather*. I was absolutely convinced of this and warned the ambulance men that if they attempted to take me away they would sleep with the fishes. I was told later that I even had an Italian accent.

My love, I prayed for him to go to bed that night. I thought he never would. When he finally did come up the stairs it was well after midnight. I heard the radio go on in his room, waited another half an hour, threw some clothes on over my pyjamas and slipped down the stairs. It was cold outside. A light rain had started to fall. I was shaking, I half-expected him to appear behind me at any moment and call out my name – if I even got that much warning before the gun blast. Gently I opened the car door and let the handbrake off. Tender splashing sounds seemed to come from the dark trees. I pushed the car down the drive so that he would not hear me starting it up.

Outside the gate, the wind was whipping down the avenue. Drizzle speckled the windscreen. I climbed in and started the engine. The sky was thick with turbid, blackish clouds. I turned the heat up full blast, I was freezing, I heard my teeth chatter. The intensity of the rain suddenly increased, it seemed to surge down horizontally in sheets. A dustbin overturned, spilling its contents with a loud crash. I was about half-way down towards the village when a man stepped quickly out of the darkness at the side of the road and held up his hand for me to stop. I rolled down the window. Splashes of rain hit my face and hands. He walked over.

'Remember me, pal?'

It was the milkman, Nap, his pock-marked face pink and shiny. He was wearing a camouflage jacket and black jeans, a dirty-looking woolly hat which the rain was rapidly reducing to a wet rag.

'You look fierce warm in there, Billyboy. Can I hop in there with you for a minute?'

'I'm in a hurry,' I told him.

'You must be,' he said, 'if you're headin' out this late.'

He knows where I live, is what I was thinking, as he walked around the front of the car and opened the passenger door. He slid in beside me, wiped his wet face with the back of his sleeve and rubbed his knuckles together. He smelled of paraffin and feet. Shuddering, he reached out one finger and pushed in the cigarette lighter. I asked him what he wanted.

'I've an awful problem on me hands,' he said. 'I'm a bit financially embarrassed.'

He took a damp cigarette from behind his ear, wiped his face again and then peered at his hand. A smear of condensation began to mist across the windscreen.

'I need money,' he said, 'I thought y'might like to give me a dig-out. A bit of a loan.'

'A loan?'

'Well, a permanent loan, yeah.'

'I couldn't really do that, no. I'm sorry for your trouble but there's nothing I can do.'

The lighter clicked in the dashboard. He took it out and peered at its glowing tip for a few seconds. Two men in wellington boots and thick yellow oilskins strode urgently past the car in the direction of the village. The rain drummed on the roof. He lit his cigarette.

'No, see, yeh don't follow me, Mr Sweeney,' he said. 'The thing is, if y'cant see any way clear to giving me a dig-out there might be a problem for me. And if there's a problem for me, I'll be makin' fuckin' sure there's a problem for a few other people too.'

'Meaning?'

'Meanin' that chap Quinn now. That poor fucker you got

347

the job done on. I talked to yer friend Sheehan about it, Mr Sweeney.' He shook his wet head and frowned 'Only I'm not sure he's yer friend any more. Said he'd never seen the like. Told me yeh flipped out, went spare altogether. Anyways, there's a lot of talk about the same Quinn around town at the minute. All sorts of funny rumours, Mr Sweeney. His ma's tellin' everyone he's after goin' to England. Only he's not in England, is he, Mr Sweeney?'

'How would I know where he is?'

He grinned. 'There's talk around the place of some very fuckin' dangerous people lookin' to have a little word with him. I'd hate if it was me had to let them know where to look.'

More smoke, a hacking cough, a leery smile.

'Have you been in my house?' I said.

He laughed. 'Christ, Mr Sweeney, that's an awful thing to say.'

His fingertips traced parallel lines through the condensation on the windscreen.

'You're a businessman,' he said. 'I won't insult yeh.'

'What does that mean?'

He shrugged. 'Well, it means a grand,' he said. 'To start.'

'I don't have that kind of dough.'

He nodded. Suddenly he seemed to notice a white plastic supermarket bag twisted into a ball at his feet. He snatched it up and began smoothing it out across his knees. 'Yer bank opens at ten in the morning. Yer bank down in Dalkey. Yer well in with the manager, McDermott's his name. I'll be down at the tower in Sandycove at half-past. Y'can bring it then. And try and be on time, Mr Sweeney. I'd hate to have to drop in on y'at home. Disturb your privacy.'

'Fuck off,' I said.

He laughed and stubbed his cigarette out in the ashtray. 'I don't want to hurt anyone,' he said. 'I promise, nobody's gonna get hurt here, Mr Sweeney, if y'do what I say. I mean it now. Y'can trust me. I'm yer friend. Now I'll see y'in the mornin'.'

Shivering, he wrapped the plastic bag around his head like a scarf, leapt out of the car, stared up maliciously at the sky and began to trot off quickly down the avenue. A thunderclap boomed. I turned around and drove back up to the house with my heart hammering. When I came in, Quinn was sitting at the kitchen table, with screwdrivers and parts from the old iron spread out in front of him. He gaped across at me.

'Marge,' he said. 'I thought you were up in the scratcher.'

'I went out for a drive.'

'What's the matter? Y'look like shit.'

After I had told him, he was quiet for a long time. His face took on a strange kind of almost religious seriousness. I could hear the high wind whistling through the garden. He asked me if I was tired now. I told him no, I wasn't.

'Could we go out for a drive together?' he said. 'I need to try and think straight.'

We went out to the car and got in. He asked me to drive him into town. I got to the river in less than twenty minutes; he smoked all the way, and refused to speak. I parked on the south quays and got out of the car, leaving him still smoking inside. The rain had stopped but the river was still swirling and eddying. It was about three in the morning. I leaned on the Liffey wall and looked across at this new fashionable nightclub on the Northside bank for a while. The building was white and bathed in a wash of floodlights. I could see a gang of photographers outside the door, clearly waiting for some famous person to come out. There was a violently purple laser beam on the roof, pointing up at the clouds. It would divide into two, ripple, dance, wriggle, quadruple. I do not know how long I must have watched it, but eventually the photographers began to drift away in twos and threes. A blood-red sun began to rise over the dome of the Customs House, trailing wispy crimson tentacles beneath it. Below me, a few catty gulls skimmed the surface of the river. The people in the nightclub switched off the laser and the whole city seemed suddenly to go quiet.

Quinn opened the car door and stepped out. 'I have an idea, Marge,' he said.

Chapter Eighteen

Nap was in the lane when we arrived at half-past ten, leaning against a lamp post with his arms folded, and staring hard out at the sea as though watching for something specific. The morning was dull; there were no swimmers. The martello tower looked wet and black. I parked, left the motor running and let Quinn out. He told me to stay where I was and not to turn off the engine. If he was not back in five minutes I was to come over, make some excuse and get him.

'What kind of excuse?,' I asked.

'Use your bleedin' imagination, Marge. Say I'm after winnin' the Lottery or somethin'.'

He closed the door, walked quickly over to Nap and they shook hands. They talked for a minute or two. Then they climbed over the low wall and sauntered down the beach together. Quinn took a pack of cigarettes out of his pocket and offered Nap one. He took it. They both lit up. Quinn went down on his hunkers and started skimming flat stones across the grey water. The other stood looking down at him, his hands thrust deep in his pockets, his boots disconsolately toeing the sand.

After a few minutes they came back up into the lane. Nap glanced around himself a few times, sidestepped quickly over to the black railings of a front garden, reached into a thick hedge and pulled out a black plastic rubbish bag which he handed over to Quinn. They shook hands again. He looked over at me for a second or two. He waved in my direction, beamed optimistically and made a thumbs-up sign, then he turned on his heels and walked away towards Sandycove village, beginning to jog before he had gone from my view.

Quinn strolled lazily over and got into the car. He offered me a cigarette. I took it. Then he handed me the plastic sack.

'Well, there's your heater back anyway,' he said.

'What did you tell him?'

'I told him y'were me uncle. And y'wanted to teach me a lesson.' He stretched his arms and yawned. 'Jesus, I'm fuckin' jaded, are you?'

'Your uncle?'

He grinned. 'Yeah. I told him we were an awful close family.'

'And was that him? In the house the other night?'

He nodded. 'Who else? But I said I hoped he'd be reasonable and not be a fuckin' grass. 'Cos if he wasn't reasonable I'd have Charlie Collins on to him by the end of the day. That seemed to do the trick, all right.'

'Who's that?'

'Collins? He's a crim, Marge. A big boss around town. Anyways, I told yer man he was a good friend of the brother's. Kieran. The brother who got shot by the RA. Told him Charlie Collins let the mother know at the funeral if he could ever do her a favour he would.'

'And what about him? This Collins?'

'Well see, he crucified this youngfella once. One of his own gang. Seriously. Fuckin' took him for a drive up to a house in the mountains with one of them things for hammerin' Hilti bolts into stone walls. A power hammer. Thought he was after rattin' on him to the coppers. Tied him up and asked him if the rumours was true. Poor cunt says no. Collins and his mate get him down and nail him to the floor with this thing. Bang. One bolt through each of his mitts, bang, bang, another two right through the feet and into the floorboards. Poor fucker ends up pinned to the deck.'

'Jesus.'

'Yeah, exactly. Just like Jesus. See, if there's one thing Collins doesn't like it's a rat. He'll put up with nearly anything, but not a squealer, he's known for that. And then, anyways, yer man's there stuck like a pig and he screechin' out of him and bawlin'. And then after a while it turns out Collins's convinced he's tellin' the truth after all. So what he does, he unties him, pulls out the bolts, turfs him into the back of his motor and lurries him down to the hospital. And then, as your man's gettin' out of the car, blood drippin' out of him, Collins goes to him, I'd say you've a good case for a claim, pal. A criminal compensation claim, y'know, against the State. If you need a good solicitor let me know. And he helps him into casualty and shags off home for his breakfast.'

'You've some lovely friends,' I said.

He nodded and looked out at the sea. 'Y'don't know the half of it, Marge.'

'And that's the kind of person your brother was hanging around with?'

He smiled. 'Not at all, Marge, don't be dense.'

'How do you mean?'

'Sure Kieran never met Charlie fuckin' Collins in his life. No more than I did. Are you jokin' me? Kieran was low rent. And as for me, I wouldn't know Collins if he shaped up here and gave me a foot in the arse. No, I only came out with all that to scare the shite out of our friend. Worked too. Thought he was gonna piss himself.' He chuckled. 'Look at the mug on yeh.'

'So how did you know all that stuff?'

'What stuff?'

'About the crucifixion and everything. Don't tell me you made that up too.'

'Ah no,' he said. 'I didn't make that up. I read that it in a book.'

He punched my shoulder. 'Aren't y'glad y'met me now, Marge?'

'You never really killed anyone in the Lebanon either, did you?'

He seemed to think about this for a second. 'Well, I was the unit cook,' he said. 'So probably I did, yeah.'

I pulled away slowly down the lane. 'You'd think you'd know how to boil an egg,' I told him.

'Don't fuckin' start, Marge. I'm knackered. Take me home.'

By last month the weather had changed for the worse. The morning I turned the calendar page over to October, I came out of the house to find a light dusting of frost on the grass and the tops of the bushes. The water in the bird table was covered with a thin crust of ice. Far in the distance I could see swathes of bluish snow on the peaks of the hills.

I remember work being absolutely insane that day. O'Keeffe was acting like a maniac as he stormed around the office barking and running his fingers through his perm. There was talk of a transport strike in England that would cause us big problems with distribution; the phones didn't stop ringing all afternoon. To make matters worse the new secretary had arrived. Dawn by name, a bad-tempered young one who'd eat the face off you soon as look at you. 'Zulu Dawn,' Hopper called her. When I got home I was completely exhausted. I told Quinn we would have to remove the budgies from the aviary or the cold would kill them. He rooted around the stable and found the cage, put them into it, then brought them up to the kitchen. He fed them warm water, mashed-up bread and milk. He laughed as they chirruped and hopped and flapped their wings against the bars. He seemed to get a great kick out of the budgies.

Late that night I was here in the small room by myself, writing to you as usual – it was a stormy night, just like it is tonight, very cold and blowy – when suddenly I heard slow and heavy footsteps plodding up the drive. It was almost eleven and I certainly was not expecting anybody.

The roads were icy, the radio news had said that some of the streets in town were almost impassable, and the forecast had been for heavy snow. For a moment I wondered if it was a traveller from the back field in search of money or a cup of tea. I remember rooting for change in my pocket because I felt pity for anyone out on a night like that. The footsteps stopped. There was a loud knock on the front door.

When I got to the hall Quinn was poking his head out from the living-room. He looked nervous. He slid sidelong into the kitchen like a crab and came back a moment later with a steak knife. I motioned him to leave. He slipped down the hall and quickly upstairs. When I was absolutely sure that he had hidden himself away I opened the door.

Seánie was standing in the porch with sleet whirling around him. His face was purple with the cold.

'Seánie. Jesus. Is everything OK?'

'Yeah, yeah, just passing, Liam. Thought I'd beg a coffee.'

Before I could think of an excuse to stop him, he had stepped into the hall. I closed the door and brought him in here to the small room. He brushed himself off, clapped his arms, sat down shivering in the bay window. I went and stoked up the fire. He seemed a bit distracted as he peered around and ran his fingers through his wet hair. Even when he smiled across at me I could see that he was anxious. I went to the kitchen and made a pot of coffee. When I returned, I found him standing up very straight with his head bent back and staring at the ceiling.

'Anything wrong, Seán?'

'Is there someone else here, Liam? In the house?'

My heart skipped. 'Not at all, I'm alone as usual. Worst luck, says you. If you hear of a nice blonde looking for company on a cold night you give her my number.'

I passed him a mug of coffee. He cupped his hands around it.

'Well, it's official anyhow, Liam. I'm off on my travels again. Just heard this morning.'

'Great, Seán. Whereabouts?'

He blew on the coffee. 'Nicaragua this time. Looks like I'll be gone a few years.'

'That sounds right up your street.'

I noticed him staring around the room again. 'Liam, you wouldn't have a drink in the house at all, would you?'

I laughed. 'Afraid not. If you'd tried me ten years ago I'd've had a whole brewery.'

'Yes. Well, never mind. How's Lizzie?'

'Well, fine, I think. She's settling into the new place with Franklin. To be honest, I don't see that much of her these days.'

'Good. I mean I'm glad she's well.'

'She's fine.'

He nodded and tried to smile. 'Well, you look tired, Liam. I'm sorry for calling so late.'

'Well yes, I was just about to turn in actually.'

'Do you mind if I stay just a minute or two all the same?'

'No, Jesus, of course. Look, is everything all right, Seán?'

He put his mug down on the floor and sighed. 'No, Liam. It isn't.'

I heard the floorboards creak upstairs. He moved his fingers to his face for a few moments, then stared across the room at the fire.

'Liam, I've something terrible to tell you. My conscience is at me.'

'What's that, Seán?'

He looked into his glass. 'We've been pals a long time now, haven't we?'

'Christ, yes, Seán.'

He was silent for what seemed like an age. Then he got up, went to the window, took out a pack of cigarettes and lit one. I noticed that his fingers were trembling badly.

'God, Seán, you're in a fierce bad way tonight.'

'I am, yeah.'

'Well lookat, if there's anything I can help you with.'

'It's about Lizzie,' he said.

'What about her?'

He splayed his fingers and touched the window-pane.

'I've something I need to say about her.'

I laughed. 'What's that?'

He leaned his forehead against the glass. 'You'll be hurt by what I have to say, Liam. Very hurt. I'll have to ask you to prepare yourself for a shock.'

He turned around to face me. I felt my throat go dry as I nodded at him. Out in the garden the trees were creaking in the wind. I heard the floorboards upstairs groan again, but this time he did not seem to notice. His eyes were wild with fear.

'Christ forgive me, Liam,' he said. 'But I'm Lizzie's father.'

The first thing I remember after this is the sound of hoarse laughter coming from my mouth. Perhaps I thought that it was some kind of sick joke. But then I looked closely at his face and knew that he was serious.

'I meant to tell you before, Liam. There've been so many times I was close to it.'

I heard myself quietly saying his name a few times. When he started to speak again his voice was shaking.

'What happened between Grace and myself, Liam . . . It was one time when you two were after splitting up. I bumped into her this night, walking down the street in Ringsend. She'd been up to visit your mother. You know the way she was so fond of your mother. Well, I was heading off into town but I could see she was down in herself. Whatever row you had, she was upset. So I took her to this dance in town. We had a few drinks, I suppose. We lost the run of ourselves.'

'Stop,' I said. 'I don't want to hear the details, thanks.'

'I wasn't . . . I didn't mean it like that. I was just explaining how it happened.'

For a while I listened to the logs crackling in the grate. 'This was one time when we split up, you say?'

'No. There was more than one time.'

'After we started seeing each other again?'

He bowed his head and said nothing.

'And after we got married?'

'God, no,' he said. 'Not after that, Liam. I swear to Jesus.'

I felt my hands clutching at the arms of the chair.

'The day she came to tell me about the baby being on its way, I was playing football with a couple of lads down at the dump. Beside the gasometer in Raytown. I just glanced up and there she was, running across the field. I'll never forget the sight of her. She was astray over it, absolutely despairing. She told me she'd been to the doctor, she was sure of it.'

'So what did you say?'

'I said it was a shame. I couldn't think of anything else to say.'

'And what then?'

'Well then, it was me who arranged for her to go to England.'

'It was you.'

He nodded. 'We kept in touch a bit. I sent money of course. And then after a while this letter came and asked me not to write again. So I stopped. I didn't hear from her for a few years, not until she came back to Dublin and took up with yourself again. And then the night before you got married she came up to me in the seminary. You remember I was still living there. It was late, the Father Superior came into the dormitory and told me to dress myself and come down.'

He leaned his forehead against his fist. 'She was in a dreadful state, Liam. Absolutely dreadful. She wondered

358

whether to tell you or not. She didn't think she could get married without you knowing. She was sure it would cause problems later on, that you'd turn against the child. Or turn against her.'

'And . . . ?'

'And God forgive me, Liam. But I told her not to tell you. I thought of all sorts of reasons, how it would hurt you and do no good. How it was better to let everything be. But really I was thinking about myself. I was afraid for myself. I told her on no account to tell you. We agreed that we wouldn't ever speak of it again. And we never did.'

I looked at this man sitting before me and refusing to meet my eyes. 'But you married us, Seán,' I said. 'You baptised Maeve.'

He hung his head. 'I know.'

'Jesus Christ, Seán, you gave the woman the last rites. Don't you remember that?'

His head was bowed so low that I could see a tiny circle of baldness on his crown. I stood up.

'Get out of my house,' I told him. 'Before I do something I'll regret.'

He put his mug on the table and sighed. His hands rested on his knees for a moment. He nodded a few times, then stood and reached for his coat.

'Liam, look,' he said. 'I know you're hurt, I can understand that. I know that.'

I said nothing. I felt the sinews contract in the base of my throat.

'Liam, please. Won't you shake hands at least?'

I heard the sound of my open hand striking his face before I was fully aware of what I was doing. Then I saw the fading mark of my fingers, dark pink on his cheek. He stared at me.

'I deserve that,' he said.

'You creepin' Judas,' I said. 'Get out of my sight before you get what you do deserve.'

He turned to leave. He put his hand on the doorknob. He stopped.

'Liam, Jesus. I'm asking you to forgive me. After all we've been through.'

I tried to speak calmly but my voice shook with rage. 'Me? Christ, you lot never get the fucking point, do you, Seán? *Me* forgive you. That's beautiful. What about her? What about Grace?'

He looked confused. 'How do you mean?'

'Did you ever ask her to forgive you?'

'I don't know. I don't think so.'

'How dare you come slitherin' up here and ask me to forgive you then. I pity you, Seán. I never thought I'd see the day but it's here.'

'You must know she loved you, Liam. Always.'

'A lot you'd know about love.'

'Liam, please. You'll never know the guilt I have about this.'

I believe that I actually laughed here. 'And you think I know nothing about guilt? You can't handle what you did and you want me to take it away. Like that, one word. You weren't man enough to deal with it then and you're not now either.'

'It isn't like that,' he said.

'Professional Christians,' I said. 'Look at yourself, man, take a good look, you crawlin' hypocrite. And you lot wonder why you're up shit creek in this country these days. The fuckin' God Squad.'

'Liam, look, it's the best part of thirty years ago.'

'That's right, Seán. One piece of silver for every year.'

He looked quizzical.

'It *was* thirty pieces, wasn't it, Father? Remind me, why don't you?'

He smiled his sad smile. 'You always knew how to hurt, Sweeney. You were always a fuckin' bollocks when you wanted to be. I'll give y'that much for nothing.'

He left the room. The front door slammed. I heard his footsteps going quickly down the drive.

I went out to the garden and walked around for a while in the sleet. It started to fall harder, it smacked against the dead leaves and the aviary roof. Before long I was wet to the skin but I did not care. It was dark in the garden, very quiet except for the sputtering sound of the sleet. I looked up at the white sky. That old voice from the past came into my mind again, your Uncle Stevie, close to Christmas, sleepspeaking the names of the stars.

Andromeda. Perseus. Pleiades. Camelopardalis.

I thought about your mother. I pictured her in a small, cold flat over a newsagent's shop in King's Cross on a stormy night. It was such a clear image, I could see the pale orange glow of an electric fire on her haunted face, and could almost hear the traffic moving outside in the street. How she would have hated the loneliness of a night like this. My eyes picked out a satellite moving slowly down the sky, tracing a line through the livid and ancient-looking clouds. I do not think that I had ever loved Grace Lawrence as desperately as I did at that moment.

When I finally came back into the house I did not want to continue my writing. I went into the living-room and sat on the sofa. The television was on, I turned down the sound. A few minutes later Quinn came in with a teapot and cups on a tray. He put them on the table and poured me out a mug. He sat on the floor and stared at the television. The screen showed a heavy young man in a tattered Muslim head-dress firing a machine-gun and screaming. Then it cut away to a shot of a black tank firing a puff of orange smoke, being jolted backwards by the force of the shot.

He cleared his throat.

'Listen, Billy, I heard what your man's after comin' out with. I'm sorry, pal. I couldn't help it.'

I said nothing.

'And I didn't know your missus was dead, man. I'm sorry.'

I shrugged.

'It's some slap in the gob though, isn't it? About your girl.'

I nodded.

'You must be bullin' now, are you?'

'I don't know what I am.'

'Yeah, I know.' He handed me a cigarette. 'And did you never cop it before this, no? Did your old lady never tell y'about it?'

'No, we never talked about it much.'

'Why not?'

'Why?' I said. 'What's it to you anyway?'

'I'm only askin' you, man. Put your eyes back in yer head.'

I took a light from him. 'We kind of agreed we wouldn't talk about it, when we got married. I'd one or two notions of my own. There would have been gossip, you know, in the neighbourhood. But the little bastard I figured it was, he went to Canada and got married over there. And anyway I reckoned I'd drive myself half-mad if I thought about it too much.'

'Fuckin' sure,' he said.

'But I know she'd a hard enough time in England all the same. She told me that much. That little bollocks running around Africa in his dress, waving the Bible and standing up for the oppressed. Christ, it'd make you puke up your ring. He was probably ridin' some baluba over there.'

'Yeah.'

He went to the fire and poked it a few times. The flames spurted and fizzed. He sat on the floor and stared into the fireplace, picking up bits of twig and tossing them in.

'Well look, I'd say you were a good father to her, Marge, all the same. Isn't that the main thing?'

'Oh, sure I was.'

'I'm serious,' he said, and he laughed. 'Sure my father, he was me natural father all right, but he was only a fuckin' bollocks to me. He bet me black and blue. He did it for kicks. He'd ladder me from one end of the street to the other. He'd burst me soon as look at me. When I think back now, I can see why. Because nobody ever gave him a chance, that's all. Every single time in his life he needed a break, he didn't get it.

'Like there was this one time he was in trouble in work. He worked in a paint factory. His fingernails were always manky from the paint. Because if you mix all the colours together, black's what you get. Did you know that, no? Black. Anyway, one day a few cans go missin' from the stores. He's hauled up in front of the boss. I didn't do it, says he. Fuck you, says the boss, y'did. Goes to the union. Fuck you, says the shop steward, we don't want to know. He's told to go home for the month. Came in scuttered and bet the mother around the place. Knocked lumps out of her, man. I could hear her screamin' at him, Eddie, give me a chance, would you not gimme one chance? But he didn't. Because he wasn't given a chance himself. He was shat on, so he shat on her. And they both shat on me. That's the way it went.'

'And?'

The flames leaped in the grate. He shrugged. 'And nothin'. They shat on me and I shat on everyone else. By the time I was twelve I was in Letterfrack for robbin' cars. Then it was Spike Island. And then the Joy. You name a nick, I was in there, man. I can't even sleep somewhere there isn't a locked fuckin' door any more. And still, every time I'd get out, the father'd batter me soon as he'd see me. He'd take a belt to me, a bottle, whatever was goin'. He'd beat me till I bled if he was in the humour. Put me in hospital a few times.'

He laughed. 'Only the last time he tried that crack I fuckinwell hit him back. Just once. In the chest, bang.

363

I had drink on me at the time. Doubled him up. He goes down on his knees kind of clutchin' himself and red in the mug and then he falls over on his arse. And I tell him, you lift your hand to me or the mother again and I'll kill y'stone dead, man. Stone fuckin' dead, I mean it. And I walk out the door. And I never come back.'

He took out a new pack of cigarettes and peeled off the cellophane. 'I'll never forget the sound of him hittin' the floor. It wasn't a good sound. It wasn't like the movies, y'know. I've heard it a good few times by now, Marge. It always means fuckin' trouble.'

He scrunched up the cellophane and flung it into the fire. 'Didn't speak to him for six years, man. Not a word. I'd send him up a few pound when I had it to spare, but I wouldn't see him. No way. And when me own kid was born I didn't even tell him. He never saw the kid once. I wouldn't have it.'

He lit a cigarette and coughed a bit as he breathed out.

'I didn't know you had a kid.'

'No,' he said. 'She's over in Manchester with her ma.'

He rummaged in the pocket of his shell-suit pants and pulled out a crumpled photograph which bore a thin white cross where it had been creased into four too many times. He glanced at it for a moment, then handed it across to me. It showed a beautiful, angular-faced blonde woman with dark eye make-up, holding up a fat smiling baby in a Superman suit.

'That's her,' he said. 'Niamh. We named her after the ma.'

'Whose ma?'

'Mine, y'gobshite.'

'I thought you might have meant your girlfriend's.'

He rolled his eyes. 'Yeah, right. We were going to call her after the girlfriend's ma allright, but we didn't think Frustrated Aul Bitch was much of a name for a nipper.'

'Niamh Anne Morgan,' he sighed. 'That's a name-and-a-half, isn't it?'

'Yes,' I said. 'That's a name-and-a-half.' I handed him back the picture. 'And what's the girlfriend's name?'

'Daphne,' he said. 'I think her auld dears got it out of a book. Daphne Morgan.'

'She was some beaut,' he said, and grinned. 'She was gorgeous lookin'. Like a model she was. Even that picture there, it wouldn't do her justice. We used to all go and play pool in this place down the quays on a Saturday night. And my Christ, Daphne'd come into the place with her mates and you'd nearly hear the fuckin' promises breakin' around you. Dressed up, she'd be. Like a princess, her hair piled up on her head, beautiful clothes.' He laughed. 'And she could play pool. True as God, she'd beat the arse off any bloke.

'I never thought I stood a chance with her. She had that look, y'know, that she'd swallow y'up and blow y'out in bubbles if y'went near her. She was classy, y'know, she was soft, she wasn't like me or mine. And then one night I seen her at a wedding. She was all dolled up like you wouldn't believe. It was me cousin Anne-Marie's wedding. The do was in the North Star Hotel in Amiens Street.' He clicked his fingers. 'I remember it like that.'

'And anyway, we're all there havin' a dance. Doin' the air guitar, Status Quo, the lot. Loads of drink. Great crack. I suppose I'm a bit jarred so I'm lookin' at her all day, y'know? I'm doin' the thousand-yard stare, but she doesn't look back, she's with her mates. Christ, Marge, if y'could've seen her, you'd've fallen for her yourself. She was so gorgeous that day. And anyway, there we all are, on the dance floor, it's nearly the end of the night. The band's playin' 'Stairway to Heaven'. Everyone's twisted. Fuckin' locked. And suddenly, doesn't your one walk up to me and she gives me this ten-penny piece. What's that for, I ask her. And she looks at me, givin' me the eye, y'know. It's for you to go and phone your mother, love, she says. Because you're comin' home with me tonight.'

He sniggered. 'She was mad,' he said. 'You'da liked her, Marge.'

'So what happened?'

'Ah, we just fell out,' he said. 'She didn't have any time for me when I was dealin'. Couldn't stand all that. Specially after the kid came along. And there was other women involved too, she wouldn't have it. Fucked off t'England. I was a tosser, wasn't I, man? Look at her. She was lovely.'

'And the kid never met your father?'

He shook his head and stared at the photograph, holding it very lightly in both hands as though it was on fire. 'When he was dyin' he sent a message for me. Wanted to see me. Fuck him, I said, but the sister made me go up to him. So I do. And he's lyin' in the bed in the hospital and he's already in the shroud. I didn't know they did that, Marge, but they do, they put y'in the fuckin' shroud before y'even kick it. Miraculous medals and holy water everywhere, it's like bleedin' Knock in there, they're sprayin' the holy water around like snuff at a wake. For that dozy bollocks, never in a church in his life except to rob the poor-box. It'd make you spew. Crucifix on the wall, rosary beads in his hands, the works. And they're after combin' his hair across his scalp to hide him goin' bald, like it bleedin' matters at this stage. So he looks like Jackie fuckin' Charlton lying there in the scratcher. And his fingernails are still mouldy with the paint after all that time. The stupid cunt, they can't even clean his fingernails and him dyin'.'

'And he gawks up at me in the bed, the poor tool. Was I a good father to yeh, Donie? he goes. Tell us the God's truth now, Donie. Was I?'

'What did you say?'

'I said, yeah, Da. Course y'were. The best. And then he starts coughin' and spewkin' out of him. I could never talk to me auldfella, he goes, I was afraid of him. But you could always talk to me, couldn't y'son? And I go' oh Jaze, yeah,

Da. Till the cows came fuckin' home. I could talk to you all right.'

'And when I used to hit yeh, he says, y'knew it was only because I loved yeh, didn't y'son. That was only my way of sayin' it. And I go, yeah, Da, course I knew that, don't be worryin'.'

'And why did you tell him that?

There were tears in his eyes. 'Why d'y'think, Marge?'

'I don't know. Because you loved him?'

He wiped away the tears and scoffed. 'My shite, I did. No. I couldn't stand him. Wouldn't've pissed on him if he was on fire. But it didn't matter a fuck to me any more. And it did matter to him, the stupid poor cunt. It did to him. So I just said it, 'cos it didn't cost me anythin' to say it. And that's my natural father. That's how I felt about him. He rid the mother and I was born? Well big fuckin' deal. Congratulations. There's more to a father than that, man, or supposed to be anyway.'

He picked up a log and threw it into the fire. He poked at the embers until they reddened and glowed. Then he started to laugh again.

'What's so funny?'

'Ah well, nothin'. But I go up to his grave every year on his anniversary with the mother, just to keep her sweet, and we leave him a bunch of flowers. I always tell her we'd be as well off gettin' a bottle of Johnny fuckin' Walker and pourin' it into him, but anyway. She likes goin' up there. And this one year we're up in the boneyard and the mother is saying the prayers and blessin' herself and all that crap. And this other auld one is just down the way, y'know. And she sees the mother and comes over to her.

'Oh, I'm terrible sorry for yer trouble, ma'am, she goes to the mother. Me husband knew your chap well and never had a bad word for him. You must miss him awful now he's gone.

'And the mother looks down at the old man's grave for

a sec. No, she goes, not really. I'll tell you the God's truth now, missus, he was never a man I liked.'

He throws back his head and snorts with laughter. He looks like a child when he laughs. And I can't help laughing back, despite the way I feel.

Chapter Nineteen

Next morning the snow was thick on the roads, banked up into slushy heaps on each side of the Stillorgan dual carriageway. I phoned Zulu Dawn from the car and told her I would be in late. O'Keeffe came on the line and started up with the whip-cracking act but at this stage I did not really care. In fact I was right on the point of telling him what he could do with his poxy job when there was a roar of splintering static down the line and he got cut off, which was maybe just as well.

When I got to the apartment and came up in the lift, I found Lizzie in the kitchen dressed in her overalls. She looked so happy and well, she had just finished giving a lesson. Her easel was set up near the window and she was painting a scene of the river. She told me she'd be with me in just a minute, she wanted to finish this one section. I went and looked over her shoulder. It was a big vivid picture full of blues and purples and mad greens. She had already sketched in the Ha'penny Bridge in broad black lines and now she was doing the dome of the Four Courts in copper brown and sepia. The kitchen smelt of linseed oil and paint. There were thick sheets of newspaper on the floor under the easel.

The distant sound of loud power chords being blasted out on an electric guitar told me Franklin was in the bedroom. I looked at Lizzie's face reflected in the window. Such a beautiful face, so full of longing, like a paler version of your mother's. I watched as she frowned in concentration, the tip of her tongue protruding from her mouth, her bright restless eyes darting from the board to the river down below. She caught my glance and smiled. I told her I loved to watch her painting and she scoffed at me.

'Jesus, I wouldn't call this painting, Billy. It's only a daub. But I sold one yesterday.

Some German yuppie over for the Yeats festival. Herman. Herman the German. Kept saying he loved my earthy quality. I wasn't sure whether it was me he was talkin' about or the bloody painting. I thought maybe I needed a wash.'

I said there was something I wanted to talk to her about. She took a palette-knife from the table and started smoothing out a rectangular wodge of red in the sky.

'What's that?'

'Well, it's about your mother, love. And I suppose it's about you.'

'OK. Fire away.'

I took a deep breath and started into the story. After a moment or two she stopped painting. She plopped her brush into a jamjar and stared out the window, up at the long clouds. When I started to speak again she held up her hand to interrupt me.

'Billy,' she said. 'Listen, Ma told me years ago.'

'She told you?'

'About Seánie, yeah.'

'Jesus. Why did she do that?'

She shrugged. 'I don't really know. I'd talked to her about it a bit when I was a kid. I think I might have pushed her on it, you know, trying to get the gen. But I dunno. Didn't she ever tell you about it, no?'

'No, she didn't.'

'Jesus. So you've only just found out?'

'Yeah. Last night.'

'Fuck.'

'Fuck is right. And have you ever talked to him about it?'

She shrugged again. 'I was going to a few times, but then

370

I don't know, I just didn't bother my arse. But why? What does it matter now anyway?'

'Well it bloody matters, Lizzie, that's why.'

'But Billy, why? It doesn't. It really doesn't, when you think.'

'How could it not matter, love?'

'Billy, Jesus, don't make me spell it out for you.'

'Spell what out?'

She laughed softly and pushed her hair out of her eyes. She shook her head a few times. Then she came over and touched my face. 'I have a father already.'

Franklin came ambling into the kitchen in his Karl Marx boxer shorts. He stood in the doorway for a few moments with a vaguely startled look on his sleepy face.

'Somebody kick the bucket or what?' he said. She ignored him.

I held her close to me and kissed her hair. Franklin sat down at the table and stared at us.

'I don't deserve you, love,' I said.

'No,' she said. 'That's true, you don't. But you've got me. And you've got Seánie too.'

'Don't talk to me about that creep,' I told her.

'No, I want you to forgive him,' she said. 'Just make up your mind and do it. He's not a bad man, Billy. He made a mistake, that's all. He was only a kid himself and he made a mistake. Then he got scared and he lied. It happens.'

'Some bloody mistake, though.'

'Billy, listen, if you feel there's anything you owe me from the old days, then forgive him. Just do it for me and do it fast. Please. Do that for me and we're quits.'

'Don't ask me to do that, love. I couldn't.'

'Billy . . .'

'I said I couldn't.'

Suddenly her expression darkened. She sighed bitterly and held up her hands. 'Well look, don't involve me then, Billy. You want to open it all up, then it's your fight.'

'What do you mean, my fight? The way he hurt your mother like that. Jesus. The way . . .'

'She's dead, Billy. Mum's dead. Face it, all right? She's not hurt any more.'

The abruptness of the interruption shocked me. 'And that makes it all right?'

'I'm not saying that'. She turned away and went to the window.

'So what are you saying?'

She whipped back around to face me, her nostrils flaring. 'I'm saying I don't think it's Mom's hurt you're so fucking worried about here, Billy. Or mine. If you want to know the truth.'

I sat down at the table. She went to the sink and began furiously washing her hands. Franklin blew gently through his pursed lips and lit a cigarette. A moment later Conal came tottering in and stared at us.

'Why is everyone being quiet?' he said.

He crossed the floor and climbed into Lizzie's arms. She kissed his neck. Franklin coughed ostentatiously and nodded in my direction. 'Listen, wench, did you tell Fatty here the news?'

'You tell him.'

'I'm afraid to,' he said. 'It'd be better comin' from you.'

She turned to me and grinned. 'So I'm pregnant, Billy. I'm due in April.'

Franklin put his hands in the air and stepped backwards into the doorway. 'Don't look at me, mate,' he said. 'I never bloody touched her, I swear to God.'

Late on the following Friday night, I was awoken from a deep sleep by a loud crashing noise coming from somewhere in the house. I remember thinking at first that I must be dreaming, but then it came again, a loud thump, a shattering. It was then that I realised it seemed to be coming through the wall next door, from your room. I sat up and looked at the clock. It was just after three in the morning. Another crash, then the tinkle of broken glass.

Quinn was on the landing with a sweeping brush in his hand. He looked scared. He put a finger to his lips, motioning me to be quiet. We crept towards the door together and now there was a soft swishing sound coming from inside. I unlocked the door and pushed it quickly open. Silence. Quinn reached around for the light switch, but the bulb had gone, it was pitch dark in the room. We listened. There was something alive in there.

He ran into his own room and came back with a torch. He flicked the beam around your bedroom a few times and it glinted in the dressing-table mirror. The window had a jagged, star-shaped break in it. I thought I heard a soft anxious croak. I gestured to him to move the light over towards the bed.

A fat elegant blackbird was standing on the pillow and pecking at its right wing, its beady eyes glimmering in the darkness. Quinn cursed, sighed with relief and we went in. The bird regarded us without moving its head. It allowed me to come right over and touch it.

'Poor thing,' I said, 'how did you get in? You're after scaring the life out of me, you daft bird. You put the heart crossways in me, didn't you?'

I stroked the back of its head and its dirty yellow beak. It nuzzled against me.

'Jesus,' Quinn said. 'It's like a Christian. Look at it. Tame.'

'Poor creature. You didn't see the window, did you? You're lucky you didn't break your wing.' I ran my knuckles gently down its back.

'You've a way with the birds, Marge,' Quinn laughed. 'I always said it.'

I grabbed its soft plump body with both hands. Of course it took fright then and started flapping and squawking and pecking at my fingers. Quinn rushed over to the broken

373

window and opened it wide. We let the bird out into the night and watched it beat its way against the gusting wind and off over the travellers' field.

Afterwards my hand and wrist were in rag order. We went down to the kitchen, found some band-aids and disinfectant and I washed off the blood before bandaging myself up. Quinn has turned into a medical expert now and keeps informing me that I'll need a tetanus shot but I tell him to shag off, I've been pecked by more birds, et cetera. But it was aching pretty badly, I have to say, and the thumb seemed to have gone a bit stiff. He made us toast and a pot of tea. I found some classical music on the radio, Schubert, I think. We sat there for a while just eating and drinking and listening to the music. The wind was blowing hard outside and I could hear the loose slates clacking on the roof.

'That's shite depressin' music,' he said.

'Well, that's what we're listening to,' I told him. 'So you can like it or lump it.'

He went back to his tea. I picked up a paper and started to read – I think it might have been something about the divorce referendum.

'Listen, Marge,' he said, 'I was thinkin' I might shag off over t'England after all.'

'Oh yes?'

'I thought I might go and look up Daphne and the kid. See how they're doin'. Y'never know. She might be glad to see me, what?'

'That's true. You never know.'

He nodded. 'Plenty of work over in England, isn't there? Everyone says that.'

'Yes, they say England's great for makin' money. I nearly went myself when I was your age.'

'They don't like the Paddies much though, do they?'

I took a swig. '*I* don't like the Paddies much,' I said. 'If it comes to it.'

374

'Outdoor work I'd like,' he said. 'On the sites and that. Y'can make a packet I hear.'

'So I believe.'

'They say the beer is only pisswater in England though.'

'I'm sure it isn't.'

'Yeah. Y'wouldn't mind, Marge, would yeh?'

'What the fuck are you on about now?'

He grinned. 'I just thought y'might be lost for company without me, Marge. That's all. I don't know how yer gonna manage without me sometimes.'

'I'll manage just great, believe you me. Now shut your face and listen to that music, will you?'

In the late afternoon of that same billowy day I was in the kitchen feeding the budgies when I saw him trudging up the garden in one of my old jumpers and a pair of muck-smeared wellingtons. He strolled in, pulled off the wet boots and sat down shivering in front of the Aga. For a few minutes he held out his hands, massaging them together and warming them, in between munching on a biscuit. Then he turned to me.

'I've somethin' to ask you about your daughter,' he said.

'Who? Lizzie?'

'No, the girl in the hospital. Maeve, isn't that it?'

I did not like it when he said your name. Just something about him uttering the word made me tense up. 'What about her?'

'D'y'think I could go down and see her some time?'

The budgies squawked and jabbered in the cage. He got up from the chair, came over and looked in at them. He broke off a piece of biscuit and pushed it through the bars, making a soft clucking sound with his tongue.

'I don't know if that's such a great idea,' I said.

'Well, I'd like to,' he said. 'If y'could see your way clear some time. Wouldn't have to be today or tomorrow, like. Just before I go away.'

'Why would you want to do that?'

'It'd set my mind at rest about her. Before I go away, like. T'England.'

The smaller budgie spread its wings and hopped up on to the perch.

'So what d'y'think there, Marge?'

I did actually think about it for a moment or two. I tried to picture how this could happen. If it could happen. I closed my eyes. Your powdery white face seemed to loom up at me. I saw your hands stretched out to full span, just as they had been on the video screen that day so many months ago in the courtroom.

'No. No, look, I don't think so, son. I'm sorry.'

'OK,' he nodded. 'Fair enough, so. Just thought I'd ask.'

He put his boots on and went back out to the stable. The wind seemed to die down a bit. He emerged with the old lawnmower and started cutting the grass.

Chapter Twenty

Quite early the next Tuesday morning I got up, took a long hot shower and drove down for a swim at the Forty Foot. There was nobody else around that morning, and the grey swirling water was so indescribably cold that when I plunged in I thought at first I was going to scream. Even after ten minutes of hard crawl my skin was still aching. Around me the black-headed-gulls whirled and dived low.

I was backstroking gently out in the swell when suddenly I saw this enormous freak wave coming in slowly from the middle distance. It was perhaps six feet high, but all on its own, just one towering wave. It was an odd dreamlike sight, quite beautiful, but I did not exactly have time to admire it. It was heading straight for me. I turned and began to swim as fast and strong as I could for the shore but it caught me. I actually heard it rushing up behind me, gaining on me, fizzy flecks of foam spattering through the air. I felt it lifting me, raising me up like a giant invisible hand and pulling me along with it, dangling me in space just for a moment and then dropping me down on the shore. It left me standing right there on the mossy rock.

I clambered up the rock, dried myself slowly, rubbing my still smarting skin hard to try to generate some heat. I was quivering and my knees felt weak as I began to dress. Just then a fit-looking old man with a red face and woolly beard came tiptoeing down over the damp stones with a thick towel under his arm. He nodded at me and grinned as he took off his straw hat and unbuttoned his shirt. He had a discoloured tattoo of a scallop shell on his chest.

'I see you got a bit of a lift in,' he laughed. 'I was watching you on me way down the front. The way the big wave carried you in.'

'Amazing, yes,' I said. 'I got the land of my life.'

He chuckled again. 'Happened me too the other week. Thought I was losing the marbles altogether. But it's only that damn Sea Cat.'

'The . . . ?'

'That new super-ferry they have going over to Holyhead every morning. From Dun Laoghaire, you know. The Sea Cat, it's called. Huge big thing the size of an office block but it does fifty miles an hour. It's some kind of newfangled what do you call it. Hovercraft.'

'Oh yes. I've seen it.'

'Well, it churns up the water to beat the band. But you only get the wave in this close ten minutes after it's gone past and you can't see it any more.'

He slid his trousers down. His legs had blue varicose veins showing through old porridgy skin. 'I believe they're putting up warnings about it soon,' he said.

I had tea and toast in a café in Sandycove village and met Quinn outside the ruined teetering hulk of the Pavilion cinema just after nine o'clock, like we had arranged. We were a little early for visiting hours so we decided to take a walk up the metals. He asked me why the metals were called the metals when they're only lanes beside the railway track. Would it not have been easier just to call them lanes? I told him I could not remember why, but they had always been called the metals: they had been there since the track was first built in the late years of the last century, the labourers had made them to carry the granite and marble slabs down to the shore from the quarry in Dalkey. 'So you could walk all the way home to our gaff through there?' he laughed. I told him yes.

378

Our gaff, if you don't mind.

Soon it was a lovely sharp wintery morning. A creamy sun appeared in the grey and white sky. The steep banks on each side of the track were thick with blackberries and wild roses, ferns and ivy and huge clumps of flame-yellow gorse. I told him the names of the different plants. As if he gave a shit. Young men in red corporation oilskins were swinging scythes at the long brown foliage. Near the bridge at Glasthule Dart station the cutting was strewn with rubbish. A carpet of shattered beer bottles and a pile of mouldy yellow newspapers. A warm ammoniac aroma rose from the mound. We turned back and walked down together as far as the entrance to the People's Park. We went in there for a few minutes and strolled around looking at the blackened, empty flower-beds. I could see by his face that he was getting nervous. Down in the playground, the roundabout was gently creaking as it turned in the wind.

We came back out to the street and walked slowly down in the direction of the hospital, taking our time, our breath turning to soft white globes of steam. He was very quiet now, and chain-smoking madly. We turned into the hospital. We crossed the car park. We were actually on our way up the steps to the lobby when he stopped.

'What's the matter?' I asked him.

He looked as though he was going to throw up. 'I can't,' he said. 'I can't do it.'

'Well lookat, you're here now.'

He shook his head. 'No. No, I can't do it, man. I'll catch you later.'

He whipped around and walked away very fast, weaving through a line of parked ambulances. I went after him and followed for a while, back down the main street, past the shopping mall, down Marine Road, all the way down past the Pavilion and as far as the entrance to the metals. I called out his name. He did not turn when he heard me, just started to run. He ran hard off down the metals and I let him go.

When I got back to the hospital the doctors were with you. A specialist had been called. You had contracted a minor lung infection. Ordinarily this would not be anything to worry about but your immune system was getting low. They might have to operate if the infection did not disappear or at least recede, they told me.

When I got back to Glen Bolcain his door was locked. I knocked a few times but he did not answer. I noticed that the radio was not on, and that surprised me.

I went into the office and tried to work for a while. The specialist rang several times that day to tell me how you were doing. At about four in the afternoon he called once more. You had deteriorated again, he would definitely have to operate that night. I could be in the recovery room if I wanted.

'Of course,' I said. 'But it's a minor enough thing, isn't that what you were saying earlier?'

'I said the condition was minor. But no operation involving a person in Maeve's condition is minor.'

'She will be OK, won't she?'

'Nothing is certain,' he said.

'What does that mean?'

'Just that, Mr Sweeney. Absolutely nothing is certain here.'

'Should I be prepared for the worst?' I asked him.

He sighed. 'I suppose we all should, yes.'

Next morning I slept late. When I got up Quinn was gone. Money was missing from the kitchen table – about fifty pounds and some change – and he had also taken my dictaphone. I searched around the place for a while, certain that there must at least have been a note, but there was not.

I went out to the garden and looked in the stable, thinking that he might have moved back out there for some reason. But the stable was empty. I had not been in it for a few weeks, not since the time that the gun went missing. It had

380

been completely cleaned, right down to the stone floor. It was gleaming. The window-sills had been painted white, the wooden beams stained with fresh sweet-smelling varnish.

His shaving things were gone from the bathroom. In his bedroom, his new clothes had been taken from the wardrobe. His pictures and posters from the newspapers and magazines had been taken down from the walls; even the strips of sellotape and buds of Blu-Tack had been peeled off. The radio was gone. There was no trace at all of him in the house. It was almost as though he had never even been here.

I was in the kitchen making tea when I noticed that the plaque on the wall over the Aga – Man does not live by bread alone – was gone too. I had to laugh. The four screws that had held it in place were in a beer glass on the draining board, along with the screwdriver that he must have used.

I waited by the phone all morning thinking that it might ring. But it didn't. Just before noon I was in the garden leaving out a few sultanas for the blackbirds when I thought I heard it. I ran up to the house but it was only some student selling magazine subscriptions.

Around lunch-time I drove down to the hospital to see you, making sure to bring my mobile with me. The procedure had gone better than the specialist and surgeon had anticipated. They thought you might be rallying. They thought that for a few days. Rallying. But soon they stopped thinking it again. When I saw you in the ward this morning you looked even more pale and thin than you did in the days after the operation. Your weight is down to less than seven stone now. I can hardly bear to look at your hands.

The house seemed lifeless and ludicrously empty without him. In the middle of the night I would often wake and find myself listening out for the sound of the television or the radio, for his tuneless, childish whistle, for the fall of his footsteps on the stairs. But there was only silence. Sometimes in those nights I would find myself imagining him and his girlfriend together with their child. Would he tell her what I had done to him? What would she say about it? Would I ever see him again?

On the night of Monday 10 October I came in quite late from the hospital and went straight to bed. The phone rang at about two in the morning. At first I thought it might be news of you. But when I picked it up nobody spoke. I sat up in bed and held the receiver tight to my ear. I said hello a few more times and then I said my name, but still there was no reply. 'Please speak to me,' I said. There was a soft undulating sound like a radio wave, followed by a rasp of crackles. I did not want to hang up. I thought that I could hear the sound of traffic then, but only faintly, and possibly the sound of muffled rock music. I stayed on the line for several minutes. Every so often I was sure that I could hear the clang of another coin being pushed into the slot. After a while I was certain that I could hear breathing. I said hello again and asked who it was. Nothing.

'Is that you, son?' I said.

The line clicked, bleeped and went dead.

I lay down and tried to get back to sleep. A few minutes later the phone rang again.

'Mr Sweeney?'

'Yes.'

'This is your friend here.'

'My friend?'

'Yeah. I met you a while back. In July it was. We took a spin out beyond to the seaside one night. To Bray.'

I sat up slowly. 'Sheehan?'

Silence for a moment. 'I think y'know well who it is.'

'Where are you?'

I heard the deft scrabble of mice in the walls. 'I can't tell you that. I'm not far away.'

'Do you know anything about Quinn?'

'I know a lot about him, yeah.'

Above me, a gust of wind seemed to race through the

attic. 'He's after gettin' himself into big trouble with some people. I was asked to take care of it. Can you hold on a minute there?'

'Yes.'

I could hear him whispering to somebody, the clack of feet on wood, a man's voice I did not recognise hissing the word 'No', a sharp noise that sounded like a window slamming down.

'Sorry, Mr Sweeney. We were talkin' about Quinn.'

'I heard he was gone away to England.'

'No, he's not.'

'So where is he?'

The line crackled again. 'He's closer than you think.'

'Is he in trouble?'

'You could say that, yeah.'

More whispers and footsteps. 'Can I do anything for him?'

A deep sigh. 'No, you can't, Mr Sweeney. I'm sorry. It's all taken care of now.'

'It's taken care of?'

'Yeah.'

'Can you not at least tell me where he is?'

'Go out the back garden,' he said. 'Take your mobile with you. I'll ring you back in a minute.'

'To the garden?'

'And be sure and bring your mobile.'

'How do you know I have a mobile?'

'Mr Sweeney, I don't have an awful lot of time here.'

'Will I give you the number?'

'We know the number already. Just go on. Make tracks.'

I got out of bed, pulled on a pair of slippers, an old mac over my pyjamas. It was raining hard as I stepped through the back door. The night was bitterly cold, very dark. For a moment I could see nothing except shadows. I remember the wind, screaming over the back wall. The tops of the trees shaking. The stove-pipe on the stable roof squeaking and rattling in its moorings. I went down the wet steps. I walked forwards, into the garden.

The security light blazed on.

He was slumped with his back against the apple tree, naked except for a pair of underpants and track-suit trousers which had been pulled down around his thighs, his arms tied behind him around the trunk. His head was bowed very low to one side. His legs were bent and twisted into a grotesque tangle. As I came closer I could see the thick smears of blood across the white skin on his chest. A small robin was sitting on his bony shoulder, preening its wings. It stared at me for a moment before lifting off and fluttering up towards the house. When I raised his head a thin trickle of watery blood flowed out of his bruised mouth. His nose was a wet red pulp. There was a small dark hole in the centre of his forehead.

I felt tears smoulder in my eyes as I began to untie his ice-cold hands. His wrists were scarred from the rope, his knuckles and fingertips caked with dried blood. He seemed to lurch forward into my arms before sliding down my body, his neck lolling, his ruined hands sagging, a broken leering puppet.

The mobile rang in my pocket. I laid him slowly down in the wet grass. I was crying so much that I could barely speak.

'You're out the back garden now, Mr Sweeney, are you?'

'Yes.'

Nothing for a moment. The crunch of dead leaves. Flutterings in the branches.

'Listen, I'm sorry anyway, Mr Sweeney. I was asked to take care of it.'

'Did you have to do that to him first?'

'Yeah. We had to get some information. I'm sorry. I can't really give y'the full story on it.'

'You're sorry?'

A cough. 'Well, I liked him actually. Always actin' the hardchaw. Tough little fucker. But he wasn't the worst. Just played out of his league in the end.'

'How could you do that to him? Why did you bring him back here?'

'I have t'go now,' he said. 'But I'm after bein' told to tell you somethin'.'

'What?'

'I was told to say if you breathe one word about this, Mr Sweeney, them two grandkids of yours'll get a lot worse before they get the same. Do y'understand me?'

'Yes.'

'You're sure now?'

'I understand, yes.'

'All right so, Mr Sweeney. Take care now. I'll say goodnight to you. And I'm sorry again.'

Chapter Twenty-One

Sunday 27 November 1994

And if it can be possible for me somehow to reach into that dark realm where you find yourself now, then permit me to say a last thing to you. It is a thing every father should say at least once. I cannot remember if I ever actually told you that you were cherished, that you saved my life, that you brought to the darkest of days moments of helpless sacred joy, that I did not deserve you, that your presence in my life blessed it. Simply that I loved you. It was true then. If anything, it is more true now.

If some day you do come to read these words, no doubt now as they reach their end you will be wondering why I continued to set them down when I did not know if you would ever awaken to them. I have no answer, is the truth of it. This is something I have wondered about too. Perhaps it was because I could not – would not – believe what had happened to you. Sometimes even now I see a girl of your age in the street, and I am sure she is you. One night recently, very late, when I was out on the road I stopped at a phone box on a petrol station forecourt just outside Kinnegad and rang Glen Bolcain, half-expecting you to answer. I must have stood there for five whole minutes, listening to the phone ring, while the trucks and cars thundered by through the rain outside. I do not know why I did that, just as I do not know why I have kept all this going. Maybe it was because I wanted to finish something I had started, to be faithful to some small important thing for just once in my life. To keep one promise.

Nobody will ever see these words, except you. I have arranged for what is written between these covers to be lodged in a secure place to which only you can ever have access. With the one exception of Lizzie, and that will not be for a long time yet, I promise nobody will ever see these pages. But the strange thing is that sometimes I think you can see them already. I feel you so close to me when I sit here late in the evenings and write. Sometimes I sense that you are actually here in the small room with me and looking over my shoulder. Isn't that odd?

This morning I collected Seánie at the presbytery as arranged and drove him over to the airport. We had to leave quite early and take the toll-bridge route because the traffic in Dublin is so awful these days, even on a Sunday. This is because the country is doing so well, apparently; any time Ireland is doing well it takes you a lifetime to get from one side of the city to the other. The two young priests who were going with him were already in the departure lounge when we arrived. He introduced me. I found it hard to believe that they were priests. They had fluorescent rucksacks, fashionable haircuts, T-shirts emblazoned with the names of rock groups. One was wearing a baseball cap that said 'Beavis and Butt-Head!'.

The flight had been delayed, they told us, because of a security alert at Moscow airport. We went upstairs to the canteen, I got coffees and plates of fry for everyone. The priest with the baseball cap said he was sorry and didn't mean any offence, but he couldn't eat the bacon and sausages because he was vegetarian. Seánie laughed. 'We'll see how vegetarian you are, Niall, when we get over beyond. I'll tell you what, six months in San Juan and you'll ate your own head.'

He turned to me and grinned. 'These youngsters now, Billy. Honest to Jesus, so idealistic they are.'

We talked for a while about the length of the flight, a long hard journey for them all the same. Down to Shannon, a few hours' wait to connect with the Aeroflot to Cuba, and then on to Nicaragua tomorrow night. From Managua by jeep to some tiny border town in the South, from there by steamer to their final destination, a Miskito Indian village deep in the rain forest. Seánie said that they would all feel ten years older by the time they got there.

We sat and talked for another hour or so. Then the announcement came over the loudspeaker, their flight had been called for boarding. I walked them down to the departures gate, shook hands with the two younger ones and wished them luck. Seánie put his bag on the deck and hugged me.

'Mind yourself, Liam,' he said. 'I'll see you whenever. Keep it country, what?'

After they had gone through the X-ray machine I went upstairs and out on the balcony. The wind whipped against my face and threw dust in my eyes. A few minutes later I saw the three of them walking across the tarmac to the plane and up the wheeled steps. The doors closed and the staircase was driven away. I watched the plane taxi over to the apron and pull off down the runway. It climbed very steeply into the sky, its wing lights flashing, its engines trailing plumes of white steam. I stayed until the lights had completely disappeared from view.

Ten minutes later I had just paid my car-park ticket in the automatic machine, love, and was about to get on the escalator when I saw your face. I could not believe it at first. I went closer. On the wall in front of me was a large framed backlit poster with a photograph of a group of students, all standing beside the lake on the UCD campus and wearing mortarboards. 'Welcome To The Republic Of Ireland', the slogan announced, 'The Quality Business Base In Europe'. You were standing to the far left of the group with your head tilted to one side. You had your hands on your hips and you were smiling. Dominic was beside you, with his arm around your shoulder. You looked so like your mother. It was the most extraordinary thing.

When I got home, Franklin, Lizzie and the twins were waiting for me downstairs, in front of the house. Conal and Erin had their buckets and spades and wanted me to take them down to Killiney beach. I tried to tell them it was too cold today; but no, they told me, they always go to the beach at this time of the year. In Australia, yes, I said. Not in Ireland. Conal looked as though he was about to burst into tears.

I told them all right, but we would have a cup of coffee first. We came in and sat at the kitchen table. Lizzie filled the kettle and put it on the Aga. She moved so assuredly and unthinkingly around the room, it was as though she had never left the house. Franklin took out a pen and notepad and began to scribble something. After a while I noticed that Erin was staring up at me.

'Are you Sweeney?' she wanted to know.

'Yes, love. And so is your mum.'

'And am I?'

'Well, I suppose you are, yes. If you want to be.'

'Is Daddy?'

'No. Daddy isn't.'

I gave her an apple. She tore out the back door and into the garden. Lizzie went to follow but I told her she should leave her, she'd be fine out there.

A few minutes later I went out with a cup of hot chocolate for her. There is a new flower-bed now, down beside that mis-shapen old aspen. It has worked out very well, I must say. But we won't get any growth there till the spring, of course.

Erin was sitting under the apple tree waving her plastic spade in the air. When she saw me approaching she staggered to her feet, stretched out her arms and started to race around the trunk, cackling with malevolent glee. She

389

stopped suddenly, swaying with dizziness, and gawped up into the branches.

'*Swee*-ney,' she cooed.

I went down the garden and tried to make out what she was pointing at. But when I looked up I saw nothing at all, except the long knotted branches, dark like black lace against the sky. While I was staring, she cantered away from me and straight into the new flower-bed.

I grabbed her out of it very quickly. We would not want her digging around in there after all, would we, love? That would not be a very good idea. It is never a good idea to disturb recently bedded-out plants. Bad for the roots. Any gardener can tell you that.

I must remind the builders when they come back not to go near the new flower-bed, not for any reason.

I held her for a few moments while she squirmed and kicked against me. Then I led her by the hand down to the aviary and explained it to her. She wanted to know why there were no birds inside. I told her that it was much too cold for the birds now. She gurgled and spat into her hot chocolate.

It occurred to me that the garden really is in a mess these days. I walked around for a while just looking at the state of it. Yes, the lawn is all right now. But it could be such a beautiful garden, love, were it not for those twisted and broken plants, those strange hybrids and terrible snaking weeds about the place. It needs to be dug out and raked. Really, it needs to be started all over again, by a person with a bit of imagination.

Because all gardens are stories, as somebody told me once, and all gardeners are storytellers.

I went into the stable and found the old shovel, exactly where I had left it. I took it out and kicked the hardened red muck off the blade. I selected a patch of moist grass that simply took my fancy and began to dig. Erin poured her hot chocolate into the hole and giggled.

And the earth was so soft today, even though the winter is here now. Your birthday has come and long gone. The sea at Sandycove is icy in the mornings. The nights have grown longer and darker. The siskins have settled in the stunted alder, the bramblings in the fir. The winter stars have appeared in the sky. Soon it will be Christmas again. The shovel felt good, solid in my hands. After quite a short time I was sweating, despite the cold. I took off my jumper and handed it to Erin. She hung it on the stable doorknob, tottered back to me, dropped to her knees and sank her plastic spade into the broken clay at my feet.

Monoceros. Auriga. Hercules. Pegasus.

I went back to work, my shovel slicing into the mulchy earth, the child in fervent silence digging around me.

Acknowledgements

Grateful acknowledgement is made to my family and to Anne-Marie Casey, to my agents Carole Blake and Conrad Williams, to Isobel Dixon and all the staff at the Blake Friedmann Literary Agency, to my editor Geoff Mulligan, to Peter Mullan, Móirín Ní Moynihan and Mary Ellen Ring for patiently explaining Irish court procedures and aspects of law (any errors or distortions are, of course, my own), to John McDermott at the Irish Council For Civil Liberties for further general advice on legal rights in Ireland, to Michael Paul Gallagher and once again to Bernard and Mary Loughlin at the Tyrone Guthrie Centre, Annaghmakerrig, County Monaghan, where part of this novel was written.